Praise for *Split-Level*

MW01040429

"In her latest novel, *Split-Level*, Sande Boritz Berger paints a vivid picture of the early 1970s, when the sexual revolution was making its way through the suburbs of America. With equal parts humor and heart, Berger explores the anguish of a marriage coming apart and how some will go to any lengths to mend it."

—Laurie Gelman, author of *Class Mom*

"Sande Boritz Berger eloquently takes us to a time and place where young marriages reeled with a new playbook. When the husband of New Jersey housewife Alex Pearl upends their '70s-style suburban bliss with some bad behavior, Alex knows her life might never be the same. *Split-Level* is a gripping, fast-paced story, perfect for readers of literary fiction who enjoy a mature, nuanced look at the complications of marital relationships."

—Betty Hafner, author of *Not Exactly Love: A Memoir*

"In a story dotted with Pyrex, Fresca, and dial phones, Sande Boritz Berger sets the stage for a page-turning journey through 1970s suburbia. An unsuspecting trip to 'Marriage Mountain,' a healing sanctuary, will have readers rooting for lonely housewife Alex Pearl to take a chance on the life she desires instead of the one she's settled for."

—Elizabeth McCourt, author of *Sin in the Big Easy*

"A poignant look back on suburban post-war haze during the swinging '70s, Berger has written a smart and unpredictably funny novel. Her protagonist, Alex, grappling with marriage, two small children, and the conflicting social mores of that time, is sure to win over your heart."

—Susan Tepper, author of *Monte Carlo Days & Nights* and *The Merrill Diaries*

"In *Split-Level*, Berger, a keen observer of suburban angst, takes us back to the early days of the sexual revolution in the 'burbs—to the promise and reality of bed-hopping and marital bliss—as it plays out in the lives of Alex and Donny Pearl and those of a neighboring couple whose marriage is in a parallel state of decline. Hard to put down; hard to forget."

—Barbara Donsky, author of award-winning *Veronica's Grave: A Daughter's Memoir* and the international bestseller *Missing Mother*

SPLIT-LEVEL

SPLIT-LEVEL

A NOVEL

SANDE BORITZ BERGER

SHE WRITES PRESS

Published 2019
Printed in the United States of America

ISBN: 978-1-63152-555-1
ISBN: 978-1-63152-556-8
Library of Congress Control Number: 2018961676

For information, address:
She Writes Press
1569 Solano Ave #546
Berkeley, CA 94707
She Writes Press is a division of SparkPoint Studio, LLC.

A version of the first chapter of Split-Level appeared in TriQuarterly, an international journal published by Northwestern University Press.

for Steve
my light along the path

Love never dies a natural death. It dies because we don't know how to replenish its source. It dies of blindness and errors and betrayals . . .

Anaïs Nin

The Day Before

Prime rib, rib roast, or is it silver tip? For years I have been an ovo-lacto vegetarian, but this morning I stand on a line that snakes around three blocks, securing my right of passage into Fernando & Sons Meat Emporium—this being Fernando's widely advertised yearly blow-out sale. I'm startled when two ruddy-faced workers, in a noisy pickup, hoot and honk, then brake to survey the selection as if we, the women on this line, are the beef in the offering: a curvy leg, perhaps, a lean shoulder or nice rack of ribs. But no one bats a curly lash to acknowledge them. Instead we concentrate through icy eyes, daring someone, anyone, to snag a spot in line.

Hurrying from the house, after the girls boarded the camp bus, I noticed how the freshly cut grass shimmered with dew, as if gift-wrapped in cellophane. A lazy moth struggled on the cold stone path, its wings heavy with moisture. And once again, I ached for that time: The cool, fragrant air stinging my cheeks, my heart pounding as I struggled uphill to Old Main and art class. Some days, I'd stop to dally among the morning shadows before the sun leapt through branches, capturing me in its honeyed light. True, I was alone then, but never lonely. Now I stand, chin to skull, with nearly a hundred women waiting, all waiting, for this golden opportunity: the chance to save, to stockpile for next winter—provisions made from acts of slaughter. Am I the only one watching the floating sky, streaked like

1

the inside of a conch shell, or the hydrangeas across the road weighing on their branches—violet balloons about to burst?

I mumble aloud, desperate to memorize the varied cuts of beef, needing to be prepared when it's my turn to enter Fernando's. My stomach churns as before final exams, any exam. I will not ask my friend, Rona, no never, and see that flutter of sympathy in her eyes, that downcast look bordering on pity—a look capable of turning me mute. How can I so easily distinguish each Modigliani, a Manet from a Monet, but remain pathetically lost on chuck roast, tenderloin, and filet?

ONE

I am breathless from a morning of tedious phone chatter. Long conversations about how the wallpaper is starting to lift in my powder room—a bathroom with a small pedestal sink shaped like a clamshell and a very low commode. No one will ever powder there; it's hard enough to maneuver your body, let alone relieve yourself in the miniscule space. Still, I like the way "powder room" sounds, and Rona Karl has taught me a great deal about home décor since I moved to Wheatley Heights, New Jersey, a small suburban community that boasts nothing taller than an intrusive water tower standing guard as you enter town.

The phone receiver is crushed between my ear and shoulder while I paprika a rump roast slumped in a square Pyrex dish. Struggling to stay tuned to the daily *Listen to Rona Show,* I chop an onion, then mistakenly blot my stinging eyes with a wet dish towel.

"Damn, that hurts. I can barely see!" But Rona has pumped up the volume, grumbling now over the "outrageous" price of her imported porcelain tile. Though my focus is blurred, I can see myself dividing. One of me, confident and cocky, is propped on the kitchen counter— sleek legs dangling, shaking a head of wavy blonde hair while hissing at the other me, who, appearing embarrassed, tries to continue a conversation.

"So, Rona, I was thinking, I might patch the wallpaper myself, with some Elmer's." This is how I often pose a question when speaking with Rona, whose response is usually predictable.

"Are you nuts, *Al-ex*? Do you want to *ru-in* everything you've done?"

"Of course not, you know much better about these things."

"Hold on," Rona says without curbing her exasperation.

I slide the rusty roast into the brown Magic Chef and slam the oven door. Stretching the phone cord to its uncoiled limits, I move to the den and begin dusting the bookshelves, my feather duster held high like a magic wand. *Poof! Make just one wish, Alex. Remember when you had fistfuls of wishes?*

My shoulder bumps an ancient edition of Monopoly, which sends a slew of frayed, yet dependable, cookbooks cascading to the floor. I rearrange the wobbly shelf and rub grease off the cover of *The Fifteen-Minute Quiche*. Above the culinary section sits another shelf wholly dedicated to the fine art of gardening, and how I've learned to rescue our roses from the cruelty of mealy bugs and aphids. On the bottom shelf is a tower of decorating magazines, which have replaced my fine art books, now in storage, and boast effortless projects like silk flower arranging and chic decorating with sheets. But shoved in the back of this flimsy teakwood wall unit, wrapped in a Wonder Bread bag, is my one little secret—an often-scanned, earmarked copy of *A Sensuous Life in 30 Days,* which offers a woman's-eye view, with detailed information, on how to set off fireworks in the bedroom with tantalizing chapters like "The Whipped Cream Wiggle" and "The Butterfly Flick." I'd bought the book after Becky's first birthday, not realizing I was already pregnant with Lana. So, for now, I'm sticking to decorating with sheets, giving much less thought to what I could be doing on top of them.

"Got a pencil?" Rona's voice blasts through the receiver, and I quickly stuff the book back in its hiding place.

In the kitchen I fumble through the junk drawer, ripping sales receipts for items purchased well over a year ago. A blonde Barbie head topples out and lands at my feet. Rona's breathing turns huffy. She has important things on her agenda, like removing finger marks from her white, wooden railings. Still, I think she enjoys being my personal household-hint hotline, sharing her unique bible laden with numbers of service people in a ten-mile radius. Rona never fails to toss out extra tidbits of information and local gossip: like who was last spotted slinking out of the Maplewood Motor Inn with Bernie Salter, the bald, yet incredibly handsome, kosher butcher.

"My Maybelline eye pencil will have to do," I say.

"The number is 377-Pari. You mustn't fool around. Call them now, Alex!" I love how Rona alternates between her London and Brooklyn dialects—a vernacular that conveniently distances her from her Eastern European heritage. "They must come and repair the wallpaper before your girls discover the open seam. Then you'll be sorry!"

For a second, I ponder the tragedy facing the Mylar wallpaper dotted with silver swans curling up the bathroom wall, but remarkably my pulse remains steady.

"Okay, okay, I'll call right now." I've learned it's easier to just go along, even though our banter has me exhausted. To keep Rona as my friend, I dare not scare her by reciting passages that pop into my head at inappropriate moments, like now: *This is the way the world ends, not with a bang but a whimper.* Lately I fear my world might end precisely like this—talking about nothing consequential on a lemony-yellow wall phone.

"Promise?"

"I promise." A girlish giggle escapes my throat.

Instead of hanging up, I push down the peg to get a dial tone. What I hear is silence and a few seconds of bumpy breathing. I think of slamming the phone down on the dirty caller.

"Hello? Hello?"

"Mrs. Pearl?" I am startled by a strange voice and the coincidence of a connection without the phone having rung.

"Yes, it's Alex. Who's this please?"

"You don't know me, Mrs. Pearl. I'm Colleen's mother—Colleen Byrnes, your babysitter?"

"Oh, is everything all right? Is Colleen sick?" My eyes catch the large calendar taped to the pantry door. I've already inked in Colleen for next Saturday night.

"Mrs. Pearl, this is not a pleasant call for me to make. I'm afraid my daughter will no longer be able to babysit your little girls."

Damn. I bet Donny forgot to pay her last night. It's happened twice before. I am already steaming at him when she continues:

"Colleen came home last night hysterically crying."

Something in her slow, deliberate tone irritates me, but I let her continue while my heart revs up like a new Corvette.

"Please tell me what happened."

"It seems your husband, ah, Mr. Pearl, took my daughter for a little unexpected ride."

"A ride? But where?"

"Well . . . he drove to the high school parking lot and then he got out of his car, and came around to the passenger seat . . ."

My knees start to shake and beads of perspiration pop on my lip. I drag the stretched-out, soiled phone cord over to the sink, fill a Bert and Ernie plastic cup with water, and take a sip. Mrs. Byrnes continues to measure out each word, as if she were baking a cake, as if she's rehearsed this phone call a hundred times. I look out the kitchen bay window toward the red swing set. Becky and Lana are in day camp; they won't be home until three, but I swear I hear their squeaky laughter and the familiar rattle of aluminum chains.

I wrap my fingers around the phone cord and dip it in some pink liquid soap. Grime separates from the rubber, and I hear her say: "he popped in a cassette, some piano concerto, then got out of the car and asked Colleen to slide over to the driver's side."

"What are you insinuating?" I interject.

"Mrs. Pearl, Colleen is only sixteen, and your husband decided to conduct a driver's education class at one o'clock in the morning. He insisted he keep his arm around her shoulder while they continually circled the parking lot."

I picture Colleen Byrnes's perfect apple-shaped Irish face, freckles dotting her cheeks like sheer netting. Wisps of her hair blow in the sultry breeze of a warm night. Its fiery hue reminds me of the approaching autumn. She is small-boned and flat-chested, exactly the way I was—and hated being—at sixteen.

"Could it be your daughter is exaggerating, Mrs. Byrnes? Everyone cuts through that parking lot to avoid the traffic."

"Not at that hour, Mrs. Pearl!"

I walk the phone cord like a dog leash into the powder room. My eyes dart around; my fingers trace the wall. I find the piece of wallpaper that has begun to lift. A dark vacuum sucks up space in my mind. I tug hard, harder. With one quick motion I've managed to expose a large pasty patch of wall. The relief is thrilling.

Last night I'd fallen asleep before Donny—a rare occurrence. I had the beginnings of a migraine from the cheap sangria served at Wheatley Heights' end-of-season bowling party. I have a vague recollection of opening my eyes, just once, briefly. Donny was standing beside the bed staring at me.

"What?" I mumbled, startled.

"Nothing, I'm sorry," he whispered. "Go back to sleep."

I gaze blankly at the receiver. "My husband would never do any-thing like you're describing. Perhaps you should sit Colleen down and make her tell the truth. Why not put her on the phone?" I try to keep my voice even.

"Sorry, but I do know my own child, Mrs. Pearl. She'd never make anything like this up."

"And I know my husband!" I shriek, before slamming the receiver against the wall, instantly filled with remorse. A slideshow of our oldest, Becky, pops in my head. It is as bright and neon as a Warhol poster. She's maybe fourteen and being driven home from her first babysitting job by somebody's handsome dad, a man who has leaned in extremely close to offer her a joint.

My body is in tremor, like a covered soup pot without the vent. Acid from my morning juice rises like a geyser in my throat. I gulp more water, and then with a jumbo sponge, I wipe the already spot-less Formica counter, move on to the refrigerator doors, attacking chocolate and ketchup stains made by tiny fingertips. Still, I can't wipe away the words and bold images tattooed inside my skull. They have magnified, reaching billboard proportion.

I pace and pace, then mop the kitchen floor twice and must rest to catch my breath. My red vinyl beach bag is propped on the chair next to me. I empty it upside down and find, among loose change and lollipops, a plastic bottle containing a mixture of baby oil and iodine, along with Donny's makeshift sun reflector—a Bee Gees album cov-ered in aluminum foil. Stepping over the mound of white sand I've dumped on the freshly mopped floor, I head for the patio.

Once outside, I ease myself onto the burning cushions of the chaise, and within minutes, the shivering stops. The gardeners have come and gone, so I unbutton my blouse to dot my face and chest with the soothing pink oil. Salty tears slide down my cheeks and linger on my lip. If Donny were here, I wonder if he'd kiss me and lick my tears the way he did when we were first married. I can see his youthful face; I know he'd be furious I had to listen to Mrs. Byrnes's ridiculous accusations. I bet I'd have to restrain him from going over to Colleen's house, to force her to admit how she made this whole thing up. But what if . . . what if she's telling the truth?

The phone rings and I don't budge. I try to block out ghoulish thoughts about the girls: Did they have some catastrophe at camp— get hit in the eye with an airborne rock, choke on a wad of Bazooka during afternoon swim? Or were they kidnapped at gunpoint while their stunned counselors looked on helplessly? No! It's probably Rona calling to check whether I've contacted the folks at Parisian Home Décor. If not her, then Donny asking what's for dinner. *I'll tell you what's for dinner, Donny.*

A bumblebee the size of a small passenger jet grazes the tip of my nose. I snap up, fists out, ready to fight. I have no idea how long I've been outside, no conception of time. Peeling my damp thighs off the cushions, I head back inside. An aroma of burnt onions wafts through the sliding screen door, competing with the fragrant Queen Anne roses and the freshly mowed grass. I forgot to set the timer and have charred the roast I'd shoved in the oven. A thought invades: Why not serve the black lump to Donny? Hasn't he always preferred his beef well-done? But knowing him, he'd most likely laugh, which might steal a grin from me, and now I need to remain dead serious. Until we discuss it, *he* is the only one I can tell about this call. It's tempting to pick up the receiver and dial Rona, knowing if I shared with her, our friendship might move in a whole new direction. Yet, she's more likely to brush the incident off like most things which don't directly concern her.

I'm surprised by a distorted reflection in the stainless oven door. Staring back from my own fun house mirror is a fiery pink, Modigliani face. I grab a frosty can of Fresca, press it to my lips, and gulp, trying to soothe my throat. A large sales slip escapes the refrigerator magnet and soars through the smoky air. It's an order for several T-shirts I'm supposed to first tie-dye, then paint, and deliver to All Zee Kids, a local children's boutique, before school begins in two weeks. One is for a child named Emily and shows a nearly naked girl running through a field of daisies, golden hair cascading down her back.

Hey, Missy, So, you call yourself a painter? It's that nag again, inquiring about the five-foot canvas I abandoned a year ago after coating it with primer. Primed for what, I was never quite sure. Still, I take great solace in recalling the late-life career of Grandma Moses. Over and over I tell myself: *Live first, Alex. Paint later.*

The yellow minibus honks loudly in the driveway, stirring me from my trance. Pasting a smile on my face, I sprint out the front door to see my Lana, four and a half, cradled in the arms of a young counselor in training. She has fallen asleep on the bus ride home, and her russet curls are soaked with perspiration. Becky will be six in September. She dashes into my arms for a lift, circle swing, and hug. I lick her flushed cheeks and call her by her pet name—Vanilla Girl. She is pale blonde, her skin golden in summer. Becky's inky blues squint up at me, scrutinizing my face.

"Mommy, are you sad today?" She startles me with her old lady observation.

"No, but I *am* very busy."

"Oh no, what do I smell?" Becky sniffs my hands and looks up at me, wide-eyed.

"I burned our dinner, that's all. Hey, cookie, what's that you're wearing around your neck?"

"It's a lanyard for Daddy's keys. We made them in arts and crafts."

"I'm sure Daddy will love it. Will you teach me?"

"It's pretty hard, Mommy, but I'll try."

I take Lana from the counselor's arms and rock her gently. Lana has dolls that weigh more than she does. Her thick lashes begin to flutter as she sucks her two middle fingers. When I tickle her, I see her little smirk, but she pretends to be asleep. This one is a bundle of energy, a born actress named after my father's mother, Layla, who lived long enough to bury three adoring husbands. Playing along, I carry Lana into the house while Becky runs ahead to hold open the door. "Heavy, heavy sack of potatoes," I tease.

When I plop Lana on the den couch, she does a deliberate flip onto the shag carpeting, then jumps to her feet, wide-awake with outstretched arms, her own imitation of Shirley Temple.

"Mommy . . . hug!"

Usually, I'd wait for Donny to help get the girls bathed, but I need this time alone with them to quiet the engine roaring inside my head. After a snack of crackers, I usher Becky and Lana up the stairs and follow them, collecting the dirty socks and panties they drop along the way to the bathroom. Standing on either side of my crouched body, they rival two naked cherubs out of an ancient fresco. I pour bubble bath under the spigot; Lana squeals as bubbles escape in the air. She is already in the tub splashing, while Becky holds my arm until her chubby legs are firmly planted in the tub.

After a few cries of dread, they press washcloths to their eyes while I swiftly pour lukewarm water over their locks and rinse out the shampoo. I wrap them in one large beach towel and they collide, giggling as I inhale the phenomenon of their healing scent. For these few minutes, nothing in the world troubles me.

Downstairs again, at precisely five o'clock, Fred Rogers's hypnotic voice fills the cozy, rustic den. Mesmerized by the hospitable gentleman inviting them on his daily journey, Lana and Becky sit squeezed together holding hands on Donny's faux leather recliner. Their tiny pink tongues poke out and lick the dryness from their lips, and my heart aches with tenderness. *Look, Nana, these are your great-granddaughters. Becky's named for you. She has your long, beautiful fingers and straight silken hair.* I have always maintained an open line to my maternal grandmother, who disappointed me only once, by dying.

The automatic garage door rumbles, and I swallow hard. This, the only sound the girls hear over the clanging of the trolley in Mr. Rogers's neighborhood.

"Daddy's home," Lana announces before returning her fingers to her mouth.

I hear the familiar heavy shuffle of Donny's feet as he walks through the doorway connecting our garage to the den. His wiry brows are knit together and his shoulders are hunched to his ears, hinting he's had one rough day at the factory. Donny is no longer the aspiring musician his parents once bragged about. Since his father put him in charge of a new division at H. Pearl and Sons, he is an employee, capable of screwing up like all the others.

I cower behind the dining room wall like a cat that's been shooed from the dinner table. Donny makes a pit stop into the powder room. I listen to his long, never-ending stream. Though he's left the door wide open, I refrain from scolding. But as soon as he charges into the den and lifts Becky and Lana to give them rough nuzzles on their necks, I rush forward and tug at his shirtsleeve. I've never done this before. In fact, watching Donny with our girls has always filled me with immense pleasure, but now I need him separate—no fragile props like our children.

"Hi," he says, his kiss missing my cheek as I pull back and stiffen. "What's up? Okay, what did you burn?" He follows me into the kitchen, glancing at a few bills on the table and the blackened Pyrex dish soaking in the sink. He shoots a sympathetic grin. "I can pick up Chinese?"

"I'm not hungry. We need to talk. Let's go sit in the living room."

Becky and Lana, having abandoned their fish sticks, are slurping chocolate milk through straws. Their rapt attention is on Mr. Rogers, who has just zipped up his beige cardigan.

Donny's concern is woven with impatience. He passes our white, spinet piano and lingers, hitting a C chord hard, like in a television drama. Looking at his watch, he plops down on the loveseat beside me. I wait while he removes his lenses. Here comes the ritual of rubbing his eyes. If only he could see me now, really see me; but without his "eyes" he's close to legally blind. He hasn't noticed my sunburn or the mascara smudged beneath my lashes.

"Shoot," he says.

"I got a call this morning from Mrs. Byrnes." He looks blank.

"Who's that?"

"She's the mother of Colleen . . . our sitter, remember, Don?" My voice cracks. I take a deep breath and rally to regain my composure. Donny leans forward, resting his elbows on his knees. He pushes his glossy, auburn hair back with his fingers, and I see his smooth profile, how uniquely handsome he is—how any teenage girl might confuse his intentions.

"Mrs. Byrnes said you drove Colleen to the high school parking lot late last night. Why didn't you take her straight home? What the hell were you thinking?"

Donny turns mute, which only frightens me more. I wish he'd say something, anything. When I turn and look at him, he appears filmy through my tears. His jaw, once hidden by a scrawny goatee, sets firmly.

"I thought Mrs. Byrnes was lying, Donny—I screamed and hung up on the woman. But she wasn't lying, was she? Was she?" Donny's face is bloated as if it's about to explode, but he grabs me and presses me hard against his chest. "Tell me why," I say into his soiled work shirt, inhaling the dizzying aroma of sewing machine grease.

"I don't know, Alex," he answers somberly. "It was nothing, really. The kid said she was afraid to drive. I told her *driving* was a snap. All I did was ask if she wanted to try. She said *yes*. I swear! We were in the parking lot for ten minutes at the most."

I try to wiggle away, afraid that I'll scratch out Donny's beautiful hazel eyes. He holds me tighter as if to say: *Yes, do it if it'll make you feel better, go ahead and hurt me back.*

Maybe because I'm tired, I begin to picture the stupidity, even innocence in Donny's act—a childish need of his to feel important. It was a trait I noticed from the get-go—something I hoped might dissipate, though clearly it never did. But what I can't forget is that the incident occurred past midnight, and that Colleen Byrnes is in high school, and he might have been arrested, which may have ruined our lives.

One month before we were to be married, nearly seven years ago, Donny flew in from Boston to help with some last-minute details. We were spending a relaxing Sunday afternoon at his parents' townhouse in Brooklyn: his father and I in the small, sunny backyard picking cherry tomatoes; his mother fussing in the kitchen, trying out a sausage and peppers dish from her bible, *The Joy of Cooking*. About to finish grad school for his MBA, Donny had been cramming for finals. Complaining all day of a headache, he chose to stay inside.

I carried a few ripened tomatoes indoors to Donny's mother.

"Here, Mom, don't these look great?" She'd insisted I call her Mom since our engagement last summer. "Where's Donny?" I asked, opening the fridge to get some iced tea.

Louise shrugged, but the scowl on her face told me she was annoyed at someone, or something. I expected to find Donny sprawled on the living room couch listening to an album, or buried under a stack of books in the cozy den. Then I checked upstairs where he'd sleep later on that day after taking me back home—no Donny. Downstairs again, I entered the long hallway leading to the master bedroom, a guest room, and the bedroom that belonged to Ivy, Donny's affable and popular thirteen-year-old sister. As I walked past her room, I heard high-pitched squealing—what you would expect to hear from any teenage girl's room. But when I listened closely, I identified Donny's hoarse voice interspersed with laughter. Pushing in the door just a few inches gave me a clear view of Donny propped against the lavender organdy pillows on his sister's bed. While Ivy chatted on the phone without paying him much attention, Donny read passages aloud from *Mad* magazine to three of her giggling girlfriends. Flanking Ivy's bed, two of them leaned on bent knees, eager as poodles begging treats. A third girl tucked herself cozily next to him, while his fingers occasionally reached out to tug her ropey braids, as if he were ringing a bell.

A tight smile stretched across Donny's face, as though he were posed before an audience and had only just realized no one either heard or cared about anything he uttered. For an instant I thought about barging in the room, wondering what, if anything, my appearance might change. Instead, like an obedient servant, not wishing to intrude, I stepped backward into the darkened hallway and quietly shut the door. I felt embarrassed for Donny, but mostly for me—a stranger, roaming around the house of people I hardly knew. I was lost, not knowing where to put myself, or where, if anywhere, I belonged.

Donny trails behind me to the den where we discover Becky and Lana without their bathrobes; they are rolling around the shag carpet, gathering orange fuzz balls in their damp hair and on their buttocks. Donny bites the inside of his cheek, waiting for my reaction. Yes, they are adorable and funny, but how can I laugh? Nothing he can say will make me feel better.

Though, in the stillness of the next few minutes, I do begin to wonder if maybe, without knowing it, Colleen lured Donny into taking her to the parking lot. Perhaps later she was overcome with guilt and decided she could never look me in the face again—so it was easier to twist the truth, to fling her fanciful muddle onto Donny. The tightness in my chest slowly begins to loosen. I stand up and get busy. Busy always helps.

While I settle the girls upstairs, Donny insists on scrambling some onions and eggs—soothing, easy-to-go-down food. We don't talk much; I have one-word answers and grunts. I take birdlike nibbles from my plate while the Moody Blues sing *Nights in White Satin*. It's a little before eight, still light. There is a hint of autumn in the air, the slightest smell of ragweed. I sneeze loudly, surprising us both. "Well, God bless you," Donny says, and I nod my thanks, thinking how often civility restores normalcy. I carry my coffee mug outside to the patio and sit down. Donny stands while he lights up a joint. We both stare at the pink marbled sky. He passes the joint to me; I hesitate but take a tiny drag.

"Hold it in," he says, coaching me as usual. I imagine he hopes getting me stoned will tuck my angry thoughts away, but I've never felt safe enough to just let go.

"Enough! Take the stupid thing." I blow the smoke out, but it's already singed my nasal passages.

"Are you okay?" he asks, watching me recover. "Al, I meant to ask, what happened to the paper in the bathroom?" I watch him take a long, deep drag.

"The adhesive dried out. They're coming back to repair it." I only just realize I never got to make the call.

Donny shoots me his best piercing look: head cocked and eyes big as rain puddles. Is he waiting for me to crack wide-open, ooze like a farm fresh egg? I remember when I first took a shot at trusting him: how I'd offered my smooth upturned hand like an anxious child, hoping for sweets. He leans forward in the cold metal chair, and I put out my hand, automatically, as if accepting an invitation to dance. Standing, he takes it and pulls me to my feet. His breath is soft and smoky against my ear.

"Damn you, Donny, damn you."

"I'm sorry, honey, really sorry." His arms move up and down my hips while he kisses my face. Nervous, I look up to notice the sporadic dance of lights in all the surrounding houses. I hear sliding doors open, then close. There are people, people I hardly know, just yards away from us beyond the woven fence and the aphid-free roses. I smell the rich perfume of perennials, the charring of well-priced filets. *Good fences make good neighbors.* My mind has become a cafeteria serving up stored one-liners.

Back inside, Donny takes the kitchen phone off the hook and tosses it in the junk drawer. Smiling, he leads me to the powder room and locks the door behind us. I am braced against the wall, exactly where I'd yanked the section of silver wallpaper. He presses against me, his thin yet dexterous fingers moving up and down my body as if I were a keyboard—a place to feel at home. My arms reach for him, helping while he quickly unzips his jeans, and before I change my mind. This is the first time in months Donny's been this excited, pulsing . . . hard. I give him all the control he wants.

I balance one leg on the dwarf-size commode while Donny pushes himself deep inside me. Like always, it hurts for only a second. *Relax, relax.* My fingers grasp and glide through the oily redness of his hair. And I am certain this is all that I want—what I have always wanted.

TWO The next morning, when Donny leans over to kiss me good-bye, I feign sleep. His cool, minty breath tickles my neck, but I keep my eyes shut until I hear him fly down the stairs and slam the front door. An hour later, once I feed the girls and put them on the camp bus, I crawl back in bed and bury myself under the soft, eyelet covers. I dream weird, fragmented dreams. In one, Colleen's mother is announcing over the PA system at the A&P: *Customers, for one day only, Alex Pearl's husband, Donald, will be giving free driving lessons in the parking lot.* Followed by: *For the next half hour, get 50 percent off on Boar's Head bologna at the deli counter.*

In one particular Jabberwocky scene, I'm Alice, not Alex, tumbling through the dark hole of my imagination. My teeth are chipped and blackened, and my pumpkin dyed hair stands stalk-like at the roots. Upon waking, I find my nightgown up to my belly button, soaked in sweat, but I'm not interested in figuring out the hidden meaning in dreams. All I want is to push Donny's incident away, swallow it down as if it were a pungent dose of penicillin insuring no relapse. I need to trust him again so I won't waste away the hours daydreaming and rehashing events. Yet, the truth is I feel humiliated and want to hide.

Out of bed around ten, I tackle two weeks of dirty laundry. While folding Donny's boxer shorts, I wiggle my fingers through the convenient *little* opening, and scan the fabric for telltale stains. Though I find nothing, my heartbeat gallops through my eardrums. I try calming myself and choose rationalization over meditation; meditation has always made me nervous, like watching myself, watching myself.

Wait! Hey, of course! Didn't I have a humongous crush a couple of years ago on Becky and Lana's pediatrician—a slightly balding, yet terribly sexy man I'd nicknamed Dr. Hot? I actually called his office once and lied, saying Lana was burning up with fever, when her temperature barely reached 100. All I wanted was to hear his soothing voice, his *Okay, Alex, why don't you bring her right in*. So, what if he was so much older than me? When he strode into the examining cubicle and placed his stethoscope on Lana's small quivering chest, I felt that God himself had descended upon the room. Once I leaned against the wall while he was examining Lana and accidentally hit the light switch. Though my poor baby wailed in fear, there were several moments charged with a weird sexual energy. Oh, and when I was often housebound in our cramped apartment in Brooklyn . . . yes, I remember now . . . there was this swarthy young guy, with amazing emerald eyes, who made greasy falafels at a Middle Eastern take-out place. I'm embarrassed to think that I'd once bundled up the girls to go out in snow flurries to feast on those eyes and strong, angular face—just to hear him say in his mysterious accent: *Hi there, Sunshine. How you doing today?* So, I wonder, why now this strong urge to play Brenda Starr?

I stuff Donny's clothing back in his drawers and search for the shirt he wore the night he drove our babysitter home. I don't want to think of her name. The mustard yellow, short-sleeved Lacoste is balled up on the floor of his closet. Down on my hands and knees, I sniff the garment like an anxious cocker spaniel but uncover no clues. Only Donny's dried perspiration from three games of really lousy bowling. He did say I'd be sorry for beating him that night.

Perhaps, I should have taken him seriously. Other images pervade, though I am a master of forgetting, especially when I am damn close to knowing what I'm too scared to know.

I met Donald Pearl when I was nineteen, technically a virgin, and positive I'd graduate college unattached, forcing me to live with my parents until they died. We were both counselors at The Weeping Willow Day Camp—me, working after my junior year of college, he, having dropped out of dental school to enter a music academy in Boston. When that escalated into enormous pressure because of fierce competition, Donny left, but soon after landed at a small business college where he finally felt like he belonged.

I'd observed him during the summer, a few times nodding hello—taking note of the variety of Betty and Veronica counselor types he paired with, a different girl each week. Donny doubled as the music counselor, and when he played the beaten-up white baby grand propped across the camp's stage, his head bobbed, rhythmically, reminding me of Paul McCartney. Maybe it was the spell of the upbeat music, or just being surrounded by the chaotic energy of two dozen admiring and adorable tots, but I felt an immediate tie to Donny—something unspoken, yet upbeat and lyrical, telling me he could be *it*. Though I wasn't thrilled to learn *it* had a waistline two inches slimmer than mine. Donny camouflaged his boyishness and ruddy complexion by sporting a goatee and wearing his wavy auburn hair long and tucked behind his ears. Near the end of the camp season, our grins grew broader whenever we passed each other, an assortment of squinty-eyed campers trailing us like twitchy caterpillars. Once, I'd thought I was being nonchalant, but we both turned around to look back. We knew we were running out of time. Then one day after most of the minibuses left to return campers to their respective neighborhoods, Donny sauntered up to me and asked in a low, husky voice for me to hold out my hand. Taken aback, my heartbeat accelerated and I obeyed, as if it were perfectly natural for him to give me a command, as if he and I were already that well acquainted.

"What are you doing?" I asked, giggling.

"You'll see," he whispered. His eyelids were slightly droopy. Yes, just like my favorite Beatle, Paul. Donny leaned his head over my shaky outstretched hand and tugged on his eyelashes a few times until a moist contact lens popped into my palm. The little sphere tickled, and I held my arm out stiffly, afraid to move.

"It was in wrong," he said, wearing a lopsided grin. Then he peeled the nearly invisible lens from my hand and popped it inside his mouth.

"Don't do that, you'll get an infection," I said. Here I was having a hard time remembering his name, but I was already taking care of him. Had I just passed some test? I wondered if all of Donny's girlfriends got to feel the warm wetness of his contact lenses swirling around in their open palm. He walked alongside me to the counselors' parking lot, and as I slipped into my slightly dented, white Dodge Dart convertible, he leaned in and asked for my number.

"What about . . . ?" I started to ask.

"Betsy?"

"Oh, so that's her name."

"Betsy and I are just friends," he said.

I looked at him, coyly, tempted to say, *Come on, do you think I'm an idiot?*

I guessed he was just another cute charmer and yet, I scribbled my number on a gasoline receipt and handed it to him. What the hell, there were only two weeks of camp left, and we'd both be heading back to school. He called me an hour later, and we went out that night, and every night after for the remainder of the summer.

Each morning, when we lined up for roll call, Betsy and her junior counselor threw me murderous looks. I was sure one of them would sprinkle arsenic on my orange sherbet at lunchtime. Perhaps, Betsy had her own interpretation of what it meant to be Donny's good friend.

Then, on our third date, Donny brought me home to meet his folks: Louise and Benjamin Pearl, a charismatic couple, with whom I became enamored before falling for their son. They presented themselves as a united front in matters involving both family and business—a foundations firm started by Ben's father in the late 1930s. I didn't believe Donny when he announced his family was *in* ladies' underwear. He'd said it with such a sweet, flirtatious grin that I thought he might be telling a bad joke. The truth is when first hearing *foundations,* I'd envisioned hard hats, cranes, even cement mixers. I was sure the Pearls were involved in building and construction and that *foundation* referred to basements, rather than a line of lacy, sexy, push-up bras. But, not ten minutes after the introduction, Donny mortified me by asking:

"What do you think, Dad? I'd say she's probably a full C." Louise, noticing my jaw drop, assured me this was standard father-son shoptalk. She said that any woman, young or old, entering the Pearl household was immediately scrutinized, then mentally fitted with the proper brassiere. Because they were in the business of breast support, the Pearls felt it their duty.

Later that evening we uncovered a huge coincidence, which may have sealed our fate. Our grandfathers had done business together decades before; mine owned Bliss on Lexington Avenue, a well-known wedding gown salon specializing in designer gowns and accessories at discount prices. For years, H. Pearl and Sons had been one of their steady suppliers and manufacturer of strapless-bra styles for that *most* memorable occasion in a young woman's life.

"Are you saying that standing before me now is Charlie Kane's precious granddaughter?" Ben stretched out his arms to embrace me.

"Louise! The girl's practically family!"

I stood shyly in front of the Pearls like a schoolgirl receiving kudos on her first A. Though I felt proud, I worried I might not live up to any future expectations. Something about these warm, gentle folks jolted me back to when I was a carefree and jubilant girl frolicking around my grandparents' home. My senses were stirred by the aromas of baked chicken, mushrooms, and onions, as well as the soft flickering of Sabbath candles, and the melodic clinking of stemware in the china closet when anyone moved past—a familiarity melding my past and present, sending a tingling warmth throughout my bones.

I couldn't wait to get home to call my grandfather who, when hearing about this new boyfriend, boasted how he'd loaned Donny's grandfather a "nice" sum of money during the Great Depression. As a Polish immigrant, who arrived in America with a suitcase and five bucks in his pocket, Papa was insanely proud.

"Well, tell me, Papa," I asked. "Did he repay you?"

"Sure, sure, *shaina maidel*," Papa answered. "It was a thousand bucks, and I crossed it off in my little black book." Though relieved there'd be no bad blood between our families, it took some time before I felt comfortable enough to relay the story of my grandfather's diligence in keeping track of what he had, so generously, loaned his cronies.

Then, on the eve before we were both to return to school, after

Thanksgiving, the Pearls insisted on taking us to dinner at The Quilted Giraffe in Manhattan, where they often entertained important customers. Dinner out, for *my* family, usually meant Sunday nights at Gam Wah's Chinese Palace, written up once, not for its ambience, but the discovery of cat skeletons in the garbage bins. When it came to patisserie, we savored the weekly gift bestowed by my father, a box of Dunkin' Donuts, but only if we'd completed our assigned chores and homework. So, when the slightly aloof French waiter, bent on one knee to offer something I recognized from the dessert wagon, an éclair, I sighed with relief. The truth was: fancy anything made me suspicious.

Donny squeezed my hand under the table while his father, sipping Sambuca, told me that Donny wouldn't stop talking about this "knock-out" he met at camp. I immediately asked if her name was Betsy, but he shook his head *no*.

"Me?" I mustered the courage to ask, while Donny sat there grinning and enjoying a Singapore Sling.

Ben circled the glass with his fingers. "My son said, 'Dad, I'd like to ask her out, but I doubt she'll give me a shot.'"

"So, is this true?" I asked, leaning against Donny's shoulder. He squirmed a bit in his chair and adjusted his tie to free his Adam's apple. Louise's smile looked a bit strained as she chewed the celery from a Bloody Mary. I truly liked Louise and hoped she didn't mind the fuss her men were now making over me.

"Of course, I say, 'If you don't call the girl tomorrow and ask her out, you are definitely not my son.'"

"Well, I guess I should thank *you* then," I said, leaning in and barely touching Ben's sleeve. I hadn't spent a great deal of time with older men other than my dad, grandfather, and an uncle or two, and was still unsure of the physical boundaries. Ben winked, and we raised our glasses. I gripped the skinny stem of my wineglass, wondering what the Pearls might say if they knew I'd lost my virginity, just days before, in their enormous brass bed, on top of the four-hundred-thread-count, Porthault sheets—the same sheets I'd frantically scrubbed, afterwards, for an hour, because of one teensy speck of blood.

My eyes met Ben's and then landed on Donny. Maybe it was the champagne, but seconds later, my mood plummeted. I excused myself and found the ladies' room. Leaning into the marble vanity, I splashed cold water on my wrists and dabbed at my face. Not then, but someday soon, I vowed to ask Donny who he was *really* trying to please when he made that very first call to ask me out.

It is nearly noon before I realize the phone receiver spent the night trapped in the kitchen drawer. As always, Rona manages to be the first to get through to me.

"Well, aren't you the little chatterbox today," she says, with an acidic hint of possessiveness that signals: it is definitely time to make new friends.

"No, Rona, I took the phone off the hook and forgot about it. I've been in the bathroom all morning. It must've been the chopped meat. Donny and the girls ate spaghetti and they're fine."

"Are you saying it was the chopped chuck from Fernando's?"

"Uh-huh, probably that order we split of frozen patties."

"Don't tell me this, Alex. I just read in *Family Circle* that you can actually die from bacteria in spoiled meat!"

I hear doors opening and closing, a frantic shuffle coming through the phone as Rona begins emptying her freezer. Like a seasoned cashier, she tabulates aloud: "That's six filet mignons for forty-eight bucks, eight shoulder chops, twenty-five dollars, two prime ribs, thirty-five dollars, and a jumbo package of beef patties for fifteen dollars—in the garbage."

"But it might only be a little virus." I don't know whether to laugh, cry, or come clean and tell Rona I had scrambled eggs, coffee, followed by a toke or two, and pretty decent sex against the bathroom wall.

"I'm not taking any chances," Rona says. Then I hear: "Hey, do you feel well enough to come over? I'll fix you something light—tea, toast, and scrambled eggs. I'd come get you but Hy brought the car in for the five-thousand-mile check-up. So, maybe you'll drive me there later so I can pick it up. Of course, only if you're feeling up to it."

It serves me right. Though I'm full up on eggs, I agree to lunch in half an hour. Without going into details, over the phone, I mention the lovely babysitter, Colleen Byrnes, saying she is no longer under my employment. Rona gasps with the identical intensity she had demonstrated over the possibility of food poisoning.

The Karls' home is an immaculate split-level on the north side of town, "done" in muted tones of beige and mocha—reminiscent of a Danish modern furniture showroom and sterile as a dentist's office. I often picture Rona and Hy sitting down to a Pillsbury-perfect dinner with their young son, Ethan—a sweet, nervous boy forbidden to tumble and soil his clothes. As their forks and spoons lift in unison, they appear futuristic and comically robotic. As part of her vows, I'd bet Rona has included a policy promising no crumbs, spilled milk, or indelible stains. Yet, secretly, I envy her strict dedication to order. She would have been the model daughter for my mother—the one she would have chosen had she been able to foretell the future. "Oh, Alex, how's that darling friend of yours?" My mother never fails to ask this when she calls weekly from Florida, her question reminding me that I, too, was raised in a home where the pursuit for perfection was revered, and tidiness was the true religion.

"I thought you and Donny loved your babysitter," Rona says, daintily dabbing tuna salad from the corners of her mouth. I wouldn't mind a taste of her tuna, but I'm stuck with the dry rye toast and gooey eggs. She stares me down with her thickly coated lashes. Here in Rona's spotless Formica kitchen, there is no place to hide. I pretend to look for the dry-cleaning receipt in my bag, stalling to collect my thoughts.

"Yes, we both liked her a lot"—my voice falters on *both*—"and she was great with the girls, but there's this new boyfriend she met this summer. The thing is . . . she's just not as dependable."

"I'm not surprised she has boyfriends. That kid is drop-dead gorgeous."

"You really think so? Personally, I think she's too damn skinny." Heat wraps around my collarbone. My teeth gnaw through a triangle of toast.

"Well, maybe she is a bit thin, but I'd kill for her hair."

"But it's red, Rona! How would you, of all people, manage all that wild red hair?"

"Relax, Alex, take a breath. I see you're upset, but you'll find another sitter soon. There are zillions of homely teenage girls trolling the mall each weekend with nothing to do."

"That's depressing as hell, plus I hate having to look for someone all over again." Tears spring to my eyes. I'm on the brink of spilling the beans. It's a struggle to keep everything inside.

"Hey, all we are talking about is a few hours on a Saturday night, and an afternoon here and there. Alex, no big deal."

"You know, maybe you're right. I'll find someone even more competent and reliable." I sit up straight and finish my slice of rye. The soggy scrambled eggs remain buried underneath my napkin.

"I bet you're feeling better already, right?" Rona asks, picking at her molars with a wooden toothpick.

"Yes, I think so. Thanks. And thanks for the delicious lunch."

Rona glances at the chrome clock above her stove. "Come on, we've still got some time. Let's get some shopping in while our little monsters are still in camp, and then you can drop me at the car dealer."

She stands and, in seconds, loads the dishwasher, grabs her handbag, dabs on her shimmery gloss, and is ready to go. I stare at her, amazed at how easily she analyzes any crisis, minor or major, produces a solution, and then ties it into a bundle like worn-out clothes to dump in the Goodwill bin. There is not a trace of sentimentality in deciding to let go. Finished. Done. Next! I am certain Rona and I live not only on the opposite sides of town, but on opposite poles of the earth. Still, since moving to Wheatley Heights, I am drawn to her like a piglet to teats, searching for any semblance of nourishment. The truth is: it's much less lonely to sleepwalk alongside her.

Later that afternoon, at Rona's suggestion, I place an ad in the *Wheatley Heights Tattler*. By the following week, I have ten teenage girls scheduled for interviews. One of them is a fourteen-year-old named Agnes who lives half a mile away. She is ebullient in spite of severe acne and the silver fences imprisoning her teeth. I hire her on the spot.

THREE

Since camp has officially ended for the season, the days are no longer just mine. Gone are the blissful hours of planting my garden while the sun, a quiet but reliable lover, tenderly kisses my back. Gone are the warm, breezy nights, the girls spread across a blanket like paper dolls, gazing up to count the stars.

Today, while Agnes babysits the girls, I drive to the drugstore to pick up a cream for Becky's eczema before stopping at the shoemaker to have taps put on Lana's first pair of tap shoes. Strolling past Fernando's, I see that the sign advertising the blow-out sale remains pasted in the window, but for the first time there's no need to take a number. Three butchers wave their bloody choppers in the air, anxious to serve me. I stare at the sawdust floor looking for footprints and wonder how many people Rona has already cautioned not to buy Fernando's meat—how many heard about a woman named Alex Pearl, who resides on Daisy Lane, ate chopped chuck last week, and took violently ill?

Mr. Fernando, a kind, jovial Sicilian with eight children, doubles as the fire chief of Wheatley Heights and is a very solid citizen. I'd feel personally responsible if his reputation was now tainted, forcing him to close up shop. I buy two farm fresh chickens and ask to have them cut up in eighths. It's the least I can do.

Back again in the car, I press my foot to the accelerator and soon realize I am chauffeuring raw poultry in eighty-degree heat, inside a car with a leaky air conditioner.

Sweat dripping, I remember the other night's fast and furious bathroom sex and ponder whether it had burgeoned out of Donny's grit or guilt. I wish I could let it go, but I keep imagining him in the high school parking lot helping Colleen master her first parallel park.

I make a sharp right into the A&P lot and, going too fast, I can't stop in time to avoid a Chevy wagon backing out of a space. I clip the left rear bumper and watch the vehicle shimmy. Terrified, I jump from my car, hands clasped on top of my head like *The Fugitive* finally surrendering. This is my first "fender bender" and, although I sense the damage is minor, the sheer surprise of the impact, and loss of control, has me quaking with fear. Tears start in my throat and slide down my cheeks.

A petite, delicate-looking young woman jumps from her station wagon and inspects her bumper. She looks up at me and shrugs. "Oh, please don't fret, this car is a tank," she says. "See all those battle scars? What's one more?"

"Oh, but look at you, you're pregnant! Are you sure that you're okay?"

She deep sighs *yes* and runs her hand over a protruding belly, then steps forward to shake mine. It's a small hand with the power of a tugboat. Her demeanor is tranquil and serene, something, which along with her pregnant belly, I can't help but envy.

"I guess I better move my car," I say, dabbing my nose. "I'm blocking traffic."

"You can take this spot. You've more than claimed it." She laughs.

She is about to leave when I notice a bold, colorful emblem adorning the rear window of her wagon. The design is simple, two red hearts with wings floating atop a tall mountain. Across the middle are the words: *Marriage Mountain*.

"Marriage Mountain. I like that, it's so intriguing." I'm afraid to sound cheerful in case this is a serious deal, something related to drugs, alcohol, or spousal abuse. Her doe-like eyes turn wistful. "Oh, forgive me. Sometimes, I'm much too nosy."

"No, no, please. I'm glad you asked. Joe and I joined Marriage Mountain six months ago, and it's made a huge difference in both our lives. There's a sanctuary for married couples about thirty minutes from here—a weekend retreat, held in a monastery, run by the Jesuits," she says, in a timbre as smooth and angelic as her face. I see a flash frame of Mia Farrow in *Rosemary's Baby.*

"Uh-huh, I see." I know little about the Jesuits except that they are priests. Perhaps, it would have served me better to take an elective in world religions instead of all those credits in oil painting and mixed media.

"It's totally non secular," she says, as if reading the trepidation in my face. "The program is designed mostly to help couples of all faiths rededicate themselves to the relationship. After a while we all need to renew our marriage vows. You are married, I assume? Come on . . . how long?"

"Um . . . almost seven years." My voice sounds as tiny as a third grader's. Maybe it's her softness or the surprise impact made by our car bumpers, but because I feel she sees through me and how scared I am, I begin telling this complete stranger everything. I talk so fast I can hardly catch my breath. She observes me, quietly, and as I babble on, all she keeps saying is "breathe honey, breathe."

A gum-chewing, Brillo-haired woman pulls up in her sleek, shiny Corvette and honks. "Girls! Ya' leavin' ta-day or ta-morrow?"

"In one minute!" my Marriage Mountain woman shouts back. Holding up her hand with the authority of a crossing guard, she takes her sweet-ass time. She fishes for a pen and paper in a suede-fringed shoulder bag and scribbles on a flyer. "Call me when you get home for all the information. By the way, what's your name?"

I glance around, then whisper, as if I'm Deep Throat exchanging life-altering information, "Alex, Alex Pearl."

"I'm Jillian. Today is your lucky day, Alex. You'll see." Jillian pivots around to the seething woman still waiting and smiles a Cheshire smile. "Sorry, my girlfriend, *Alex*, is taking my spot."

For the rest of the day I'm super-hyper, elated about the prospect of a weekend away with Donny and sold on the idea of forcing our intimacy in order to reinforce it. I'm determined to use Donny's midnight ride with our babysitter as a turning point and fresh start.

Alex, admit it, there have been plenty of times when you weren't exactly the perfect mate. Tired or under stress, you can be hypercritical and a bit of a nag. If I'm the one responsible for pushing Donny away, then it's up to me to find the way to tug him back. Split again, from what's real or imagined, I must fix whatever needs fixing.

I call Jillian before Donny gets home from work. She sounds surprised to hear from me. Practically bursts my eardrum with her, "Hi!" But doesn't recall if I'm the woman she met at the dry cleaner, the car wash, or locked bumpers with in the parking lot. In the background, I hear dogs barking, playfully, and the warm tones of a man's voice trying to still them. Again, I feel a pang of envy toward this stranger who seems to possess some secret marital code I have yet to figure out. Jillian gives me the phone number for Marriage Mountain, then mentions the total cost of $200. I've got at least that hidden under the bedroom carpet—money from my T-shirt painting that I've saved for new window treatments. The sliding Japanese panels for our den can wait.

"If you mention my name when you register," Jillian says, "you'll get a twenty percent discount, and my husband and I get fifty percent off on the next brush-up weekend."

"Oh, I didn't think we'd have to return. Doesn't that get pretty costly?"

"Alex, would you stop taking a lifesaving drug if it was working for you—showing evidence of a cure?"

"Well no, of course not." I spot my face in our mirrored armoire. My cheeks are brick red and blotchy.

"So, basically you're saying you'll do anything to make your marriage work?"

"Yes, I'd be foolish not to."

"Trust me, you're already halfway there." Jillian signs off before I can say *thank you.*

The next morning, when I call the toll-free number for Marriage Mountain—1-800-FOR-LOVE—I'm informed the first available opening is the third weekend in October. "I'll take it!" I shout to an automated-sounding operator, as if I've just garnered the last set of Ginsu knives in North America.

"You are incredibly lucky, Mrs. Donald Pearl of Wheatley Heights, New Jersey, to have gotten a spot onboard," the operator recites, "to be included among the many couples, seven hundred sixty in the fine state of New Jersey alone, selecting the same route for the same destination: a happy, healthier marriage."

Yes, I think, *I am incredibly lucky, and Marriage Mountain sounds much less intimidating than a trip to marriage counseling.*

I drive the very manageable twenty-five minutes to Brooklyn so I can ask Donny's mom if it'll be okay to leave the girls that particular weekend of the retreat. Plus, I think it's better to deliver this information in person. Louise is off from work today, waiting to meet with her decorator. Multi-textured fabric swatches are spread out in front of her, according to color scheme. I point to a group of soft, celery greens and nod an enthusiastic yes. I'm trying to be upbeat, but the instant I mumble the words "Marriage Mountain," Louise digs at her temples, as if she's locked in a vise, suffering from one of her debilitating migraines.

"Oh no," she says, mussing her fabric display, laying her upper body across the butcher-block cooking island. The exact same spot Ben usually carves the Thanksgiving turkey. "I knew it. I just knew something was wrong."

Hearing this, I'm struck, momentarily, with a sinking feeling. What does she know that I don't know? What can she see that eludes me? Still, I continue to peddle enthusiasm. "No, no," I assure her. "This is the biggest thing now. Young couples just like us, alone on a retreat, exploring their relationship, hoping to open the lines of communication."

"Your lines are *closed* already? You're married what? Six, seven years?"

"Mom, this is a positive thing. Hey, a bit like redecorating or sprucing up." I point to the wide array of swatches, many of which have fallen on the floor.

"Let me tell you something, Alex. In our day, Ben and I didn't think of such things. We were too busy raising children, trying to scrape up enough dough to pay the rent. We worked hard at everything—together."

I'm waiting for the infamous mousetrap story: when Louise tells how, when they were first married and destitute, living in a basement apartment and not this renovated mini-mansion on Ocean Parkway, she and Ben had to pry the shriveled mice out of the mousetraps in order to use them again. Instead, she drags herself to the double-door freezer and pours a glass of Smirnoff on the rocks, which she chases down with Excedrin. Her hands shake lately; and I hold my breath as the glass dips like a sailboat on a wave, meeting her pale mouth for the first gulp. Few signs remain of the woman who proudly marched on Washington for civil rights over a decade ago. Though she complains she's going through her *changes*, if I ask about it, she waves me off, fanning herself with spatulas, place mats, or any flexible aid within reach.

"Sometimes, darling, it's not wise to dig so deep—or you may uncover a fat, juicy worm."

"But what if things don't feel right, and I'm already hurting?" Why mention the lovely teenage girl, whose flawless smile resides permanently behind my burning irises?

"That's marriage, my sweet. What, you think *our* lives have been completely unblemished? Ben's a very fine man, and I love him dearly, but there are things that all women must learn to expect and accept within a marriage. That is what we do! Nothing is perfect, Alex, nothing." Louise glances out the huge bay window, and the years roll backward in her eyes, like numbers on a calculator. I reach up and place her cool hand in mine. If this were *my* mother pouring out her heart, I'd be shifting my feet, wanting to cover my ears and run from the room. *No, Mother, don't. I do not want to know!* I was intent on learning about men through trial and error. Like most daughters I knew, I'd resisted the wisdom born out of my own mother's experience. *Feh!* Why did I need to hear all the gory details?

"So how are we to know that the one we ultimately choose will remain faithful?" my baby voice asks.

"Ah, but you never *really* know, honey, unless you chain him to your leg." Louise grabs a tissue from the counter. "There are some who eventually spill their guts, but you become the receptacle."

She puts down her glass and stretches out her arms. They are covered with freckles and dime-sized liver spots. "Of course, now *they* feel so much better while you remain in a constant state of queasy. And no matter how hard you try to forget, a vague picture of *them* follows you around like a cold draft—at work, in the car, the supermarket, at three in the morning, when you look over and he's sleeping like an angel. Yes, that's when, that's when!" Louise's voice builds to a crescendo.

"What?" It's as if we're both looking into the same crystal ball.

"You remember things down the hall—sharp objects shoved in the back of the utensil drawer. You lie awake, afraid if you let yourself fall asleep some maniacal rage will take over, forcing you from the bed into the kitchen."

The muddy dam collapses, and for the second time today, tears drip onto my cheeks and chin. I'd never focused on all the possible distractions from a marriage, the time when two people vowed to love one another forever. I feel like a complete idiot, a naïve teenage girl raised on films starring Doris Day and Debbie Reynolds, or maybe I've conveniently forgotten.

"Oh darling, everything will be fine, you'll see."

Louise clutches my hand and strokes it tenderly. I haven't shared a thing, but I feel as if I've been inducted into some club, one she's belonged to for years, where she keeps renewing her membership. Now visibly tired and wobbly on her heels, Louise turns and exits the room.

A few minutes later, she returns, toting her Louis Vuitton satchel on both wrists, like a pair of handcuffs. She pulls two crisp hundred-dollar bills from a wad of cash held together with red rubber bands—a symbol of her meager beginnings.

"Here, sweetheart," she says, kissing my forehead, her red lips chilled. "Go, buy yourself a pretty new winter coat.

I think of all the stunning coats sandwiched together in Louise's closet, the several pairs of suede leather boots, not to mention the imported handbags and designer scarves. I stuff the bills deep into my jeans' pocket. *Groceries*, I think. Yes, I will use this gift, this extra cash, for nourishment and buy my family food.

FOUR

Donny jokingly refers to Marriage Mountain as "The Treat of Retreat." Sitting behind the wheel of our leaf-laden car, he tosses me his best half-mocking, half-flirtatious grin. Even now, minutes from our arrival, I can't help wondering whether Donny's incessant teasing isn't substitution for a more vigilant restraint—a convenient cover for his inability to refuse to attend the weekend. Or perhaps he thinks this encounter will turn out to be one gigantic couples' party with goody bags stuffed with Trojans, massage oil, and fun games like "pin the tail on the boobies."

Noting the whimsical pumpkins adorning porches in the surrounding neighborhood, I correct him: "Trick! And then retreat."

How long must I punish him for humiliating me?

"Tricky Dick." Donny laughs, missing the innuendo. "Can you imagine how many crazy people will be dressed as Nixon this Halloween?"

"I guess politics and Halloween have a lot in common. But don't you have to do something terribly notorious to wind up a caricature?"

"Nah, you have to be *scary*, that's all. Nixon? That's scary." Donny feigns shuddering.

"It's because he lied, of course, but how did he manage to get away with lying to an entire nation? Whatever happened to the principles held by Honest Abe?" I ask.

Donny leans in and pats my thigh. Puffing on an imaginary cigar, he says, "Another century, my dear, another century."

"Well, I guess *everyone* lies from time to time, but our president went way overboard." I could be trying to stir something up, but Donny's either unaware or exercising extreme patience.

"Hey, see that sign? The place is a half a mile down that winding road. Some nice spot these Jesuits have picked out. Did you know they're considered a very hip order of priests?"

"No, Donny." I sigh. "I thought priests were priests."

"The Jesuits have founded over a thousand colleges around the world," Donny recites as though reading from the World Book. Since learning about this weekend, he has asked every Christian we know to fill him in on the Jesuit order. When asked why he was interested, Donny concocted a story saying his brother, Bobby, was dating a girl whose brother had just become a Jesuit priest. I reminded him that Bobby lives on a commune near Woodstock where sex with multiple bed partners has replaced the ancient practice of monogamy. Dating is definitely not part of the agenda. A pinch of fear goes through me when I imagine Donny, so taken with the event, considering his abandonment of Judaism, traveling the country as a Marriage Mountain advocate and leader.

The gravelly road dips and rises again, then stays up, until we feel like we're climbing Everest. Donny shifts the car's gears for the first time since we've lived on the mostly flat, former farmlands of Northern New Jersey. The car jolts, and surprisingly, we are level again, our heads upright. Wrapped in palatial splendor, before our eyes, is an ivy-covered monastery, turrets and all. This seems the antithesis of suburbia and all the cookie-cutter towns devoid of origin. Even the parking lot, with its bold yellow lines, appears comically out of place. Donny and I appear out of place. People should travel to somewhere as beautiful as this, only on foot. I picture myself adorned in a flowing, gossamer skirt, while Donny momentarily appears in a suede vest, a feathered hat, and tights. While he seems excited, his eyes owllike and alert, I'm steeped in trepidation. "Hey, Don, let's leave our stuff in the car and walk a little. I'm guessing we'll be indoors for most of the weekend."

"Sure, babe, whatever you want. You know I still can't believe Ben gave me the afternoon off," Donny says, locking the doors.

I'm not surprised at all; Louise probably encouraged it, crying to Ben that the kids were in "Big, capital B, trouble." I wrap my arm around Donny's tiny waist as we stroll among the dense foliage. While our feet crunch through piles of curled, burnished leaves, we both become unusually quiet. Neither of us rushes to fill the silence. It would be nice to trap a patch of warm sun between our bodies to heal whatever hurt exists, to hold one another for a long time. But because I don't make the move, and Donny doesn't make the move, the moment slips away, disintegrates like the airy fuzz of a dandelion.

Two noble-looking men, dressed in white robes with belts looped with crucifixes and medallions, greet us inside a colossal carved wooden door. Huge candles, like Roman pillars, emit smells of frankincense and myrrh, which I remember singing about in chorus. For the first time ever, I'm wishing I'd smoked a joint.

"Hello, fathers," Donny says, softly, like he's said it a thousand times. I purse my lips and squeeze his ribs with my fingers.

"You must be the Pearls," says a rosy-cheeked man holding a roster. I have no idea how he knows this, and again I'm a tinge past queasy. "Now, if you would, please go right through those double doors. Brother Mac will help get you settled. Oh, and for dinner will you be ordering fish or broiled chicken?"

"Chicken," I answer.

"It's fish for me!" Donny says. "Friday, they always eat fish," he whispers in my ear. "Remember, when in Rome, Alex . . ."

We walk through the doors to a pleasant surprise. It turns out Brother Mac is Ricky Nelson adorable. He is sans the loose priestly garb, dressed in a navy crew neck and cords.

"He must be what they call a novice," Donny informs me while we wait our turn.

"He doesn't look like a novice." For some strange reason, my nausea switches to giddy as hell. Donny whispers into my hair as we wait our turn to be greeted by Ricky.

"Alex, you should know that a novice is a priest who hasn't taken his vows."

"Oh, so he's not yet celibate?" My eyes roll over Father Mac like a lint brush. "It must be so difficult to have to suddenly stop all . . . . activity." I wipe perspiration from my brow and move up in line. Grinning, I hand the father my overnight bag. I can swear he winks at me, right before he fixes a pink tag on the bag's shoulder strap. Donny gets a tag that's royal blue.

"What's this?" we both ask in a birdlike naïveté.

"Your things will be delivered to your separate rooms in a different wing of the building." Brother Mac says this so softly we both need to hear it again, and then once more. Turns out, the exuberant Jillian had left out this one tiny detail—we, too, are to be celibate for the entire weekend. It seems like such a waste to have Louise babysitting and not be able to fool around. The jumping on the bedsprings, make-noise kind of fooling around we abandoned after Becky and Lana were born. I was certain I had lost my libido in order to be primed for the difficult task of child-rearing. Yet, I had grand hopes for the future. That's when I'd rushed out to buy my now stashed copy of *A Sensuous Woman in 30 Days*; I'd planned to be ready the instant our sex life returned.

"Think how exciting it will be when we can finally *do it*," Donny says; he seems to accept all the rules we hear without question, while I mash down persistent pangs of doubt. I'm surprised by how much I'm thinking about sex. I glance once more at Brother Mac, who is already helping the next couple. He reminds me of the guys I'd been attracted to in college—they drank beer Friday nights, stared at you across the bar, yet always left the hang-out alone. Or maybe they returned to another bar to meet up with their first choice.

"I'd hoped to get the most out of this time together," I say, feeling my mood plummet.

"Hey Al, we're here to work, remember?" Donny says, scooping up reading material from an ornately carved banquet table. I shake my head in agreement, hoping we get off to a positive start. I should be thrilled Donny's this focused, but I'm not. Maybe a trip to the Wheatley Heights Motor Lodge to screw under their mirrored ceiling would have been a better idea—cheaper for sure.

Later that evening during the bland filet of sole, or chicken and boiled potato, dinner held in a hot, stuffy hall, we are introduced to *the team*: a cherubic priest named Father Doyle, and three married couples who have already experienced the retreat. The Father explains that the weekend should be thought of as a getaway from the necessary distractions and daily routines of everyday life.

"Ladies and gentleman," he begins, in a tone not unlike the late Ed Sullivan, *Tonight we've got a really big show!* "This weekend is designed to provide you with an opportunity to pause and reflect—invaluable time to refocus your attention on one another."

An interesting challenge since we will hardly see one another.

Endorsements pour readily from couples of varied ages. A husband stands and comments: "I discovered that my wife is a beautiful mystery. Now loving her has become a lifelong process." There are loud applauds and strained smiles. A wife speaks: "I was searching for a way to share the *real* me with my husband—all my longings and needs. Now through my daily *dialogue*, I've found a way." The third couple, dressed in matching Marriage Mountain navy blue T's, pop up like two jacks-in-the-same-box and say: "We have fallen in love again after twenty, miraculous years." I pull at my ear. I could swear she said *miserable*. Donny claps and hoots with the rest while my mouth suddenly feels parched. Broccoli gurgles above my ribcage. I remind myself this retreat was my idea.

While we eat our angel cake dessert (with gold paper wings), each of us is handed two black-and-white spotted notebooks like the kind we used in second grade. Inside these books we are to write passages to one another—an open dialogue of our deepest thoughts and feelings. We are reminded there are no TVs, radios, or phones in the rooms, no distractions from our writing. I tug at Donny's shirt, embarrassed, when he raises his hand and asks Father Doyle, "Is it okay, Father sir, if we write on both sides of the paper?" I avoid eye contact with some guy mumbling "asshole" under his breath. No one else dares ask a question. And Donny hasn't stopped gaping at a cute, pixie-haired brunette with sumptuous (DD) breasts whose husband has dozed off at the table.

When I awaken Saturday morning, I can't wait to see Donny. Last night, when I wasn't writing or dreaming, I sat propped in bed staring at the mighty cross over the door, made from twisted grape vines. After a breakfast of plasterboard pancakes, Donny and I, clutching our notebooks, search for a quiet place to read. It occurs to me that here there are only quiet places. No laughter, only an occasional sneeze or chair scraping the floor. We sit opposite each other on a crackled burgundy couch. The smell of the leather is surprisingly comforting. We nod, grin. *Ready, set, go.* We really are like children. Donny raises his hand, offering to read first.

Dear Alex,

I've said most of this already, but I wanted to write it down, here and now, so you'll know, once and for all, how truly sorry I am. I wish you never had to suffer the embarrassment of that awful phone call. When our sitter (see babe, I've already forgotten her name) said she was terrified about learning to drive, I became a little too eager to help her. I think it had something to do with feeling fatherly toward her. No doubt it turned out to be a really stupid move, especially late at night. Dumb and careless! Please know I will never let anything like that happen again. I don't want to jeopardize our love or make you lose respect for me. I couldn't bear that, Alex. I need your respect. God knows I don't get much at work. I spend so much time trying to please my father lately, but somehow always come up short. He seems to have a knack for uncovering all my fuck-ups. Lately, I've been thinking that it was a grave mistake taking him up on his offer. I should have listened to you when you urged me years ago to go back to school. It's just that his offer came when we learned you were pregnant with Becky, and we certainly needed the money. At the time it seemed like the right thing to do. Who was it that

said you learn by your mistakes? Not Richard Nixon. Will
you forgive me? Please?
I love you . . . Don

Dear Donny:
Here's my truth. Nobody knows me better than you, and yet
after all this time together, I am still so hesitant to share my
deepest thoughts and worries with you. Why that is I am
trying to figure out. To feel safe and be happy, I need to trust
you completely. I want to believe that your daily mantra is:
you would never intentionally hurt me or our family. I'm not
sure why but I am scared a great deal of the time, feeling as
if I'm walking under rain clouds that are about to burst. I try
but can't seem to shake my chronic worrying about the girls,
my crazy fear about dying and being replaced—what haunts
me at times, making me vulnerable and so insecure. I hold
on to these fears as if they are part of an incurable disease
preventing me from being happy and free. There I said it. I feel
better, but just a little.
Alex

I share tiny glimpses of the agony I often put myself through: my
daily endless struggle for perfection, and the naïve belief that I can
control our future. Writing it down, as though confessing, seems to
loosen those chains of anxiety. I hear myself take deep sighs while
my tears drop and blur the letters. This notebook exchange happens
three times a day, so we can read what the other has been afraid to
say—ruminations each has been harboring. Many of the couples
here appear at the family-style meals with their eyes red-rimmed,

cheeks streaked from tears. Yet, most of the time, *we*, the Pearls, are as cheerful as our hosts Father Doyle and Brother Mac and the three happily encountered couples headlining the show.

On Saturday afternoon, after a quick trip to the outside (I'd actually gasped taking in the fresh autumn air), we have our first Creative Touching Workshop led by Father Doyle and Brother Mac. They sit side by side, Father Doyle dangling his cloaked arm affectionately across Brother Mac's shoulder.

"Touching," the holy Father says, "a simple act, and yet we either lose or pass on the opportunity many times each day. It *is* the first step in intimacy, the most important part of communication." Father Doyle asks us all to stand and circle the room a few times, then change directions. I get mixed up and walk in the wrong direction. He tells us to reach out and grab the hand of the person passing us, *right now*! I try to catch up to Donny, but he's already tapping the shoulder of the pixie-haired, DD woman in front of him. His eyes never scan the line to find me. It's as if he's forgotten I'm here. Though I'm trapped in a familiar feeling, the veins in my head begin pulsing and my mouth becomes parched. I am six or seven *again*, and my father is walking toward a crowded parking lot. We'd been at the beach all day, and now I'm lingering, as usual, digging my toes in the warm white sand, searching for one last sand crab. When I look up and see my father, he seems miles away—unreachable. I run to catch up, my heart about to explode inside my fluttering chest. But I can't cry; my tears are stuck beneath squeezed-shut lids. I am furious at my father but don't know how to tell him. Finally caught up, I lean against the burning car trunk and vomit my hot dog and fries across my bare feet.

Donny seems intent on following directions, pleasing the Father, pleasing himself. *See Donny touch; see Donny having fun.* Some couples have broken the rules and walked paces ahead, seeking each other, to embrace or share a smile. Not us. With peaked interest, Donny observes the other couples. And filled with fresh melancholy, I observe Donny, wondering what he's really thinking.

Later, during dinner, Donny tells a complete stranger that the two of us have made this investment as a way of warding off "the seven-year itch." I had forgotten there was such a marital prediction and recall the entertaining movie starring Marilyn Monroe. Wasn't it a comedy? The paunchy, bald stranger glances over at me but quickly returns to slurping his tomato soup, which makes his lips blood red. Just minutes later the skin across my belly is attacked by a case of hives. It occurs to me we will be married seven years come May.

When I stand and say good night, Donny takes my hand and pulls me aside. "These people have bigger problems than us, Alex. Trust me."

I flinch, annoyed by Donny's nonchalance and the easy comparisons he makes to the other couples. Yet, at the top of what I label my Bitchin' list is his obvious attraction to the pixie-haired wife of the big dozer.

"How can you be so sure? We don't know a damn thing about these people. Besides Don, I care about us, not anyone else."

"Al, nobody looks at one another. Have you watched the way they sit and do nothing but move the food around on their plates?"

"Some people take this very seriously. It takes a hell of a lot of courage to talk about certain things, to really delve," I say, my voice quavering.

"Yeah, that's part of the problem," Donny says. "We make things worse if we take them too seriously."

"Do you mean *me*, the one who brought us here hoping to make things better?"

"Shush . . . calm down. I'm referring to *people* in general." When Donny pats my shoulder, I'm aware of the lightness of his touch, as if I were a figurine on a mantle admired on occasion, like while dusting.

"Donny, do you realize you often do things, which makes it hard for me to trust you?"

"Yes, and I've said I'm sorry. Do you want to hear it again? I'm sor-ry, sor-ry, sor-ry!" My husband of almost seven years mimics a vaudeville act, bending on one knee. Other times, I might have laughed, but all I can do is whisper a good night, before walking down the dark hallway alone.

Back in my chamber, I'm convinced the crucifix on the door has tripled in size. I recall the time my best friend, Stacy Keenan, and I snuck into her church to steal the special wafers she raved about, making me envious I hadn't been born Christian. When Stacy informed me that they were symbolic for the body of Christ, I was certain I'd committed a horrible sin and spit the rest into a tissue.

My reliable Bulova reads ten after nine, and I realize, except for illness, I haven't spent a Saturday night alone since high school. I wonder if Donny is sorry and misses me, if he's writing to me this very moment to say, once again, he acted like a complete and total ass. The pen rolls out of my throbbing fingers onto the floor, and I stand up and stretch my arms toward the ceiling. I open and close my bedroom door, then open it again to peek into the gray cave of the hallway. The place is funeral-home quiet. A stale, musty smell lingers in the air—the aroma of thrift shop clothing. I turn the latch so not to lock myself out and walk in the direction of the male-only wing, toward Donny's room. What can they do to me? Throw me out into the woods, banish me from the grounds? *Forgive me father for I have sinned*—something I've always wanted to say anyway.

"I had a headache," I'll say, if caught, and "my husband had the drugs." Surely that would be acceptable, despite the double meaning. A rare excitement takes over my body as I move quickly down the hall. I am ready for a confrontation in any shape or form. I stop to listen. Is that laughter I hear up ahead? I can barely make out two figures several yards in front of me: one leaning against the doorframe, the other standing just inside a room. I hear a deep, husky laugh, followed by a duet of whispering men. There's Donny, half in, half out, of what I imagine to be his room, wearing plaid pajama bottoms and a white undershirt. He is talking to the husband who proudly announced the first night that he and his wife have been married twenty *miraculous years*! Sporting a dark green Marriage Mountain T-shirt, the guy looks around before handing Donny what appears to be a large red envelope or portfolio. *Whoops*, I think, *danger, danger, no reading of outside materials.* But I am curious, not to mention bored out of my Marriage Mountain mind. Squinting into the darkness, the men turn from their friendly exchange to focus on the slightly disheveled apparition moving toward them—me, a female, intruding upon their budding kinship.

"Al, hon, *what-cha* doing?"

"Don, I was just about to ask you the same thing."

"Well good night, you two lovebirds. I hope you have another great day tomorrow. It only gets better Mrs.?"

"Pearl, my name is Alex Pearl."

"I'm George, nice to meet you, Alex. I'm right next door to your hubby so you better keep it down in there." George smacks Donny so hard on the back that Donny drops the portfolio, then bends quickly to retrieve it. Maybe George gave Donny some back issues of *Playboy* to keep him occupied; George did have a familiar guilty expression that I often associate with sex.

"Hey, Don, don't forget what I told you," George whispers loud enough for me to hear. "It's all there between those pretty little pages. You want to know how to make it to twenty years? Read it, share it, then do it!"

The instant George shuts his door, I turn to Donny. "Hey, I thought we were told no distractions. I've been sitting in my mouse hole of a room since dinner writing my fingers off. Show me what he just handed you. Come on . . . *pot* or *porn*?"

More energized than I've seen him in months, Donny raises the mysterious red portfolio above his head and out of my reach. I jump up high to grab it and miss. This becomes our exercise of the day—a childish, yet laughable game, which miraculously dissolves the tension.

The next thing I know we are spread out, side by side, on Donny's mattress, under which I saw him tuck the mystery read, but I'm almost too tired to care.

"So, what the heck was that about?" Donny blinks in sync with my question. "Don't tell me the guy signed you up for Amway? He sure sounded like he was trying to recruit you."

"Now that you mention it, I guess, in a way. Though I assure you it was not Amway. Now, come here, you," Donny says.

"What? Are you crazy?" Why is Donny always so eager to break the rules? And why can't I say no and mean no? I lie stiff as a statue on his lumpy bed, while Donny peels off my jeans. I'm aware of a vague stirring, something old and buried, excavated from a mountain of mud. Marriage Mountain.

Donny kisses my nose, my eyes; he wiggles his tongue inside my ear, which he forgets I hate. Then his face deserts my face, and before long his warm tongue is circling my navel, then the slight curve of my hips. I lift my neck to look down and see only a patch of Donny's wavy head; it's as if he's disappearing into the depths of a cave. The skinny red portfolio flops to the floor. I no longer care what's inside. I'm surprised by what he's doing and how assuredly he's maneuvered us into position. For the very first time, Donny *goes down* on me—an expression I have always disliked because it sounds so very *Travel and Leisure.* I try concentrating on my body and all its delicate parts, on what will ultimately give me pleasure, but I am captured by a faded print of Mary Magdalene, which hangs lopsided on a poorly lit wall. I assume she is Mary because of her potato sack gown, the halo, and how tenderly she cradles the cherub of a naked child, which reminds me of what I truly want to do: to leave this place . . . now, go home where I belong—with my girls.

It's a week later and we're out eating Chinese food with Rona, Hy, and all our kids. I have just shared how our retreat weekend culminated with a chamber music ceremony and us renewing our vows, when Rona, the neatest human I know, spits a mouthful of fried rice all over the starchy white tablecloth. "You did what?"

"Oh, you think that's funny?" Fuming at her smugness, I lean over my plate. "I thought, Rona, you might say, how nice!" Our children's chatter halts at my piercing voice. Ethan picks up a limp, lonely shrimp and pops it in his mouth. Rona cringes and grabs the tail before he swallows the creature whole.

"Alex, it's their problem," Donny whispers, while he dives in for the last fatty sparerib. Something in the way Rona glances toward Hy infuriates me.

"Oh, so wait! You two have it all figured out, no surprises *ever* in your perfectly blissful union?" Though my heart gallops, I feel strong.

"Sorry, Alex," Rona says, through a tiny smirk. Her eyes dart like guppies to connect with Hy, and I can't help but think they are the only couple I know sure to stay married forever.

On Monday morning, seconds after Donny leaves for work, I find myself crawling on the floor again, this time searching for the mysterious red portfolio, which I'd nearly forgotten about until witnessing the smug look on Rona's face—a look telegraphing the message that she knows something even I don't know about my own marriage—specifically Donny.

After an hour of searching each drawer, closet, even the stinky oil burner room, which I'd never even seen, I give up. I decide I no longer give a damn. Yet, for the rest of the day, I battle with both detest and pity for this new pathetic version of me.

FIVE

Our attachment to Donny's folks intensified as a result of my own parents' absence from our daily lives. Miriam and Nathan Shore moved to Florida two weeks after I returned from my Jamaican honeymoon. They had planned my wedding and their escape from Brooklyn, simultaneously, as if telegraphing the message: life was on hold until their only daughter got hitched.

It felt peculiar to rush back home, soon after I'd left, to immerse myself in the sifting of childhood memorabilia. Just when I'd made the gallant attempt to try out the new me—*Mrs. Donald Pearl*—I was whirled down memory lane, swept up in a tornado, the funnel holding all my dashed hopes, needless fears, and follies. I spent hours sprawled on the floor rummaging through milk crates of old 45s and scrapbooks bulging with browned, crumbling corsages that reeked from mold and prom night photos of boys all shorter than me. Forced back in that chilly pink room with its faux fireplace, I mourned the youth of a painfully thin, nervous girl—a girl who shoved fingers down her throat each morning to try and vomit because she awakened nauseous and desperate to feel some relief, even if only stringy phlegm rising from her gut.

For the last time, my eyes searched the cabbage rose wallpaper on which I'd scrawled secret messages in a girlish cursive between green vines in every corner of the room. I filled the trunk of my Dodge Dart and transferred everything to the spacious home of the Pearls—folks who seemed to offer the taste of freedom I'd always hungered for.

Part of me has never forgiven my parents for making me move the neat pink montage of my childhood—the flash cards of another time I'd left in their safekeeping. So, when they call tonight, as they do every Sunday, after the rates go down, and I hear their upbeat duet, I revert back to become their onerous teenage daughter. Even though I'd wanted to leave them for quite some time, how dare they leave me?

"Hi, dear, it's us. How's every little thing in Wheatley Heights?"

"Ah, pretty good, I guess." *Who else could you possibly be?*

"It must be quite chilly up there in Jersey."

"No. It's not bad, really."

"How are *our* little girls?"

"Fine, I told you, Mom, everything's fine."

As soon as my father reminds me he'll be sending the plane tickets for our visit over Christmas, I feel guilty for sounding like an ungrateful brat. I attempt some oomph to match his enthusiasm, though I imagine Dad, phone pressed to his ear, watching grains of salt slip through an hourglass.

"So, how's the weather down there, Dad?"

"Gorgeous! Sunny and in the eighties."

I've learned most Floridians lie about their weather, especially northerners who left everything, once dear, to move twelve hundred miles away.

"Hey, Mom, remember last year when I sat at the pool with my ski jacket over my bathing suit?"

"Of course, Manny Gluck still talks about your crocheted bikini. He thinks you're the spitting image of me."

"Wow, Mom, nice compliment from the *Man*!"

"There's more, but I don't want to get your father jealous. So, please put those darlings on the phone, oh, and one more thing . . . when will Donny be joining you?"

"You know how backed up the factory gets around the holidays, so he can't be sure."

"That's nice. So, you'll have some time apart." A tinge of worry kicks at my belly as I digest my mother's words. She's great at making pronouncements about all the things I stuff down and try to forget.

"Becky! Lana! Pick up the phone."

While my father hangs up precisely at five minutes, Miriam lingers on her extension, until Dad hisses in the background, "Okay, wrap it up." Frugality defines him.

At 3:00 a.m. I sit up, ruler straight, thinking I hear my mother's familiar gabble coming from our cedar-lined walk-in closet. She is whispering, "What you've always needed, Alexandra, is a real man." Her words spark some interest, then dwindle. Later in the day, while I'm loading a wash of mostly Donny's jeans, they return. *Real man* catches me by surprise, resounding in my ears like the dull chant of a transcendental mantra.

In the back of my mind lives the fact that for the past seven years, my mother has gathered a plethora of ammunition to prove Donny's immaturity—ever since I first said, "I want to marry him." She actually tried to give me an out on the night of my engagement party after everyone had gone home. Mom sat at her gilded vanity table pulling off her false eyelashes, storing them in a plastic box the way a child might store an insect. Staring into the mirror, she said that to her *deep dismay*, during the festivities, she'd discovered Donny in her bedroom rummaging through her drawers. He was in the company of his old high school flame, Julie. Julie, a C cup, just happened to be married as well as very pregnant.

I fled the room crying, but my mother followed me. She refused to budge while I telephoned Donny to press for details. Shocked by my accusation, Donny swore up, down, and sideways, he was only trying to help Julie who'd felt chilly and asked for a sweater. My adorable fiancé convinced me his attempt at chivalry was no big deal.

"We can send back the gifts," my mother coaxed, perhaps testing me. An instant later she lifted a Baccarat vase and held it to the light, her aqua eyes multiplying through the crevices of the crystal. "Alex, darling, look, isn't this spectacular?"

She'd already arranged an elaborate display of Gorham silver and Noritake china. Alongside these gifts she'd stacked a set of embroidered bed linens with our soon-to-be initials—APD—the indelible stamp of my new identity.

I'm on my third cup of black coffee, heart racing, when I get the urge to sneak a peek at *A Sensuous Life in 30 Days* wisdom. I skip the chapter on masturbation (but dog-ear the pages) and jump directly to maintenance—addressing issues exclusively of the upper body. It is definitely time for a tune-up, and the trip to Florida has become my incentive for change. Just yesterday I was overjoyed to receive an invitation from my only Florida friend, Sophie Woodman, to attend her husband's birthday party a few days after Xmas.

I turn to the section on hair and makeup, which professes one should: *Accent the good features and hide the bad.* Thumbing through some women's magazines, I dismember the bodies of seriously thin models that make Twiggy appear chubby while I contemplate a new hairdo. I'd like something manageable, yet sexy, and stylish.

I think of Rona, crowned with a head of thick chestnut hair. She travels two hours monthly to have it coiffed short and sleek. "Mario really knows my hair," she has said so often I worry I'm beginning to understand the importance of that statement. *And what, I wonder, does my hair say about me?*

In McCall's I find a softer, less severe version of the Jane Fonda shag. But, unlike me, Jane has a perfectly chiseled nose and could wear a dripping mop and look terrific. I'd refused my mother's offer of a nose job as a sweet sixteen gift after she pressed a black comb against the bridge of my nose to show me how much better I could look.

I call Perry's Place—an upscale Wheatley Heights salon, never expecting to hear an appointment has opened up for this afternoon. The time works well with my schedule. I'll get Lana from nursery school and then shoot over to pick up Becky. I grab the slot before I change my mind, because the prices at Perry's are outrageous, more than I've ever paid for a haircut in my life. Since the salon is just thirty minutes from Louise and Ben's, it makes sense to leave the girls with Gussie, the Pearls' sometimes caustic, rarely cheerful housekeeper.

I have some time before my appointment, and while Gussie plays a game of Old Maid with the girls, an idea comes to me: I'll try on my wedding dress and surprise Becky and Lana, but especially me if I can fit into the size 6 silk organza gown that has been stored in a special box provided by Bliss, my grandfather's bridal store, and placed in a basement closet with my other memorabilia.

I sneak away from the cozy warmth of the kitchen and walk down the one flight to the basement. Immediately my nostrils take in a strong mildewed aroma, one I remember from other basements, but never the Pearls. I open the heavy steel door behind the staircase and am surprised to see the interior so clean, if not barren. A large water stain, resembling a small pond, is spread across the curled carpeting. Pushed into a corner is one dilapidated carton. My scrawl, in black magic marker, is visible on the outside. I tug open the cardboard flaps, relieved to find several pieces of Nana's Noritake china. I'd never had the complete set, but I'd planned to find white plates someday to coordinate with the ornate edging—when I turned fifty and needed to set a formal table. *This is a good sign,* I think; maybe my other things have been moved around as well. I take the steps two at a time, anxious to ask Gussie, who is known for locating misplaced objects.

Upstairs, I find Lana sitting with her head in her hands; she has crocodile tears spilling across her cards. "Mommy, I'm going to be an Old Maid, Gussie said so."

"Lana, angel, that'll never happen, *but* it's not the worst thing in the world. Lots of women decide to never get married." *Who do I know besides my poor Aunt Leda, crippled at ten years old with polio?*

I stare through a slightly embarrassed Gussie. "Do you know what happened to all my things that were stored downstairs?"

"Nope, can't really say. All I know is it got awful damp down there in September. That week was something else, it rained cats and dogs."

"You're telling a fib, Gussie," Lana says, sticking her chin out. "It can't rain animals." Gussie chuckles but diverts her glance. She seems to prefer the girls' attention at this moment.

Guessing Ben must have moved the boxes to one of the bedroom closets, I search, frantically, until I decide to call the factory. As soon as she hears my voice, two octaves higher in the middle of the day, Louise shrieks, "Is everything all right!"

"Yes, yes, but I'm at your house, and I can't find my *stuff,* all I'd stored in your basement after my folks moved to Florida. Remember all the cartons and a long garment bag holding a gown . . . my wedding gown?"

Louise's long pause gives my stomach time to rise and curl. The organ ingests the news before my brain. "Oh, Alex, they were all ruined," my mother-in-law answers. "We had quite the flood from all that rain."

"What? Why didn't anyone tell me?"

"You had a lot on your mind at the time. We didn't want to upset you."

Tears rush to my eyes, surprising me. Gussie hands me a box of Kleenex. Becky and Lana are squealing, running up and down the hallway, playing tag. "And I guess after a few weeks, we forgot to mention it. You know, Alex, when you moved to New Jersey, you should have picked up those boxes. And the gown, well, the thing was stinking up the entire basement. It was unfortunately mildewed."

I feel trampled upon, flattened like the silvery water bugs lying dead upon the basement floor. I imagine my beautiful gown floating on a sea of tears, buoyant, but formless and empty—the satiny label of *Bliss Bridals* sewn beside the zipper. *Bliss, Bliss, Bliss.* My grandfather's one-of-a-kind creation for me—a labor of love.

"I'm saying I wish I'd known."

"Sorry, dear, I assumed Donny would have told you by now," Louise says.

"Donny saw the boxes?"

"Well, of course. They were sopping, and he had to help Ben carry them to the curb. Listen, honey, you're busy now making a new past, new memories every day with your beautiful children and your wonderful husband. Can you try to let this go?"

"I guess I have no choice." I am on the verge of losing my patience with Louise, but Becky and Lana are within earshot.

I sink into a chair at the kitchen table, half listening, as Louise changes the subject to her dear friend's recent diagnosis of melanoma. I rub my aching temples. All we are talking about are scraps of moldy paper stuffed into scrapbooks, and yards and yards of wrinkled fabric, what was once my wedding dress. While tangible, everything I saved told a story. I'd carted these things into an unknown future, allowing glimpses at who I used to be.

There were letters and unrhymed poems from a first love, my high school boyfriend, Jonathan Tanner—words I wanted to read again. On a rainy afternoon, the day I had selected my wedding gown, Jonathan appeared out of a guilty daydream and leaped onto the same car of my train. Rain-soaked and shivering, we sat beside each other, speechless, like limp marionettes the entire ride home. Just as the train was pulling in to our station, he took my hand and squeezed it till it hurt. The doors opened, and he rushed out, disappearing onto the crowded platform into the pounding rain.

Now, six years later, sitting in the hairdresser's chair at Perry's Place, I'm aware of the rapid clip-clip of razor-sharp scissors. If I turn into them, I'd be maimed for life. I squeeze my eyes shut. I couldn't care less what happens to my hair. It's only hair. It has roots. It grows back. I take a mental inventory of all that may have been lost in the great flood of September—the unremarkable event that sent the relics of my past to the curb, where they were crushed by the undiscriminating jaws of a Brooklyn garbage truck.

Donny walks in later than usual. The girls, already fed, are downstairs hosting a tea party for their stuffed animals. He checks through a stack of mail, glances up, and begins peeling open a manila envelope. Not a word about my hair. How can he not notice my new shaggy layers? How the cosmetician taught me to highlight my eyes using a brush and a tiny pot of kohl.

"Donny, did your mother mention I called this afternoon?" I'm standing alongside him, peering over his shoulder at a catalogue for barbecue tools.

"No, I was out most of the day buying supplies."

"She told me what happened to the boxes I'd stored in their basement. How everything had to be thrown out."

"Boxes?" Donny rips the piece of mail in half, checks the table for more.

"Do you think you could at least look at me?"

"Hey, babe, your hair looks amazing! Come on, turn around!" It's hard not to grin at his compliment. Automatically I become a spinning top for him. Donny sees me now, therefore I exist.

"Were you ever going to tell me that my wedding gown, scrapbooks, letters, and God knows what else were dumped?"

"Are you positive I didn't tell you? I'm certain—"

"I think I'd remember something as important as that. Did you happen to go through any of my stuff?"

"Huh?"

"Was anything salvaged? There were letters I've had forever."

"Oh, you mean from that goofball you went with who couldn't spell for shit."

"I knew it! Mr. Curiosity wouldn't have missed an opportunity to snoop through my things."

"Well, it's true." Donny laughs. "The guy bordered on illiterate."

"You're so wrong!" I grab the barbecue catalogue and toss it like a Frisbee; Donny ducks.

"Yeah, like I give a rat's ass."

"That's the problem, Donny. What *do* you give a rat's ass about? Me? Work? Let me know when you figure it out."

"I sure will *schweetheart*." Donny winks, gathers his mail, and heads for the powder room.

I picture him spread out on the vinyl beanbag in his parents' basement, dissecting the letters from Jonathan and other short-lived romances I'd scampered through. Could he have plagiarized a romantic line, stolen it and used it on me again—words which might have sounded sweet to me only because they were vaguely familiar?

Two weeks later, just days before we are to leave for Florida, Becky, Lana, and I come down with the wretched Hong Kong flu. "Your resistance must be terribly low," says Dr. Carner, the former Dr. Hot, giving his explanation for all he can't explain. Still I love his mellow, Perry Como delivery of diagnoses and remedies. I'm *delirious*, a beautiful word for a truly horrible state. My body feels like it was run over by an eighteen-wheeler—trucks that rumble on the turnpike, causing car windows to vibrate in their wake.

Once fairly tidy, our bedroom resembles a Red Cross station during wartime. Formless pieces of laundry are scattered about the room, dripping off nightstands, much like the watch faces in a favorite Dali painting. The girls have brought books, stuffed animals, and Candyland to the foot of my bed, where they camp out on sleeping bags. While Becky deals with her illness by reading quietly, Lana, burning with fever, circles the room like a rabid dog. She climbs up on my bed, walks over my back, and then jumps off the other side. If I die here now, who will feed them?

I hear voices coming from downstairs and wonder what Maria Callas is doing in my den. I'm relieved when I realize it's a Saturday, and Donny is home blasting *Madame Butterfly*. Soon he appears beside our bed, carrying a wicker tray of hot tea, Uneeda biscuits, and jam. *Ta da*, presenting Donald Pearl at his best. I watch him place the tray on a chair and vigorously shake the thermometer. I'm hoping he's using the oral kind and not the bulbous rectal as he shoves the tip under my tongue. I try to mumble: *What time is it? How's the weather? Am I ovulating?* He jots something on a pad, reminding me of how, when I was in labor with Becky, curled and moaning on our bed, he'd kept a meticulous chart timing my labor pains. Sometimes Donny mothers more naturally than me. I studied tediously for the role and just happened to win the audition.

Kneeling at my bedside, he stares into my face. I want to vaporize like the Vicks vapor rub all over my chest. My hair, my, oh so stylish, feathery cut, resembles an abandoned robin's nest, and my pajamas are as dank as dust rags. Not a word is uttered, not a single word, and I think how convenient caring for an ill spouse can be, what an easy way to dodge all conversation. The sickness usurps the norm, replacing affection, sexual longing—all matters of the day. The metal blinds rattle in agreement as a cool draft races past my head, reminding me that winter never waits for an invitation. I dread the cruel isolation I feel when it arrives, the holding pattern created by the onset of shorter days, and the gloom paired with early darkness.

Lana jumps on me again, this time knocking out my air. "Please send her away," I moan, my face buried in my pillow. Donny scoops up Lana in his arms, and while she resists, her flailing legs hit a glass of water on the nightstand. "Leave it, just go, please."

"Come on, pumpkin," he says. "Come downstairs and keep me company."

Lana throws her arms around Donny's neck and peeks at me. I hear her whisper in his ear. "Is Mommy going to die?"

"No, sweetie, of course not." Donny chuckles.

"Will I get a new mommy if she dies, Daddy? One who paints pictures too?"

"Shhh! Let Mommy rest now, okay?"

Lana's words are perfectly enunciated in their terrifying inquiry. I hear them above the hum of the cold mist humidifier and the irregular rhythms of my heart. In her innocence, my child has raised the possibility of me being replaced. She has sounded the loudest bell of fear. It's all I needed to hear to pull myself up in bed, to unravel my chapped feet from the blanket. Yet, when I stand, my whole body feels leaden.

"Hi, Mommy, are you better?" I have forgotten Becky—below me, spread out on the floor, drawing a picture on a jumbo pad. She's drawn us, her family; everyone sucking on thermometers, except Donny.

"Yes, angel, and you?" I kneel, holding the mattress for support, and touch her forehead with my lips. Her scorching hands are the real giveaway; her fever hasn't broken.

"Maybe now," she says, "because you're better."

I slip on my green sick-robe and move cautiously down the hallway. I try bumping down the steps like the girls often do, but every bone in my body throbs.

The kitchen is surprisingly neat, except for an array of pastel Tupperware containers that had contained meals sent over from neighbors. News of our dreaded illness has spread faster than a lawn fungus. Mothers all over Wheatley Heights, no doubt, are checking their calendars to see the last time their children were exposed to Lana or Becky Pearl. Even Rona stopped by with a barbecued chicken, though, slave to her germ phobia, she'd left the meal and a get-well note on our doorstep. I imagined her speeding away as if she'd abandoned a baby.

The doorbell rings and rings but Donny can't hear a thing. Headphones in place, he's slumped in the leather recliner, his eyes closed, while my baby girl lies at his feet dozing like a puppy. Donny wiggles his head-phoned head back and forth to a song I can't hear; in his face there is such apparent joy. He is so much happier away from work.

Louise and Ben let themselves in with their own set of keys. They're bringing in half a dozen shopping bags and intruding gusts of frosty air. For an instant I forget this is where *I* live. They look shocked to see me out of bed, shuffling around in my robe and sweat socks. Hopefully, they'll quit nagging me to postpone my trip. I need to get away, to bake my bones until my body heals and this Hong Kong flu is just a bad memory.

Donny's eyes widen, feeling his father's not-so-gentle rap on the top of his head. Ben then plops himself down at my kitchen table to finish the *Times* puzzle in fountain pen. Legs rubbery and weak, I saunter over and sit next to him. My lips curl down like the mask of tragedy. He kisses my forehead and checks for fever.

"You're warm, get back in bed. We're here now."

"I'm so much better."

Donny joins us at the table and before long the two men are talking business, the buzz of which circling my head like a toy plane. All I hear over and over again are Ben's words:

"You will leave when all the orders are finished and shipped."

Donny chews the inside of his cheek; he runs his fingers through his hair. He blinks his eyes and starts to stutter. Ben slips into his ski jacket and motions Donny to go outside. When Louise returns from visiting Becky, I ask if there's anything's wrong.

"When it comes to business, darling, I'm Switzerland."

A minute later, I hear Donny's voice booming from the backyard. "Stop blaming me for everything that goes wrong! I suppose I'm the reason you're always playing catch up, why half your loyal customers quit wearing bras."

I brush my hands across my pajama top and pat my very over-heated bare breasts. There was a time, after Becky was born, when I joined the thousands of women, in protest, and went braless. Business took a real nosedive then, but I never once felt guilty.

"Why is Daddy screaming?" Lana asks, waking from her nap. She scampers across the room and presses her face against the cold glass.

Louise bends her head down and lights a cigarette using the gas burner. I hear a loud pop, and I'm glad Lana didn't get to see her grandmother's neatly coifed hair just inches from flames. She scoops up Lana, her cigarette dangling, and flips on the outside lights to reveal Donny and Ben standing on opposite sides of the plastic-covered barbecue, their necks cranked up above their shoulders.

"Ben, come inside! What's wrong with you?" Louise shouts.

"I'll tell you what's wrong with him," Donny answers. "He cares more about his imported, lying manager than the workers who have been with you for years . . . including me!"

Donny rushes in past his mother and plops down at the kitchen table where I sit sipping my soup. He blows out air as if inflating a flaccid pool float. His father follows next, rubbing together crimson hands. Louise scurries to bring bowls of steaming chicken soup, and maybe because Lana climbs into Donny's lap, the men suddenly cease arguing. A deliberate silence fills the kitchen. All that's audible is the slurping of broth, a noise which Lana brings to our attention by mimicking. It's an effort to cut my food, but I might feel better if I eat something. They think I don't know, but everyone is watching me out of the corners of their eyes.

"Hold your compliments, people. I know I'm utterly breathtaking."

Stifling laughter, Louise chokes and takes a sip of her ice water.

"Do you really think you can get on a plane with Becky and Lana next week?" she asks.

"They'll be fine," Donny answers, scooping mashed potatoes onto my plate.

"Thank you," I say, "for the comment and the potatoes." I feel a surge of affection for Donny and the familiar urgency to muster up forgiveness, to once again wipe the slate clean. "I need to get back to bed." I struggle to stand, pushing my chair back. I turn once before I climb the stairs, and notice Ben and Donny, stone-faced, scooping second helpings onto their plates.

With all my strength, I grasp the railing leading up the stairs to sweet Becky, and the shelter of the electric blanket I bought on sale at Sears.

Only after his parents leave, and he calms down, does Donny give me bits and pieces of what occurred. Beside me in bed, he attacks a one-pound bag of pistachios, his fingers turning purplish from cracking them open. I've never seen his mouth move so fast with such unleashed fury. Between sucks and chews, he mentions that a highly skilled, well-paid machine operator and assistant plant manager, Karl, has a real problem with him.

Whenever there's a faux pas—like the one that occurred Friday, whereby hundreds of underwires were never inserted into style #007, Luverly Lace, a best-selling bustier, sold exclusively in the Frederick's of Hollywood's catalogue—Karl blames it on Donny, who, as plant manager, is in charge of production and quality control.

"So, you're saying there was no *boost* in the bustier?"

"I'm not kidding, Alex. He's out to destroy me. Karl knows he is supposed to check all finished garments and report all defects and mistakes directly to me before they are shipped to customers."

"I'm really sorry, Don. It sounds like Ben went too far, but maybe he was trying to be fair and, afraid of favoring you, he made a point by chewing you out in front of Karl, which was terribly wrong. Damage to so many garments *is* quite a deficit, but it pales in comparison to the humiliation you must feel."

"Hey, how'd you think he'd like it if we were up in God's country, growing vegetables and chopping wood?" Donny says, while he stares ahead at a blank wall.

"Who knows," I answer, at the start of a coughing spasm, "we might . . . all be . . . a lot happier." I wish I were more honest, but I'm telling Donny what he thinks he wants to hear, instead of the truth.

SIX

On a frosty December morning, Donny drops us at the airport on his way to work. I watch him pull away with the speed of a downhill skier. My eyes are fixed to the back of his head as our car disappears down the curvy ramp. I imagine him chanting the words of the late, great Martin Luther King: *Free at last!* The girls continue to shout, "Bye, Daddy!" They are excited about flying, not focusing on the fact that Daddy's already gone. My heart jitterbugs in my chest, and I'm aware of a weird, momentary pull, like wanting to be in two places at the same time. Donny and I have been apart like this before, but this time I am wary of our physical separation, as if it might do us harm instead of good.

Seconds before the departure of National's flight 509 to Miami, I give Lana and Becky each a tiny dose of children's Dimetapp, hoping to clear their nasal passages and make them just a tad drowsy. I make a mental note to tell my father he can no longer save money by not buying Lana her own ticket. This is the absolute last time I will pass her off as under two, dressing her in a pastel knitted cap and cradling her against my breasts while we board. A young stewardess, sugary as a Georgia peach, asks, "Can I fill a bottle for your sweet baby?" And I can't help but interpret sarcasm.

"No, thanks, we're fine." I try not to make unnecessary eye contact and pray Lana doesn't awaken and open her precocious, close-to-adolescent mouth. Becky spends the flight reading *Highlights* magazine, chewing a wad of bubble gum to reduce the pressure in her ears. She suffers quietly and pushes her head into my ribs whenever it hurts.

Precisely three hours later, while dozing, I feel a loud, terrifying bump—a sensation of speed followed by a round of applause signaling our plane has landed. The girls look puzzled by this outburst but join in with giggles and clapping. I remind Lana she must keep her hat on, even though the temperature outside the cabin has reached the high seventies.

Along with several other sets of transplanted Floridian grandparents, a montage of white duck-cloth and pastels, Miriam and Nathan have been staked out at the gate since our flight left Newark. They wave wildly the moment they spot us, longing springing to their eyes. They are usually reserved in public; it's rare to see them unable to contain their pride. With this distance between us, during the long walk down the narrow corridor, I have the time to take them in without feeling smothered.

They grasp each other's arms—pinching, as if they can't believe we're here. I move in slow motion toward them, clutching what they've awaited—the tiny hands of two gems, named for each of their deceased mothers. As the gap between us closes, Becky and Lana dash into their open arms. I weep, secretly, behind my big round sunglasses, from observing the purity of my parents' emotions, and how rapidly they've aged since moving away. It's true. They've missed a great deal living so far from us.

Looking around, I notice scenes of sleepy grandchildren being hoisted and squeezed while leathery, sun-bleached women warn their husbands, "Don't lift, your back!" A chorus of cooing surrounds us like rooftop pigeons, gray feathers shedding everywhere.

"Hi, darlings, let me have a look at you. Nate, look, aren't they something? Pale, a little thin, but we'll fix that, right? My, my, and look at your mommy."

Yes, Mommy, look at me. I push back my hair and lift my chin, instantly conscious of my less than perfect nose.

My father glues his chest to mine, and I peel away, always uncomfortable hugging him in front of my mother. She and I move toward each other to kiss—tiny, cheeky pecks, weightless as down. When she smiles, I see myself in twenty years: the crow's-feet etched deep in the corners of her eyes, the vertical folds of flesh jiggling under her neck. Today she is radiant, healthier looking than last year. She's gained back some weight after "that lousy bout with the *doldrums.*" That's how she refers to the condition that caused her to show up on my doorstep three days after her fiftieth birthday. Twice weekly, with the girls in tow, I chauffeured Miriam to her psychiatrist an hour away, and on the ride home, she'd deliver an encapsulated version of the session—a one-sided view, which blamed her misery solely on my father. How he'd dragged her away from everyone and everything dear. When I asked if she ever put up a fight, or thought about saying no, she looked blankly out the window. But I knew, by the tightness in her jaw, there was something else she was revisiting, my guess, for the zillionth time.

Since our arrival in sunny Florida, my mother, Miriam, has become a woman of purpose. She rises early and adorns herself in Tropicana colors before preparing a sumptuous breakfast of scrambled eggs and kosher bacon, which tastes like salty cardboard. While I relax at the pool, scanning her collection of *House Beautiful* magazines, my mother parades Becky and Lana, door to door, to neighbors who will be "aghast, simply aghast" that such a young, stunning woman could possibly be a grandmother. When she tells us this, later in the day, I bet my father will roll his eyes. And, as always, I hope she doesn't notice.

Dad, with at least five Phillips screwdrivers spread out before him, spends hours assembling the Fisher Price miniature kitchen they bought the girls for Christmas—because, even though we are Jews, my mother has always adored Christmas. She doesn't consider it a religious holiday, only an opportunity for giving. And parked in front of the heavy brocade drapes that always remain closed is a shiny silver tree decorated with miniature candy canes. On top of the marble sideboard is an ornate brass menorah of eight monkeys. All routes to heaven are covered.

By the second night of my visit, I'm convinced that the stale, humid air of this condo may choke me. Though I plead, Dad refuses to turn on the air-conditioning until June. Looking disheveled, Miriam and Nathan are propped up in bed, exhausted from a day at Parrot Jungle, where it took ten minutes to untangle a macaw's claws from my mother's shellacked hair. They are laughing in sync with the dubbed-in laughter of *All in the Family*. Because the volume is deafening, I must shout in order to be heard.

"I'm going out for a while. I think I'll see if Sophie is home, so don't wait up, okay? I've got my key."

"What?" they yell back, eyes glued to the tube.

"Never mind. I'll be back soon."

"You've got great color, honey," my father shouts after me. "Tomorrow's going to be another sunny day." Since moving south, Dad's added meteorology to his many skills. His imaginary weather wand points to high and low pressure areas across the entire country. Whenever I visit, there are rarely storms in his forecasts—his love for me magically puffs away the clouds.

Alone finally, I take the glass elevator to the penthouse floor. High-pitched children's voices ricochet down the hallway. A variety of crayoned menorahs and snowmen are taped on the door, the latter, perhaps memories of past Chicago winters. Since moving from their windy city, Sophie and Rob have invested in huge sectors of Florida real estate. Most of their properties are low-income residence buildings, with a few luxury high-rise condominiums that stand majestically on the coastline of Biscayne Bay. One of the latter is this building, Pelican Plaza. They've moved temporarily into this penthouse while renovating their sprawling Spanish-style home a few blocks away.

It was last winter, while I was teaching Lana to swim, when Sophie strolled over, and using her son as a prop, suggested I hold Lana by her feet and dip her headfirst into the deep end. The boy surfaced, gasping for air, but Sophie didn't blink.

"Nah, don't think so," I said, choosing a more conventional method.

"Believe you me, she'll learn how to swim." Sophie laughed.

I am about to leave when Rob Woodman, bare-chested and beaming, opens the door.

"Hey, hi honeybun, come on in." Rob hugs me, and I smell his English Leather mingling with minty toothpaste. The heat from my sunburn intensifies as Rob's eyes move directly to my chest. I guess I've missed a button and try to act nonchalant while using one hand to conceal my cleavage. More than a little saggy since giving birth to Lana, my breasts appear perkier than usual, thanks to the magical plumping power of H. Pearl's newest entry in ladies' foundations— The Bubble Bra, which is quilted with multilayers of soft nylon promising a lot more lift for the flaccid.

"I'm on my way out, but I'm sure Sophie will love the company— hey, when's Donny due in?"

"By the weekend, hopefully," I say, thinking how Ben warned Donny he couldn't leave New York until every last order was filled.

"Super, we're counting on you to show for my big birthday bash."

"I . . . we've been looking forward to it."

"Cool. There's another couple from Jersey we want you to meet, our friend Peter's brother and wife. Sophie thinks they may actually live near you."

"Sure, I'll be happy to meet them." I become super polite around people like Rob, hoping they'll respect my desire to maintain some physical distance, but Rob is now inches from my face. So close, I notice the beads of perspiration rising from his huge pores.

On a few occasions, we'd gone to dinner with Sophie and Rob, and even though Rob flirted openly with me, Sophie seemed amused. I got the feeling she was analyzing me, watching my maneuvering so not to piss anyone off. Donny? He didn't seem to care.

"Well, I know he'd like to meet you, who wouldn't?" Rob's sweaty hand moves sneakily up my arm. I take a step back and hit my head on a closet door. "Whoops, you okay?"

"Yes, fine." I rub the back of my skull and check my fingers for blood.

"Sophie, Alex Pearl's here!" Rob yells down the hallway. "Saturday night, be there," he says, slipping into a palm tree printed shirt while rushing out the door.

"Alex, I'm in here!"

I follow Sophie's voice and find her on her knees, rummaging through a black camp trunk. Her children, clad in underpants only, bounce on the bed as if it were a trampoline. Sophie, whose tranquil demeanor I usually envy, seems a bit harried.

"They have a Coppertone audition tomorrow, and I don't know if I packed their bathing suits. Unlike her two striking children,

Sophie is petite and plain, yet there's something quietly exotic deep within her green eyes. I have surmised this means she has a fantastic sex life—something I automatically ponder when meeting any new couple, making me certain I'm missing out.

"God, I can't wait to get back to my own house," she says, her voice muffled—her torso half buried in the trunk.

"I can give you one of Becky's suits for Wendy, but Jake's another story."

"You know what?" Sophie says, standing up and pecking me on the cheek. "Fuck it, the kid's going naked! I'll bring our dog, Jasper— it'll look like the original Coppertone ad, except the dog will have to bite his little un-sunburned ass!"

"Cute, but will Jake agree to it?"

"He's got no choice unless we drive to the house. Want to go for a little ride?"

"It's getting late, who'll watch the kids?" I ask, looking around.

"Oh, right, silly me! I forgot. It's nanny's night off—which means nanny's night on the town. You got to keep these young girls happy, or they go running straight back to Dublin."

"Hey, why don't I go?" I say, surprised by my own words. "I think I remember how to get there."

"Alex, fabulous, would you? I have to bathe the little monsters."

"Sure, but I better take your car. If I ask to borrow my father's at this hour, he'll ask a million questions."

Sophie reaches into her pocket. "Here, this key is for the side door, near the kitchen. In the laundry room, you'll find a basket of the kids' clothes, grab something—anything."

I call downstairs to say good night and check on the girls. "Mom, I'm hanging out in the stratosphere with Sophie. Guess what? These people actually believe in Freon."

Missing my sarcasm, my mother says, "Be sure to say hello for me." She is thrilled that Sophie and I are friends, which distinguishes her from the rest of the tenants.

"By the way, did Donny call?" I practice my best blasé.

"No, dear, he did not," and through the wires, I hear the judgment mounting in her mind.

About to pull out of the parking garage, I adjust the seat in Sophie's '74 silver Porsche, wondering how she could feel safe driving her kids around in this sleek sports car. I don't trust the power of this machine, and for several blocks my speed is about twenty miles per hour.

The radio is tuned to a station playing golden oldies from the '50s and '60s. The deejay's voice is barrel deep, reminding me of my own favorite, Cousin Brucie. My mood shifts when "Wake Up, Little Susie" comes on, and I begin belting the words out loud. I drive in the opposite direction of Sophie's for many blocks just to hear the song finish. There's a dedication: *To the boy I have always loved, wherever you are, I hope I am in your thoughts. Katie.* The Skyliners are singing *This I Swear,* and I am fifteen again, making out against the garage door with Jonathan who smells like a wet puppy after playing basketball. He looks at me and is about to say something, then changes his mind, then starts again: "I love you," we whisper at the exact millimeter of a second. How could he know he'd ruined things for me, right then; silly me believed passion was something one could savor, play again and again, like a favorite cut on a record.

As I am rounding the corner leading to the Woodmans' house, I notice a car, lights on, parked in the driveway. What? My vitals are pumping as I increase my speed. Turning for no more than a few seconds, I spot Rob, that tropical shirt of his, unmistakable, and the blurry image of a lanky young woman. They are walking up the driveway toward the well-lit house, him leading her by the hand as if she were a toddler unsure of the terrain. Through my rearview mirror, I see them turn and gape in my direction.

Faster now, I reach an enclave of dark, narrow streets where the houses are all pitch black. More than one ferocious-sounding dog begins to bark, and as lights switch on like some syncopated dance, I lose control, plowing the Porsche through a neat row of privets. Branches and leaves hit the dashboard like confetti. My hands are sweaty, and I struggle to grasp the wheel. As soon as I'm in the clear, I pull over to catch my breath. I really have to pee but squatting here is out of the question. Instead, I begin concocting my story for Sophie:

Well, I guess you're wondering why I'm not carrying any swimsuits. The thing is—when I got to your driveway, there were three workmen idling in a rusty pickup. I couldn't imagine what they were doing there, especially at that hour. Sorry but I got scared. I decided it best to turn around. Oh, I might have hit a bush or two during my getaway. Check your car.

I picture Sophie listening, intently, her eyes bright as high beams, forcing me to look down and smooth the wrinkles in my shorts. I embellish this tale while exhausting myself in the process—for the want of her friendship, my budding confusion, and the prickly sensation across my neck, the slow gestation of fear.

Back in the hallway, I knock softly, figuring, by now, Sophie's children are asleep. She opens the door as if she had x-ray eyes and knew I'd be standing there at that precise instant.

"Oh, so you couldn't find anything for them to wear?" Sophie says, her face dewy, her eyes as I imagined: star bright with anticipation.

"Well, the thing is when I got to your—"

"Oh, so you saw them?" Sophie asks, smiling broadly. "It's really fine. I'm completely cool with it, Alex. Relax, breathe."

"Sophie, I'm not quite sure what I saw." This is when I smooth the wrinkles in my shorts, again.

"Alex, please, you can't be *that* naïve. Rob and I have an agreement. It's good for him, good for me, and therefore our marriage."

I shiver, victim to her words plus the efficiency of the Woodmans' air-conditioning. I wish I had a soft woolen blanket to wrap around my shoulders. As Sophie continues to chatter, I stare at her lips. The room becomes vacant of sound, as if watching a silent movie. Laughing faces dance before my tired eyes. I see a parade of familiar men, doing what they like to do. Look, there's Donny, Ben, Dad, and Rob, and all those who came before.

Donny calls the next morning while we're eating breakfast. Words stick in my mouth like thickened oatmeal. When he asks about the girls, I report with clips, like excerpts from a travel journal. There are long pauses in our conversation; we are walking along some dangerous edge. I look for a hidden meaning in every little thing he says, annoying him by interjecting "What?" constantly. He's forced to repeat things, pacing his answers to avoid a fight. My mother's presence in the kitchen keeps me from going overboard. She sips her coffee, but I know she hasn't missed one of my sour intonations.

Later, despite my suggestion he leave extra time for holiday traffic, Donny misses his flight. He calls from a boisterous airport lounge, and I can barely make out his words, except that he has to connect in Atlanta, making his arrival after midnight and certainly past the girls' bedtime.

I break the news to Becky and Lana while we are sitting around the table having the usual five o'clock dinner. Upon hearing this, Becky, child of reason, says, "Well, then I'll have to get in your bed and tickle Daddy in the morning." Lana, however, is inconsolable. She cries throughout the entire meal and eventually tosses her macaroni and cheese in my mother's direction. Ducking the plastic bowl before it hits the floor, my mother laughs, infuriating Lana even more.

"No laughing, Nana!" Lana pouts.

"Lana, sweetie, calm down. I promise you'll see Daddy in the morning," I say, kissing her curly head.

"Oh boy, what a mouth on her. Well, we know whose daughter she is," my mother says.

"Mom, not now, she's really upset."

"She's a little actress, a regular Sarah Bernhardt like her Momma."

"Miriam, enough!" My father's head pops out of the *Herald*. He's been sitting at the table waiting for the blowup, something he did all through my teenage years. When I was really "fresh," he would jump up from the dinner table, holding his belt that he'd already quietly unbuckled. In one swift motion he'd push back his chair, yank the belt from his waistband, and hold it high in the air, ready to tame the unruly lioness, me. I'd run screaming to my room and lock the door, terrified, not of the belt, so much, but at the fury lurking in his eyes.

"All right! I guess everything's my fault, but I bet Alex would never open her mouth to Mrs. Wonderful, Louise Pearl!" I have the notion I am about to pay hard for my father's remark to her.

"Mom, what on earth are you talking about? I said Lana was upset, and you were making her even crazier."

"You don't have to tell me the truth—I know the truth. If your father and I had loaned you money to buy a house, you'd kiss our asses too!"

"Dad, make her stop, the girls!"

My father says nothing as he stands and pushes back his chair, scraping the tiles below. Becky and Lana watch transfixed as if this were early morning cartoons. I flinch when he walks toward me, my eyes fixed on his waistband, but he is wearing beige polyester slacks, the kind with a sewn-in self-buckle. Dad grabs his newspaper and locks himself in the bathroom, where he will remain until God knows when.

Hands shaking, I pull Lana out of the booster seat. I wipe Becky's sticky fingers and kiss her forehead. "Go, go play on the terrace."

The silence is awful and yet so very familiar, like a second language I learned while growing up.

"Give me the sponge, Mom. I can clean that. It's not good for your back."

"What's the difference?" she says, handing me the sponge, getting up slowly.

Instead of being furious at her for hurting me and upsetting Lana, all I feel is a punch of ancient, nagging guilt. I imagine reaching out to hold her face, forcing her to look at me. I might smile, even stick out my tongue, anything to break this nauseating tension—maybe I might stand tippy-toe next to her tall, imposing frame and give her a feathery kiss on her cheek. But I do none of these things. My arms are like dumbbells, and my stomach churns from a half-eaten dinner. Again, my mother's words are the mortar for the wall she builds between us. I am too tired, and much too sad to drill through it. Instead, we finish cleaning up the kitchen in a hammering silence.

Almost three years ago, when Becky and Lana were still babies, Donny and I stayed here for the very first time. My parents had just moved in and were excited to have a place big enough to house us all. Although this trip was a badly needed respite from winter and the clutter of our mousetrap of an apartment, I arrived in Florida without my usual enthusiasm. For months I'd been hiding out—not sharing the disturbing, haunting thoughts that kept me awake each night and prohibited me from shopping for, cooking, or swallowing food. I barely functioned as a mother. While the girls napped, I'd lie on the couch in a fetal position, riveted to the TV. I'd turn the volume down low while I stared at soap opera stars, beautiful women—who looked older than me—embracing lovers, caring for babies, having heart-to-heart chats with caring friends or mothers. I had difficulty moving from my spot and had concluded the worst—I was probably dying. I watched and listened to my body as intently as an air traffic controller keeping planes out of danger. But I was about to crash. Every heartbeat became a string of palpitations; each swallow produced nausea. I focused on the numbness on the right side of my face, and a strange tingling in my fingertips. At the library, while browsing through medical books, I was sure I'd found my diagnosis: a brain tumor. My symptoms worsened and still, I told no one. Not even Donny. He had just given up some of his own dreams to work in his parents' business. We had to put off looking for a home, even though our apartment was cluttered with two cribs, two strollers, and cardboard boxes stacked with toys. When Donny came home from work, he'd bathe Becky, while I tended to four-month-old Lana. Then he'd put on his headphones to listen to some opera until his father called and they would talk about something that might have occurred during the day, or what had gone wrong and was probably Donny's fault. After the call, Donny closed his eyes and returned to his music. No, he didn't want to talk to me. It could be days before he'd touch me. Donny just wanted to be alone. And all I could think was: *Well, now he will finally get his wish.*

Then somehow, that December, we managed to get on a plane to visit my parents in their beautiful new condo. And a few nights into the trip, at the dinner table someone called out my name, but it sounded muffled, as if I was hearing it underwater.

"Alex, what the hell is wrong with you?" my father yelled, snapping his fingers in front of me, getting me to open my eyes wide. But I was too tired to answer him, too tired to even feel embarrassment. My plate was clean, just the remnants of a roll on its shiny surface. He couldn't be angry at me because I'd wasted my food. I hadn't eaten a single morsel. The very next day my father made an appointment for me with his internist. I agreed to go but insisted he wait outside, next to the thirty-gallon tank of tropical fish. As soon as I sat down across the desk from Dr. Unger, I burst into tears. He reminded me of the old grandfather in my favorite childhood book, *Heidi*. How he ran through the snowy streets looking for her, thinking she was lost. I, too, was lost. And I was hoping, just maybe, Dr. Unger might find me. He stood up, finally, from his leather chair, came around the desk, and patted my shoulder a few times, waiting patiently for me to stop weeping.

"Well," he said, "you've lost some weight, and you've written here that you can't sleep, suffer from headaches, numbness in your fingers, and now a new baby, added to your toddler. Married four years—are things okay?" He peered down at me from gold wired spectacles.

"It's my mother," I said, grasping for the one convenient place to put the blame for whatever I didn't understand. It seemed so easy; the words felt so right. "She's driving me nuts, making me absolutely crazy."

"Mothers can often do that, I'm told," he said. But I knew he was placating me, hoping I'd say much more. He suggested, for "peace of mind only," that I undergo some further testing. Then he handed me the name of someone to talk to when I returned home, but I never went. Nearly all my symptoms vanished a few days later. Maybe I just needed to cry with a kind stranger, someone who demanded nothing from me.

The 11:00 p.m. news has ended, and my father insists on driving me to the airport to pick up Donny. Like a commandant in the Russian Army, he says, "Alex, get in the goddamn car—you're crazy if you think I'd let you drive on I-95 alone. Don't you read? Most of the refugees who live in Miami carry pistols in their glove compartments. Shootings, every day, that's all you hear on the news."

"Really? Are you sure you aren't afraid I'd wreck your precious Caddy."

"Cut it out," he says, exhaling slowly, and blowing air through his lips.

"Dad, are you okay?" He's already had one mild heart attack, when I was in college, and I don't wish to be responsible for another.

"I'm fine, fine—just sick of the same bullshit. You think it's easy? Do you have any idea what I deal with?"

"Mom?"

"All she does is dwell on the past—the same crap that happened forty years ago: If her father hadn't pulled her out of design school, if her mother hadn't died, and at the top of the list is—"

"I know, Dad, if you hadn't taken her away from her children and grandchildren—her life would be perfect."

"Exactly. So tell me, what has she done to make her life better down here?"

"Does she have any real friends?"

"Nah, you know how particular she can be. Oh, excuse me, I forgot, she does like your friend."

"Sophie?"

"Yes, and those *fancy* guys, the decorators who live down the hall." I hear his narrow-minded disdain, reminding me I'm with the tough sailor from Flatbush.

"Dad, I think you've been watching too much Archie."

"Yeah, well they swarm all over your mother. They're the bees and she's the honey."

"Listen, it's got to be hard feeling like she's missing out on everything, thinking Donny's folks are getting a bigger piece of us."

"But you're here now, right? So why did she have to bring that up? Maybe if you visited us more or called her more often…"

"Come on, Dad. I've got my own life to juggle. Sorry, but you're the one who moved away—not me."

For the remainder of the ride, my mood turns sullen. I can't help but wonder what my father's real intent was on driving me to the airport. Does he expect me to solve his problems with my mother, as well? Fix it, Alex. Come on, kiddo, show me that A+. And yet I have taken a front seat on this guilt trip; I've bought the ticket he continues to sell me.

He's been whistling the theme from *The High and the Mighty* for the last five minutes, driving me nuts. He knows he's upset me—his one dependable ally. I'd love to blast the radio and drown him out, but it would be an act of defiance, something I can more easily save for my mother.

As we approach the sign for arrivals, I spot Donny standing below the greenish glow of the taxi stand, swatting night bugs with his hand. I am surprised to see him looking so rested—as if he'd been on vacation instead of me. Hadn't he switched planes and spent hours traveling? And yet, this is what scares me most: for the first time in our seven years together, I am aware that my heart is not stirring in anticipation of our embrace. The more I try to shake this thought, the more I feel as if my blood has been replaced with blue coolant. I blame it on the hour, the discussion with my father, and number one—the blowup at tonight's dinner. But I hate the sensation; it's as if I've been cut open and revealed to have nothing inside these bones. *Naught*, as Dad always corrects me whenever I say *zero*.

My father puts the car in park and gives a shrill whistle in Donny's direction.

"Stay here," he commands.

From the car, I watch them embrace warmly. In my mother's absence, I adopt her annoyance when my father hoists Donny's bag. She has been known to scold Dad for carrying a gallon jug of skim.

As soon as the trunk slams, my stomach churns.

"Hi," Donny says, peeking through the open window before getting in the car.

"Pretty tired huh?" A strange shyness wraps itself around me.

"Whipped!" Donny opens the door and slides in the front seat, moist heat emanates from his body. Though he smells of wintergreen Life Savers, layered underneath is the vinegary aroma of cheap wine. When Donny throws his arm around me, I inch closer to my father.

"I thought you'd surprise me with the girls," he says casually.

"After midnight, are you crazy?"

He retreats, looking hurt, but I continue, "I was going to bring them. We had a scene at dinner because you were going to be late—"

"All right, all right, how's business, son?" My father interjects, hoping to change the subject. Stuck now between him and my husband, I sit brooding like a ten-year-old. I left one and made a beeline to the other. Nothing has changed, as I am still reacting, always reacting to their words, actions, or inactions. Maybe they change, these men: they get to walk in and out of so many doors, some, if lucky, break through walls; yet too often they hide, and when it works for them—they lie.

We lie in the dark like mimes, beating our pillows, trying to get comfortable in this torture chamber my parents call a high-riser. Before Donny's arrival, I slept restfully across the large living room couch, having promised my mother I'd tuck sheets over her cut velvet cushions. Now on one of my super-dramatic flips onto my stomach, I notice Donny's eyes are open, his mouth taut. My parents are asleep in the next bedroom, Dad's snoring audible through the wall, and though I know it's the worst time to pick a fight, I can't help myself. Venom oozes from every pore of me like garlic.

"I spoke to you twice the entire week. Don . . . I know you're up."

"Not now, Al, I'm so tired." He flips over and left jabs his pillow.

"Oh, and I'm not, after being with the kids, running around, meals, baths, and bedtime!" There, now I can't stop even if I want to.

"I thought you were having a good time," Donny says, crooked up on his elbow now, his head resting on his hand.

"Sounds like *you* were the one having a ball!" I lean in so we are face-to-face, nose-to-nose.

"What's that supposed to mean? And why are you acting like a bitch ever since I got off the plane?"

All of a sudden, Rob, all sweaty, wearing his palm tree shirt, pops

into my head, and I think about telling Donny what I saw and heard
from Sophie, but he'd probably say, "Oh, so that's what this is about."
I don't want to hear it, even if he's right.

"You know, I think you loved having us gone."

"That's not true. Stop looking for things that don't exist." Donny
turns on the bamboo lamp on his side of the bed. "Come here."

"No, I don't want to." I'm on the verge of crying, and I think I want
Donny to hold me, but I can't ask. I just can't.

"I'll come to you then." Instead of rolling toward me, Donny
stands on the severely, dilapidated mattress and walks over my head.
His stance is Mr. Clean, hands on hips. Looking up at his boxers, I
have a telescopic view of his precious *jewels*. Though I plead with him
to get down, he jumps up and down, trying to make me laugh. The
sounds of the grinding metal are sure to awaken my parents, giving
them the wrong idea. Because we are in *their* home and not ours, it
will always be the wrong idea. But if we were making love, instead of
bickering like adolescents, maybe I'd feel less like I'm afloat at sea—
on one of those budget cruises to nowhere. Truth is it's easier to spar
with Donny than to expose any glimmer of sexual yearning. I grew
up hearing hints of: *good girls* played hard to get, while *really good
girls* learned to suppress desire.

Donny plops back down on his side of the bed and yawns. I've
never been much of a gambler, but I'm on the brink of anteing the
entire pot by screaming: DO YOU FUCKING LOVE ME?

"Come on, babe, give me a juicy one," Donny says, puckering
like a blowfish. I watch as his eyelids struggle before losing the fight.
Within seconds, he is fast asleep.

SEVEN

Since tonight is Rob Woodman's birthday bash, Donny has been working arduously on his George Hamilton tan—a golden glow he will preserve, back home, with several treatments under his number one favorite appliance—the sun lamp. Now he repositions his chaise so that the searing noon rays are directly overhead.

I'm startled when my mother, like an eclipse, halts in front of my lounge and blocks out the sun. Dressed in skintight white capris and a lavender blouse, my mother practically lassoes us from our stakeout beside the kiddie pool. It is her intention, she says, hands on hips, to serve lunch "immediately" on the terrace. She then tugs the beach towel free from my chair and holds it bullfighter fashion for Becky and Lana. They are in the pool, kicking like tadpoles, tucked under my father's arms.

"Let's dry-off my little girls," Miriam sings with Debbie Reynolds glee. "Time for lunch."

"Don't want yucky lunch, Nana. Watch me swim!" Lana shrieks.

"Let's go now, you'll swim later." Abruptly Miriam changes her tone, her voice deepening like a seasoned truck driver. She has no intention of waiting. When she spots her neighbors, "the decorator guys," she waves wildly, her bangle bracelets jingling and capturing the sunlight. I watch her strike a pose for these trim, handsome men named Oscar and Giorgio, who she refuses to believe are lovers. They wave back from their chairs, and Oscar, wearing a gold bikini bottom, blows an exaggerated kiss in my mother's direction. He has an enormous bulge in the crotch of his bathing suit that I surmise has little to do with my mother.

"They're both European and so very *continental*," she mentions, at every sighting. And they simply love her, especially Oscar, who thinks she is absolutely stunning.

"That's so nice, Mom," I say. "You *are* stunning. So how long have they been lovers?"

"What? Alex, dear, you are *so* wrong. I can assure you they are not lovers." Miriam laughs, hinting she knows their sexual proclivity from firsthand experience. She has been redecorating her bedroom for over a year now, much to my father's chagrin. I feel a wave of embarrassment imagining her throwing herself into Oscar's arms after he delivers the fantastically expensive Etoile bedspread with matching pillows.

I nudge Donny to help gather the surplus of water toys, towels, and lotions scattered near the pool. "But we just got here, babe. These rays arc the best."

"Donny, we haven't had a meal together yet. Besides, look at you, your chest is purple."

"And yours is sizzling." Donny reaches into my bikini top and cups my breast as if it wasn't live flesh, like it was the breast on a plastic torso displaying lingerie in his showroom. I slap his arm as I might a junior high boy messing with me in the hallway. He thinks I'm kidding, but I'm not. My mother flashes us a quick, disgusted look—a warning to behave on her turf. She has to know Manny Gluck has been peeking at me through the pages of his *Miami Sun* all morning.

"Donny, why do you pick the most inopportune time to be, shall we say, sexual, or was this your attempt at being romantic?"

"Call it whatever, babe." Donny gathers up an arsenal of lotions and gives my father a hand with the tubes and pool toys. We walk several yards to my parents' terrace on the ground floor, which has an expansive view of Biscayne Bay. The morning's syrupy fog has lifted, revealing a horseshoe of high rise coral and aqua buildings along the shoreline. Today the water is a deep azure blue, calm except for the occasional ripples left by passing yachts. A smiling stranger waving from a bough shouts, "Hi folks, what's for lunch?"

Lana and Becky keep waving way after each yacht passes. They're like miniature movie stars in sparkly sunglasses. Donny plops Lana into the wrought-iron loveseat, then finds himself a spot facing the sun.

"Great day, heh kids?" my dad asks. He looks at the sky and scolds, "You better get the hell out of here!" For an instant, I think he's spotted an intruder on the rooftop, or a swarm of palmettos, but no, Dad's actually wagging his finger at a hovering, nimbus cloud—as though the sun is the remedy for all his problems.

Six hours later, we arrive at Embers Steakhouse to find five couples already seated at a long rectangular table. For Rob's party we've dressed in our finest cruise-wear ensembles: Donny in a navy Ban-Lon shirt worn over white ducks, and after changing three times, I decided on a faded-blue denim jacket and torso-clinging white bell-bottoms. For the first time, in a long time, I am aware of my attractiveness, which I attribute to spending time outdoors, and a few dabs of terra cotta blush.

Silver place cards, adorned with Rob's baby picture, direct us to a rectangular table where we are each seated parallel to our spouses. Once settled, I wave to Donny, who looks as awkward as I feel, not knowing a soul except our hostess, Sophie, and her birthday boy, Rob. Introductions fly through the air despite pings of crystal glasses and the clatter of flatware. I try to remember names but become distracted by one woman's Miss Piggy nose job, another's diamond ring the size of Rockefeller Center's skating rink, and a bold, silver streak threaded through the bangs of an unsmiling brunette.

After a few gulps of wine, we learn, compared to most, Donny and I are practically newlyweds. Sophie, buoyant as usual, announces she and Rob have been together twelve "heavenly" years. I glance over at Rob to see him gaping at me and quickly turn away. Of course, he knows it was me the other night who whizzed by his house, driving Sophie's little Targa. Guess Big Rob thinks he's going to have himself some fun.

Throughout this sumptuous steak dinner, we hear toasts by Rob's friends, a tender love poem written and read aloud by Sophie, and lastly, a roast, alluding to Rob's raucous side. There are blatant references to him being a slumlord, and to his charming the pants (someone yells "diapers") off the elderly women residing at his hotels. A few of the guys howl when Rob's golf course demeanor is described: temper tantrums ending with golf carts driven into ditches, and manicured greens machete-d by his putter. As proper guests, we merrily laugh along, but I can't help but see Rob in a bold new light— living on the edge.

Donny's sporting his shy face, which, instinctively, makes me want to protect him. Tentative in the company of other men, he prefers talking about "us" to avoid talking about him. He gestures toward me while speaking to a very attractive man sitting beside him, who appears a bit older, almost fatherly. I catch myself staring more than a few times. The first time we lock eyes, my heart races. I look down, feigning interest in the floral pattern of the dishes. What's in this wine anyway? The effects have slowly moved down my hips to settle in my groin. A minute later I look back. The guy's face is angular, his cheekbones high, reflecting the glow from the candelabra above the table. Though he's begun to lose his hair, it's the older persona I find most appealing—that, and dark, deep-set brown eyes.

It's his turn to talk, and he looks as though he's telling Donny a joke. I can tell from the rhythm he uses, the way his hands move in tiny circles as if juggling. When the punch line is delivered, his arm reaches over and rests on Donny's shoulder. Donny, protective of his space, winces before he laughs. Perhaps relieved Donny got his joke, the guy laughs again. His warm eyes twinkle, and though I haven't heard the joke or punch line, I find myself caught in its rippling effect. He looks up and sees me smiling at them—at him. The place is so noisy I can barely hear his name, even when he says it a second time. "Charlie," he says, finally reaching over the table to take my hand in his firm grip. "Charlie Bell."

"That was my grandfather's name," I answer, as a hand automatically goes to my heart like *I pledge allegiance to the flag.*

"Mine was Carl. Papa Carl," he says, with a melancholy grin, hints of pride evident in his voice.

"Mine was a *Papa,* too," I shout over the racket of voices and colliding dinner plates.

"*Oh my Papa, to me he was so wonderful . . .* by . . . ?" Charlie asks.

"Eddie Fisher!" I answer, having sung the sappy song as a girl eager to entertain her grandfather.

"Give that girl a trip to the Bahamas!" Charlie toasts me with his wineglass held high. *Come on, ask me another tune,* I want to say.

The woman beside me with the silver streak has not spoken a word to me. She's been in deep conversation with the woman next to her, whose arm must throb from carrying her skating rink–size diamond ring. Noticing me chatting with Charlie, she now turns to stare at me. And because I'm already nervous, I speak first.

"I'm sorry, I forgot your name," I say.

"Paula. Paula Bell."

"I'm Alex. It's short for Alexandra." I haven't referred to myself this way since signing my marriage certificate.

Her pale hand motions vaguely across the table. "He's my husband."

"Oh, right!" I just then realize Charlie and Paula must be the couple Sophie and Rob had wanted us to meet. Maybe we should make some new friends, something that seemed so much easier to do when I was single. Now I have to worry if Donny will like the husband. In the name of diplomacy, I've limited my socializing to before dusk sets in. "Sophie and Rob thought we might be neighbors," I say. "We live in Wheatley Heights, New Jersey."

"Ah, yes," Paula says, without enthusiasm, as if she knew, "so do we."

I wonder why I've never seen her before back home, but couldn't she say the same about me? I turn back to my food; a few slices of coagulated filet mignon on top of soggy onion rings. Glancing over at Paula's plate, I notice she's hardly eaten a thing. She pushes her food around, carefully separating her double-baked potato from her meat. And, as if he knew this as a given, Charlie, her handsome, quizmaster husband, reaches over with his fork to stab a huge chunk of red rare meat.

Sophie jumps up and clinks a spoon against her wineglass to get everyone's attention. Wearing her signature mischievous grin, she announces we'll be going back to her house for a special dessert and "munchies." I predict, as the evening's finale, most of the people at this table will soon be stoned. I, for one, am not thrilled at the idea of using an illegal drug with my parents only two miles away, especially while watching our children. My mother once shunned me for a month when I took Becky out into a cool summer evening with a slight fever. I can only imagine what she might do if I was part of a drug bust. Don't drug busts happen all the time in Miami?

Lifting my glass, I take a dainty sip, then gulp the rest to the bottom. I look up thinking I've caught Charlie admiring his wife, then turn away, flushed. There's a throbbing beat of pure excitement when I realize he's been studying me.

We are gathered in the Woodmans' newly renovated den, renamed the *entertainment center*. Where a northerner anticipating cold winters might have put a fireplace, Sophie and Rob have placed a magnificent Steinway—an ebony baby grand that is making Donny drool. When we were first married, he played almost every evening. He diligently practiced Beethoven sonatas when he should have been studying. Music, not people, has always provided safety for Donny, so I'm not surprised when he pulls out the bench and sits down to play.

As the first joint is passed, a few people join Donny around the piano. A book of Christmas carols sits propped on the music stand, and before long, we are caroling our hearts out, performing like kids in a holiday assembly.

When Sophie gives a tour, Rob saunters over to the piano. Beads of sweat drip down his face like melted ice cream, while steam rises from his entire body. He is singing—no, screaming—the loudest. I feel his clammy hand reach under my jacket, inches from my bra closure. Donny begins "Oh, Holy Night" and perhaps it's the sacredness of the melody that causes Rob to release his grip on my spine.

"So, Alex, how'd you like driving Sophie's car?" Rob whispers, pressing into my hipbone. I think that's what he said, but the wine and grass has rendered me unreliable. At that very moment, Sophie and Miss Piggy, who makes me grateful I'd nixed that nose job, carry in an enormous cake and place it on what looks like a steel table. Devilish Sophie has used those trick candles that keep relighting, and Rob plays along, struggling to blow them out. I make a mental note not to eat the cake after his spittle flies through the air and lands on the icing.

"Enough of this shit!" Rob starts pulling them out, not caring who or what he burns in the process. A candle falls on the plush beige carpeting, yet Sophie hardly blinks. I get a weird, masochistic pang for Rona. If she were here, which is a real stretch of the imagination, she'd be the first to stomp it out.

The guests move in to get a better look at the cake: a huge rectangle colorfully frosted to show a young man with a baby face who truly resembles Rob. In profile, he's pointing what appears to be his *member* toward the golf green while peeing—displayed with curls of lemon icing. The lettering reads "Happy Birthday Rob, *You Little Pisser.*" Donny, still at the piano, bangs out a jazzy version of "Happy Birthday."

"Donny, come have some cake!" Sophie yells, but he is caught up in the happy childhood melody, his eyes fixed on the ivory keys.

Rob's golf buddies howl, having seen him in action on many golf courses. The women roll their eyes, sharing that *boys will be boys* look, part of the silent code of a universal society. The laughing subsides, stealing with it the energy in the room. One by one, we settle into the deep furniture. Furniture you can live in for a day or two at least. Beanbag chairs in wild-animal prints are scattered among three couches. A wall of travertine built-ins house stereo equipment, and the largest television I've ever seen. Rob turns up the volume on Cat Steven's "Tea for the Tillerman," making me ponder for the hundredth time: *What the heck is a tillerman?* I'm more than a tiny bit stoned and hope it doesn't show. I hate that shit-eating grin some get after a few tokes. Once I became totally paranoid when my ex-neighbor Ellie baked a batch of brownies that we devoured on the way to tennis. While serving, I felt the court closing in, as if the net was wrapped around my body like seaweed on an ocean floor.

Sophie announces, "Everyone—listen up!" These people, vibrant and colorful at dinner, have now taken on the muted tones of the room. Paula and the woman I learn is her sister-in-law continue their sidebar chatter. They ignore my smiles and attempt at small talk. Sophie once told me that while she personally isn't intimidated by anyone, she was certain some women would find *me* threatening.

"Are you kidding?" I said, hearing this for the first time.

"Oh Alex, don't be coy," she answered. "You're attractive, sensual, and you carry yourself with extreme confidence."

My extreme confidence had me unsure whether this petite woman with the elfish grin was paying me a compliment or putting me down.

"Come on people, wake up, it's not even midnight," Sophie says, clapping her hands three times. "The game's called Wink and it goes like this: Everyone has to pick a piece of paper from this wicker basket. Only one of the papers is marked with an *X*. So, whoever gets the *X* is the killer. It's the killer's job to kill as many people in the room as he or she can without getting caught."

"How, pray tell, does the killer do the deed?" Rob asks, as if the question was a setup.

"By winking, silly, that's why the game's called Wink." Sophie continues, "Remember: Do not reveal yourself as the killer. Make sure no one else is watching, but if you are winked at by the killer, then immediately yell: 'I'm dead' to let us know you are not the killer. Got it, everyone?"

Nervous giggles dart about the room. Why are adults so dumb when following simple directions?

"But first," Rob says, "some A-1 stuff!"

God, no, please. Another fat joint is passed around. One by one, Sophie and Rob's guests take a hit of the "good stuff." It's hashish, which I try to avoid since the vapors are too harsh for my respiratory system. But Donny gets up and presents the joint to me. All eyes are upon me. Once again, I'm at the blackboard in fourth grade reciting The Declaration of Independence. I fake a deeper inhale than I take. Still, the fumes singe my throat.

Sophie places the basket under my nose. I think of tossing in the joint, but I'd probably start a fire. Instead, I reach for a tiny piece of folded paper. I unfold it in slow motion, stalling, trying to recap the rules of this ridiculous game, which I've already forgotten. I look at my paper quickly, then squeeze it down into the pocket of my hip-huggers.

Donny, wedged between Sophie and Rob on the couch, tosses me a smile. He appears shrunken, dwarfed by big bad Rob, or it could be the pot. Sophie's eyes dart around the room, intent to catch the killer in action—to give them up and away. I try another deep breath because the pressure is more than I can bear. The red *X* on the crumpled paper feels as though it's branded through my sweaty palm. I actually hear the sizzle. My eyes scan the array of faces. Paula and her sister-in-law are already dismissing the game, and I wonder what the hell could they be talking about this long? Rob's eyes bulge as he forces a huge slice of cake down his throat. Sophie cackles, enjoying him enjoying. The coast seems clear. Yet, I feel him watching me, waiting for my move. Standing in the glow of candlelight, he looks very kind and more handsome than I imagined.

I look at . . . Carl? Charles? Nope, it's Charlie. He leans against the wall, half listening to his brother beside him. Our eyes lock, and my arms and legs go limp. Only my lashes flutter, as they move up and down, taking on a life of their own, heading straight for my target.

"*I'm dead!*" Charlie Bell announces. He stares down at the swirling carpet to avoid my eyes, protecting me from being caught. At once I'm filled with this strange and penetrating warmth, as if wrapped in a rainbow. Who cares if I'm caught?

"It's Alex!" Sophie squeals, jumping up from the couch to point to my sun-roasted face. "Alex Pearl's the killer!"

It is half past three in the morning, and Donny's at the wheel of my father's plane-like, cherished Caddy.

"Well, did you ever think Sophie and Rob were so out there?" Donny says, widening his eyes, trying to focus on the road.

"Out there and outrageous, but I admit I had a really good time."

"Yeah, I could tell. Hey babe, you looked real pretty tonight. Come here—why are you sitting so far away?"

I slide over and rest my hand casually on Donny's thigh. Instinctively, he clamps his hand over it. Testing . . . one . . . two . . . three. I've been reluctant to reach out, to make the first move toward closeness. I'm not holding back on purpose. It's just that I need to be sure I'm really wanted.

"Thank you. I hope I didn't look out of it. I hate that zombie look."

"Nah, but that couple from our neighborhood and his brother were wacked."

"You mean Paula and Charlie? Oh, so that's why she was so quiet. I only saw her chatting with her sister-in-law."

"And me," Donny says. "I spoke to her in the kitchen while having coffee. She seems a bit withdrawn, but nice—most likely, a loner. You might like her once you got to know her. I suggested we make plans to see them back home."

"Really, Don? You never do that. So, I guess that means you liked Charlie?"

Donny slides his hand up and down my thigh, letting it rest near my groin. "The guy's definitely a performer," Donny continues. "He's with some firm downtown, a trial lawyer."

"Well, they do look like a down-to-earth couple, not snobby or nouveau riche."

"He complained he was still paying off some hefty loans from law school. These corporate guys have to bust their butts for years before they reap any benefits. Oh, and he's away practically all the time." Donny reports this, dreamily, as if imagining what it might be like living in Charlie's shoes.

"I'd hate that. I think they have young kids like us. He's missing their entire childhood."

"So, maybe working for Pop isn't such a bad thing after all. But I'd prefer it if I had a choice in the matter."

"Donny, it's never too late to go back to school or return to your first love, music. We'd manage. I'd find something part-time." It would be the best thing for Donny to know he could walk away from H. Pearl and Sons if he wanted to. His parents would probably be the first to give him their blessings. He'd probably trade places with Charlie Bell in a blink.

"What are you thinking about, tell me?" Donny asks. We are walking through the stifling parking garage, swinging hands. The echo of my sandals on the cement forces me to keep looking behind me. The effect of the hashish has faded but only slightly.

"He's not how I'd picture a corporate lawyer, all stuffy and con-servative. He reminds me of this actor, Ben something, but I can't remember his name." I quickly become cautious, aware I might be showing too much interest.

"Well, there's usually a great deal of theater in the courtroom—it's all about who tells the best story." A hint of envy in Donny's voice saddens me. I put my arms around him for a big hug. He begins rub-bing his body side by side against mine.

"Not here in the scary garage," I say. "Let's hurry upstairs."

The pressure has been mounting all weekend, making our attempt at lovemaking frenzied and distracted. Dad has raised the thermostat, and we are sweating profusely beneath the cheap, acrylic blanket used to shield us from surprises: Lana's need to go potty, my mother's midnight stroll to see if we double-locked the front door, or, hearing our voices, her standard: "Did you have a good time, children?"

Faces appear in my head, staccato, like quarter notes on a scale. I'm not able to hold an image long enough to reach orgasm. Our bodies stick, then separate, and I taste the salt of Donny's perspira-tion dripping above me. At first, I want it to be unrushed—loving and romantic. But I become bored, and at the same time I'm afraid if we stop, each unsatisfied, it might damage us in some irreparable way. I try focusing on the image of the shy, but sexy, wallpaper hanger, who I'd hired in the fall, selected from Rona's golden list of community service men. Damn. What was his name? Oh yes, Tommy. Tommy dressed in tight white overalls worn over a torn white tank shirt, his arms splattered with paste and paint from a full day's work. Only once his sharp hip had bumped mine as we stood in my miniscule powder room, when I showed him the damage done to the bathroom wall. As he talked, I noticed the tiniest drop of white paint on his top lip. I shocked myself when I leaned in to scrape it gently with my fingernail, while Tommy stood there frozen, staring at the wall. Turns out, I had picked a very professional wallpaper hanger. Now though, I imagine his lean body pressed to mine, and how holding a flat trowel, dipped in plaster, he butters me up and down, up and down, covering every tiny imperfection, all my cracks and fissures. Wait! There's a new face in the picture that I try blinking away, but he remains in sharp focus. He's dressed in a suit, a well-tailored, navy pinstriped suit. Oh, it's you! I wink.

"I'm dead." He smiles. Charlie's hands caress my bare shoulders, my back, moving down my thighs. They push up and underneath my nightgown. They are rough hands, strong enough to catch me if I fall.

I lie sweating in the dark, my body limp as Becky's favorite "drowsy doll" that says, "Good night, I love you." Donny withdraws, abruptly, without a kiss, while my body trembles. He takes my hand, and I know without us talking, he wants me to help. Though I could be anyone at this moment, I kiss his face, tenderly, and as my eyes become accustomed to the shadows, I see that Donny's are squeezed shut. His cheekbones glisten in the dark. When I reach out to touch his face, I find it wet with tears.

"Don, it's the wine and all the stupid grass, relax."

"It's hot as fucking hell!" He jumps up, groping for the door.

"Where are you going? It's late."

"The shower," he says. "I'm going to take a goddamn cold shower."

I follow Donny into the hallway and peek in on Becky and Lana. They're asleep on an air mattress in the dining alcove off the living room. They have kicked off their covers and their nightgowns are twisted around their waists. I lean over their bodies and kiss them each on the neck. Though their hair is damp, they smell fresh as lavender.

Lana opens her eyes and grins at me; two fingers are curled inside her lips. She doesn't say anything, but she pops up and looks around, as if reminding herself this is not her room. Then she folds back down and throws her arm around Becky's neck. I sit there listening to their breathing, twirling a curl of Lana's hair. Thinking she's asleep, I start to get up, only to have her reach for my hand. When I finally return to bed, Donny doesn't stir, but I know from the sharpness of his breath he is still awake.

"Do you feel better now, Donny?"

"Oh yeah," he whispers, turning away from me toward the wall, "so much better."

EIGHT

I would give anything to be lounging under a breezy palm in Florida. But I'm back on Daisy Lane, staring out the window at our only apple tree, now hunched and skeletal. All the gray stalks against the fence, once fertile rose bushes, show little promise. I try to accept this wintry bleakness as a form of punishment—a chilly price to pay for the glory of summer.

Housebound for weeks, I have become what my Lithuanian grandmother called a *balabusteh*, a woman of many domestic talents. I've made eyelet curtains for Lana's bedroom, antiqued a small desk for Becky, and cooked chicken soup from scratch, stashing pints away in our freezer. Since my T-shirt business has slowed down, considerably, I find it necessary to keep my hands moving. That's why I began knitting an Irish Fisherman's sweater for Donny, which I'll probably keep for myself out of superstition, because in college whenever I finished a sweater for a guy and handed it over, we broke up within hours. And since we haven't done *it* for three and a half weeks, the longest break in our seven years together, I'm definitely not taking any chances.

For exercise, I make several trips downstairs, where propped against the playroom wall is the *blank* canvas, angled like a steep white cliff I've refused to climb. If I reached the top, might I discover the challenge to adopt a new perspective? This kind of thinking causes me to rush upstairs, raid the pantry, and devour half a bag of chocolate kisses. Yet even sweeter, because of school closings, the girls and I take long naps cuddled together, warm and toasty in my bed. This is the deepest sleep for me because they are nowhere but home, tucked beside me and completely safe.

Since I nap during the day, unfortunately, I toss and turn like flapjacks most nights. The neon digits of the alarm clock glow a frustrating 2:00 a.m. When I turn on the light, Donny squints before crunching a pillow over his head. In our first few years together, we'd lie in the dark talking about so many things—discovering one another's childhood secrets. Now there's no need to respond to my apology for having stirred him. Instead of warm affection, a kiss, and the stirrings of sexual arousal, my nourishment is the growing stack of *Gourmet* magazine—a gift subscription from Louise, the best cook I know. While the world is sleeping, I read long, intricate recipes for dishes like Saucisson en Croute, Rumaki, and Chicken Divan in a similar way I once read Frost and Whitman, intrigued by content, the language of the ingredients, and the promise of a satisfying culmination.

It's another snowy Friday night, and hoping to lure him with food, I serve Donny a new concoction—Golden Mushroom Chicken. In *A Sensuous Life in 30 Days*, I've read how certain foods, like mushrooms and oysters, are terrific aphrodisiacs though they often cause flatulence. Although the dish is far from gourmet, I need to start out slowly—sort of a fifty-yard stroll for cooks.

I study Donny intently as he scrapes the remainder of sauce from his plate. This must be how my grandmother beamed while watching Papa dissect an entire whitefish, leaving only the gold casement of scaly skin and needle-like bones. Nana lived to please Papa but did he return the favor? A year after her death, he moved in with her best friend, a woman who painted her face like a geisha and couldn't boil water.

"Well?" I am tapping my foot, waiting for a response.

"Delicious!" Donny stands from the captain's chair, his hands massaging his belly. "Is this one of my mom's latest creations?" His skin, pushing through his shirt, resembles an inner tube. Why hadn't I noticed this before?

"No, but it is probably somebody else's mom's. It was a snap to make—took no time at all."

"No kidding?"

"Well, not that easy," I add too late. Donny's headphones are already firmly in place. His eyes are tightly closed, and his lips curl into a flirty smile. And then, within minutes there is flatulence, lots and lots, only I am privy to hear—and I think: *So much for the sexual power of mushrooms.*

"Bye, bye, Donny," I shout, forcing him to take the headphones off.

"What did you say?"

"Not a thing." I'm left standing in the kitchen wondering why I couldn't take Donny's compliment or any compliment and just say thank you.

You look great, Alex usually gets: "Oh, but my hair is terrible!"

You have a lovely voice, Alex and I'll answer: "Are you sure there's nothing wrong with your hearing?"

And, *I simply love the paintings you did in the girls' bedrooms* is sure to hear: "Oh, those, well, if you look closely, you'll see the mistake I made right *there*. I covered it with a tiny cloud . . . see?"

Donny finishes his catnap, shuts off the stereo, and joins me in the kitchen. He opens the broom closet and glances at the school calendar tacked inside. I live my entire life by that calendar. "Al, I've got a really cool idea," he says. "What do you think about us throwing our first Valentine's party? We can keep it simple, not crazy or terribly expensive."

"You want a house full of people on Valentine's Day?"

"Yeah, why not?"

"Sorry for asking a dumb question, but in the past, you preferred spending that particular night alone—getting a sitter and sharing a quiet dinner somewhere. And then later we get to exchange predictable presents of sleazy underwear."

The truth is I planned on making this Valentine's Day as sensuous as it could be. I was prepared to stand naked on my head, instead of *on ceremony.*

Donny responds by pulling the scotch-taped calendar off the wall. "Fear not, Juliet, we can still do that. Turns out, VD is during the week. We can have the party the Saturday night before."

"VD? Isn't that a sexually transmitted disease?"

Donny's sudden enthusiasm regarding socializing surprises me. He has seemed quieter than usual lately, more introspective, something I found both puzzling and mildly attractive. Now he's talking *party.*

"Okay, Don, I guess, but absolutely no fondue. Dr. Carner blames fondue for most of the streptococcus he sees each winter. We've all been sick enough."

"I have an idea! Why don't I help you cook?" Donny says.

Here's a perfect opportunity for Donny to mimic Ben, who after a week of screaming in the factory, and a weekend of playing eight-handicap golf, can be found sitting in the kitchen, scooping honey and chopped nuts into his prize-winning baklava.

Donny sits at the kitchen table while I finish loading the dishwasher; he thumbs through my paperback copy of *The Elegant Cook.* "I've got it," he says. "How about I make baklava?"

"Baklava would be terrific, Donny."

Together in bed, we are propped on corduroy pillows, doing a mock roll call of our guest list. My leg is crossed over Donny's leg. His curly leg hairs are mingling with my bristles. I am thrilled to be touching like this; it feels warm and cozy, but mostly safe. With a pad and pen, he's jotting down, crossing out, and enjoying our kindergarten fun. It takes no time to realize in our two years living in Wheatley Heights, we've made some acquaintances, are surrounded by nice neighbors, but other than Rona and Hy, we have few new friends.

"What about Nina and Noel?" Donny first suggests. Nina and Noel still live in our old apartment building in Brooklyn. I've always thought Donny had a thing for Nina. She's a bit of a chameleon—the kind of woman whose demeanor transforms the instant a man walks in the room, and she's often too damn attentive to Donny. There were times when, watching them interact, I'd feel my stomach tighten. Was there something I didn't know? What I wanted to say to each of them but didn't was: *Stay away, he's mine*, or *Stop, she's my friend*. It often felt like a toss-up.

"Sure, I guess, fine."

"And Alvin . . . and you know who?" Donny teases.

"Ohhhhh." A bellyache moan escapes me. We occasionally see Donny's high school buddy, Alvin, and his wife, Michele. Alvin has a terrible stomach, probably caused by the ever-whiny Michele. The theory is he spends so much time in the bathroom to escape her.

"To smoke or not to smoke—that is the question," I say, putting our list making on pause. Our neighbors Norm and Sue, across the street, are a few years older and very conservative. Norm is the only person we know who admits he voted for Nixon. There is no way Norm has ever smoked a joint. And just a few doors down from them, fairly new on the block, are Jake and Ellen. Word travels fast in these parts, and the word is Jake's got a nice little business going on the side. He's been tagged *The Man*—the main supplier of "the good stuff." Last summer, while making a deal for some of that *good* stuff, he was arrested in Harlem. Rumor had it that he was in the company of a young, gorgeous Spanish girl when the cops nabbed him. Two weeks and he was out, which made our neighborhood's heads very happy.

"Why not go for it?" Donny says, his head sinking deep into his pillow. "It's best not to slight anyone. As a matter of fact, we should probably invite that couple," he adds.

"Ah, who?" I sometimes do this, even though I can usually predict what Donny is about to say. Am I so starved for adult conversation that I need to string him along?

"Oh, you know, Charlie and his wife, Paula . . . we met them at Sophie's, remember?"

"Right, that's an idea. Do you think they'd come?"

"Hey, you wanted to make new friends . . . well, go ahead," Donny's voice sounds garbled as he slides down on his pillow.

I can feel my face brighten as if someone's shined a floodlight on me. Even though Paula Bell and I had exchanged numbers the night of Rob's birthday bash, I put off calling her, what with fevers running rampant. It was my guess Paula would never be the first to call; she was either a snob or terribly insecure and needed to be pursued. I wasn't sure if I wanted to find out. Though, it had been harder to forget her husband, Charlie Bell. I remember his warm eyes, bright and pressing, as if asking some young girl he liked to dance—expecting an enthusiastic response.

Within seconds Donny's mouth is wide open and he's asleep, making little puffing noises. I'm too hyper to fall asleep; there must have been a heavy dose of MSG in the mushroom soup plus nine hundred milligrams of sodium. I rise and sip cool water from the bathroom faucet. Pacing the bedroom, I am already worried about the party with its weird concoction of people. A party, sure to be whispered about—by those I did not invite—for days down Aisle #8, alongside the Tidy Bowl rebate display.

When I do fall asleep, I dream about competing in a nationwide event called the Gourmet Olympics, where women donning identical white aprons are stationed on an assembly line, cracking egg after egg, frantically beating hundreds of egg whites until they form a tall, frothy monumental peak. I awake a few hours later, hungrier than usual, and notice that on a pad, sometime in the night, I'd scribbled the words:

My life . . . like batter swirling in a crepe pan . . . what to fill, fill, fill?

The next evening, I give in to an impulse and do something I've never done before. After picking up another bottle of cough syrup at the drugstore, I take a different route home in order to drive past Charlie and Paula's house. The streetlights help me make out the square wooden sign that reads Bell. At first, I feel excited I've found their house and surprised they live so close by. But then I notice a greenish glow coming from an upstairs window, most likely from their TV. I picture Charlie and Paula rolling around in their big brass bed, or their waterbed, making wild, carnivorous love. My jaw tightens. I'm flooded with green-eyed envy. I hate this feeling and myself for feeling it. Right then, I decide not to invite them to our goddamn party.

I realize it's too late to mail out invitations, so I have to call everyone on our guest list. I get *our* family out of the way first. Donny's brother Bobby can't make it. He is busy running the commune and taking care of Rainbow, the baby girl he and his girlfriend Melody delivered last year. My brother Marky and his fiancée also refuse. They have lots of preparations for their wedding, which is less than a year away. I'm guessing he figures that any party his older sister throws will be deadly boring and drug-free. Wrong!

We also hadn't figured that since Valentine's Day falls during Presidents' Week, some of our friends might be heading south. Norm and Sue are off with their girls to Puerto Rico, and Alvin, Michelle, and his stomach will be yachting with Alvin's folks in the Bahamas. Positive that Rona and Hy are a *yes*, I forget to formally invite them. I mention the party while jabbering a week later on the telephone.

"Alex, I'd told you we were going to visit Hy's brother that weekend in Tampa!" Rona wails, maiming my eardrum.

"Gosh, I'm so sorry. I'd forgotten. We just decided, Rona—completely spur of the moment. It'll probably bomb since most of my guests have never even met."

"Damn! I had the perfect outfit to wear. Remember the stunning black velvet pantsuit we both bought at Annie Sez?"

You bet. That day, last month, when we'd shopped together, Rona was faster than a crow in strewn trash as she pecked through the rack of discounted items. I had just admired the velvet outfit, said I loved it, when Rona scooped one up in her size and took it to the checkout counter without trying it on. Did she think I'd go anywhere with her dressed like the doublemint twins?

"Yes, the velvet one." Since Rona won't be coming, the black velvet outfit with the red piping is exactly what I'll wear.

A few days later, while thinking about our shrinking guest list, I spot Paula Bell in the parking lot of a convenience store. I think this must be fate, and so follow her to her car, taking notice of her badly hunched shoulders—probably because she's cold. As she leans to put a bag in her car, I tap her arm. Still she doesn't move. I tap her again and clear my throat.

"Paula, is that you?" She turns, looking slightly annoyed but mostly puzzled. I see an imprint of *Alex Pearl* register in her brain, slowly, like the credits rolling at the end of a film. Her neck strains to look around before returning to my face.

"Alex . . . Alex Pearl. Miami and the Woodmans?" Like in charades, I cheat to help her along.

"Oh sure, Alex, how are you?" A white cloud of air slips from Paula's lips. She looks so cold I resist an urge to hug her.

"Me? I'm dreaming of springtime. My girls are home with the sniffles," I say, shifting from foot to foot, hands buried deep in the pockets of my grandmother's black Persian jacket. "Our sitter is close by, so I'm able to get out for a while."

"My two are tough to handle now, so I leave them with my folks or not at all." As if on cue, there is a bloodcurdling scream from the back seat of Paula's station wagon. She throws her body over the seat and flails at the butts of two children who are wrapped up like Eskimos—two fluffy balls of earmuffs and snowsuits. Their faces are hardly visible except for their big white teeth, which now hold a firm grip on each other's gloved fingers.

"Cut it out, I'm warning both of you!" Like a boxing referee, Paula separates them. This is a much different woman from the one I'd met in Florida. Her aggression with the children surprises me. I watch with my mouth open, trying to peek in and get a look at them. There's a little girl and a boy, I think, bundled up in snow gear, so it's hard to distinguish them. Their faces are flushed; they shoot me sidelong glances filled with mistrust.

"Sorry about that," Paula says, her hair wild and full of static, the bold white streak blowing across her misty eyes. "When Charlie's away, they are uncontrollable."

"Please do not apologize, it must be hard. How long has he been gone?"

"Almost two weeks. He's on trial." *Oh, so the other night, she was watching TV alone.* A cool gust of relief slaps me gently on the face. And before I know it, words leave my mouth and fall like invisible snowflakes between us.

"It's crazy that we ran into each other. I was just about to call and invite you and your husband to a get-together a week from Saturday—you know, since it's Valentine's."

"Mom, let's go!" the girl screams from the back seat. "I want to bash his ugly head in! Why do I have to have this stupid *brother*?"

"Can I let you know this weekend?" Paula asks, her eyes shifting toward the back seat. "I'll have to check with Charlie about his workload."

"Sure, whenever—last minute's fine. Bye, bye kids." *Some handful there,* I'm thinking while I act nonchalant about her kids' behavior. Paula flashes me a weak smile and gets behind the wheel and revs up her car. As she backs out of her spot, she bangs into a shopping cart, sending it careening into a parked car. She doesn't stop or turn around. Standing in the chill air, I watch her maneuver like a race-car driver, heedlessly and determined, straight out of the parking lot entrance, nearly colliding with the brown panel truck belonging to UPS.

NINE Donny has taken the girls to his parents for the afternoon, allowing me to cook in peace with little interruption. I am so concentrated on my spinach-feta rolls that my body jumps when the phone rings.

"Alex Pearl?"

"Yes?"

"Is this really you?" he says. I recognize the deep, mellow voice immediately. His words intermingle with long, breezy breaths, and I'm surprised when I feel my heartbeat quicken. He states my name as if he had said it thousands of times, and yet I am instantly aware that this is the very first time. I tuck the receiver under my chin and button my pajama top. I'm so glad he can't see me. Picking up the spatula, I turn a batch of sizzling crab croquettes that are starting to turn black.

"Who's this?" I lie. I am my mother's daughter after all.

"It's Charlie, Charlie Bell. How are you, Mrs. Pearl? It's been a long time."

"I'm great . . . and you? Are you home? I mean, in town? Whoops, sorry for all the questions." Charlie laughs—a Jack-and-Jill-rolling-down-the-hill laugh.

"I was home for the weekend but I'll be leaving again tomorrow."

I'm so disappointed; I might burn the whole batch of croquettes.

"However," he continues, "if the invitation is still open, Paula and I would love to come to your shindig next Saturday night."

"Yes, sure—I'd love it. We'd love it!"

"Can we bring anything? Wine, a bottle of scotch, gin?"

"No, but thanks, we're pretty much organized," I say, thinking I sound really dumb. Miriam would have said, *Please . . . just bring yourselves.*

"How's Donny? Can I say a quick hello?"

"Actually, he's out with our girls visiting his folks, while I cook."

"You mean he left you all alone?" I hear Charlie, the sexy actor, asking: *Do you want to play?*

"Actually, sometimes, I enjoy being alone so I can concentrate on just me," I say, my heart now in gallop mode. I read that line when I glanced at the cover of *Ms.* magazine while checking out at the A&P.

"I think I know what you mean," Charlie says. "It's certainly tough work, staying home and raising kids, plus I hear the pay is lousy."

"Most of the time I enjoy being home," I answer. "Though there *are* other aspects of me that often get pushed aside."

"Hmm, like what? I'd really like to know."

"Oh, I paint . . . at least I did once upon a time. I'd studied art in college. Then there's writing poetry, and believe it or not, cooking. I'm learning that I really love to cook. It's the only thing that relaxes me."

"And I love to eat. I find that tremendously relaxing." Charlie's smiling, I can tell.

"Well, if I don't burn everything while talking to you, you'll have a chance to sample my culinary arts." *Why did I do that? This conversation is over.*

"Sure, I'll let you go, but just one more thing . . ."

"What?" He's making me nervous with such long pauses.

"Is that David Gates in the background?"

"Yes, Bread's new album. You like them?"

"I love the ballads—I find them very melodic and smooth."

Smooth. Right. Charlie Bell surely identifies with smooth. "Well then, guess we'll see you Saturday. Got the address?"

"Yep, I'd jotted it down on that little piece of paper . . . you know."

"What paper?"

"The one you dropped with the big red *X* that made you my killer."

"Oh, sorry about that." I feel myself blush.

"Don't be. I was flattered you chose me to knock off. It was quick and painless—a great way to go. I'll see you soon, Alex Pearl."

"Yes. See you Saturday."

Standing beside the phone, I freeze like a mannequin. I play the words of our short conversation over and over, like a favorite cut on an album. I'm obsessed by simply the idea of something, the idea of someone I hardly know. *Charlie.* I can't believe he saved the paper marked *X* as a memento from our first encounter. My body is overheated, and I toss my pajama top on the floor, then slip out of the flannel bottoms. It is Sunday, and I am wearing ripped cotton panties that say *Tuesday.*

The instant Donny returns from his folks, he begins a mini-tasting of my hors d'oeuvres. *Gourmet* states that presentation is everything, which is why I've left the misshapen ones on a plate until his return. He gobbles up a few and gives me a greasy kiss on the cheek, followed by a high sign. After it cools, I'll pack everything in our basement freezer, but first I must spend time with Becky and Lana, who requested one of my stories about Benji—a sweet, but naughty, pink teddy bear who tries to behave but consistently gets into trouble. I imbed simple life lessons within these little tales, adding bits of humor to keep their attention. Tonight's is a repeat about remembering to look left, right, left before crossing the street, but the girls, looking as tired as I feel, don't seem to mind.

I rush downstairs, after a sixty-second shower, to find Donny sprawled across the couch, his head peeking out of a thin red book, a book I recognize, instantly, as the same book he was intent on hiding from me on our last night at Marriage Mountain—the book I had tirelessly searched the house for but couldn't find.

Though surprised, I say nothing and head for the kitchen. Then, just as I begin wrapping shrimp rolls in shimmering sheets of foil, images of bleak darkness turn into flashing lights. My reliable memory returns with a bang, whether I like it or not, forcing me to see the burly guy, standing in the dingy hallway of the retreat, who hands Donny a thin red book, pitching his wares like Allstate. Yes, *that* guy: the happily married man, married to the same woman for twenty *miraculous* years.

I recall our silly grappling for the book before Donny pinned me down. What followed was the so-so sex, Mother Mary—our witness on the wall, me on the edge or was it the ledge, desperately wanting to go home? Was it fear that stopped me from learning the secrets between the pages of this mysterious manual, and what, pray tell, does he want me to know right now?

Back in the den, I collapse on the recliner beside him. How I'd love a massage. Testing, I whistle for Donny's attention, but he is engrossed in the book, his brows peaked like rooftops.

"Interesting?" I lean over, pretending to be as stupid as he needs me to be.

"Quite the amazing read," Donny says, placing the scarlet book across his chest and taking a deep, dramatic breath.

"What's the title?" I ask, stifling a yawn.

"It's called *A Different Proposition*, which describes how an entire community has existed in California for almost three years."

"Let me guess. Ah, is it a commune?" Tired, I don't even try to hide my sarcasm.

"It says here, couples are able to share each other's mates and/or spouses in a nonthreatening environment, drawing on each other's strengths and weaknesses," Donny recites aloud from a blurb on the book's back cover.

"Wait! Do you mean they screw everybody, and anybody, and no one ever gets jealous? Give me a break!"

"From time to time I imagine there might be some problems."

"You better believe it. Throw that stupid book away, Donny, right now!"

"It's only a book, hon. Relax."

"Why are you so hopped up on this principle? Look at you, you're drooling!" I toss a pillow at Donny, which knocks the book out of his hands. His childlike fascination with this concept has me wondering: Could it be he envies his brother's unconventional life? In spite of all his screwing, screw-ups, protests, and experimental drugs, Bobby remains the son who took "the road less traveled," securing the bulk of attention.

Out of nowhere, I shriek a hyena-like sound.

"What, what's so funny?" Donny sits up taller.

"Oh, I just imagined you—me, oh God, with Rona and Hy. I saw them running after us with mops and cans of Lysol. Me have sex with Hy? I would choke to death on his Mennen's."

Donny can't help but chuckle. "You're right, pretty damn weird."

"Actually, I don't find the thought of you and Rona sleeping together all that threatening," I say.

"See? That's precisely the way I'd feel about you and Hy. I suppose that's when the concept of sharing works best."

I notice that my outstretched hands have begun to tremble. "I think you've lost your mind, Donny. What exactly is the point? Variety? *Marriage* is the complete opposite of variety. It's about compromise and acceptance."

"Sure, sure, but the book also talks about the arrangement being appropriate in certain economic situations. Let's say someone loses their job. There's another person bringing in the dough. And there are benefits for children, like exposing them to varied parental values."

"Oh, and what if Grammy and Gramps want to bring a brisket over on Sunday afternoon? This could be just a tad confusing, don't you think?"

"I suppose the challenge is to find the perfect combination where this premise might work," Donny says, thumbing through pages.

"Do me a favor. Don't you dare mention this to anyone, especially your folks. Remember how upset your mother was when we went to Marriage Mountain? She has a very traditional view of marriage."

"So," Donny says, "I suppose that would make any indiscretions by our fathers palatable, as if our mothers expected it?"

Donny's words sadden me. I feel like I'm protecting someone, but I'm not sure who and from what exactly.

"Can we keep this chat current please?" I ask. "So, are you saying couples who choose this arrangement aren't violating their marriages because they know who their spouse is sleeping with?"

I just now think of Sophie and Rob and how I never told Donny what Sophie alluded to regarding her own marriage. I know him well enough to spot the areas in which he'd be acutely impressionistic.

I shimmy off the recliner and stand in front of Donny, hoping to block his light. He flinches, shielding himself with his arms, while I grab a cushion and pound it into shape. Part of him must be stirred by this controversy between us—like a body rash that fascinates while it starts to spread, before leaving you crazy with a nagging itch. I sense the whole idea of what it would be like in an open marriage has sent an electrical charge directly to his groin. I should reach down and grab the damn thing, check it out myself—bare Donny's pre-masturbatory fantasy.

"Please, sit down, Al, this is kind of interesting, don't you think?"

"No, Donny—you know what I think?"

"Uh-oh, here it comes," he says. His head stares up to the den ceiling, his mouth goes slack.

"If you're looking for adventure, Donny, consider rereading the Hardy Boys."

"Right, ha, ha. And . . . perhaps it's time you cancel that subscription to *Family Circle*." Donny reaches down and grasps my ankle as I pass between the coffee table and couch.

"Quit it. I'm tired."

Out of habit, I expect him to playfully tag after me as I head for the stairs. But the manifesto wins. Donny makes himself cozy among the fluffed-up cushions. All he's missing is a harem. First, I am relieved and then faintly disappointed, thinking his fantasy may have percolated some deep, hidden desire. Desire for me—Alex—the woman he chose to be his partner, his one and only, *till death do us part*.

I awaken Saturday morning instantly aware of an abundance of light stealing through the bedroom shades. Lifting one, I see snowflakes as large as ticker tape swirling around the ochre glow of the street lamps. There are no car tracks yet; it is still early, but I hear the harsh, scraping sounds as trucks reduce their speed on the highway exit down the road. Chilly, I jump back into bed, thinking how excited Becky and

Lana will be. I will let them make a Valentine's snowman—a whimsical white butler, in a red hat, to greet our Saturday night guests.

A few hours later, I unravel myself from the covers when I hear Donny yell: "Holy shit, it's a goddamn blizzard."

I think immediately of the six dozen canapés in the basement freezer, and am relieved to learn we've not lost our electrical power. I also imagine Rona and Hy, basting like chickens under the Florida sun, poking each other with glee while they listen to the New Jersey weather report.

By noon, the Kahns from Westchester call. They're sorry they won't be joining us since their garage door is barricaded by a "monstrous" snowdrift. Next, Nina and Noel phone and offer to take the train, but they'd have to sleep over with their little girl, Sasha.

"Hey, don't worry, we'll do it another time," I assure Nina. I can tell by how she almost begs that Nina was looking forward to this as another adventure. I am secretly relieved they can't make it. When I relay the news to Donny, I scan his face extra hard—the verdict: regret. It doesn't bother me that I've stolen his Peter Pan fun.

Sitting at the kitchen table, Lana and Becky listen to Bernstein's *Peter and the Wolf*, while cutting out paper hearts from construction paper. Becky keeps one eye on Lana while she draws a large heart, occasionally sliding off her chair to help her sister maneuver the tiny scissors with the rounded blades. Lana wears her Stan Laurel pout, which means momentarily confetti may cover my freshly swept kitchen floor. Their father has been practicing the perfect log fire since noon, depleting our winter supply of firewood. When there's a loud pop from the fireplace, the girls stop what they're doing to check on Donny's safety.

"Daddy, better be careful," Becky says, peering up from her artwork, her eager eyes waiting for disaster. Donny pokes at a burning white log, causing a spray of orange sparks. Becky runs upstairs to the safe haven of her bedroom. Why Donny's picked this day of all days to practice his Boy Scout skills is beyond me, until I realize this keeps him from doing other things—like shoveling our buried walk.

Our neighbor Jake, dressed like an Eskimo, bangs at our storm door. His two children are double-parked on the barren street, back to back on a long, wooden sled.

"Ellen wants to know if you guys need anything for tonight, wine, cheese, you know." He winks, and I wonder if this is how he does his pot deals in inclement weather—door to door like the Avon Lady.

"Thanks, but we've got plenty of *everything*. Just bring yourselves." This time I remember the proper thing to say. When we were in Miami, Rob had given us, gratis, an ounce of the *good stuff* that he'd smuggled in from God knows where. And I knew Jake would be passing around his own special *hooch*, hoping to attract new customers to his thriving enterprise.

He wipes a drip from his nose with his woolen mitten. "Baby, you sure now?"

"I'm sure. See you later and tell Ellen thanks for the offer."

"I will. And tell that lazy shit husband of yours to shovel your goddamned driveway. I almost broke my neck."

"It's on his list, Jake, I promise."

Hearing the phone ring, I rush back to the kitchen. Lana's already standing on the kitchen chair, the yellow receiver pressed to her tiny ear.

"No, this isn't Lana Turner, you're silly. I'm Lana Pearl!"

"Who is it, honeybun?" I ask.

"He says he's Charlie the Tuna, Mommy." Lana giggles and hands me the phone. Oh, please, don't be canceling. I hide crossed fingers behind my back. I walk the phone cord to the front door. Outside, the wind blows powdery dust around Jake as he struggles with a long wooden sled, trying to pull his children up the sloping road.

I listen for a few seconds before speaking. It's him; I recognize his breathing.

"I hope you still plan on coming, Mr. Bell."

"Alex, is that a question to ask someone you've met just once?" He waits for my response.

"Oh, ha, I get it." I feel myself blush.

Charlie clears his throat. "No, really, we wouldn't miss this for the world. But I must say you really know when to pick a party. It will be a memorable evening, I'm sure," he says. I focus on *yes*, he will be here.

"Well, thanks to this lovely weather, we're going to be a small group."

"I like that. It's more intimate, don't you think?" His voice sends a wave of tropical heat up my neck to my ears.

"That's true, but I was thinking about the amount of food I've prepared."

"Pretty, and she cooks! Wow, that Donny Pearl is one hell of a lucky guy."

Yes, and you Charlie Bell are so smooth. But weird as it is . . . I like it, simply, because the attention feels so good. Smooth is okay; what's wrong with a little smooth?

"We're both lucky," I say, half believing my words. Donny, now outside, presses his red, puffy face into the storm door. I jump, holding the receiver against my cheek. Though I haven't done a thing wrong, I feel guilty. Snow shovel in hand, Donny's mouthing to me: "Who's on the phone?" I stare blankly at my husband as if I've never ever seen him before. And then I remember. He's Donny. It is remarkable how Lana, when she knits her brows together, and turns down her tiny mouth, looks exactly like him.

Rushing, I kiss Becky and Lana good night. They promise to stay upstairs if I allow them to sleep together in what they've always called *Mommy's bed*. Something about the request feels déjà vu. And then I recall the Scotch and cigarettes that lingered on my father's breath, as he carried me back to my room after one of my parents' marathon poker games. I'd shut my eyes, tightly, but I was really wide-awake, praying he'd remember to kiss me, which he always did.

Before the guests arrive, I'm like a Waring blender operating at grind speed. More than a few times, my head lunges deep inside the oven. I sting my fingertips testing the doneness of things. Perspiration, tinged with Revlon Nearly Nude, drips down my face.

"Donny, where are you?" He rushes down the stairs, his hair damp and glistening. He looks fantastic. "You didn't?" I ask, touching his hot and oily sun-lamped cheeks.

"Yup, but only for a minute. I looked ghastly green."

"Here, please fill this bucket with ice. By the way, did I mention I'm never, ever, doing this again?"

The doorbell chimes. Donny yells, "It's open, come in."

Jake and Ellen stamp the snow on the doormat and slip out of their heavy snow boots. They have surprised us with another couple. "Hi, guys, meet Beth and Len. They moved next door to us just yesterday," Jake says. Everyone mumbles niceties, but I don't catch the last name. Why is it I never catch the last name?

"Jake," Ellen scolds, "you were supposed to tell Alex this afternoon. Did you forget, honey?" Beth cowers, looking embarrassed.

I'm aware of how hard I'm trying to smile. "It's totally fine!

Welcome to the neighborhood, so nice to meet you . . . please, follow me to our den. I promise it's cozy and warm."

I pass the two couples off to Donny and fly upstairs to pee. No surprise that Becky and Lana are out of my bed, rifling through Donny's night table drawers. Lana is about to shove a chunk of Ex-Lax in her mouth. I didn't know they still made this stuff nor that Donny ever bought it.

"Drop it! That is definitely not candy! It is yucky medicine that will make you poop all night long—probably in your PJs. Under the covers now with lights out or back to your own rooms! Pick one."

"Here!" Lana whines, handing over the Ex-Lax.

The stuff doesn't smell half bad. Maybe if things don't go well, I'll melt a package of it over my cheesecake. I can imagine the frenzy, everyone clutching their keys, begging for their hats and coats to rush home.

From the landing upstairs, I hear more people arriving. I straighten my shoulders and grab on to the banister. Downstairs, Donny is helping Paula remove her coat. I avoid looking at Charlie, but I can feel him watching me as I descend the stairs.

"I'm glad you were able to . . . get out," I say, stepping down, allowing Charlie to capture my hand in his soft leather glove.

He hugs me quickly and close, and I'm cooled by the frostiness of his breath.

"Try to relax," he whispers into my neck, and then to the three of us, he says, "We've been looking forward to this all week."

I don't know what to do first. I break from him and move toward Paula. Her pale cheek feels icy against my lips. Her hair is surprisingly darker, a sharp contrast to her blanched complexion. As she looks around the foyer, Paula's eyes flutter, reminding me of one of Lana's dolls. There's a burst of laughter from the den, and I sense

Paula's genuine discomfort. I think she would like to stand here all
night and not have to budge.

"Is that for me?" I reach for the white box gripped in her fingers.

"Ah yes, I brought you a pie," she says, "from Richter's Bakery in
town. It's apple, is that okay?"

"Apple's perfect, thank you." I gesture for Donny to escort the
Bells, but it takes him several seconds to read me. He is sporting his
spacey look, staring at Paula's full bow lips. My guess, he's already
downed some liquor and had himself a toke or two. "Donny will
introduce you guys—Don?"

"Yes, right this way." Donny's arm rests limply around Paula's
shoulder as Charlie follows them down the hall.

I grab a batch of shrimp rolls from the oven and transfer them to
a tray. Spying from the safety of my kitchen, sucking burned fingers,
I glance toward the den. What's surprising is a measure of shyness
evident in Charlie—his strained smile, a vulnerability I'd not yet
witnessed. Yet, he manages to tackle this bashfulness without pause,
shaking hands like a politician campaigning through a sleepy upstate
town. Our eyes meet, and he motions for me to come over, to leave
whatever it is I'm doing. I hold up a finger, indicating one minute.
I turn to the hot oven, hiding the smile spreading across my face,
my heart racing. It is this, his constant attention that I find exciting.
It feels as though we are sharing the same secret, but what that is
remains a mystery.

I return with more food, relieved when Jake and Len reach out to
him, and soon all three are near the fireplace, sampling one of Jake's
finest blends. Jake, a master salesman, has the forceful stance of a
barker at a carnival.

Donny makes the rounds with Paula and introduces her to a few
of our female neighbors. Her eyes appear apologetic as she struggles

to answer the simplest of inquiries: where she lives, her kids' names and ages. At her first opportunity, Paula joins me in the kitchen, where the temperature must have spiked a hundred degrees higher.

"You made all of this yourself?" she asks.

"It's no big deal," I say, my head lodged in a cabinet. "I'm looking for another tray. I never seem to know what to use for *what*. Our wedding gifts were much too formal . . . lots of sterling silver, not practical."

"We received mostly Corning Ware," Paula says, her lips curled down.

"My mother warned: 'Alex, do not return anything. You'll need that grape cutter, and that well-and-tree platter.'"

"What's a well-and-tree platter?" Paula laughs, revealing a sweet smile and perfect teeth. She'd appear extremely young if not for the white streak of hair, her distinct signature. I knew a boy in high school who had the same streak. The mean kids labeled him a mutant. I wondered if Paula was ever teased, and whether that may have contributed to her shyness.

"It's supposed to hold the juices from meat and poultry in a *well* that's shaped like a *tree*. I have an extra if you'd like one for your next holiday dinner."

"Thanks, but I can't cook."

"Well, don't think I do this all the time, not with my girls and their finicky, macaroni and cheese appetites." This is the most we've ever spoken, and I wonder if Paula's clinging is to avoid the group of glassy-eyed strangers in the den now singing along with Queen. "Oh, look what a mess I've made." The sleeve of my satin blouse is saturated with the dipping sauce for the Rumaki.

"Here, let me help." Paula grabs a bottle of seltzer from the counter and dabs at my sleeve with a dish towel.

"Thanks, I think I got it all out." At once Paula seems more self-assured, and maybe as a frazzled hostess, I've become less threatening. There is something in the way she comports herself that makes me want to shield her—from what, I haven't a clue.

Donny has been standing near us and rinsing out glasses at the sink. He tries to disarm Paula with a joke. I half listen to this joke, which I've heard maybe thirty times. Paula's laugh is not convincing. "That's okay," I whisper in her ear, "I didn't get it either. Donny, I think Paula needs something to drink."

"I love your kitchen, the way it steps down into the den," Paula says, taking a glass of wine from Donny's hands. Her face blushes, nearly matching the color of the liquid swirling in her glass.

"Come," Donny says, "I'll show you the rest of the house. I'm the official tour guide." Donny loves showing people our home but also uses the tour as an excuse to sneak away whenever he's bored. Paula glances back in my direction as if she needs my approval. I shrug. I'm too busy to think; all I want is a place to rest my aching feet. Donny takes Paula by the elbow and leads her from the smoke-filled downstairs. He looks determined, gallant, and only slightly drunk. All he is missing is an ebony horse and a sweeping Zorro cape.

"Donny, remember that the girls are asleep in our bed."

I carry in a tray of canapés to cheers and whistles. I fake a curtsy. Ellen makes room for me beside her on the couch. She offers me a joint that's near its end but quite potent. The smoke makes my eyes water. I look around the room to find Charlie observing me as one might a constellation. He's got that wacky look, having smoked quite a bit. Jake's been doling out joints like a proud papa celebrating the birth of his firstborn son. His new neighbor, whose name I've already forgotten, doesn't know what the hell hit him. Like a magic trick, Charlie digs out a Meerschaum pipe and lights it.

"Something new?" I ask, shouting over the music. He shakes his head no, sucking at the pipe stem, working the tobacco with his long fingers. I think I like this version of him holding a pipe—wise and scholarly, reminding me of my English professor, Harry Bloom, who used to pack tobacco into his pipe but never once lit it. Maybe the pipe is a convenient prop Charlie uses to buy time, to veil his vulnerability, which makes him even more appealing. The pipe, clenched between his teeth, makes his dark eyes squint. His gaze is so intense I quickly turn away, as if yanking down a shade after being spotted naked.

I don't realize Donny's missing from the room until he shows up about a half hour later. The tip of his nose and ears are bunny rabbit red.

"Where's Paula? Did she run away after all?"

"Using the powder room," he answers.

"Are you all right, Donny? You look smashed."

"Yeah, fine. We went outside to look at the snowfall. It's such a beautiful night."

"But it has to be freezing." Not sure what I expect to find, I peer outside and see footprints, many footprints, big, little, hard to distinguish.

"Nah, not really, actually it was surprisingly warm." We stare at each other for a few awkward seconds, waiting for the other to blink or turn away.

"Hey, by the way, great party, babe," Donny says. "A really fun time had by all."

The hateful clock broadcasts 4:00 a.m. and a slim ray of light bounces off Donny's cheekbone. He sleeps soundly, his lips slightly parted. I trace my fingers lightly around his cheek, longing for him to awaken and pull me on top of him, hold me as if we're floating in a gentle tide. The planning, the party, it all being over, has me a bit let down.

"Donny, are you awake?" He scratches his nose, missing my eager hands. I can't stay in this bed another second. Slipping into my robe, I leave the drafty hallway and head downstairs. For the third time this evening, I check to see if all the doors are locked, and the oven knobs turned in the off position. I wrap my icy toes in an old crocheted throw and sit staring at the glow from the remaining embers in the fireplace. The den is drafty and cold. Just hours ago, it was steamy with laughter, warm food, and the friction of anxious bodies, each of them desperate to connect in some small, significant way.

With heavy lids, I scan the picture frames arranged perfectly on the mantle. Seven years of revelations, joys, and tired mistakes pulse in my head like a slideshow carousal, making me blink and blink. I take in the bookshelves, the scratched furniture, frayed rugs, and nicked walls, cramming now, wide-awake, as if there might be answers hidden deep between the fissures of the golden fieldstone. My sighs are deep, like some tired old hag. I rest my head on a couch pillow and slowly drift off. Spring will arrive before I know it, and in a few more weeks, I'll turn thirty. Time to close the curtain on my pocket version of *Godot*—an elusive thing called *happy*.

"Are you happy, darling?" I can hear my grandmother's sweet, faltering voice. I am fifteen years old and, though I don't yet know it, she is quite ill, resting in my canopy bed, cuddled up close to me. As I touch the sleeve of her satiny gown, stroke the deep folds of her failing flesh, I breathe bouquets of her—lavender, lilac, a hint of Pond's cream. "Yes, Nana," I always lied. "Of course, I'm happy."

TEN

"Happy birthday, darling, and many more happy returns of the day!"

While I ponder my mother's standard yearly greeting, she yells for my father to pick up the phone. She slips in a quick inquiry about what the Pearls bought me for my thirtieth.

"Oh, a '75 silver Maserati."

"Really? How wonderful."

"Mother, I'm joking! What they bought was a gift certificate from my local art supply store—Flax Pen and Paint."

"Well, that's thoughtful too. I didn't know you were painting again, dear. That's good, isn't it, Natie? Nate, are you on?"

"Hey, happy birthday, kiddo. Wow the big 3 . . . 0," my father says. He sounds melancholy or is it me?

"Thanks, Dad. I'm not actually *painting*, painting. It's March and almost spring, so once again *it's T-shirt time*," I mock sing.

"Don't knock it. You bought a lot of nice furnishings with that little hobby of yours."

"Right, Dad. *My hobby*." I bristle at my father's words even though I know he means no harm. Making money, at anything, is his equivalent of success.

There was a time though when I actually called myself an artist, although the only people who hung my paintings were friends, my parents, and Ben and Louise. I once painted a watercolor of a young girl in a pinafore, playing the piano, a long-haired cat curled at her feet. I was sure when Louise redecorated, the painting would disappear, but she had it reframed, and placed on a wall—not far from an authentic Chagall of stained glass windows. A kind gesture I will never forget.

Yesterday, the March wind pummeled at my back, nearly lifting me off my feet in the parking lot behind Flax's. I was eager to spend the one-hundred-dollar gift certificate. After picking up a fresh supply of permanent markers, I'd browsed the kaleidoscope of aisles, stopping to caress soft sable brushes like a starved lover, imagining the textures they might impart using shades like Kilimanjaro yellow and Parisian red. Then, as I headed to the cash register, I put most of the brushes back. I remembered how backed-up I am with T-shirt orders. And though there's little time in my life for serious art, the yearning never leaves. It's attached like an invisible body stocking that I wear and remove each night, only to pull on the very next morning.

"And what did Donny and the girls give you?" my mother asks. I imagine her jingling a set of measuring spoons, comparing, always comparing.

"Mom, I have no idea yet, I'm hoping for a new bathrobe. I've actually dropped some hints."

"We must always drop those hints, dear, or we'd get nothing." *Did you hear that, Dad? That one's for you.* "Oh, if only I were thirty again," my mother sighs before signing off. Dad clunks the phone down, leaving me with clear images of my thirty-year-old mother, tenable as a result of my lifelong fixation with our family's home movies. The movies were mostly black and white, but there was one with her as a flaming redhead, her long wavy hair worn back in a snood. In one shot her long legs chase after me, as I maneuver my two-wheeler down her parents' sloping driveway—here she is a vibrant, sensual woman running with open arms toward life and a bountiful future. There is not a trace of regret.

Rona calls next. It seems she can't conceal her ecstasy that I've turned these digits before her. "I still have two years to prepare for it," she reminds me, as if she's talking about a famine. Before Rona's call, I was almost happy about the watershed event. I've always looked at each decade as an adventure, writing a poem on every big birthday. This year's creation was scribbled on the back of a grocery list at a traffic light. Seeping through the creased paper are the bold red letters listing the staples I needed at the A&P and my (thirty-second) poem:

Ode to the End

The beginning was nice	*apples*
yes, I admit	*bananas*
the pleasures seemed trite	*eggs*
but nevertheless we laughed	*yogurt*
the middle was stronger	*margarine*
as we tore off old ties	*Oreos*
and then the spring came	*Ivory soap*
Hold me, hold me	*tissues*
I'm falling into the future;	*baby aspirin*
will you be there	*sugar*
this time?	*grape jelly*

"So, would you like to hear my poem?" I can't believe I'm taking this giant leap with Rona.

"I must tell you, Alex, I just don't get poetry. Much too depressing, that stuff we were forced to read in high school, but sure, go ahead."

I take a deep breath and recite my poem. Silence. I read again. Finally, I hear Rona's voice, softer than usual.

"Alex, is everything all right with you and Donny?"

My stomach churns. What have I done?

"Oh, I can see why you'd ask, but I'm only expressing melancholy about the turning point, you know: the end of the decade. Goodbye to the *twenties*. Rona, are you still on?"

"Oh no, damn it!" she says.

"What Rona, what's wrong?"

"I can't believe I didn't notice. There's a huge yellow mark on my marble countertop. Hy must be sneaking cigarettes again. Damn, this will never come out."

"Try leaving some Comet on overnight," I say, sounding exactly like her.

"That's brilliant," Rona says, hanging up before saying goodbye.

On a surprisingly warm, practically windless Sunday in March, we decide to meet up with Charlie, Paula, and their children at the Wheatley Heights Community Park less than a mile from each of our homes. This is the exact place where Rona and I met, two and a half years ago, while dumping soiled diapers into the garbage.

Paula has overdressed her children, a girl named Ricki, and her brother, Ross. They are bound by stiff jackets and hats, but it's not my place to say anything. This is the first time I'm seeing Charlie Bell in broad daylight. His hair looks lighter in the sunshine—the color of chestnuts, and when there's the slightest breeze, he appears self-conscious, quick to smooth it in place. We take turns introducing our children, who wait for us to finish before running helter-skelter to the swings and slides.

We, the parents, sit opposite one another on green wooden benches placed at the edge of the playground. This allows a good peripheral view of all our kids. I can't help but think how different people seem as soon as they're around their children. Instantly, all our senses are fine-tuned, our energies pumped up. No longer are we limited to two eyes, but like potatoes, we sprout them in all directions.

Becky watches Lana, who has learned to pump her legs on the swings, allowing her to swing longer than her usual sixty seconds. Yet, the serenity is broken when Ross angrily shrieks at his younger sister.

"Hey, move, stupid, or I'll kill you!" Ricki stands Buddha-like at the bottom of the slide, blocking Ross so he can't slide all the way down.

Paula runs to Ricki and ushers her away. Out of earshot, she crouches down to scold her, wagging a finger in front of Ricki's impish face, which remains hidden under a red corduroy hat. Donny and I avert our eyes from the scene. It's one of those weird moments when, not knowing people well, or not knowing what to say, you say nothing at all. The truth is most parents feel a bit relieved when it's someone else's kid misbehaving.

When Charlie catches my eye, he shrugs. He doesn't seem to be embarrassed or frazzled by his kids' behavior, and I imagine with all his traveling, Paula has become the one doling out the discipline. How exhausting it must be to tote that load solo. Donny shares some of that burden with me, although, at times, he's pretty tough on Lana. Once, when she was going through the "terrible twos," she lay on the kitchen floor kicking and screaming, and then holding her breath until her skin turned an iridescent blue. Donny tried to lift her, but because she resisted, he accidentally pulled her arm out of its socket. She sat up and told Donny *she* was broken: "Like Barbie." Lana would know, having mutilated many of her dolls.

Paula plops down on the bench, reentering the world of adults.

She manages a grin but her expression twists to a wild look bordering on fury.

"This is *exactly* what I'm talking about," she says, through clenched teeth, to Charlie. "They don't stop fighting, not for a single minute."

Charlie listens, his head cocked sideways. He lights his pipe with a blue plastic lighter and puffs swirls of gray smoke through his lips. The air is made calmer, sweeter by the aroma of his cherry tobacco. A halo of smoke floats over our heads as if it were a blessing.

"I'll have a long talk with them, I promise," he says softly, brushing Paula's hand.

"Right," she says, stealing back her hand and tucking it in her pocket. This has embarrassed him; I'm certain. When Charlie looks toward me, his face reddened, I turn away. I am uncomfortable, yet grateful, because Lana and Becky hardly ever fight. My guess, they're saving it all for their teenage years.

During the droning silence, I notice Donny's smug expression. I know him well enough to guess he likes having observed flaws in the Bells' relationship: that maybe Charlie and Paula don't see eye-to-eye on everything.

"Hey, is anyone hungry?" Donny shouts through funneled hands, breaking the remnants of tension.

"I am, Daddy," Becky yells back. She's swinging on the inner tube that's suspended on heavy chains.

"Me, too," Lana adds.

From their perch on top of the monkey bars, hanging upside down like orangutans, Ricki and Ross, the little Bells, wave their arms.

I'd picked up hero sandwiches at the deli, and Paula, wanting to contribute, said she'd bake brownies for dessert. Jingling the car keys in front of my face, perhaps noticing me gazing at Charlie, Donny announces, "I'll be back in a few."

"The picnic basket is under the blue blanket in the trunk. Donny, don't forget we'll need the beach blanket," I say.

"Would you like me to help with the brownies?" Charlie asks Paula.

"No, I'd better carry them. They were still warm when I packed everything. Hey, wait up," Paula calls out to Donny.

As I watch them jog together up the winding path, which leads to the parking lot, my stomach does a weird somersault. Still, I ignore the tiny voice urging me to go back to the car with Donny. I stand and sit again, aware of the warm body now next to me on the bench, and the leathery aroma of his jacket. The fact hits me with the unmistakable awareness of a bee sting. I'm alone with Charlie.

Rifling through my canvas tote, I drop a tampon on the ground before finding my sunglasses. I put them on even though we're sitting in complete shade. Wordless, Charlie follows my motions like an easy connect-the-dots drawing. Feeling the penetration of his gaze, I try humor with a flash of a toothy smile. He leans in closer, an elbow on his knee, the pipe clenched in his mouth. I need air, the gap between us rapidly shrinking. Off the bench again, I try an overhead stretch while taking inventory of all the children. I run to Becky who needs some help rolling up the floppy sleeves of her sweater. When I turn back, the man is still beaming. His eyes dance like the flames of a campfire. As they burn through me, all my layers, I imagine a slow, erotic sizzle. Perhaps I'll disintegrate, right here in this park, in front of my own children—"Like the Wicked Witch of the West," Becky might say. If Donny and Paula don't get here soon, they may find a smoldering pile of my clothing: clogs, jeans, and fishnet sweater. When did I ever receive this much attention from a man?

"What?" I pivot and ask Charlie, startling us both.

"Nothing," he says, straightening his posture. "Your daughter Becky looks so much like you. Quite an amazing study in genetics."

"Oh, my poor little kid." I dig the dewy grass with my heel and sit down beside him on the shrinking bench.

"I was going to say she's beautiful like her mother, but I was afraid of how that would sound." There's a fluttering within my stomach, like something trapped, begging for release, or maybe I'm just hungry.

"Actually, that might sound very nice." I am surprised at my boldness but compelled to switch the subject. "Hey, so how's your case progressing? I'd like to hear more about it." This is my absolute most mature voice. The one I left, years ago, in the smoke-filled coffee shop of a small college town. The one lost in the daily rituals of *this*, my split-level life.

"You want to talk about my case, Alex, you sure?"

"Yep, I'm sure."

"Well, it's doubtful you'll find this interesting. Are you ready?"

"Ready." I say, mock bracing myself against the bench. What else might I like Charlie Bell to be? *A butcher, a baker, a candlestick maker?*

"So, here goes: for the last few years I've been involved with this case having to do with the shutdowns of plants by several public utility companies, nuclear power plants, to be precise." A long pause, and the pipe returns for a deep inhale. Oh, is he testing me? Should I raise my hand? I search his hot fudge eyes to see if he is telling me the truth.

"Well, that sounds like excellent news to me. The thought of all those power plants scattered throughout the country scares the hell out of me. I grew up in a house stocked, at all times, for nuclear disaster. My dad made sure there was a big supply of Sterno for cooking. We had cans of sardines, salmon, and some strange powdery drink."

Charlie tosses his head back and laughs. "And, do you remember those frightening duck-and-cover drills when we'd have to crunch down under our desks?"

"Oh God, yes, we thought it was *the bomb*. I hated the sound of the siren and that awful image of the fallout—a charcoal mushroom spreading through the sky, enveloping everything. It still makes me shudder. As if crouching under a little pine desk could protect us from the consequences of such a disaster. So, I have to ask . . . you're for the good guys, right? Those who want to shut the plants down?"

"Well now, Alex, I wouldn't exactly call them the good guys. It's more complicated than that."

"Try me," I say, already feeling nervous about his answer.

Charlie loses the pipe. "You see, first the power companies were going to build all these low-cost plants. Then, because of safety and environmental concerns, it became too costly, so they changed their minds. It's because of this, the members of the community, the rate payers, lost huge amounts of money. So now they want to recoup their losses . . . therefore . . . the lawsuits."

"So, you're defending these power companies?"

"Yes, Alex, I am. After they reneged on the deals they made, they pissed a lot of people off." Charlie picks up a small twig, snaps it, and throws it down. He looks up at me, waiting for some reaction. *What to say? What to say?*

"Well, I, for one, am happy to know there won't be as many plants built in the future. That is the bottom line, right? Not to mention all that nuclear waste going into the soil, tainting our drinking water and poisoning our children!"

"Hey, it's only a job. Don't be angry with me," Charlie says, while I struggle with a sinking disappointment over what he does for a living. I'd conjured up a different persona for him, something a lot more grassroots.

"Alex, do I look like a monster?" He crouches down near me and twists his face and neck grotesquely.

"What's so funny, Mommy?" Lana asks, climbing into my lap, her little hands pulling strands of my hair over my mouth and nose.

"You're funny," I say, tickling her exposed belly.

Ricki and Ross race each other, heading in our direction. They bang into the back of the bench, sending me catapulting to the ground with Lana on my lap.

"Whoa! Take it easy, you two," Charlie scolds. "Here, let me help you up." He had flung one arm in front of me—abrupt and strong, but too late. I stand up, Lana still clinging, and assure Charlie we're fine.

"Dad, she cheated," Ross whines, complaining about his sister again. "She started before I said go."

"No, I didn't, you baby!" Ricki jabs at Ross's arm.

"Enough!" Charlie grabs them by the collars of their parkas and marches them to the shade of a hunched oak. I notice the wide expanse of his shoulders stretching through his jacket when he crouches down to talk to them. Though he looks to be speaking gently to his feisty daughter and whiny son, there is firmness in his expression. Within seconds both children burst into tears. They hug Charlie, reluctantly each other, and walk crestfallen back to my bench.

"I'm sorry, Mrs. Pearl," they each recite, a beat apart, looking down at their dusty sneakers.

"Thank you. It's okay."

"Thank you!" Lana mimics, making Charlie stifle a laugh.

"Not funny, Dad," Ross glares at Lana.

"You're right, Ross. Lana's my little parrot sometimes."

In the distance, I see Donny and Paula walking back over the hill toward us. Their arms are bountiful, carrying our lunch and dessert. With the orangey sun as their backdrop, they look as mystical as flower children returning from Woodstock. Donny's hair falls below his eyes, but hands full, he's unable to brush it back. Paula laughs, heartily, at whatever Donny has said, her head flinging back in the breeze. A velvety smile transforms her into someone new and vivacious. An old feeling of possessiveness clutches me, and I brace to pounce.

"Donny, did you forget the blanket?"

He stops dead in his tracks, starts to do an about-face.

"I'll run back," he says. I am surprised to see someone has stuck a large candle into the batch of brownies.

"Oh, so thoughtful, but I don't remember mentioning my birthday. Never mind about the blanket," I say, "the kids are starved."

"So, has everyone been behaving?" Paula poses to Ricki and Ross. Her mood has elevated several notches, causing an irritating thought to cross my mind: I wonder if she and Donny shared a joint.

"All is super, duper," I answer, emptying the tote bag of sandwiches and cans of Tab and Fresca. "Charlie and I have everything under control."

Ricki and Ross sit on a mound of pebbles they have claimed as their own private picnic area.

"Stay far away," Ross squawks at Becky when she saunters over to sit near them. Obviously, these children have short memory spans. Becky looks like she wants to cry but fights it hard, not wanting them to see. For a moment, I think of her all grown up, in love with some idiot who loses his patience with her and flies off the handle—someone who might break her precious heart a hundred times.

"Come here, Becky girl." I hug her close, letting her hide her humiliation against my chest. "Don't show them it hurts, baby." *Please don't show them.*

The next day, Rona stops by on her way to the dentist for her quarterly cleaning. She sits at my kitchen table slurping coffee, a safe distance from my work area, but she's been up and down three times, making me crazy and distracting me from getting my work done. Cleo, my favorite shop owner, called a few days ago, her voice resembling a croaking frog. She said she had some early spring orders she wanted immediately! And now watching Rona, I can't help but picture her, twenty years from now, working at her own chic fashion boutique: hair and makeup flawless, rhinestone bifocals worn on a long gold chain, her style the magnet for some young insecure woman filling her loneliness and walk-in closet with glitzy, overpriced apparel. She's been tossing me a glacial shoulder, lately, and talking to her is like shucking corn—it takes forever to uncover what might be irking her.

"Rona, what the hell are you looking for?" I ask, watching her slam the doors of my pantry for the third time.

"Don't you have any goddamn cookies in this house?"

"Nope, I haven't had time to shop since I started this T-shirt order—sorry. Do you want some saltines?"

"No! I must have something sweet or I'll die."

"How about preserves? I've got apricot and raspberry."

"Forget it," she says, pouting, reminding me of Lana. Could a part of Rona be rubbing off on my own child? She does spend many afternoons there when Agnes can't babysit, or Lana and Ethan want to play together.

Silence for a few seconds, but I feel her eyes slicing through me while I shade the petals of a red rose on a powder blue shirt. I can end this or just let her stew. I put down the marker and stare at Rona across the table. The stare down lasts until I stick my tongue out, and we share a strained laugh. Truth is I would get more pleasure out of smacking her skinny little ass.

"I just don't get the attraction," she says, referring to Paula. "Does the woman even speak?"

"Rona, come on. You don't even know her. You've spoken for what, five minutes? She's actually very nice, just shy." *And at least she doesn't look at me like I'm speaking Arabic when I say something intelligent.* I don't understand why Rona is so possessive. It's always been fine for her to have other friends, women she's known since grade school, a slew of neighbors, but as soon as I introduce her to anyone who I've met on my own, without her involvement, she has something negative to say. A trait, most likely, carried over from adolescence and what occurred in every girl's locker room during gym period.

"So, tell me," Rona says, moving in closer, her lips pursed in a perfect bow. "Has he made a pass at you yet?"

"Who?"

"You know who. Sexy, smoky, Charlie." Rona shimmies her shoulders right above my face.

I look down at the shirt I'm decorating with petite roses and feel my neck redden. "Are you crazy? When would that have happened?"

"Well, you've certainly gone out with them enough times in the last few weeks. And for sure he has a roving eye. I'll admit he's even given me the once-over," Rona says, leaning back, smug.

"When was that?" I ask a little too quickly. How could Charlie be attracted to Rona, if he's attracted to me?

"Oh, last Sunday, when you *finally* decided to have us over. I was beginning to think you were embarrassed by us, keeping your new little pals all to yourself." A gong resounds inside my head; embarrassed *is* the magic word.

"Here we go again." I stand and roll my stiff shoulders.

"Anyway," she says, scooping up her car keys, "first, I saw him studying you as you were carrying a tray of coffee. He was sitting all comfy on your couch and smoking that weird pipe—next thing I know, he's checking me out, too."

"Well, let's just say the guy's got great taste." I taste a drop of blood on the inside of my lower lip. Turns out, inviting Rona and Hy over was truly an asinine mistake.

"Yes, but what about Pamela?" Rona asks.

"For the tenth time, her name is Paula."

"Right, what about her?"

"I imagine he finds his wife appealing. What's the big deal if she's not terribly cool or stylish like you? Actually, Donny thinks she's very nice."

"Donny, oh right." I watch as Rona's nostrils flair, making her ugly. Seeing her transform like this, even temporarily, is more than pleasurable.

"What's that supposed to mean?" I turn on the faucet and let cold water gush.

"Not a thing." Rona turns from me and heads toward the front door. She's wearing her superior look, one I've noticed many times before. If only I had the guts to grab her arm and yank her toward me, to blast her for scattering little snippets of crap she knows will hurt me. But I don't, mostly because I can't. Because, even though I'm older and wiser now, less than a week past thirty, like Rona, I, too, am a terrific coward.

ELEVEN

There's a sudden break from the monotony of April's showers just in time for Passover—Becky and Lana's favorite holiday. They love haggling over the price of the *afikomen*, the hidden *matzah* for the children to find after the meal. And they always do, because friends and relatives, bloated to their gills and thrilled to be finally standing, give away the most obvious hints. The highlight of the evening is hearing the girls try to top last year's price when selling the crumbled piece of unleavened bread back to Ben, who sits at the table, stone-faced and official, trying to conceal his laughter. I am always impressed by Louise's enthusiasm and dedication in making her home a traditional Jewish home. No one would ever figure my mother-in-law a convert, and yet I've heard it said that women who convert to their husband's religion work especially hard to be taken seriously in all aspects of that new life.

Yesterday, for the first of the two seders traditionally held in the Pearls' rotunda-style dining room, I'd dressed the girls in matching navy jumpers, which they wore with white lace peasant blouses underneath. Even I was grateful for an opportunity to dress up for a change, although I had to paint and deliver a dozen T-shirts in order to splurge on my own new outfit: a creamy doeskin shirt, and a calf-length denim skirt, which I wore with faux lizard boots. *On sale, on sale at Macy's.* I could actually hear myself explaining, my father's frugality attached, like a price tag, to whatever garment

I was wearing. I also imagined Louise with thoughts of her ancestors during the great potato famine saying: "Boots? Who would ever dream of leather boots?"

But tonight, the second night of the holiday, we are already an hour late for dinner. Donny, who said he'd be back in *no time*, is still at the Bells'. We were getting dressed when Paula called saying she found one of the four kissing garomis dead—the big orange fish we had jokingly given our first names. Charlie had flown to DC for an emergency conference and might have set the thermostat too low. I envisioned the poor fish floating at the top of the tank, its mouth pursed and frozen in one final smooch. I wondered which of our namesakes had kicked the bucket.

Donny, who'd professed to be an expert (he had one goldfish in college), helped the Bells set up their aquarium, and now he was out the door in seconds. I had never seen him move so fast. I thought, *Hey, where's the fire? We're talking about a goddamn fish.*

"It's Passover, Donny, and we're supposed to be at your folks in an hour." I shouted after him, but he'd already pulled out of our driveway, tires screeching around the Belgian block curb of Daisy Lane and headed to the Bells'.

Another half hour goes by, and I'm slumped on the den couch, still waiting. Warned not to mess their matching navy velour pants sets, Becky and Lana march like majorettes around the patio, twirling toy batons. As soon as the sun exits behind the clouds, they clutch their upper arms, trying to keep themselves warm. I should probably get up to bring sweaters, but I can't move. There is a gnawing in my stomach that isn't hunger—hunger subsides with nourishment. This feels like a permanent void.

Although the girls are just yards away, completely visible through the mesh of the sliding screen, I can't see them. My eyes begin to sting, and I touch the corners of my lashes, pressing my fingers against my lids. "Not today," I say out loud. I do not want to cry. This is a joyous holiday. The children are wonderful and healthy. I have a roof over my head. But loneliness has crept in and taken me by surprise, most likely, the only way it could. I look over at the built-in log bin, where just a few pieces of kindling remain. Before it became the log bin, it was a small aquarium with beautiful, exotic fish of our own. Fish, that Donny had sworn he would never, ever neglect.

The phone startles me when it rings. I jump from the couch. It's Louise checking on our whereabouts.

"He's where?!" she practically screams into the phone. I answer in a slow staccato rhythm.

"He's helping our friend, Paula, with their new aquarium."

"Why can't her husband take care of this? Don't they know today's a holiday?"

"*The husband* was needed in Washington—*the wife*, Paula, called asking for Donny's help."

There is an abrupt pause on Louise's end. Then quickly, as if she'd discovered some grave error while balancing the books at H. Pearl and Sons, she changes her tone.

"Oh, I see, well I'm sure he'll be home any minute. Why don't you call over there?"

"No, I don't want to! He should know better than to keep us waiting like this."

"You're right, dear. I'll tell everyone we'll be starting a little later. When you get here, you get here."

An hour later, Donny honks for us in the driveway. Getting in the front seat, I avoid his face and his look of pure, unadulterated innocence. I don't want to hear, to know, to see. I am a puppet. *Just drive me to the goddamn holiday dinner*, I would like to say, but I can't find my voice.

We are finally gathered, all together, under the glittering lights of the Pearls' crystal chandelier. Ben is conducting the service and, trying to make up for our lateness, he is inventing an abbreviated version. I look across the table and study Donny as if he were a specimen pressed between thin glass slides in a bio lab. Remembering the dissection of the earthworm, I stifle a gag when the ceremonial plate of bitter herbs is passed around for me to taste. Donny's brother, Bobby, wearing a black yarmulke pinned to his ponytail, reads from a portion of the prayer book—the Haggadah. He is up to the part where he dips his pinky onto the red wine while shouting out the names of the plagues. Locusts are one, but he forgets sly husbands who habitually show up late.

For each plague he dips, then drops the wine onto his dinner plate. But with the zest of someone who has spoken at too many anti-war rallies, Bobby keeps missing the plate, dousing my mother-in-law's ivory embroidered tablecloth from Budapest, and the sleeve of my doeskin shirt. Not wanting to make a scene, I slip into the kitchen for some seltzer. Gussie, in her holiday whites, waits for the signal that food can be served. The counter is covered with shimmering platters filled with my most favorite foods, potato *kugel* and brisket, but I've lost my appetite. She notices me dabbing my shirt and shakes her head. "That won't do no good, child. Might as well cut it up into rags."

"All right, Gussie, just tell me where Pop keeps the Pepto?"

"What, you carrying again?" Gussie asks, her large palms lifting a bowl, moving it out of the way to reach into a cabinet for the bottle. I chug the thick pink liquid right from the bottle, pretending it's a Bud.

"Don't think so," I answer, patting my flat belly and thinking of my nearly nonexistent sex life.

"Well, that's good since you already got your hands full."

"The girls are wonderful, Gussie, what are you talking about?"

"I'm not talkin' about your girls. I'm talkin' about your boy in there tryin' to be a man."

Just then, the saloon doors swing into the kitchen. In marches Louise followed by Bobby's common-law wife, Melody, and Donny's sister, Ivy, a college freshman, who appears a bit wobbly on her feet. She bangs into me, sending a heap of *tzimmes* into the bodice of my blouse. I instantly recall what the buttered carrot and prunes dish symbolizes: a bother, a muddle—just like me.

"Now look."

"Sorry, sis," Ivy slurs. She loves thinking of me as her older sister. I wish I could return the favor at this very moment, give her a strong dose of older sister, but I control myself. Louise and Melody have food on their minds; they don't notice me pressed against the butcher block rubbing seltzer all over my shirt, swigging it from the bottle while contemplating one of Gussie's salient zingers. I slink back to the dining room more apprehensive than ever.

Ben gives us the green light to eat, and the prayer books are laid aside. I help serve the string beans *almondine* and cut up some brisket in tiny manageable pieces for Becky and Lana. Too much goes on for anyone to notice the topography of my plate. As usual, I use it to serve up the girls' food so it appears full.

Through the flickering flames of the Sabbath candles, Donny's eyes find mine. I am surprised by my glare, telegraphing the message I'm still furious he left us waiting today, nearly two hours—because of some stupid dead fish. Then a fierce pain presses against my lids, forcing me to widen my eyes, to really look at Donny. He grins at me—a taunting grin, which in the past might have eased my discontent, even softened me. This time though, I don't give in. Just as Gussie said: I see a child sitting across from me. I already have two children.

"Alex?"

"What?" I answer, startled.

"Don't think I didn't notice," Louise whispers, her chin grazing my shoulder. "Darling, you hardly ate a thing." She ladles a mound of sweet potato mousse onto my plate, just missing my fist that jerks up and nearly punches her jaw. I smear the glob over muddy beef gravy, watching it congeal and harden, like the paint on one of my many abandoned palettes.

Donny and I drive home in our own exodus of traffic, while I conjure up images of hordes of Jews fleeing Egypt. Neither of us has uttered one word since we got in the car. Louise said she'd be taking the week off and offered to have the girls sleep over. Hesitant at first, I said yes. Donny reaches over to take my hand, but I pull away. His exasperated exhale inflates more anger. He puts the car in park and stares at me. It hardly matters; we're at a complete standstill on the turnpike.

"Come on, Al. I don't want to fight with you."

"Fight? We don't fight. You just go your merry own way, doing sneaky things while I just, just . . ."

"Get really pissed off?" Donny says.

"You bet. I do have a thimble of self-respect left, believe it or not." My voice cracks and tears drip onto my, no longer special, doeskin shirt.

"Tell me what you mean," Donny says, jolting the car into drive.

"Never mind, I'm so damn tired," I say, wiping my nose on my sleeve.

"And . . . I'm more than a bit confused." He uses a tone wholly unsympathetic that cuts deeper.

"Okay then, so I'll tell you. Do you know what it feels like to think that you're missing some vital, intrinsic element in your personality that will make your mate love you, truly love you? And that, day after day, no matter how hard you try, you are just not good enough?"

Donny stares ahead into the blinding taillights leading us back home. Immediately, I wish I could take back the question. Why does honesty have to be so demanding?

"Yes, Alex, I think I do," he answers. I shrink back into the cold leather cushion and close my eyes.

The next morning, I awaken after Donny has left for the factory, feeling slightly disoriented. There are no familiar sounds like the children's nasal breathing heard down the hall. I'd forgotten I left Becky and Lana with Louise. I rub my eyes and the ensemble of silver frames on my dresser comes into focus. There's Donny and me, prideful and rigid as a young bride and groom, and Becky, swollen and bruised, a one-day-old prizefighter. And a cherished picture of Lana on her first birthday, cheeks coated in vanilla frosting. I'd always paid attention to the minute details of each and every passing day. How then did seven years rocket past me? It's as though I've been catapulted from a cannon and missed the billboards advertising *a life*—one, which, coincidently, belongs to me.

I drag myself out of bed, knowing if I fall back to sleep, I'll awaken dry-mouthed and logy. I brew fresh coffee and scramble up some eggs. Without the girls running around under my feet, I take my time, actually eat sitting down. I pry open a jar of apricot preserves and spread some on a toasted English muffin. It is so quiet I notice my sighs between each crunchy bite. I look around the kitchen like a nosy unwelcome guest checking for fingermarks and neglected crumbs. The sun beats through the picture window, enveloping my body like a heated cloak. And then there's a familiar guilty pang—an aching disconnection. I look toward the rosebushes for a sign, wondering if my future is as predictable as the buds beginning to sprout in our garden.

I use this leisure time to work on back orders of T-shirts. In between I take a few breaks, lie across the shaggy rug, and stretch. I brace myself against the sliding glass door and try a headstand. I move my knees and legs slowly upward until I'm stick-straight. My brain fills with blood until I no longer feel my limbs. Actually, I don't feel anything except a strange pressure in my skull. Could this be an embolism? The phone rings five times before I answer.

"Alex, I'm so glad I caught you," my mother says, sounding out of breath.

I'd failed to reach her for a couple of days and felt awful that she and my father had no place to celebrate Passover. They settled on a seder for ten bucks a head at their local JCC. I visualized them dining in a pungent-smelling room, packed with ailing and aging strangers eyeing one another, all slightly humiliated that some child or relative hadn't recued them. Now, I take the dour tone of her voice as an attempt to manipulate me for having a poster-perfect life without her. But then I hear a fissure in her speech, a holding back—not true to Miriam's style.

"I'm sitting here stunned," she continues. My heart does an unexpected drum roll.

"What's happened, Mom? Is Daddy okay?" I hear myself yell, as if saving a child from a speeding truck.

"Your father's fine. He's out buying extra copies of the *Herald*."

"Why? Why extras?"

My mother finally releases her grip. "Rob Woodman dropped dead last night . . . a heart attack."

"Oh God, no, I don't believe it. He was only . . ."

"Thirty-five."

There's a throbbing in my neck that shoots directly to my throat. I begin pacing the room, looking for my image in every reflective surface.

"Poor Sophie, and the kids. He was crazy over those kids."

"Yes, honey, it's a horrible tragedy, and everyone here is shocked. Dad and I saw Rob at a condo meeting two days ago. And now he's laid out in a box down the road at Kronick's Chapel on Lincoln Road."

I imagine Rob squeezed into a plain pine box, his head and neck distorted. He's wearing his palm tree shirt, the one he wore the night I saw him in his driveway with the tall, skinny girl. His eyes are open—the color of swirled aqua marbles. Rob wouldn't want to miss a thing. But for some weird reason he appears happy. Come to think of it, Rob laughed all the time, either with you or about you. And now he is a *was*. In an instant, anyone is capable of becoming past tense.

"Where did it happen?"

"Rumors are spreading through the building faster than mildew." My mother clears her throat and whispers, "The housekeeper told our doorman he was with the nanny. Supposedly, the girl was so terrified she ran into the street, wrapped up like a cocoon, wearing only a sheet."

"But where were Sophie and the kids?"

"In the Bahamas for spring break . . . obviously, without their nanny."

I conjure up my car ride in Sophie's jazzy Targa, and how I nearly crashed into a barrier of privet after spotting Rob and the waiflike figure in the driveway.

"Is there news yet about his funeral?"

"With the holidays, I imagine the family will wait before they can, you know, put him in the ground."

I'm immediately reminded of my lack of religious training, all rituals involving birth and death. "That's horrible having to drag the thing out. I'll try to make arrangements to come down. It's only right."

"No, dear, don't put yourself through that. People will understand. You, too, have small children who depend on you."

Talk of death, any death, sends me scuttling back to infancy. My mother is well aware of this. While growing up, an event like this rarely invaded my parentally controlled, sterilized life. If it did, the result would be many sleepless nights and fears of any recurring trauma.

"Call Sophie when you can and what you say is *this*: 'I'm terribly sorry to hear of your tragic loss.'"

These are words my mother has written in perfect calligraphy, dozens of times, on custom-designed note cards, painstakingly selected for acquaintances, friends, and family members, including the wives of heads of state. In her dining room, on display, is a gold-framed thank-you note from "Jackie" sent soon after JFK's assassination.

"Thank goodness, dear, you can't afford one of those live-in nannies," my mother says, jarring me. Right then, she validates the decision I made, in August, not to tell her about Donny's midnight ride with the babysitter. Fury sinks back in, like the dull ache from an old fracture. I try shaking it off, but notice I've left a Sharpie resting on a pale blue shirt. The ruby ink spreads bloodily through the back of the shirt, leaving its mark on the surface of our kitchen table.

"Mom, I have to go. Call when you hear more."

"But dear, you didn't tell me. How was Louise's dinner last night?" I hear the envy in "Louise's dinner," not to mention how my mother shifts gears faster than anyone I know.

"Fine, Mom, it was fine. Everyone loved your ambrosia recipe. But I must try and catch Donny. He'll be leaving the factory any minute."

"Don't tell him now, honey. Let him drive home with a clear head," Miriam says, protecting her son-in-law, which, to my recollection, she has never done before.

I call, but Donny's already left work. Filled with an overabundance of nervous energy, I must call someone and punch in Paula's number, which I'd glanced at once and memorized. The connection seems perfectly clear: if it weren't for Sophie and Rob, the Pearls and the Bells might never have met. I almost hang up when I hear her low, struggling—"Hello."

"Paula, it's Alex." I don't presume she recognizes my voice, although hers is unmistakable.

"Oh hi, Alex, how was your holiday?" Paula had mentioned her mother was Italian, and her father a nonpracticing Jew. She and Charlie were married in a judge's chambers—no church, no synagogue. Religion? No big deal.

"Yes, *our* holidays were fine." *Even though we were almost two hours late.* "Donny told me Charlie had to rush back to DC. That's too bad."

"It was okay. My folks took the kids for the weekend, so I got the chance to do some spring cleaning."

"Oh, so, they weren't home to witness the unfortunate demise of your fish?" My heart's a locomotive picking up speed and puffing out invisible smoke.

"No, and thanks to Donny, they'll never have to know. Wasn't his idea to drive to Pet Land for a replacement, clever?"

I rush through the stale silence before I puke. "Yes, well, Donny's very inventive that way." I smother the revelation that while I was sitting home and waiting to go to his parents, Donny was fish-hunting with Paula. I think of strangling him and then remember Rob.

"Paula, I have some very sad news. Rob Woodman died last night."

She responds in that London foggy way of hers, as if this happened years ago, and she'd forgotten.

"Oh my, this is awful. How?"

"He suffered a massive heart attack."

"Gosh, that's so frightening. I think Peter and Cheryl were out with them just last weekend. I'm surprised they haven't called us."

"Maybe they tried Charlie. Is he back in town?" I'm already wondering how Charlie Bell reacts to terrible news.

"Actually, he's flying home right now, hopefully in time for dinner."

I envision Charlie walking through the door, throwing down his bulky lit bag, and dipping Paula in his arms. Ravenous, he searches for something to eat. Tiptoeing toward him, Paula presents an ornate sterling-silver well-and-tree platter full of bloody roast beef.

"Listen, why don't the two of you come over tonight, say around eight? I haven't mentioned this to Donny yet, but I know he'll be happy to see you both."

"Um, I guess that would be fine, if Charlie's not too tired."

Tired is nothing! Tired isn't dead. "I thought it might be good if we got together. You know, for Sophie and Rob."

"They were certainly a very unusual couple or maybe you didn't know," Paula says flatly.

"Know what?"

"For one thing, they have, I mean *had*, a crazy relationship—some call it an *open marriage*."

Have I been entombed, residing here on Daisy Lane? So, even Paula knew what I failed to completely digest. I let her words settle in while trying to stay focused on the facts of Rob's death, rather than rumors of his extramarital activities. No need to share with her now that I'd witnessed one in the making. As Paula dreamily singsongs, I recollect thoughts about Sophie and Rob: His late-night business meeting, which he attended in shorts. Her mentioning his chauffeuring their au pair to rock concerts, malls, and movies. Sophie had said over and over again, smiling that devilish smile of hers, "You've got to keep them happy, Alex, or they will pick up and leave."

I was certain she meant the nanny.

TWELVE

When Donny walks in and greets me an hour later, I make a point of not looking at him. I sit at the table, buffing my nails, hoping to hide the fuchsia dye stains. A sidelong glance tells me he's wearing his usual ridiculous smirk, which only half admits to being a fool. It's hard not to fold when I see that look. This is how we've always shown our connection—it's our native dance, the one *we* have choreographed into the intricate pattern that became our marriage. Usually, I find comfort knowing I can expect this, but a sudden change, like a rip tide, warns me: it just isn't enough.

"Donny, I've got something to tell you. You better sit down." He pulls out the captain's chair and glances out the window, needing a few seconds to settle in. It's challenging, this game we play, but I don't dare laugh when I'm about to tell him something horrible, even though I'm fighting off a strange, nervous grin.

"Rob Woodman had a heart attack last night."

"Was it bad?"

"Bad enough—he's dead." I sneak a peek at Donny's reflection in the windowpane. He runs his fingers through his hair, then grips my hand.

"Holy shit!" he says. "Holy, fucking shit. I bet it was drugs; maybe he was coked-up."

"Maybe it was strenuous sex. My mother said he was with their nanny when it happened. Sophie was with the kids in the Islands."

My new contralto voice reverberates through the kitchen. *Warning, warning: this is what happens to selfish, indulgent men who fool around.*

Donny looks at me, his head cocked to one side. There is genuine fear in his eyes, the purest look I've seen from him in years.

"I know it's hard to believe. We just watched him blow out thirty-five birthday candles," I say. Donny just sits staring into space. "Oh, by the way, you might want to freshen up, we may be having company. I've invited Paula and Charlie over."

"Tonight? Why tonight?"

"Especially tonight with Rob gone and all. If it weren't for Rob, we might never have met Charlie and Paula. I thought you'd be happy. Don't you like them? Aren't they the *perfect* couple, you know, as couples go?"

Donny pushes his chair back, stands, then sits back down. He lets me get it all out, but there's a trace of loathing in the way he looks at me. It hurts to see his disgust, yet it makes me persist. Why worry about limits now? I'm in, whether I understand the rules or not. That's what he wants. That's what he'll get.

Donny stares out the window. A light crystal rain streaks the panes.

"Alex, I know how much you despise games. I've always respected that about you."

I can feel myself starting to back down; here comes the about-face. Is it a perpetual rash? "So why are you toying with your own version of follow-the-leader?"

"No one is making you do anything. It's all in that pretty head of yours." Donny gives the top of my skull a gentle *knock, knock* as he leaves the table to go wash up. I think of saying, "Who's there?" Or, who are you? Are you my husband or an adolescent son concocting a noxious potion with your chemistry set—something to blow us into smithereens?

While Donny showers, I do a quick fix on my hair and makeup. My eyes stop me when I pass the bathroom mirror. Have they always been this feral? Tonight, they are greener, what happens when I weep, and I can't stop crying about Rob, even though I was far from his biggest fan. It's the children my heart breaks for, the memory of them riding his broad shoulders, Rob patiently teaching them to play croquet on a burnt patch of condo grass.

I choose my tightest-fitting jeans, which I must lie down flat across the bed in order to zip. There's this bulge protruding from my belly like dough rising in a cupcake pan—an extra five pounds from hibernating.

I glance at Donny while he rigorously dries himself off. I'm waiting for some electrical twinge that will raise the hairs on my neck. You'd think that with his weekly sunlamp treatments, he'd have a wrinkle or two, but his skin is flawless. Donny is actually pretty. Our eyes meet, and again that smirk—a look that takes the place of hours, days, and weeks of conversations we have not had. I can't help but think we may be out of time. Someone our age has passed away, a shocking reminder that we can run from almost anything, anyplace, but not from fate.

Downstairs, we go about our host and hostess activities, blanketed in stubborn silence. He opens a bottle of Canei. I stir Lipton's onion soup mix into sour cream. He says it's too warm to build a fire. To create an atmosphere of respect, what one might find at a vigil, I light an array of scented candles on the mantle, surprised by the knot in my throat.

The Bells arrive and we peck each other's cheeks, making a tense and comical round of it. Charlie kisses me twice. Changing to the more appropriate somber mood, each of us mumbles our reflection on Rob's death:

"So crazy, yeah."

"Hard to believe, uh-huh."

"Those poor little kids."

"Who could imagine?"

Paula and Donny make no eye contact, and I can't help but think it's deliberate. Whenever Donny speaks, she stares down at her feet, a weak smile stamped on her face. I can tell she's spent time on her hair, flipped the long ends back and off her cheeks. The frosted pink lipstick makes her appear younger and *mod*. And so, it's the first time in her presence that I feel a twinge of competition. *In this corner, folks, we've got the fair, perky streaked blonde, and here's the dark mysterious brunette.*

Donny leans in to hear Paula speak. His eyes offer genuine sympathy for the difficulty she has expressing herself.

"Oh, I wanted to say something. Shoot, I've forgotten, oh well," Paula stammers. Charlie seems tense, as if he were socially responsible for her, the way I sometimes act with Donny.

"Let's go inside," I suggest, heading for the den.

Charlie and Paula sit side by side on our burlap-fabric sofa, and before long their fingers fumble like spiders to find one another. Envy shoots a BB through my gut.

We drag two vinyl beanbags over and sit facing the Bells. Between us is a toy-damaged, highly distressed teak table on which I've placed a platter of cheese and dip, kosher for Passover Tam Tam crackers, cut-up veggies, and seedless grapes.

"It's not much, sorry. I hope you've eaten."

"It's fine. We had leftover roast beef," Paula says, still pensive.

"Roast beef! Oh, good," I say, instead of *I knew it!* I am certain that I've acquired clairvoyant powers. Donny pours the wine; it's bubbly and goes down easily like ginger ale. When Charlie reaches for some chips, I'm fascinated by the spread of his hands, and how they push like a steam shovel in and out of the bowl.

"To Rob," Donny toasts, "a guy who sure knew how to have a good time."

I glance at Paula for some small validation of our afternoon conversation. She sips her wine while scanning the glowing candles on the mantle.

"I didn't know Rob well, but he seemed a bit too fearless at times," Charlie says. "You should have seen him on the golf course. Pretty crazy."

"How crazy?" I ask, wanting to hear him speak some more.

"If he wasn't doing well, Rob would become a one-man excavation team, swinging his club like a maniac, making divots everywhere. Peter said—you remember my brother Peter, right?" Charlie asks.

Donny and I both nod yes like two polite hosts.

"Peter thought some of Rob's dealings were a bit shady. He avoided handling many of his legal affairs for that reason. But Rob managed to get what he wanted."

"Yeah, well now he's a dead guy, and two children are without a dad," I answer.

Quiet fills the room with the serenity of a prayer service. *Funny,* I think, *that no one mentions the nanny.* I'm learning that men, most men, will run from the room rather than knock a member of their species—especially if the subject has been caught with his "slacks in the sewer," as my grandfather was fond of saying, and which now I understand.

We decide to send a Harry and David premier fruit basket from the four of us, and our prattle about Rob ends abruptly. Donny flashes the new Bread album for our approval and stacks a pile of records on the turntable. When he finishes, instead of returning to the beanbag, he stretches out on the recliner, his foot, a shoe sole from Paula's crossed knees. Through the amber streaks of candlelight, I see her skin tone deepen, yet her expression remains grim. I think of the famed *Mona Lisa*, and the first time Mr. LeBlanc had shown a slide of the painting in freshman art class. Yes, I had this same vague disappointment. When he'd gone to the blackboard to mark out the actual size of the renowned masterpiece that hung in the Louvre, I'd thought he was joking. Perhaps Rona is right. Am I inventing a persona for Paula that doesn't exist? Yet, why I would do this is unclear.

I shift my gaze to Donny. He knows damn well I'm looking at him. Donny has become my own personal cartoon show. Except cartoons are supposed to be funny. He takes a joint from his breast pocket, lights it, and passes it to Paula. They lock eyes for a second, right before her fingers graze lightly over his. I don't like watching this, but I'm fascinated. I should just excuse myself and go upstairs and take a bubble bath. I'm as malleable as all the melting candles, wicks suddenly ablaze. Donny preens when Paula takes a long deep toke of the joint. He's like a music master with a new protégé. Ah, so that's what he sees in her: an unresisting Eliza to his Henry Higgins. What has my Dr. Higgins taught her so far? My brain is performing acrobatics. One second, I'm viciously jealous and the next, I don't give a rat's ass.

I try pouring myself a second glass of wine, and Charlie takes the bottle from my shaky hands. "Here, let me do it." I hold my breath, watching the liquid nearly overflow. "Whoops," Charlie says. I lift the delicate glass with both hands. My head moves slowly to the brim, but I take too large a gulp. I start to choke. The bubbly liquid has gone down my windpipe. This is how I will end, dying in front of people I hardly know, and yes, even my own husband, who is about to play footsy with another man's wife. Charlie leaps from the couch and, with one hand grasping a joint, he pats my back.

"You okay?" All ask in unison.

I lift a finger to signal *wait*, but when I try to speak, I sound raspy, like an old witch on her deathbed. "Gee, I hate when that happens, thanks for saving me."

"Oh, a small payback," he says, smiling broadly, reminding me of the first time we'd met. Charlie had looked so manly the night of Rob's party while he stood talking to his brother, making Donny appear more boyish than usual. Now sitting catty-corner to Paula, my husband appears more self-assured and in control.

Donny and Paula sit, side by side, reading the cover of our new special edition Beatles album. This was one of my gifts to Donny on his thirtieth birthday after moving into our house, a time when we often fantasized we were Linda and Paul—Donny delivering a Liverpool accent while he banged on the keys, our heads touching in many strained attempts at harmony.

Charlie offers me his hand as I struggle to rise from the beanbag chair, but I lose my footing on my platform clogs and collapse against his chest. I grip his upper arms to regain my balance. Through his shirt I feel the rock hardness of his muscles. His skin smells musky and fresh, like the aroma you inhale when walking into a steamy Laundromat—the anticipation that everything will come out clean. I'd like to linger here awhile and feel hopeful again. He holds me at arm's length, and we gape at each other, not saying a word. Tossed in with his obvious fatigue from traveling is his warm flannel sexiness.

I decline the last toke that Donny shoves under my nose. Is he trying to momentarily distract me? Charlie trails after me into the kitchen, carrying the empty bowl of dip. He looks a bit comical, slightly clumsy in this domestic role, but I don't dare laugh.

"So?" I say, rummaging through the cracker box, stuffing one in my mouth automatically.

"So?" Charlie answers. He's leaning against the kitchen sink, his feet crossed in front of him. I take a swig of my remaining wine. "Careful, pretty. Don't hurt yourself." I hear the heartiness in his laugh, before it winds down to a light chuckle. Our spouses, who I've temporarily forgotten, glance in our direction before resuming their whispery conversation. Here I go again, splitting in half. One half, watching and worrying about Donny—the other, craving this pleasure, the attention Charlie's paying me. He glances toward the den, and I wonder if he, too, is denying possessive thoughts. I open my fridge to check the date on a container of milk, then lift open the fruit bin, as if buried among the fuzzy, month-old strawberries I'll find clues to what happens next.

"Come here, you." Charlie's words send chills shooting through my scalp. His hand slides down my shoulder and arm until it clasps my cool, damp fingers. Instinctively, I look back to the den. In the fading candlelight, I see Donny moving onto the couch, taking Charlie's spot. One arm is already draped over Paula's shoulder. I know exactly what I see. It is as clear to me as a sheet of shimmering glass, and perhaps for that reason I don't falter or unlatch my fingers from Charlie's firm hold. He leads me, as if I were blind, from the kitchen through the dining room, to the adjoining living room. A room rarely used, sparsely decorated with the piano, a white ceramic cocktail table, and two loveseats—one of which I am now sitting on, staring into the soft caramel eyes of Charlie Bell.

I slip off my clogs and cross my legs Indian-style. I'm waiting for Charlie to say something. The numbing effects of the hashish Donny ground through my flour sifter earlier are still with me. Charlie strains to hear the groaning sounds of Barry White, the lyrics barely audible. Listening to Barry's deep baritone is embarrassing, like eavesdropping on some lascivious sexual act. I peek out of the corner of my eye at Charlie. His eyes are closed. Again, I study his hands. Rough hands—the hands of a laborer, not a lawyer. The phonograph changes abruptly to another album. While I'm pondering what other tunes Donny has prepared for our listening enjoyment, the hallway light dims. The only light in the living room emanates from a yellow lamppost outside. It filters through the pattern of the drapes, creating interesting shapes around the loveseats, leaving the rest of the room inky black.

The feathery stubble along Charlie's jaw is captured by the light, and I resist the temptation to reach out and touch him. His hands move up to his tired face to rub both eyes, massaging them, probing hard. Opening his eyes wide, he stares at me, as if surprised.

"Oh, it's you," he says, and in the quiet laughter, he manages to rest his hand on my kneecap. How many times would I have peeled or bent back fingers I had not wanted to touch me? I take "one giant step," placing my hand over his. There are tiny bristles on his knuckles. The comparison is startling. Donny's hands are softer; his fingers long—piano hands meant to slide across keyboards, not bases.

"If a picture paints a thousand words then why can't I paint you?" The ballad is seriously romantic, and I am aware of my organs in the following order: my heart pirouetting within my ribs, my bowels squeezed into a pulsing vise, and my brain vacillating between projecting blame and sweet exaltation.

Charlie pitches his head toward mine, stopping an inch from my upturned face, his hand still clamped to my knee. I shut my eyes as all the dancing shadows fall into place. His kiss, though soft, is infused with a mysterious brilliance. Out of the corner of my eye, I see sparks but realize it's only static. Charlie taunts me, pulls away, and begs to be kissed back. Taking the deepest breath, I plunge willingly into the night with this stranger, memorizing all particles of light, smell, sound, and touch.

I drift away to a time, half a lifetime ago, when I learned how erotic kissing could be, how primitive in its stirrings. I was with Jonathan Tanner in the boiler room of his friend Jerry's house, at a "gathering"— what we called random get-togethers on Friday nights. After days of listening to my pleading, my father agreed to drop me off with the cold-eyed warning he'd be back to get me in exactly two hours. And sure enough, when I wasn't waiting at the front door for him (I'd lost track of time), I had to suffer the humiliation of having my father march, like a member of the KGB, through the door of Jerry's parentless home. There he encountered a sweaty couple pressed against an oven door, others sprawled like puppies on the floor, and the hasty hiding of beer cans behind closed drapes. Silent and only a little bit scared, Jonathan claimed me. He took my hand and walked me to my father's idling car. Turning me away, blocking me completely, he kissed me, first deeply, then tenderly.

"Hey, it's okay, relax," Charlie says, putting his arm around me.

"I am," I lie.

We are nose to nose, and I have the impression Charlie is waiting for my reaction, perhaps my rating on his kiss. I guess he's used to kudos, but, being old-fashioned, I'm used to playing hard-to-get. As his lips travel down my neck, I grip the tasseled pillow on the loveseat. He is leaning into me now, and it is all up to me. If I lie back against the loveseat's arm, he is sure to climb upon me, and I might not say no. I'm aware of a throbbing deep within my jeans—a warm, gentle current flowing inward. Saved by the abrupt click of the turntable shutting off in the den, I am scared to leave the room. I envision Donny and Paula sprawled Sumo-style upon the orange shag carpeting.

"What's the matter?" Charlie asks.

"This is much too weird," I say, searching for my clogs.

"I've wanted to do that for a long time, Alex. But you know that, don't you?"

"Shh! Not now. I can't handle this." I unravel my legs to stand, and switch on the Stiffel lamp on top of the piano. The first thing I notice is the lamp's brass finial of a monkey covering its eyes as in: *see no evil.* Charlie's eyes, however, are like hot coals searing my back.

The hallway seems brighter, and there's the clatter of glasses being placed in the sink, my sink. Donny clears his throat. The toilet flushes, and I picture Paula sitting on the cushiony seat, admiring my wallpaper. With Charlie close behind, I rush into the kitchen, squinting from the harshness of fluorescent lights.

"We're here!" I announce. I'm like a guest entering my own home.

"Hi, guys," Donny says. But I don't dare look at him. I don't want him to see my face when I don't know what it reveals. I open the dishwasher and begin unloading a batch of soiled dishes. Paula walks out of the bathroom and, when seeing us, freezes like a child in a game of "statues." Her cheeks are blotchy, the blotchy from a bad case of beard-burn. Maybe I have it too. My eyes scan every inch of her. I am looking for something invisible, some mysterious quality that would make her desirable—first to Charlie, and now, Donny. Paula smiles a weak, innocent smile, and I realize she doesn't care as much about me, as I do about her. There is no measuring tape afloat in Paula's eyes.

"Charlie," she says, looking up and over me at our sunflower of a clock, "we've really got to go. It's late, and my folks are bringing the

kids back in the morning." I think of Becky and Lana sleeping peace-
fully at Louise and Ben's.

"Are you sure I can't make us all some coffee?" Donny asks no
one in particular. I throw him an *are you out of your mind* kind of
look. I've had enough for one evening. With eyes shut, I give Paula
a peck on her cheek, noting Donny's citrus cologne lingering in her
hair. While Donny escorts Paula to the front door, Charlie hangs
back in the kitchen. He looks like he'd like to pull out a chair and
stay forever.

"I'll miss you," he says.

"Don't say that! You're not supposed to miss me."

He runs his fingers through my hair and whispers: "Sister
Golden Hair Surprise." Who is this guy? At times he seems older,
as if he's lived a hundred lives, and then I see past the quiet, settled
demeanor—a sweet, insecure boy.

"Charlie, please!" Paula yells from our front door. Maybe she, too,
has had enough, and wishes to flee.

I can hardly wait for Donny to walk back into the kitchen after
locking the front door. Here he is, taking out his lenses and rubbing
his eyes, a small ritual that's bought him much time over the years.

"Donny, did you consider that Charlie might have wanted to
punch you out tonight?" Funny, but the shame pinching me, just
minutes ago, is suddenly gone.

"Why's that?"

"Tell me you didn't orchestrate the entire evening so you could
make a move on his wife? Like in the music you selected, where you
sat, how we divided so conveniently: Donny and Paula, Charlie and
me."

"Oh, so I guess you had nothing to do with this? May I remind you
darlin', it was you who'd invited them over tonight, not me." Donny

performs a tap step on the kitchen tile and ends with his arms out. "Gotcha!"

"That was because of Rob . . . him being dead . . . and you . . . when were *you* going to tell me about your pilgrimage with Paula to the pet store?"

"I was only being helpful."

"Not your job, Donny."

"Alex, why not enjoy the fact that Charlie's flipped for you. He couldn't care less what his wife was doing with me."

Hearing this evening's summary delivered by Donny feels incredibly strange. How am I to respond? The validation of his words causes an explosion in my head. I am glad to hear the news, though furious at the messenger.

"Anyone might have *flipped* watching you and little Miss Helpless-When-It-Serves-Me. Did you expect me to just hang out and watch your Casanova routine? I truly didn't know where to put myself."

"Oh right, Alex. When did anyone force you into anything?"

"Well, I didn't *do* anything!"

"Did you kiss him? Come on, come on, I bet you kissed him." Donny sticks his face closer under my chin. Needing air, I turn to open the cafe curtains, but all I see is a sprinkling of stars above the blackness in the backyard. Familiar shadows of our sleepy neighborhood have vanished from view.

Donny's voice is somber. "It was great, babe, wasn't it? I bet you heard harp strings and everything." My husband of nearly seven years stands beside me, appearing anxious for my answer. All he is missing is a pad and pencil to jot down some notes. This, the same man who kept a precise log of my contractions for each of my deliveries wants to know how much I enjoyed making out with another man. So, this is it, I guess. These are the words he has chosen to let me go or *let go of me.* They are stronger than anything Donny's ever said to me. In using them, he has abandoned all claims to me and the principle of—us. Is it true? My husband wishes to trade me in.

"You know what, Don? I won't talk to you about any of this," I say, wiping my hands on the legs of my jeans.

"I want you to be happy, Alex, and I believe Charlie Bell is what you need."

"Please, can you just leave me alone now?"

Fragments of the evening and Donny's words march in my head as he follows me through the hallway and up the stairs to our bedroom. We struggle on the way. He grabs my leg, and I jab him in the ribs. I mumble for him to fuck off. Once upstairs he tackles me, pushing me down on the bed that still has garments strewn across it. The room is much too light. I'm able to see Donny's weird expression; it's a rare peek at lust. At first, I'm shy and embarrassed, and then this sudden strangeness between us excites me. He pushes himself inside me, hard, almost angry, as if he's hitting a car horn in rush hour traffic. I am able to separate completely as if engaged in a crucial stage of metamorphosis. Inside my head an imaginary paintbrush transforms all the contours of Donny's face. I raise his cheekbones, deepen his eyes, and thicken the vertical cords of his neck. The image appears so real I worry I might call out his name. Charlie. Charlie Bell. It takes only minutes, this exercise in mutual fulfillment. Donny rolls off me, pants bunched at the ankles, and for several minutes we lie on our backs, side by side.

As I sometimes do, I begin counting the holes in the ceiling—ugly black nail heads that pop through the plasterboard. When I'd first learned the cracks and holes were caused by our house finally settling into the foundation, I felt overjoyed. *What good news,* I'd thought, *how enormously comforting.*

THIRTEEN

An unusual calm permeates our home. Words are suspended like dust trapped in a ray of sunlight. Donny and I are extremely polite with each other, acting like you might with the people in your life you often see, yet never get to know: the gardener, the cleaner, the neighbor on the corner whose name you forgot, but who never fails to wave. People whose faces you see perfectly when you close your eyes: a splattering of freckles, an intrusive mole, the slight overlap of a front tooth. But you may never get to touch their hand, or glimpse inside their troubled heads.

And, as if barometers of our internal weather, Becky and Lana command a bit more attention. Lana has begun wetting her bed again—the first time in over a year. When I call to consult with Dr. Carner, he asks if anything out of the ordinary has been going on.

"No!" I bellow into the receiver. My mouth goes dry when I scan the den and notice two empty wineglasses perched on the mantle above the fireplace. They have been there since Saturday night, or maybe the Saturday night before, or the one before that, which were spent in the company of the Bells—scheduled get-togethers during which the four of us first relax, chat, smoke, and eventually break off: splitting with the other's spouse to either the darkened den or living room to neck feverishly. The raw excitement of all of this seems to mimic our younger years—a time seeped in the sweet juices of unrequited love. Like then, we have imposed certain guidelines on ourselves as individuals—first base, second base—*and* on our *four-some*, a word we are yet to utter aloud. Never is any one couple to enter a bedroom; without discussion, bedrooms remain off-limits. We are to meet in the kitchen at eleven o'clock sharp to say our sheep-ish good nights. Donny and I check on the children, and then crawl into bed, where little is said. Yet I lie awake, all night, reliving the last hours—wondering if, perhaps, I might be losing my mind.

I regain my composure and answer the doctor. "Nothing has changed, not a thing." He assures me Lana's bed-wetting is most likely a stage—a slight regression. Most children grow out of these "unpleasant" incidents without requiring further treatment. But his answer doesn't offer insight on how to help Lana or to allay her fears that we'll be angry with her for what she's smart enough to label: her little accident. *Accidents do happen* is all that comes to mind.

I make a quick trip to our library, which I'm surprised to find is under complete renovation. The only usable area is an old stucco section, the size of a Carvel stand, and after researching through *enuresis and bedwetting* on microfilm, I discover a recent article from *Psychology Today*. It suggests explaining to the child in simple terms the parts of the anatomy and their function—kidney, bladder, and the storage of urine after digestion. I make a few copies and rush back home.

After bath time, I sit alone with Lana and try to explain that sometimes her tiny bladder can't hold all the fluid in her body, but when she's a bit older or bigger, it definitely will. And it is no big deal, because some kids, even twice her age, still wet their beds. I tell her a true story, which she loves so much I repeat it every night for a week:

When I was twelve, I had a friend named Jill, who had a ten-year-old sister, Kate, who wet her bed almost every single night. One evening, while I was at a sleepover at Jill's house, lying next to her in

Kate's bed (Kate slept in the den that night), their father came home from a party and checked on both his daughters as usual. Having had a drink or two (the part I omit), he scooped me up from Kate's bed, thinking I was her—*Come here, my little girl*—and carried me to the bathroom, hoping to ward off the usual accident. Not until the bathroom light glared in his foggy eyes did he realize the young girl he'd placed on the potty seat was not his precious little Kate. *It was me, schnookims! Mommy!* I was too stunned to utter a sound. Plus, I had to pee.

When I see Lana's sparkly eyes anticipating the end of my story, how they brim with happy tears, for a moment the shroud of guilt slips from my shoulders. I almost convince myself that what's happening in my marriage has had no effect on my children. And then what enters is this awful sinking sensation—a foreboding that looms over me like an out-of-reach cobweb. I am accustomed to managing my guilt in the form of superstition. If I expose a trace of joy, whisper its existence aloud, it will be snatched away like bait. It's safer to walk around feeling guilty and mildly miserable.

It's just past noon, and I am at the kitchen table wrapped in my new peach robe, protected by the calm, domestic hum of the clothes dryer in the background. My mind drifts to Charlie. I picture his eyes, how they capture finite specs of amber light. I'm getting used to the texture of him, his buttery soft skin, a strong jutting chin, and the salty taste of his lips. How when he smiles at me, I like the person he thinks he sees.

I've been busy for hours, tie-dyeing and drying piles of T-shirts, readying them for their design. The markers are spread across the

table, some resting on my half-eaten bagel. I have already finished a
Lucy on ice skates for a girl named Jessica, a silver moon and golden
star design for Mia, and a Big Bird frolicking at the beach for someone's infant girl, Jennifer. Before the day ends, I promise myself to
make something new for Becky and Lana. In *House and Garden*, I'd
found a beautiful rose, which I stenciled and saved as a pattern. This,
I'll make for myself on a blue shirt with lace trim around the neckline,
to wear the next time I'm with Charlie. I imagine him fascinated by
the way the skimpy garment clings—how the petals, deep red above
my heart, expand with every breath. I catch myself daydreaming, my
head and hand completely disconnected.

There are a dozen items to finish before Memorial Day, and if I
don't deliver on time I may lose the chance for several camp orders
in June. Just last week Cleo dropped a hint when she said, batting her
false lashes, "You know, Alex, there are so many of you gals selling
these T-shirts now—so many more choices out there."

"Yes, I realize that," I said, taking time to gather my thoughts.
"That's why I choose to take only the higher-priced custom orders.
Did you know, Cleo, that my markers are more expensive so colors
won't fade in the wash? Actually, I've been thinking of limiting the
amount of work I take on or raising my prices."

"Oh, I hope you'll wait until the camp rush is over," Cleo answered,
immediately, pulling two twenties from the register to pay me for
the work I had just delivered. I tucked the money in my pocket and
headed for the door, aware of the pummeling inside my chest. I was
energized by my deep dislike for this woman and proud of how I
stood up to her. Why it took me this long, I really can't say.

A rush of warmth levitates me, Ouija-style, from the kitchen
chair. I stretch my arms out, move my legs up and down. I mimic a
fighter about to enter the ring. Something electric propels me down

the stairs and points me in the direction of the already primed canvas propped against the playroom wall. Yes, it is still there, waiting like an unmarked tomb. Until it is complete, the work will have no identity or meaning. My body keeps its momentum while I switch on the high-hat lights and begin randomly shaking cans of abandoned paint. They sit like orphans on the wooden workbench. "Choose me, choose me," I hear each of them say. I think of the works which inspired me—the sprawling canvasses of Pollock and de Kooning and how their paintings bled with color, telling stories of elation or despair. It was as if they had cut a vein, dripped their own blood. Like the lives they lived, their paintings were compulsive—unforgivably wild. But I am just a housewife, I remind myself—a housewife painting in torn underwear, worn inside out.

I throw off my robe and grab the blue denim work shirt hanging on the back of the door. I've kept this ragged shirt since college—a promise to myself I'd never give up. It is faded around the collar and streaked with a rainbow of dried paint, a creation in itself—Rorschach in design.

My first pick is a can of yellow spray paint, a sunny and hopeful color. I shake the can murderously. And with the first burst of spray, within seconds, I enter a safe haven, as if I've walked through a vault into bright light. Taking a huge breath, I dip a wide bristle brush into a can of orchard green and splash color across the canvas past all unprotected margins. Rummaging through a tool box for nails, tacks, glue, I stick my finger but keep going. I clip pieces and pieces of waxed string and copper wire. Up and down the stairs, huffing and jubilant, I'm an eager scavenger collecting fragments of broken toys, fabric swatches, supermarket coupons, bank receipts, birthday cards, and photos. I am on a frantic hunt, not caring or knowing what will be captured. I paint for what feels like hours, days, years, moving farther and farther away from the outside edges of the canvas. The creation slowly evolves, and begins to resemble a muted web of my own existence. A one-armed stick figure that could be me is at its core, pushed far into the distance and swallowed up by the surroundings: domino houses, rosebushes, a lawn mower floating over a carpet of bluegrass, a barbeque pit on fire, marijuana plants with jagged edges sprouting from windowsills. There are televisions, telephones, and telephone poles. All represented by bold lines that I draw with a thick, black marker. There are fishbowls without fish—kissing garomis floating in pairs above nimbus clouds. My feet move constantly as I lunge toward the canvas, adding stroke after stroke. I am like a swordsman taunting the enemy and embracing his fear. Tears stream down my face. Sweat drips from my neck. When the phone rings, I don't answer, but add another telephone to the canvas—a yellow wall phone with a cord that twists around the stick figure's body. Her mouth is open. Is she calling for help? She is a strange apparition wearing a bibbed apron. Black smoke billows from a red-brick fireplace. What? What is burning?

The garage door rattles, announcing Donny. I quickly seal the paint cans and throw the brushes in the work sink as if I'm hiding a murder weapon. I scrub my hands, wipe them on my work shirt, and slip back into my robe. Damn! If Donny's home, that means I was supposed to pick up the girls from Rona's over an hour ago. It must have been she who phoned. I run upstairs and punch in Rona's number. Breathless, I start to apologize, but she cuts me off.

"That's okay," Rona says in a slow drawl, making me wonder when she turned Southern. "The girls kept Ethan busy while I finished my spring cleaning. By the way, Lana had another little accident. I had to put her in Ethan's Spider-Man underpants."

"Oh, was she very upset?"

"No, I think it bothered her more that you weren't here on time. She was waiting at the front door, looking for you. What's up with you, Alex? You never even called to say you'd be late?"

"I know. I'm really sorry, but I started painting again today, Rona, really painting. It felt so amazing that I lost all track of time."

"Alex, tell me, when are you not painting?"

"Never mind," I answer, "I'll be there in a few minutes. Don't bother with dinner, please have them ready." I hang up hard. Why must she always find a way to attach a price to her good deeds? Or did I sound too buoyant for her to handle?

I yell up to Donny in the bedroom that I'm taking Becky and Lana to Friendly's for fried chicken. I ask if he'd like me to bring him back dinner. The violet hue illuminating the hallway tells me the sun lamp is in use.

"Nope, I'm fine," he yells back, not coming to the stairs. He'll make himself something later. *Great*, I think. See how simple life can be after the fizzle is gone?

Friendly's Cafe is anything but amicable. Instead it's earsplitting loud, bustling with mostly mothers and kids, families where fathers work late, commute, or don't live at home anymore.

Becky asks, "Mommy, why is your hair green?" I take out a hand mirror, and while I'm a bit disheveled, my skin is aglow. I want to say aloud to someone, "I think I may be happy." Whatever this feeling is I'd like to have them wrap it up, so I can bring it home and freeze it in Tupperware. My wrists are caked with yellow paint and a piece of gold twine is glued between my thumb and index finger.

"Pull it," I tell Lana, who is staring at me with such sweet curiosity. "Pull the string, angel, and you'll get a prize."

"What's the prize?" Both girls are eager to know.

"Me, that's what you get . . . your crazy old Mama."

"Aw no fair," Lana says, but she's laughing, while ketchup dribbles from her little kitty mouth. "We already have you."

The next day Donny calls from work to say he's gotten the okay from his cousin George to use his summer place upstate for the upcoming Memorial Day weekend. This is a trip we only casually discussed with the Bells that now seems to be materializing.

"So, how many bedrooms are there?" I ask, already worrying about the communal aspect of this mini vacation.

"There's one big bedroom and two smaller ones. I guess we can put all the kids in the large one—it'll be fine," Donny answers. I imagine the girls sharing a room with Ricki and Ross Bell, and the hairs on my arms stand at attention. "Oh, and we're just a short walk down to the lake. George said we can use his old canoe if we like."

"Uh-huh." I fail to suppress my chuckle.

"What's so funny?"

"Remember when we lived in Boston, how we wanted to rent a canoe and take it out on the Charles River? We said that every weekend and then I got pregnant with Becky and was vomiting all the time."

"Yeah, and I recall how you liked those hunky guys from Harvard's rowing team, practicing when it was thirty or forty degrees out . . . Listen, I got to go. I'm being paged."

I'm glad Donny cuts me off, bringing me back to reality and sparing me an extra stay on memory lane.

"Why don't you call Paula and decide what you will need in the way of supplies. I have to run. Pop is as red as a lobster."

I picture Ben's crimson cheeks and figure it's probably because Donny has spent much of his valuable work time arranging this little getaway. This idea for a multifamily vacation springs directly from the pages of Donny's favorite read of the year. Just a few days ago, I found *A Different Proposition* in Donny's night table where, since sharing its wisdom, he now keeps it. I noticed he'd made asterisks on several of the passages.

Opening the book to a random page, a childhood habit, I closed my eyes and pointed. My nail grazed the words *marital discord,* and I slammed the book shut. *Fuck you, Donny*! I could still decide my own fate, refusing to be guided by theories spouting the merits of communal living. I ran outside with the book and buried it in the garbage, but not our garbage. I shoved the red manifesto in our neighbors Norm and Sue's tall vinyl pail in case our ruddy-faced garbage man just happened to find it, even read a few pages before mashing it in the compactor. Better he sneaks a peek at Sue and thinks: *Whoa, that chick sure don't look like one of those hippie-dippy types.*

When I call Paula to fill her in about George's Carmel house, that it's surely a go, she interrupts me to say she already knows. I'm not surprised Donny and Paula speak during the day. What does surprise me is not a hair on my body stands at attention. There are a couple of hours left until school lets out, and Paula agrees to meet me at the coffee shop near the A&P, equidistant from both of our homes. While waiting, I prepare a list of things we'll need for our trip. I try to concentrate on staples like peanut butter and grape jelly, but my mind drifts to lace panties, silky pajamas, and where is my bottle of Musk cologne?

Paula rushes through the door and plops down in the booth. She is out of breath, which makes her unusually vibrant. While she pats her fluffy hair with her fingers, I study Paula, pretending I'm a guy, a guy like Donny. Yes, she's definitely pretty—thin, with small, perky breasts. But I bet she was one of those girls who hardly ever smiled, not even for her yearbook shot. I imagine her lips puckered, while her eyes held the icy stare of someone annoyed at having to concentrate—removing her from the habitual state of distraction.

We're on our second cup of coffee when, feeling restless, I start firing away about Charlie: Is he always so funny and cheerful? My questions elicit such a sardonic laugh from Paula that I'm startled. *What?* "He has a temper, really?" Yet, everything she shares about him, even that once, when they were out of milk, he went bat shit, stirs me.

Our voices hush as we move into the area of finance. Territory I've shied away from with Rona. Paula says they are still paying off loans from law school. She then asks about Donny's parents, whom she met last Sunday, at our house, when Louise and Ben made one of their unannounced visits. Thank God they have a frenetic social life, which keeps them from popping in Saturday nights.

I mention Donny's desperation to please Ben and how working together often causes a burdensome strain on the relationship. Paula's mouth turns down in quiet sympathy. She cares for Donny, I can tell. I expect to feel mildly possessive, but instead this revelation nudges me closer to her, like discovering the same affection for a particular piece of music or favorite childhood rhyme: *Peter, Peter Pumpkin eater, had a wife and couldn't keep her.*

"How long have you been designing T-shirts?" Paula asks, breaking her own silence.

"I started about four years ago when we lived in Queens. I was pregnant with Lana, and home taking care of Becky. My grandmother used to lecture me that it was wise to keep a *pushke*: a bit of money stashed away for a rainy day. In her era, the money was used to buy food and clothing. Me, I buy paint supplies and stuff for our house, but my ten grand for the girls' college fund stays intact."

"Ten thousand! Isn't that a lot of money to keep in a *pushke*?"

"Donny thinks we've only got five." I realize I've taken a huge step with Paula. But it's too late to take it back.

Paula's face opens like a silk Japanese fan. "I've always taken care of the bills," she says, "and there's never any *extra*."

"Didn't you once work in the city?"

"Yes, for a small accounting firm downtown, but I quit right before Ross was born. When Charlie began traveling, we thought one of us should stay home."

I envision Paula adept with numbers and bottom lines, having the skills and concentration to be exact, something I'd fail at miserably.

We finish jotting down our list, and I stand to pay the check. "Come on," I say, "let's walk a little. I, for one, have been in the house too long."

Together, we stroll past the stores of a small strip mall and pause in front of the bakery window. I inhale aromas of freshly baked bread, which brings back the memory of buying a challah for my mother on the way home from school on Fridays. Women pass and study us, some so blatantly curious they stop to stare as if troubled someone exists who they don't know.

"We should bring some warmer things just in case. It can be chilly upstate, especially at night," Paula says, out of the blue.

"So, you're familiar with the area?"

"Not Carmel but farther up, in the Catskills." Paula hesitates. "It's where Charlie and I first met."

"Ah, a resort, I bet."

"Gillison's in South Fallsburg. I was visiting a friend vacationing there, and Charlie was our waiter."

"A waiter, yes, I can see that—fast, funny and glib, right?" Paula smiles, and something in her eyes relays a jealous jab, but I push on. "So, was it love at first sight?"

"Not really. He was, well, big."

The double meaning makes me giggle.

"Oh, no." Paula blushes, noting my frisky expression. "I meant he was sort of manly. Before him, I'd dated mostly boyish guys."

Oh, I think, *more like Donny.*

"What about you two?" Paula asks, checking her watch.

"Well, I'd just broken up with my high school sweetheart for the tenth time, when Donny and I met while working at a day camp."

"So, Donny was your rebound?" Paula asks, her eyes widening.

Something in her tone makes me feel like I committed a sin. "Not really. I only went with my boyfriend for so many years out of habit."

"But you loved him, right?"

"Who?"

"The boyfriend," she reminds me.

"Yes, yes, of course, but after a while we were more like a brother and sister taking each other for granted."

"I don't mind being taken for granted," Paula states proudly. "I like taking care of most everything, as long as Charlie takes care of us."

I wipe away my *you've got to be kidding* expression. I'm wrong to judge and don't want to put her off. But I do recall hearing from Donny how she ironed Charlie's shirts and underwear. I had replied to this domestic news bulletin with, "Well then, lucky Charlie."

We pause in front of Marty's Male Boutique. In the window are two mustached mannequins wearing skintight, Ban-Lon shirts over navy bell-bottoms.

"I'm not a fan of mustaches. They usually advertise a guy's last meal, but I do like that shirt. Should we browse?" I ask. Paula nods yes, and I push the heavy door leading into a narrow, claustrophobic space. An array of cowbells ring and my nostrils are accosted by the heady smell of incense.

Standing side by side, Paula and I thumb through cellophane packages of brightly colored shirts. "What size is Charlie?"

"Large," she answers, and I whisper *large* to myself.

"Donny's a medium. At least I think so. It's been a while since I've bought him anything," I say, my voice trailing off. I used to always surprise Donny with small gifts like shirts, and albums, and books. It once gave me enormous pleasure.

Paula pulls a blue paisley from the messy pile, and holds it out for me to see. "A medium, for Donny," she says assuredly.

"Oh, here's the same exact one in khaki. It's a large, should we?" I ask, chuckling like an adolescent girl.

Paula's face beams. There's a mischievous crinkling in the corners of her eyes.

"Will you gift wrap these please?" I ask the curly-headed Marty of Marty's Male Boutique. "Wow, this aroma is pungent. What is it?"

"Vanilla, doll, like you," Marty says, swiping the twenty from my hand. "It covers a myriad of sins, if you get what I mean." Marty's wearing an onyx beaded choker. His face has an orangey cast; I guess, from a heavy application of Man-Tan.

"Whew!" I wave my hand in front of my face, trying to clear the suffocating air.

Then, from the back of the store, I hear someone shout out my name. Immediately, I recognize the "Al-lux!" I panic, as if caught in the midst of a jewel heist.

"Hi, gorgeous," Marty bellows toward Rona. Having spotted me with Paula, she has already put on her *I'm superior, you're a peasant* puss.

"So, what's with the gift?" Rona asks, after saying an almost inaudible "hi" to Paula.

"Ah . . ."

"For Charlie," Paula interjects. "I'm throwing him a party next week."

"Oh, nice," Rona says, turning toward me. "Alex, I thought you were working 'all day' on your T-shirt orders, and that's why you couldn't have lunch with me."

"I was. I mean, I am. But I needed a break."

Rona half listens while eyeing Paula's outfit: a pair of baggy jeans and a faded red T-shirt. In contrast, Rona looks like an ad for Saks. Her navy blue slacks fit perfectly on her small frame, and her pin-striped blouse is tucked in—worn with a thin, faux alligator belt. When I see Rona looking at Paula like this, I want to leap forward and mess her, but I realize that's impossible. How do you mess polished marble? Still, she has the power to make me feel guilty, as if she were my mother catching me in a porn shop dressed in chains and chaps, holding a whip instead of a gift-wrapped shirt . . . no big deal . . . for another woman's husband.

FOURTEEN

We leave the house at six o'clock on Friday morning, our intent to beat the predicted holiday traffic. Donny had originally wanted to rent a van so we'd all be able to travel together, but I nixed the idea, when Becky cried, saying that she hated the *bad girl*, Ricki, and her bossy brother, Ross.

"They leave me out, Mommy. Every time I want to play with them, they say 'No! You are a big, ugly doody.'"

"Well, once we get to the vacation house, you can play with your sister, and read your favorite books. You don't have to be with them if you don't want to."

"But what if they sneak up and kill me while I'm asleep in my bed?"

"They can't kill you. First, because Daddy and I won't let them. Second, because their daddy's a lawyer and lawyers' kids are not allowed to kill people." Sometimes I can't believe what comes out of my mouth.

"Oh," she said, considering my words in her pretty sun-streaked head before walking away. I had a flash fantasy of the Bells' kids behind bars as young adults—Paula visiting, bringing freshly ironed underthings, boxes of Dunkin' Donuts, while Charlie stood before a jury, arguing in their defense.

Donny pulls our car in front of the Bells' redbrick split-level and shuts off the motor. The sun is bursting through a gunmetal sky, and the entire block is quiet except for the occasional caw of a crow

186

perched on a rooftop. A garage door lifts, crankily, and Charlie's copper-colored Buick backs out of the driveway onto the road. Our cars are parallel, nearly touching. Donny rolls down his window, and I see Charlie straining forward—maybe to glimpse at me. I'm besieged by a strange erotic surge, up from my legs to my chest, everything I've denied and suppressed for weeks. It's been years since I felt so sexually charged, in touch with the stirrings in my body. *Hello, you, sensuous woman, you; you exist after all.*

I wave back, then pat my hand over a fake yawn. Lana, our journalist, reports to Becky in a loud whisper. "Becky, guess what? The bad girl and her mean brother are asleep in the back seat."

Paula, looking in the visor, applies a frosty gloss to her lips, which gives her eyes a mysterious opaqueness in the morning light. She smiles broadly at Donny. They lock eyes, and for a few uneasy seconds, I don't know where to put myself.

"So you'll follow me," Donny tells Charlie, "but in case we get separated, here are the directions."

"Sounds good to me, guy," Charlie mumbles back, the pipe stem clamped in his mouth. I hope he won't smoke and drive at the same time. I want to shout, *You be careful now, Charlie Bell.*

We are on the road for less than half an hour when Lana crosses her heart and swears she has to pee. Donny pulls into the rest stop on the turnpike and both men get out of their cars. Donny hops out quickly, and runs with Lana to the bathroom, but first I see Charlie stop them. He kisses Lana on top of her beautiful curls. She beams, clutching an envelope-sized piece of faded pink nylon fabric, what once was her blankie and now stinks from spoiled milk since she won't allow me to wash it.

"Donny, don't forget to line the seat." He waves his hand in response. Charlie strolls over to my open window, and I am officially awake.

"Good morning, Mrs. P." Leaning in, he adds, "Hi, Miss Beck-a-roo."

Becky answers, "Hello." Her pretty blues are glued to our interaction, her lashes fluttering like a doll's.

"Good morning to you, Mr. Bell. So did you guys have breakfast?"

"No, I thought we'd grab something on the road. I figured we'd have to stop along the way for the kids."

I decide not to mention Lana's new porcelain habit, her fascination with toilets in every house, of every town or city we've visited. And how lately, she's more aware of the mechanism of her kidneys.

Charlie starts humming along with my car radio as it plays *Fly Me to the Moon,* above the whisking sounds of trucks and cars already filling all lanes of the highway. I blush, embarrassed by his attention, and now he's singing real words. I have to look away. He's handsome, yes, nice, yes, and definitely old beyond his years. I want to say: *Show me your birth certificate, Charlie Bell. Prove you didn't live in the '40s—didn't fox-trot to Sinatra at the Paramount.* As we talk, I notice his heart rising and falling through the fabric of his shirt, and then he no longer looks as old—no, not at all.

Donny walks back to the car, carrying Lana. "All aboard!" he yells. This elicits a grin from Paula, who has been sitting in her car eating a donut, the white sugar now clinging to her chin. We wait for Charlie to use the men's room before we hit the road again. I like watching him walk away, quick and decisive. Becky, smelling from grape bubble gum, leans over and kisses me on the cheek, bringing me out of a delicious daze.

Not an hour goes by before Lana threatens to make "something" in her sand pail while we are driving sixty miles per hour. We signal to Charlie and Paula, and begin slowing down at the approach to a combo gas station and Hot Shoppe. We get out of the car, stretch our legs, and decide we might as well find a table, relax, and eat breakfast. Donny and Charlie take our orders and go to stand on line, while Paula and I take the children to what's clearly labeled *Ladies*. Ross, seven, refuses to go in, and sits cross-legged on the damp floor outside the restroom, swirling the propeller of a toy plane.

"Okay," Paula says, "but I'm warning you, don't move!"

"Do you want me to take Ricki in with me and my girls?" I ask. "That way you can stand outside the men's room with Ross." I can't believe she's planning on leaving him here.

"No, thanks," she whispers, "he'd kill me."

Should I be surprised she lets her six-year-old boss her around?

We leave Ross behind and join the line inside the ladies' room. While Ricki hides between Paula's knees, Becky and Lana keep busy depositing coins into a slot machine containing miniature perfumes.

"Okay, girls, we're next." The three of us are sandwiched into the stall. Becky knows the routine and carefully lines the seat with several squares of tissue. Lana sits first and is off the seat in seconds.

"Lana, we stopped for you—maybe you should sit awhile."

"All done," Lana says, pulling up her red Health-Tex bell-bottoms. The floor is strewn with wet squares I must peel from her sneakers.

While we're washing our hands, I scan the bathroom for Paula. I assume she's gone back to the table with her kids, but as I pass the gift shop, I see her, one arm clutching Ricki. Ross is not with her. I look back to the spot where he had slumped down to wait and see a man pacing while smoking a cigarette, most likely waiting for someone in the ladies' room.

"Paula, where's Ross?" I ask, rushing into the gift shop. She is describing Ross to a young woman behind the counter, who shrugs and shakes her head no. I grab the girls' hands, urging them to keep up with my pace. I scan Charlie and Donny's table, hoping Ross is with them, perhaps even hiding underneath.

"Why do you look so harried?" Charlie says. "Did you forget you're on vacation?"

"Paula can't find Ross."

He jumps up, immediately, and is already running when I shout, "She's near the gift shop."

"Mommy," Lana says, "maybe he went away with a stranger."

"I don't think so, honey. Ross is smart, like you and Becky. He would never do that. He'd scream, yell, and kick first. We'll find him. He's probably just lost."

Donny has wrapped up everyone's breakfast, and I grab a couple of the Styrofoam cups. The girls cling to the tail of my blouse while we walk to the front entrance. I look at my watch; it feels like midday, but it's barely eight o'clock. As we approach the entrance, I notice a small crowd huddled together—folks with coffee and looks of consternation, all looking in the same direction: up.

"What's going on?" I ask a young couple, both with shoulder-length hair.

"Man, there's some crazy friggin' kid up there—see, on the overpass?"

"Ed, watch your shit-hole mouth. Can't you see she's got kiddies?"

My terror sensor slides up several notches, and the warm coffee slips out of my hands, splattering across my feet.

"Sorry ma'am, I lost my place. The kid . . . well, he looked like he was going to jump from up there, but something flew right out of his hands. Man, he nearly caused a pileup. The little fucker could have gotten people killed."

I watch, clutching the girls' hands as Paula and Charlie walk Ross down the steep ramp of the overpass, and back to the parking lot.

Charlie yanks Ross's arm, then hauls off and wallops his backside, elevating Ross a foot off the ground. Most onlookers have scattered; those who remain applaud Charlie's choice of physical force. His demeanor remains solidly serious, and I wonder if he hit his boy thinking it might teach him an indelible lesson. When they reach the end of the ramp, Ross buries his head in Paula's stomach. She bends over and rubs his sandy hair. A ponytailed older man hops from the cab of an eighteen-wheeler, and yells something to Charlie. The man crouches down, taps Ross on the shoulder, and hands him the remains of his wooden Cessna.

Minutes later, without a word, each family climbs back into their car. The warm congeniality of the morning has been smashed along with Ross's toy airplane. As car engines begin to roar, stirring the taut silence, Lana, as if waiting for the car to shift gears, announces, once more, "Mommy, I have to . . . !"

We are gathered, finally, on the gravelly driveway, looking down a winding path, which leads to the lake. Cousin George's house is a simple cedar saltbox, more of a beach house, not the house you'd expect to see upstate, tucked behind a wall of pink dogwoods and lilac bushes in full bloom. It reminds me of my grandmother's house, always lush with flowers and honeysuckle, climbing the fence in her backyard, the tiny buds deliciously sweet on my tongue.

Soon Paula and I are in the kitchen unpacking our coolers of food and staples, while Charlie and Donny survey the surroundings to check for possible hazards: old mousetraps, random wires, anything dangerous for curious fingers. They seem to get along nicely, Donny and Charlie; so different, yet complementing each other well. The truth is I never noticed how handy Donny was until now, seeing him around Charlie, who admits to being all thumbs. "Lug wrench? What the hell's a lug wrench?" he'd asked Donny while searching through a box of tools. But when it comes to organizing the kids for a game of Simon Sez outside, on the lawn, Charlie has the energy of a pep-rally coach. He's fast and funny, like an animated cartoon, a sturdy, yet moveable tree. The children climb up his legs, onto his hips, until they are on his shoulders, stroking the top of his head. That's where Lana is now—on top of Charlie's broad shoulders. She is busy rearranging his hair while he laughs heartily out loud.

Ricki and Ross don't seem to mind that Lana has usurped their father. Fortunately, they appear mellowed by the serenity of these new surroundings. I haven't seen them pinch or punch since we arrived.

After a late lunch, both families stroll down the long slate path to the edge of the lake. Donny removes his shoes and socks and dips his feet into the pea-green water.

"Yikes, like a tub of ice!"

Four children stare at him and frown.

"Dad, does that mean we can't go swimming?" Ricki asks Charlie.

Charlie hoists Lana from his shoulders and hands her back to me.

"Don't worry, I'm sure it'll warm up. We just arrived—maybe you'll swim tomorrow."

"Maybe in July," I whisper in Charlie's ear.

"I heard you, Mommy." Lana pouts.

"I know what we can do, Dad," Ricki says. "Let's take a boat ride."

"Yeah, Dad!" says Ross, who's been skimming rocks on the water's surface, sullen since his scolding this morning. I've tried smiling at him, but he scowls and turns away. I'm not used to children not liking me, and this boy has sent me a clear message.

Barely visible among dozens of bent cattails, sits the one and only rowboat, tied loosely to the dock by a rope caked with algae.

"Charlie, why don't you and Donny take the kids out and we'll sit here," Paula suggests. She has already settled into an antique white wrought iron bench with a matching tea table. She's even paler in sunlight, resembling a Victorian doll, a fine collectible made of porcelain.

"I want to stay too, Mom," Becky says, with the same look she gets when she doesn't want to go to someone's party.

"Are you sure, Beck?" I think she wants to tell me something but is too polite to snub Paula. I've taught her it's not nice to tell secrets in front of others.

"Come on, Becky, we're just going to row right there to those trees. It's not that far," Donny says.

Becky shakes her head no. She does not like the Bells' children one bit. Lana, taking care of her older sister, says, "I'll stay with you, Becky. We can pick flowers for our new house!" Becky beams, and they are off, running up a hill, Becky tripping a few times, looking back at me with her sweet, self-conscious smile.

"That's my Becky girl. Cute and *klutzy* . . . takes after her daddy, now that I think of it."

"Gee, I didn't picture Donny clumsy," Paula says, with just a hint of disappointment.

"Haven't you noticed? He's probably what you'd call accident-prone."

"Oh, I guess it's a good thing then that Charlie was once a champion swimmer," Paula boasts.

"That makes me feel so much better." We share a laugh as we wave to the kids, Charlie, and Donny, who have managed to undo the thick rope mooring the boat to the dock. Charlie's holding the oars, and I watch his broad back fan in and out, as effortless as an accordion.

"Watch out for sharks," I yell, instantly sorry when I see the worried look on Ross's face. Donny shoots me his scornful look, but Charlie doesn't seem frazzled. He lets Ross have a go at rowing, which plants a huge smile on the boy's face.

Knee-deep in a dense field covered with Queen Anne's lace, Becky and Lana wave from their spot on the hill. The sun's rays blur the edges of their delicate bodies. I should be sketching them now—this precious moment of their young sisterhood. I imagine them in pastel shades, lines barely defined, like in the paintings of Mary Cassatt. Dandelions stick out from behind their ears, and their shirts, stretched out in front of them, cradle their collection.

Ross's and Ricki's voices echo over the lake, cutting the silence shared with the distant *knock, knock* of a woodpecker.

"I bet they'll sleep well tonight," I say.

Paula stands to look after the rowboat. A cool breeze sweeps over us from the lake, a reminder the day is slipping by. I'm looking forward to the evening, but I'm scared as well. I daydream a snapshot of the four of us, a blurred image of us laughing together, then quickly becoming silent, as if struck with an awareness of a powerful allure. I can't hide the fact that the moment our car turned into the driveway, and I heard the sound of crunching pebbles, I had the piercing thought that, after this weekend, nothing might ever be the same.

The children are asleep in the largest bedroom, all exhausted from a day of exploring and discovery. The girls on two single beds; Ricki and her brother, Ross, on the floor in sleeping bags. Using several batik pillows, they've constructed a barrier, which Becky and Lana dare not cross.

Outside, Charlie leans against the porch's railing to face us, while Donny sits squeezed between Paula and me on a wooden swing. I'm uncomfortable sitting on the swing with Paula and Donny and resist the natural urge to lean in to Donny. Charlie pauses, deeply inhales a joint, and hands it to Donny.

I notice a healthy tinge of pink clinging to Charlie's cheekbones. I think he's trying not to look at me. The night air is crisp and the evening sky illuminates with a creamy streak of stars forecasting another beautiful day. Charlie hands the joint to me but I shake my head no. I am too jumpy to smoke.

"You sure?" he asks, his voice hoarse while smoke escapes his lips. I nod and he passes the joint to Donny. We have been talking about our childhood—sharing like kids do at Show and Tell. It's Charlie's turn. He looks around, shuffles his feet, and takes a dramatic deep breath before speaking.

"Yeah, well my father, unfortunately, dropped dead at forty-nine—two days before my college graduation." There's a block of silence, out of respect, or not knowing what to say.

"That must have been tough on all of you," I respond.

"Yes, but it was hardest on my little sister. She was only five, and my folks had just split up."

"How did your mother handle being alone with a small child?" I ask. Paula sighs deeply as if slightly bored. I wonder how often she's heard this story.

"Her parents moved in with us. They were very supportive."

"Oh, was that your Papa Carl?" I recall Charlie's fondness for his grandfather.

Charlie's mood changes and he smiles brightly. "Yes, he took care of everything from then on. Carl was a tough, stand-up, stand-in kind of guy."

"Was it a bitter divorce?" Donny asks, taking it in, stirring ingredients in his invisible cauldron.

"Ugly, if another woman is involved," Charlie says, "especially when there's not enough cash to go around."

"It's getting chilly," Paula mumbles. And we stare at her, having already forgotten her presence. Without hesitating, Donny pulls off his fisherman's sweater, the one I'd knitted during the winter. I decided not to be superstitious and gave it to Donny, instead of keeping it for myself. Now, he, accidentally, jabs my ribs as he places the sweater around Paula's shoulders.

Charlie stares at me. "Alex? Are *you* cold?"

"Actually yes, I think I'll go inside. I better put the dishes in the washer before they attract bugs. This *is* the country, right?"

"Come on, let me help. Hey, you guys need anything?" Charlie asks, holding the screen door for me.

"Nope, everything's fine." Donny slides closer to Paula. In the mustard glow of the porch light, they look like boy-girl hillbilly dolls with their denim legs bent, dangling from the swing. Once inside, Charlie's close at my heels, making me shaky. He tries to distract me by going after a horsefly buzzing noisily around my head. I jerk backward to avoid the fly, and fall into Charlie, nearly slamming into his face.

"Steady girl," he says, grabbing my shoulders.

"There, there he is, get him, get him." I'm about to give Charlie the fly swatter when his hand shoots like a rocket in the air, then clamps around the unfortunate insect. He opens his hand to show me the carnage before flinging the mangled fly in the garbage.

"I can't believe you did that."

"Something I picked up from Papa Carl, who had the fastest hands in the Bronx."

"Oh?"

"Once I saw him grab a rat with his bare hands and smash him against the basement wall." Charlie appears sweet and boyish as he pantomimes the act while washing his hands.

"Please, not another word. I'm terrified of rodents. We'd be sitting and eating dinner when suddenly there'd be this loud snap. My brothers ran from the table to peek under the stove, but I'd already disappeared to my room."

"Okay, okay, let's change the subject. How about this? Alex, do you realize there isn't a dishwasher anywhere in this kitchen?" Charlie has seen me opening and closing cabinets, assuming Cousin George's summer home was modernly equipped. I close my eyes and lean against the sink and giggle. I haven't smoked; maybe I have a contact high.

Charlie grabs a dish towel, does that man thing—the annoying snap—and begins to dry.

"You wash. Paula complains I leave the dishes grungy."

"Well, I heard you were once a terrific waiter—how you charmed her when you first met."

"Did she mention how my friends and I treated the people who nudged us all summer long, asking for more bread, extra slices of cake, or the end cut of a prime rib?"

"No, but I'm sure you'll tell me." I'm fascinated watching Charlie's animated face. Yes, he's an actor, but I'm truly enjoying the show.

Charlie takes the damp dish towel and puts it over his arm, imitating a waiter. He pushes me, his only audience, gently into a ladder-back chair.

"Ma'am, is there anything else you'd like this evening? Perhaps a piece of pickled herring?"

"Oh no, no, I just couldn't," I answer.

"And Mr. Pearl," Charlie says to an empty chair, "let me tell you how nice it has been serving you and your hubbie this summer, if you don't mind my saying so." Charlie pauses. "Then the guy would hand me an envelope. I'd run to the kitchen and tear it open because I had loans up the wazoo. Our tips were supposed to offset the lousy wages we received. Tips were everything!"

"And what happened if this Mr. Pearl, with the beautiful wife, happened to be less than generous in the tip department?"

"Glad you asked," Charlie says, pulling up the chair and sitting so close I can smell the dizzying smoke on his breath. "It was usually the last night of the season, so none of us cared. We'd smile a wide, Cheshire grin, like this, and say, 'Oh, Mr. Pearl, *fuck you very much!*' We said it quickly. You know, as if speaking in Chinese: Fuck you very much, fuck you very much."

"You didn't?"

"Absolutely, and they'd say 'Charlie, ah, what was that you said?' We then leaned over really close to their face to enunciate, 'Thank you very much.' But the wives, they figured you'd been stiffed. Some tried to make up for their stingy men by slipping us extra cash. To this day, when I have lunch with my friend, Ivan, now a successful anti-trust attorney who'd also waited tables, and *our* waiter starts thanking us, profusely, we can't help but crack up. We know exactly what the other is thinking."

Charlie finishes his story, then lifts a strand of my hair and tucks it behind my ear. I turn away, but he tilts my chin, forcing me to look directly in his eyes. I'm aware of the deep quiet, and then I hear the squeaking of the porch swing just a few yards away. What is Donny doing now? Is he having a warm, lovely chat? Charlie takes my hands, rubs the palms, places them together, and sandwiches them between his own. I wonder what would happen if I screamed. All it might take is a loud, witchy shriek to end whatever it is that has begun. I picture all the wineglasses shattering and the children waking and rubbing their eyes. I see Charlie and Paula gathering their belongings, including Ricki and Ross, the children who hate my children, who my children hate more, and everyone running out of this house into the mothy, chill evening.

My heart is throbbing as if red balloons are trapped in my chest. *Can he hear it,* I wonder, *the slow hiss as they deflate, one by one, to float to him?* Charlie reaches for my face. His soft lips brush my eyelids and move to my mouth. My jaw relaxes, and I feel the tip of his tongue gently play with mine. Then, harder, it darts in and out of my mouth, tickling my palate, sliding over my teeth. He is holding my head so gently, his hands covering my ears.

"I want to hold you closer," he says. But, I can barely hear him.

"I'm frightened," I say, all of me quaking. "This isn't right."

"Can't you see what's been going on? It's not just us." Charlie looks over his shoulder and gestures toward the porch.

"What's that?" I ask, hearing the sound of a car's ignition turning over. Through the screen door I watch as Donny backs out of the driveway. The dark silhouette of Paula sits stiffly beside him. I think of waving goodbye. *Have a great time, you two, and don't forget to write.* "Where the hell are they going?" I ask, my teeth chattering.

"I'd guess somewhere to be alone. Why? Does that bother you?"

I shake my head no. But I'm not sure I mean it. Anger, fear, and worry are rolled up in a hard ball, pressing against my belly. Am I a participant or onlooker? I am not used to going along with things, especially important things—things of multilayered consequence. But I came here, didn't I? I am not exactly *Saint Alex*.

Charlie locks the front door, making the house instantly *our* house.

"Follow me," he says, leading me by the hand. We walk silently down the hallway past the bedroom where the sounds of children's nasal breathing rise and fall like fluttering moths outside the window. I hesitate before entering a small alcove that's barely a room, appearing larger than its size because of the sloping skylight cut like a piece of pie into the beamed ceiling. I hear the faint click of Charlie locking the door.

Below the enveloping white light of a full crystal moon, we stand together as hopeful as a young bride and groom. As Charlie draws me closer, I glance up at the moon, its face a kind but imposing deity, and ask permission for what I am about to do.

"I'm not good at this," he whispers, fumbling with the tiny seed buttons on my blouse.

"Neither am I," I stammer. A button pops off and my eyes follow while it rolls lazily across the floor. Am I innocent because I've been taken by surprise, and not planned easier clothes? I finish unbuttoning while his soft lips cover my neck and the blouse slips from my shoulders. So, this is how it happens, not difficult at all, not once you begin. My breasts throb as he kisses them; my nipples rubber hard against the silky fabric of Charlie's shirt. Like ice skaters we glide to the darkest corner of the room, both of us shy and hovering. In seconds Charlie stands before me naked, his arms loose and long beside his hips. He is so angular, so manly. I can see the outline of his body hair and, even in the darkness, how the moonlight clings to his shoulders. He steps forward and reaches for me. I balance myself on my toes and toss my panties into a corner. Aware of my dampness, I'm shy when his searching fingers touch me. I guide him with my hand, feeling him pulsate and thicken. We are still standing, and it is nearly perfect except for my nerves—totally electrified.

"Alex." To hear him say my name is startling. I have the anxious thought that he's moving too quickly. I want to hold him here as long as possible. I need to think some more, to decide this for myself.

"Wait," I say. But Charlie lifts me, and I wrap my legs around his waist, my back braced against the rough pine wall. Every part of me that touches Charlie springs to life, each lonely spot he kisses—the side of my neck, underneath my shaggy hair. I will never, ever cut my hair. I start to cry, a whimper really, realizing how certain I'd been that I'd never feel anything like this again. The free spirit in me, my sexuality, has not vanished as I had thought.

"It's okay, don't cry."

"I want you," I say, shocked at my words, so guttural I don't recognize the sound. I am lost memorizing the saltiness that drips from Charlie's cheeks to mine. "Now," I breathe into his neck. I am all wanting. Then some distraction, a glint of light off a shooting star, stops me, makes me shiver. Charlie pulls back, then collapses into me, his hands braced against the wall. There's that familiar feeling of emptiness, rushing in, when I cease feeling human and more like a machine. He cradles me, still hard, pressing against the curve of my hip. His fingers brush my mouth, and I smell us both—the warm musky scent of our lovemaking. I face the wall pressing my buttocks against him. With one hand Charlie cups my breast, the other moves between my damp thighs, until we slump to the floor like tired marionettes. We crawl to the middle of the room, the straw rug skinning our knees, to find that one pure patch of light, all the promise in the face of a grand and watchful moon on this—our first night.

I open my eyes the next morning to find Donny sitting at the edge of my bed with a ridiculous grin pasted across his face. He reminds me of my favorite children's show of the '50s—*Howdy Doody*. Donny is dressed in his shiny Ban-Lon shirt, the gift bestowed on him by Paula, which I'd forgotten to pack for Charlie. I'm thrilled now that these two men in my life won't be matching.

"Where's Charlie?" I ask, sitting up so fast that I'm lightheaded. He shrugs. It's not important. He doesn't care. I back into the metal headboard, trying to get farther away from Donny. All I have on is my rumpled blouse and panties. I'm bombarded by thoughts of last night. Donny leaving, Charlie and I walking down the hall, Charlie's lips on my neck, Charlie falling asleep inside me. I pull the scratchy Americana quilt up to my chin, feeling enormous modesty with Donny. "Where are the children?"

"Playing outside. Paula's watching them while I fix breakfast." He sees me bristle; he knows I'd never leave the girls alone, especially with Paula, who left Ross sitting outside a public bathroom on the turnpike. Donny leans over and kisses my forehead. My eyes shrink from his. I see my jeans on the back of a chair and remember that Charlie and I moved into this bedroom before falling asleep.

"So, tell me, how was it?" Donny tries to look pleasant, but he's scrutinizing like a doctor checking for symptoms. "I mean, you know—did you hear harps and all that crap?" I expected he'd ask if I was feeling okay. This is so crazy that part of me wants to laugh in his face.

"I have a small question of my own."

"Yes?"

"Where did you and Paula go last night?"

"Just down the road. There's this little place, a dump really, but I thought it might be better if, you know, both couples got the chance to be alone."

"That was very thoughtful."

"Yeah, I think it made things a lot less awkward. So, come on . . . share . . . how'd it go?"

"I won't talk to you about this, Donny, so please don't ask. From now on, it's private—at least to me."

"Well, I guess you're right, but I'd tell you anything you wanted to know about Paula and me. Anything. Frankly, I was a little—"

"No! That's okay." My hand goes up to stop him. I turn and stare at a red-framed print of *American Gothic* tilted on the wall, which is both comical and soothing.

There's a knock at the bedroom door. Charlie, smiling broadly, walks in, offering me a steamy mug of coffee. His expression changes and his eyes turn darker as they settle upon Donny's curved back, his hand claiming ownership of my bare kneecap.

"Hey, we're talking," Donny says, raising an arm to block him. But Charlie ignores him and walks over and kisses me full on the lips. I can't look at Donny. I need to open a window and get some air. Instead, I gulp hot coffee.

"How'd you sleep?" Charlie asks. There's an awkward silence. Donny waits while Charlie and I look at each other. Our fingers clasp together naturally, as if they were north and south magnets.

"Better get back to my omelets," Donny says. He walks out and closes the door behind him.

Charlie kisses me again; this time tenderly. But with daylight comes the reality of four children and their parents. We have each taken a step toward someplace not on the map, and the destination remains unclear.

"Is something wrong?" he asks.

"That's a loaded question. Did you know they went to a motel last night?"

"I won't lie to you. Yes, I knew Donny made plans, but it was never a definite thing. I told him weeks ago I wasn't about to force myself on you. We'd talked once or twice about the stirrings that were obvious among all of us. And when he pressed for an answer, I was open about my deep attraction for you."

"So, it was a setup and prearranged, part of Donny's house of games. It all feels so . . . so clinical, so by the book." I fling the blanket off me, then, realizing I'm nearly naked, I cover up again. Charlie grins at my sudden display of modesty.

"Alex, this, you, me—no one could have planned."

Charlie squeezes on the edge of the bed. "Look at me, please," he whispers. His head is next to mine, and the aroma of strong coffee is the only thing that seems real. "I'll do whatever I have to do to know you, to have you in my life. I don't give a rat's ass about Donny's plans— let him plan away. Some things just happen, Alex. I knew I wanted you the moment I laid eyes on you."

"Well, I should have stopped the whole damn thing. I could have you know. All I had to do was say S-T-O-P!"

"But you didn't?" Charlie stares at me, coyly, allowing me time to study his rugged face, and all the sharp angles still so new. He's the only man I have ever slept with besides Donny. Me, Alex Pearl, an almost, but not quite, virgin bride. I bet Charlie would be scared to know how important that little fact makes him, how I can't take what's happened between us lightly. And, as if I've done it a thousand times, I place my arms around his neck to straighten the collar of his denim shirt—a shirt his wife has, most likely, washed and ironed.

FIFTEEN

On the day I return from enrolling the girls in Miss Susannah's Country Day Camp, Donny comes speeding around our cul-de-sac, jumps the Belgian block curb, and stops short, nearly mowing down all the hydrangeas on our lawn. A mound of sod sits piled up like an escalator, revealing the russet earth below.

I shield my face from the flying dirt, as I rush to meet him. Sue, across the street, looks up from her pruning and waves, as though this were an ordinary occurrence: husbands driving over lawns in the middle of the afternoon. Having planned to finish another painting, I'd only just lifted two gallons of paint out of my trunk and carried them to the garage. I shudder, imagining what might have happened had Donny actually driven up our driveway with the same lack of control: HUSBAND NAILS WIFE AND CHILDREN TO GARAGE WALL WITH COMPANY CAR. ALL SPLATTERED IN BENJAMIN MOORE BUNGALOW BEIGE. MARIJUANA SUSPECTED!

Becky and Lana come running out from the house.

"Daddy's home!" Lana squeals. They stop dead in their tracks. Their hands are glued to their cheeks, like little old ladies in disbelief.

I thank God a hundred times. Just seconds before, I'd sent Becky and Lana into the house to wash their sticky hands. It was the first time I allowed them to eat Popsicles in the car. Why did I say yes this time and no dozens of times before?

Donny's early summer tan has faded to chartreuse. He paces our lawn with his hands folded on top of his head, inspecting and tabulating the damage.

"You better sit down, Donny. Forget the stupid lawn."

"Hi, Daddy! We're going to camp again, real soon." Lana is jumping from leg to leg, like she has to use the bathroom.

"Girls, please go inside. We'll be right in." I turn to Donny, looping my arm through his. "Are you okay?"

"Jesus, I don't know what the hell happened. My foot just slipped off the brake as I was making the turn."

"It's okay. I'm sure this stuff can be laid back into place."

"Yeah, well, I certainly hope so, because the gardener might have to go. My division was closed down today." While Donny stares at the disheveled grass, his words begin to register, first in my chest and then my brain.

"Does that mean you're fired? How can you be fired if your father owns the company?" I try not to show my fear, although there's a part of me that wants to lie down on the ruined lawn and scream: *Do we have to sell the house—are we now poor?* Instead, what I finally say is: "Tell me what happened."

"I've been demoted, big time. Pop says we're losing a shitload of money. After two years our catalogue business is still in the red."

Red's bad, I remind myself. "But why now, why not give it some more time? Catalogues are big. We get dozens in the mail."

"To stay alive, we need to develop products that are less costly for the mass market. Women are tired of all that fancy lace, hard bones, and polyester. It's become a thing of the past, like the corset. All the trades are saying that the demand is for natural fibers in all clothing, including lingerie. Women want only cotton," Donny tells me, but I know his speech was coined by Ben. Overwhelmed with guilt, I bite my lower lip. I am wearing yellow cotton shorts with a striped cotton tee, and matching cotton socks. Underneath the tee is a stretchy, cotton bra I'd bought at JC Penney for $3.99. Actually, it's one of those new "jogging" bras that are great under T-shirts.

"So, did he or didn't he fire you?"

"No. And that would've been a blessing. Since Uncle Louie is retiring to Florida, I'll be taking over his position in teen lingerie, which consists of a limited line of day-of-the-week panties, and a training bra we make in just two sizes: zero and the more hopeful, plus one."

"Well, that sounds okay, Donny, doesn't it? I bet you'll enjoy something new and different. Hey, maybe you can add your own signature sports bra to the line."

I envision Donny during the busy fall market week, among a bevy of shy, emaciated teenage models. He is pleasant and warm, eager to stop their shivering modesty, to put a smile on their pure, innocent faces. I glance down again at the damage to our lawn, feeling a fresh wave of annoyance.

Donny's face is pale, his eyes red-rimmed. "The company can't afford to pay me what it did before." These words, although anticipated, send my heart thundering. I think about the check I'd just written to Miss Susannah.

"Maybe I can help out by teaching again, or I can try to pick up additional stores, sell higher-priced painted items. If we have to move, we'll move," I say in a whisper. My eyes scan the budding hydrangeas, the bees hovering over the purple wisteria vines that border the driveway.

"Let's shelve that discussion for now. It's been a shitty day and now this," Donny says, toeing a piece of the butchered grass. Across the street, Sue looks up from her gardening again. She's weeding a patch of dandelions, my guess, hoping to pluck a clue or two from our conversation. Only last week, her even nosier husband, Norman, on his way to a fishing trip, saw us fly into our driveway at 4:00 a.m. As Norm crossed the road to greet us with fishing rod in hand, he reminded me of Moses on route to Sinai. Our garage door sealed in the nick of time, closing out Norman's neighborly curiosity. What could I have possibly invented as an excuse to be out cruising at this hour? *It was a trip to the emergency room. Really! We thought Donny was having a gall bladder attack. Turns out it was gas.*

"Camp starts next week!" I scream across the street, startling her. "Pain in the ass," I whisper to Donny, which makes him grin. "Smile at Sue, Donny. Let her think everything's fine," I say, through clenched teeth.

"Oh, Alex, don't forget your paint can," Sue yells back. I manage a limp thumbs-up.

Before hearing Donny's news, I'd been strangely euphoric, all day, while chauffeuring around Becky and Lana. Something intoxicating had been pumping through my veins, telling me I could do anything—learn an aria, dance the tarantella, fly a Piper Cub, hey, possibly start another painting. And of all days, today, I had the idea to drive over to the central district to enter my name into the pool of substitute teachers for Wheatley Heights and surrounding school districts. Though two permanent positions are opening up for an art teacher, one in the elementary level and one for junior high, subbing would be more manageable, what with Lana starting kindergarten come September.

I wonder if any of my actions caused this bad luck for Donny. Could I have jinxed him? I wish I could focus on the positive aspect of doing something good for myself, but Donny stands before me shell-shocked. I used to be terrific at helping him, but my heart has forgotten how.

"Come in, I'll make some iced tea." I curl my pinky around his and lead him inside as if he's blindfolded. He sits down and stares at his hands, hands soiled from sewing machinery and the dark earth. The girls have gone out in the back; they are hanging upside down on the swing set like happy chimps.

"Have you mentioned any of this to Paula?" Before he gets the chance to respond, I give myself the litmus test for envy. But I've gotten used to their daily conversations, what Donny calls *checking in*.

"Yes, she feels awful for us."

It's the "us" in his answer that rattles me. Although Paula's sleeping with Donny, she can easily separate when it serves her. Why should she worry about her lover's finances? I wonder if she's shared the details of Charlie's big summer bonus with her lover. Knowing Donny, he'd want to hear every minute detail. Painful as it might be, he'd measure himself, drawing the conclusion that Charlie is on his way to becoming his own man—one of those terrifying creatures who sometimes haunt my husband in the middle of the night.

We have established a queer ritual, the four of us. Whenever we gather, as we do now at the Bells, we sit and attempt ordinary conversation like most couples who have become good friends. Except no one sitting on this faded blue damask couch, with plastic army men stuck between the cushions, is another's bosom buddy. We know why we're here: each, going through the motions, aching for the small talk to end so we can break off into our new couple configuration. Ricki and Ross are visiting Paula's parents for the weekend, and Donny and I have booked our sitter, Agnes, until Sunday morning.

Tonight's matter at hand is Donny's business troubles. For now, we are properly paired beside our respective spouses, and I wonder if there's something in these charades we play that ignites desire. Paula's eyes are misty, deeply sympathetic, while Charlie's are pensive and respectfully inattentive to mine. Why does everyone look so forlorn when I'm feeling high? I haven't been concentrating on anything anyone is saying, even though they are talking about my life or, at the very least, my financial future. As I reach for my glass of wine, Charlie's eyes shift to look at me. He leans over to wipe a drop of liquid on my chin. I can't wait to be alone with him; words buzz around me, in and out, in and out. *Oh, come on,* I wish I could say. This chatter is one big stall—an attempt at expressing sincerity and friendship.

"What I feel the worst about is that the catalogue division was wholly mine," Donny finishes, staring at the linty carpet. Like me, Paula's slacked off on her vacuuming.

"Believe me, I understand how you feel," Charlie says, removing his pipe. "It's why I've always wanted to be a partner and not an associate. I've had nine years of people looking over my damn shoulder. It would be terrific, one day, to have a real piece of the pie."

"Donny, won't the business eventually be yours anyway? I mean, you know, when it's handed over to the next generation?" Paula interrupts, in her naturally soothing tone. It comes across like an ordinary question, not one rooted in power or money about Donny's rightful inheritance—or his financial prospects for the future. Yet she sounds as if she's given this some thought. I shake out of the haze, knowing it's time to pay better attention.

"What do you think, Alex?" Charlie asks, startling me.

"Well, given the choice, I believe Donny would like to make his living some other way entirely," I say, surprising myself above all. I direct my response to Paula, laying claim to Donny. She thinks she

knows Donny, but she doesn't. Not really. I'm the one with whom
he's shared his dreams, wishes, and every failed expectation for
the past seven years. I lean back in the sofa cushions, breathing
rapidly.

Charlie squirms in his seat, but Donny looks long and hard at me.
It's such a weird moment. I feel as though I'm betraying someone but
not sure whom it might be. There's a hint of melancholy in Donny's
eyes that pains me. He jumps up and rubs his hands together, signaling he's had enough of this conversation. Some tense moments pass,
what I might remember decades from now, when I expect Donny to
walk over and yank me off the couch. To say: *You know, kiddo, it's
time for you and me to go home.* But instead he glides shoeless into
Paula's kitchen, familiar turf, opens a cabinet, and fills an old jelly
glass with water.

"Would anyone like something to drink?" Paula asks, but I know
she's acting on cue, responding to Donny's wide-eyed glance. Some
deafening pause must be telling her he wants her near him. As if he's
sent a code: *Let's get to the fucking, already.*

It is Paula he needs now, not me. I disconnect once more, my brain
ignoring the tugging inside my chest. Is this my designated time to
choose? One final shot at *carpe diem*? I watch as Donny and Paula
move about the kitchen. It has become their kitchen. I don't budge.
There is something so powerful in watching your life shift before
your eyes, and the decision not to resist—a quiet resignation to sit
back and let things evolve.

Minutes after making love, I am staring up at the water-stained
ceiling tiles in Charlie's partially finished basement. A musty odor

permeates the mismatched sheets and pillowcases on the sunken sofa bed, making me sneeze many times in a row. Try as I might, I can't get used to the strangeness of this home—a home shaped and defined by the people living and breathing within these walls: a reticent and withdrawn wife and mother, a traveling father and part-time husband, which just might have something to do with the result of their unruly children. The colors here are not my colors. The aromas are not my aromas.

Yet I lie here as if I no longer have a choice, as if someone has chained me to the torturous bed springs. I am waiting for the next set of rules, for someone to designate and give me an order. By nature, I am a prideful person, but I have long buried my pride. It feels like I'm living the life of a stowaway—adrift between two foreign lands. Never unpacking, I live out of an old, weathered trunk—a trunk missing its destination tag.

A blast of air from the ceiling duct blows on my face, and I pull the damp sheet over my head. I try to imagine Charlie and me together in the waking hours, enjoying the small rituals that make up a day. But it is doubtful he will be taking me for a ride in his car anytime soon, or out for a neighborhood stroll.

Soon I begin thinking of Donny's problems at work, wondering if Louise will jump in as the buffer, making sure Ben's decision to close Donny's division won't disintegrate the family. Next, in my head, I replay Rona's call from yesterday, how she berated me for neglecting her. While she talked, I sat at the kitchen table thumbing through the photos from the trip to Carmel. I stopped to look long and hard at Donny's best shot of Charlie and me: a sharp image of us sitting on the porch swing, the setting sun emblazoned in our faces—eyes squinting from its blinding glow. Charlie's arm is around my shoulder, his cheek pressed against mine. What was Donny thinking when he snapped this picture? Did he wonder, even for an instant, if he'd lost me?

I copy Charlie's raspy and uneven breathing, hoping the rhythms will lull me to sleep. But right as I'm dozing off, I hear the unmistakable double flush from the bathroom directly above my head. Donny's classy signal—it's time for us, The Pearls, to go home. Hopping into my clothing, I ready myself for the five-minute road trip to my comfortable bed on Daisy Lane. *I better move,* I tell myself, *or I'll miss my ride.*

"I'm going now," I whisper, brushing against Charlie's warm cheek.

"Hmm, kiss, please," he says, eyes squeezed shut.

A bird, most likely trapped, chirps in a wild frenzy against the casement window. I'm tempted to tuck myself inside Charlie's furry warmth and pretend I'm a thousand miles away. But there's this guy at the top of the stairs waiting for me to find my sandals. In his hand are the set of keys to *our* house. I hear the faint jingle, the impatient way he clears his throat, pressing me to hurry. And for reasons still vague to me, I let him lead me, once more, into the pitch darkness of the night.

While Donny wipes dew off our car windows, I slump down in the passenger seat, not that anyone will see me. Who in their right mind strolls around at this hour? Donny belches a nasty odor, and I roll down my window without uttering a word. Glancing out, I notice an orangey glow in the sky hovering in the vicinity of our neighborhood. I blink, thinking my tired eyes are failing me. A new smell fills the car—the aroma of burning leaves, familiar and more pungent.

"Donny, do you smell that?" My heart pounds while I think: *No! It's summer, there are leaves on every tree. Becky. Lana. God, oh, God.*

"Please hurry. Something's wrong."

I lunge forward, my breastbone pressing into the dashboard. As we approach the turn onto Daisy, I hear a bunch of voices bellowing instructions—a chorus of commotion. Then I see the trucks: fire trucks lined up and blocking Daisy Lane, our street. I am out of the car, running like a rabid dog chasing its tail.

There are obstacles like thick rubber hoses and puddles of water streaming alongside the curb. Donny abandons our car, and as he catches up to me, I hear him yell, "Alex, look, there they are! It's okay, honey. They're fine."

Standing on our front lawn, wrapped in pink summer quilts, are our two baby girls. They lean against Agnes's knees, gazing up at the arc of light, what I'd first noticed in the sky. Donny and I scoop Becky and Lana into our arms and hold them tighter than anything we've held in our lives.

From our spot on the soaked grass, we see an entire neighborhood lining the sidewalk, all engaged in rapid, high-pitched chatter. A few, known to be sourpusses, are actually laughing, which puts me at ease. Most folks are wearing bedclothes except for Donny and me, who look as if we're on our way out for a lovely evening. Someone points toward Jake and Ellen's, but their house is blocked so I can't see a thing. The smell permeates the air as if the whole neighborhood is sampling the same putrid fertilizer.

"It stinks, Mommy." Lana's fingers go back in her mouth, as she rests her head on my shoulder.

"Everyone else in the world was sleeping, Mommy, where were you?" Becky pulls away from my side; her face puffy and tear-streaked. I can't answer my own child. Agnes appears shaken, and I ask if she wants to go home.

"I'm okay, just tired," she says.

"What happened? And why didn't you call us?"

"I was afraid to take the time. As soon as I heard the sirens and looked outside, I gathered up the girls."

I grab Agnes close to me and kiss the top of her head. "Yes, yes, of course, you did the right thing. Thank you!"

Donny runs back from across the street after talking to Norm. If anyone would hound out the details, it would be Norm.

"There was a fire at Jake and Ellen's," Donny says, "and big trouble."

"What? Are they okay?"

"Better bring the girls inside," he says.

As if on cue, Agnes begins leading the girls back inside our house. The girls clasp Agnes's hands and push their bodies into her hips. All I can think is my fourteen-year-old babysitter is more responsible than me.

"Jake's kids got into their stuff," Donny says, moving closer.

"*The* stuff?"

"They're saying they got their hands on a cigarette lighter and lit up Jake's entire supply."

"I can't believe it. Are his kids all right?" I ask.

"They are all in shock, but luckily no one was hurt. Norm says their downstairs is totally wrecked, and one more thing . . . the police have taken Jake in for questioning."

"I bet Norm had a smile on his face when he told you that."

"Actually, he did, but I think Norm's one of the many feeling a contact high. Look at these people. They're stoned and don't know it. Jake did have an awful lot of stash. He's lucky it went up in smoke, better than getting busted," Donny says.

"But he was busted, Donny. His own kids busted him."

I can't get Becky's scolding words out of my head, nor the censorious look on her six-year-old face. I wasn't there for her when she needed me most.

Two hours later Lana cries out, having soaked her sheets and comforter. I dash to her room, but she is already standing in my doorway, stroking her pink blankie.

"I want Daddy to change me," Lana says, surprising me.

"Wait here, pumpkin." I wake up Donny and remind him to make sure he tells Lana, "It's no big deal. This happens to all children once in a while. Soon it'll stop, she'll see." He carries her to our bed so she can kiss me again. She has the sweetest devilish smile plastered to her face, proud she's stolen moments alone with both her mother and father. For the first time in months, I feel safe and content, as if I have everything I have ever wanted.

Only later, when I start to drift back to sleep, do I realize that Agnes, asleep downstairs in our den, never heard Lana's last cry, which could have awakened the dead.

Since all the changes at work, Donny seems more reticent and withdrawn. We hardly speak at all, except about the children. He's been getting home earlier and earlier. Today's excuse is: "The air-conditioning broke down in the factory, and besides, tomorrow starts the three-day July Fourth weekend." But he doesn't hang around for long. Donny has two wives now—Paula Bell and me. The cool blue bleakness of Paula's living room has become one of his refuges. After barbequing our dinner and playing a distracted game of Old Maid with Becky, he hops in the shower and, before long, he's gone. Donny's like a fly that favors a certain spot on the screen but flees as soon as the window is open.

I'm brushing my hair up in a ponytail when he steps out of the shower, wraps himself in a towel, and sits at the edge of our bed.

His chest is red and blotchy, his auburn hair glistening. As if it were winter and not July, Donny blows into both hands, then moans. Is he too tired for tonight's trip to Paula's? Maybe he's worn himself out from marathon whiffle ball with Ricki and Ross. With Charlie traveling so much, Donny has taken on extra responsibility, evolving into a type of surrogate father. He's convinced he can teach the Bells' kids to fight without using their limbs. I've mentioned it is not his job.

"Are you okay?" I ask, putting on a fresh coat of peachy lipstick.

"No, actually, I feel like crap."

I sit down on the edge of our bed next to Donny, smelling his soapy flesh. I notice his stomach bulging over the bath towel. He turns his face toward me, his eyes sunken and red. Tears cling to his lashes like miniature icicles. And my hand reaches out, as if to catch them, ready to shore up the dam.

"Pop made Karl the new plant manager today. I'm a division manager now, that's it."

My arm automatically drapes around Donny's shoulder. "I'm so sorry. I know how bad you must feel."

"Yeah, it sucks," he says, through quivering lips. It's been so long since I've seen him cry—in fact, not since Becky's birth. I run my fingers through his rusty hair. We sit quietly for a few minutes until we hear Lana and Becky arguing, tripping up the stairs, heading for our room. And somehow I know this is a scene that I will always remember—the two of us, sitting here like this, together on our marital bed, the same mattress we'd tested years ago at Macy's, both of us giggling while faking sleep. The moment comes starkly, like a downpour from a blackened summer sky: I realize I had once wholly loved him—both the boy and the man.

"You don't have to go, Donny. Stay with us now, if you'd like."

"I promised I'd teach Ross how to fly his new kite. They're

expecting me." Donny stands and walks to his closet, where he grabs a pair of faded jeans.

"What about the things you've promised Becky and Lana?" I try hard to say this softly, and without accusation.

"I better go while it's light outside," he says, zipping his jeans and turning away from me, what he's never done before.

"Right, just go." I jump up from the edge of the bed. I don't want to sit here and watch Donny dress, something from which I once derived pleasure.

In the hallway I find the girls crouched on the floor, sharing a snack-sized bag of Cheetos, their hands and mouths smudged orange. I usher them to the bathroom and fill the tub, watching a stream of bubbles spill over and onto the tile.

"Is Daddy going out again, Mommy?" Lana asks.

"Don't ask that question," Becky says. "It will make Mommy mad."

SIXTEEN

We are together in our den listening to the new album by Queen. The music resounds, full and majestic, making me strangely jubilant. I take the green glass bong from Charlie and gulp a blast of cotton candy air—the grass, part of a hefty supply from Jake, which we plan to demolish immediately. Even though Jake got lucky when all but a few ounces went up in smoke, his one prior arrest has him, once again, under investigation. Charlie, terrified what a drug arrest might do to his career, suggested we all clean house, and fast. Having promised to do my share, I ingest more of the stuff than I can handle.

Standing on top of our club chair, I raise my arms and begin conducting the last song. Charlie is the only one who responds. He removes his brown loafers and uses them to bang out beats on the frame of the couch. Donny forces an envious smile, but as Charlie bangs louder and louder, Paula looks away. I can't tell if she's embarrassed or just annoyed. There is definitely some tension brewing between her and Donny. I've noticed it once or twice before, but who am I to intervene? Besides, I can't imagine what might happen if they decide they've had enough. If one of them said: *Okay, kids, time to stop the whole shebang*. What would I do? Return to the safety of our family cave? How could I? The solidity, once relied upon, has quickly eroded into a pile of pebbles. Donny and I are down to the last fragile layers, our marriage, chipped away like shale.

The record makes a dreadful screech with one of my exuberant jumps, which causes the turntable to stall. Everyone freezes.

"We'll be back at midnight," Donny says, reaching for Paula's hand. Yet Paula seems reluctant to leave. He announces they are going to Paula's house, and I wonder what her sitter will think when she marches through the door with a strange man. This is a first—our splitting apart and retreating to separate houses. But since the unexpected bonfire at Jake and Ellen's, I refuse to leave the girls alone in the middle of the night with Agnes. We are determined to be more cautious and responsible, yet we remain night crawlers—The Bells and The Pearls, slipping out of each other's beds as darkness is pinched by the morning light. No one in this love square questions our actions aloud, perhaps fearing a corner may fold or disappear.

Cautious around the children, we show no outward signs of affection; we lock all the doors and listen for footsteps. In order to be together, to stay together, we rationalize everything we do is fine. Before this, I never understood the power of addiction—how you can trick yourself into believing you are not at all responsible.

The instant the garage door bangs shut, meaning Donny and Paula have gone, Charlie turns to me and widens his eyes.

"Hey, ladybug . . . why don't we go outside?"

A great idea! Together, under the stars, instead of hiding in the bleakness of my bedroom. I turn off the outside lights and follow Charlie. I am heady from the pot, nervous until he reaches for my hand. The patio is so dark I stumble over a tin watering can and make a racket. A fragrance of freshly watered roses fills the night air, as thick and sweet as whipped cream. They climb wildly along the cedar fence separating us from our neighbor's yard. Muffled television voices from a second-story window next door intrude. I hear a duet of crickets, the rumbling of cars; a few doors down, someone scolds a child to get back to bed. This last sound fills me with sadness.

Charlie sprawls across the lounge chair, never once letting go of me. Our heads are sealed together while we stare at the sapphire sky. I'm aware of my trembling, always, as if his physical closeness has occurred for the very first time. One sudden Scarlett O'Hara sigh buys me time, while Charlie laughs a deep, from the belly, sound.

"Hmm, you smell so good," Charlie says.

"It must be the roses."

"No, this is *your* smell . . . like a warm summer day after it rains, when all the aromas are mingling outside."

I can't help but giggle. "Well, that's pretty poetic coming from a lawyer, Charlie."

"Hey, I'm a mushy guy." He leans closer and kisses me hard, like rapids thrashing over jagged rocks, reminding me of every possible danger. Tongues move in and out, circling our teeth, pushing against the invisible dam. Our hips shift and my leg coils around one of his. Charlie takes a deep breath and pulls his head back to look into my eyes; he looks upset.

"What's wrong?" I ask. "You're wearing your mask of tragedy."

"My brother knows everything," Charlie says. "I told him last night."

Though I've gathered how close Charlie is to his older brother, Peter, I am startled that he'd share something so personal, something which involves other people, that involves me. I uncoil my legs and sit up straight, arms tucked like a pretzel.

"Let me guess," I say. "He said you were a crazy, irresponsible fool."

"Nope, worse, he called me a *moron*. Peter can be a real pompous ass."

"You brought it up, Charlie, so shoot. I want to hear it all."

"He said, 'Now that you've had your fun, Charlie boy, it's time to end it—Cheryl and I went through the same scenario, two years ago, but we got our act together, and so can you.'"

Scenario? Peter's words make me feel like filth, like we made a porn film.

"Thanks, for sharing. Oh, I meant to say *dumping*."

"I know I'm a jerk for telling you." Charlie rotates his body around to face mine. "Alex, look at me, please."

"Go away. Did you feel better laying off all your guilty little pleasures? Sorry to be part of the crap you stuff down each day."

It's the first time Charlie's seen me really pissed. The first time I'm not floating on air by being in his presence. He takes my face in his hands, but I squirm away. Aware that my neighbors are in earshot, I keep my voice low. "I need time to think."

"Alex, I told Peter this was different. I wanted him to know I'm falling in love with you, that, for me, it's not a game."

In the slivers of fading light, I see Charlie searching my face. The sweet, mellow high I was enjoying minutes ago has been replaced by a rush of paranoia. Do I want this? The pressure and effort our being lovers might ultimately demand of me? At first, I'd gone along for the ride. Donny's ride. But at some point, I saddled up, and this became mine as well.

"Alex, I know you're mad. It's okay, I can wait."

I stall and stall. I have no place else to go. His hands begin massaging the small of my back; tiny hairs rise at the nape of my neck. I lift my head so I'm staring into his soft, pleading eyes.

"Wait? Wait for what? This has to end, and we both know it," I say, surprising myself, clinging to the notion if you say certain things aloud they may or may not come true.

On the hottest day of the summer, a record-breaking ninety-nine degrees, we sit in the Bells' living room, drinking vodka and pink lemonade. The children are in the backyard running through the circular sprinkler, their high-pitched squeals competing with the dull hum of the failing, Fedders air-conditioning unit. Donny and I take turns going to the dining room window, our cheerful waves reassuring them.

Charlie, home for an entire week, is more relaxed than I've ever seen him. We can't pass each other without touching: arms, hands, grabbing a pinky, the sneaky bump of our hips as we walk through a room. We've been together almost every day and night, taking more chances than we'd ever imagined we would. Diving deeper and deeper into this whirlpool, we never come up for air, never stick out a hand to check the climate above the surface.

Today, the heat having perhaps parboiled his brain, Donny jumps up and announces: "You know, guys, I think it's time all our parents know about us. It'll take some of the pressure off."

"Oh God, Donny, why? Maybe Louise and Ben expect to see all their children adopting avant-garde lifestyles, but as you well know, *my* parents are clearly a different story." There is just so much I can tell my parents without paying the price—their gift-wrapped biased opinions. I'd been warned once by my college roommate, Barbara, a fiery, red-headed Irish Catholic raised in New York City. "What is it about you scaredy-cat Jewish girls?" she'd asked. "Why must you always run home and report to Mommy and Daddy? This way you're giving *them* a firm hold on you forever." At the time, I thought Barb was jealous of me, what I boasted to be my family's closeness. But now I clearly see what she meant: we tell them what we need to tell them, hoping for their admonishment—the Judaic version of confession. We make our parents part of our daily checks and balances.

"How long do you think we can hide what's been going on?" Donny asks. "I never mentioned this, but my father has been suspicious for quite some time. He called me into his office right after we came back from Cousin George's house in May."

"And why is this the first time I'm hearing about it?" I ask. There's a squirmy silence, and a weird look tossed between Donny and Paula.

"It's probably my fault," Paula says, looking at a finger-smudged wall, as if a movie were projected there. "After visiting my folks, I stopped by to ask if Donny wanted to go to lunch. I had the kids with me—I thought it would be okay."

I imagine Louise rising from her desk, leaning over to peck Paula's pallid cheek. I am seized with a deep sense of possessiveness, surprised this feeling still exists.

"Well, I guess the fact that my mother-in-law has never mentioned it to me shows you made a big impression," I answer. My foot begins to jiggle uncontrollably.

"Oh, no, she wasn't at work that day. Donny's father was really nice though. He took all of us out to lunch. He was terrific with Ricki and Ross."

This jolts me, flashing a moving picture with frames hard to put into focus: Paula, her kids, Donny, and Ben breaking bread together in the middle of the work day.

"Anything else I should know before we decide to share and share alike?" I ask.

"Alex is right," Charlie says. "You two can't be running around town, making your own rules. We need to trust each other and agree not to do anything that's going to hurt or confuse the children."

"Ah, I'd say it's a tad late for that." There's a smile on my face, though I'm far from happy. Something sucks all the air out of the room. It's as quiet as a synagogue on the High Holy days. I've said what no one wants to hear. And still, nobody, not a single one of us, yells STOP.

I stand and stretch, it being my turn to check on all the kids. It's as if I'd been forewarned. Looking out the dining room window, I see Ricki Bell, the little angel, tying our Lana against a tree, while Ross and Becky look on. I tear down the steps, which lead to the Bells' backyard, and the sight of me makes the children scatter, all except Lana, of course, whose tiny body is bound at the ankles to a sappy tree by a frayed and filthy jump rope.

"Are you okay, cookie?" I find the knot and slowly unravel the rope from Lana's feet. There are reddish-blue marks already spreading around her knees where Ricki Bell has pulled the rope the tightest. What shocks me most is Lana's theatrical smile, perhaps a denial of pain, but nevertheless a nearly cherubic and happy demeanor.

"Mommy, you know what you just did? You ruined our game."

"Your game? What kind of a game is this supposed to be sweetie . . . *you* tied up with a yucky, wet rope?"

"We were playing house, Mommy. Becky is supposed to be *you*, and because my hair is the darkest, I'm the pretend *Paula*."

My mouth goes dry in the suffocating heat.

"Oh, I see. And who was Ricki, tying you against this tree?"

"You didn't see her kissing me, Mommy. She was kissing me all over from my head to my toes." Lana shoves her two middle fingers in her mouth and refuses to answer.

Donny has four Fernando's shell steaks grilling on the pit. After the fire at Jake's house, I rushed to Fernando's and doubled my meat supply. Plus, I wanted to thank Mr. Fernando personally for his dedication, and volunteering, as fire chief of Wheatley Heights, but he was on vacation in Atlantic City.

I am watching the fireflies compete with the dancing sparks, trying to memorize the sight. I've set the redwood table, and as we casually dine outside, I'm aware of a balmy stillness, like the calm before a raging hurricane.

Becky and Lana are with my in-laws who, weeks ago, stopped inquiring about our weekend plans. Now when they take the girls, they practically inspect them, scrutinizing their little faces. For what? Abandonment? Neglect? Louise has begun chain-smoking Virginia Slims, causing frightening coughing fits, while Ben's reactions to us are less subtle. He comments on my apparent weight loss and has threatened to fire Donny for his habitual lateness. Paula has recently made it a point to monitor Donny's work ethic. She seems more focused on both our families' finances.

Donny and Paula look up from their plates as Charlie slices a juicy piece of steak, puts it on his fork, and offers me a taste. He watches me intently, as if I was his infant tasting strained peaches for the very first time.

"Huh, huh, do I know? Just the way you like it, eh, kiddo?" I like when he calls me kiddo, just like my father. I nod yes, chewing carefully, aware of revelation mixed with annoyance on our respective spouses' faces. The food is piled like a beehive on Paula's plate. She picks, her shoulders hunched toward the checkered cloth. Exasperated, Donny returns to the grill, needing a bit more fire on his meat.

Charlie nudges me under the table with his knee, and my hand slips down to find his for a squeeze. We are both aware of something intense brewing between Paula and Donny. We work at not shoving any affection for one another in their faces, but it seems difficult for them to look at us or even be in the same room at the same time. We've become marionettes controlled by the unpredictable whims of our spouses—they keep altering the rules, making the time we spend together briefer and less private.

On a recent get-together Paula sat thumbing through my *House and Garden* magazine while Donny read the *Times* seated at the kitchen table. Charlie and I heard them moving about the kitchen around ten. We listened, while cuddled on the loveseat in the living room. Several times their voices raised in what appeared to be an eruption of a quarrel. Any second, I expected either Donny or Paula to say, "Okay, you guys, the jig is up."

Paula presses the napkin to her lips, blinks her eyes, and pushes herself from the table. Nearly plunging through the sliding screen, she rushes into our powder room and slams the door. We get up and follow her into the house, leaving our dinners to the hovering mosquitoes. Over the sound of faucets gushing full blast, we hear Paula's retching. She hardly ate a thing, so there's not much to toss. Waiting at the landing between the kitchen and my den, we try to avoid one another's curious glances. After several minutes, Paula opens the bathroom door. Sheet white and covered in sweat, she plops down on the slate steps next to a pair of Lana's Raggedy Ann sneakers.

"Are you feeling all right?" I ask. "Can I get you something? Paula?"

She doesn't have to speak or utter a single word. A hammering silence bangs out my answer. How in the world could I have missed this? Just looking at Charlie and how he tucks his neck like a turtle to hide from me, how Donny's expression turns to one of deep, parental concern—I know.

Donny moves to the couch and sinks into the pillows. Charlie's face looks worn, his forehead etched like stone. "What? What?" I ask. I am still holding a dish filled with greasy blood and soy marinade. It is one of my many well-and-tree platters, this one embossed with the Hebrew blessing: *L'Chaim*, which means *To Life*. Charlie tries to say something but has trouble forming the words, words that stomp in all of our heads:

No, please, not this.

SEVENTEEN

A decision needs to be made and fast, but only one makes sense, if anything makes sense at all. How can Paula, or anyone for that matter, have a baby when she doesn't know, for certain, who the father is?

In the past few days there's a type of square dance going on. I observe mouth open, while Donny and Charlie sashay and dosey doe around Paula, primed and ready to lift her the moment she falls. Utterly invisible, I am standing on the sidelines, a thirty-year-old wallflower. *Where,* I wonder, *can I unload this sharp sensation of fear coupled with slow-burning wrath?*

On a stinking hot Saturday afternoon, we gather for an emergency visit with the Pearls. Normal families are at the beach or splashing happily in the community pool. But Donny, without asking any of us, has enlightened the senior Pearls of this latest dilemma. I question the sanity of the person I've become, having refused to attend this gathering and then changing my mind at the last moment.

Ben shepherds us through the Pearls' House of Reason into the newly decorated kitchen. I am distracted by Charlie's intense expression, his dark, stormy eyes. I wait a few seconds before sitting down. Louise circles the table once, then pauses behind Ben's chair. She hasn't glanced at me, not once.

"Well, it looks as if this has gone much too far," Ben says, his hands folded, his knuckles bright red. He might as well have said, "I told you so."

Feet shuffle; a chair scrapes the floor, followed by winded sighs. Paula's cheeks are tinted rose; she looks radiant, as innocent as Botticelli's Mary. I blot my lipstick with a paper napkin, then begin shredding it into long pieces.

Will someone please take goddamn responsibility, I want to shout. An icy draft blows down upon my neck from the air-conditioning ducts. When I stand to get a drink from the fridge, Louise comes over and blocks me. She looks offended that I'd take such liberties with her new GE appliances. Reality punches me in the nose. Am I bleeding? There's a sudden urge to flee the room.

"I'll get it," she says. "What is it you want?"

"Never mind," I answer, hurt by her tone.

Donny announces he has something important to say. I wonder if it's an offering: some sacrifice he's willing to make in order for him and me to go forward, for each of us to return to our neat little cul-de-sac lives. If he does, I might vomit all over this sparkling new terra cotta tile.

"It is highly unlikely for this to be my child," he says, with starched confidence. His statement falls just short of bragging. To stuff down a scream, I envision a pool of Donny's sperm swimming breaststrokes inside Paula before changing their squiggly minds, reversing and swimming away. "We haven't been together in a long time."

Paula purses her lips to catch one trickling tear, while Charlie steadies his gaze on a bowl of overripe bananas.

"Charlie, guess that leaves you," I say, tapping both feet rapidly under the table like Lana. My nerves have traveled to my bladder, but I can't leave the room. Because I stopped having sex with Donny when I first made love to Charlie, I knew it didn't necessarily mean he'd curtailed all relations with Paula. What I can't bear imagining is if I was only an aphrodisiac for their own marital sex. Even if they were just going through the motions, it would feel like betrayal. With Donny, I was as faithful as a faithless spouse could be.

"It is a possibility," Charlie murmurs, looking only at me. I detect a dollop of pride, as if he needs to believe this could only be his child. I manage a sardonic smile, while my guts tumble like rocks down a mountainside.

"What now, Donny?" I say. "Where's your guide? The what-to-do-if-you-knock-up-your-own-wife chapter."

"Be grateful, this didn't happen to you," Louise snaps back. With a clenched fist, I push my belly and feel the hollow sac made mush by Becky and Lana. Why am I the one on display? Paula's pregnant, but now I'm the tawdry one—me, a woman who slept with only two men in thirty years. Me? Not exactly Jezebel.

"I think we've all learned a lesson here," Donny says, ignoring my outburst. "Anyway, I hope we can support Paula through this ordeal and remain great friends."

What is he talking about? I don't want new friends. I scrape my chair and head for the nearest bathroom, wondering if it's okay, or if I should leave a dollar in the bread basket on Louise's table.

I return to find Louise serving coffee and apricot Danish. Motherly, as always, I hear her direct new concern toward Paula: "Please dear, eat a little something." Paula and I have little to say, while the men seamlessly change the subject to golf, reporting their handicaps. I sit and stare, hearing everything and, as if underwater, absolutely nothing. There's a high frequency buzzing in my ears, like the sawing of an old, sturdy tree. No one yells *Timber*!

The clinic changes Paula's appointment from Saturday morning to this Wednesday. Charlie had originally planned to be there, but now, because of an emergency settlement talk, he can't get away. Donny offers to take Paula for the procedure, so it won't have to be put off another week. She says she can't remember if she's three or five weeks late, which starts me wondering about where we were, what we did, when, and with whom.

After picking up some groceries, I wait for the girls' camp bus, then rush over to Paula's to relieve her babysitter of Ricki and Ross. I try desperately to keep myself busy. I rearrange Paula's cabinets, vacuum her living room, and downstairs, in the musty laundry room, I fold a huge wash that's been neglected in the dryer. While smoothing out one of Charlie's wrinkled shirts with my hands, my knees buckle to the floor. I begin crying and can't seem to stop. Tossed in a large plastic basket are Paula's lacy bras and panties twisted around her kids' socks and pajamas—a multitude of fabrics stained by a past and waiting to be worn in the future. The future terrifies me. All is about to change and that can't mean a return to normal. Normal no longer exists. Kneeling among these formless clothes, clothes of another family, a sharp pain spikes my jaw. I feel like I no longer have a family. I blow my nose on one of Charlie's crumpled handkerchiefs. Maybe I'll dye their laundry blue, or pink, thinking about the baby again.

The banging of chairs and bickering above my head reminds me I'm supposed to be on duty. I am the woman watching her lover's children, while his wife is comforted by *her* husband, as she undergoes an abortion for the child that no one knows is whose.

Upstairs, on Paula's kitchen table, the Oreo package has been ripped wide open. Becky and Lana, in a shocking display of servitude, are separating the cookies for Ricki and Ross, who lick the sugary filling before handing them back to them. The black ring around Lana's mouth tells me this has gone on too long.

"Hand the bag over, right now!" I throw the entire package in the garbage. Have they learned about servitude from me? I imagine them as teenage concubines popping grapes in their boyfriends' mouths. I send the children to the basement and pace the kitchen—filling in for the expectant father. The phone rings. It's Charlie. I'd nearly forgotten—this is his house. I'm startled, angered, thrilled to hear his voice.

"They're not back yet, Charlie. Call later. I'm watching the kids, you remember me: sturdy, reliable Alex."

"I called to speak to you. I knew you'd be there."

All I want him to say is somehow this mess will disappear. And one day, a hundred years from now, life will be normal and terribly boring. I'd settle for boring.

"Alex, I've gone over this in my head, and yes, I slept with Paula, but we were together only—"

"Listen, you were making love to her and me at the same time, maybe on the same night. Charlie, I know I'm hopelessly naïve, but picturing this scenario makes me ill. My voice falters, but I refuse to cry. There is an amoeba of pride left inside me, struggling, though alive.

"It was something we did, I did, in order to juggle, to keep both relationships going. You and Donny might have done the same exact thing, but you chose not to."

"Right, and now Donny's punishing me."

"Are you saying it's over?"

I'm startled by my own cynical laughter. "Is what over, Charlie? Or maybe I should say who?" I tabulate the days, weeks, and months like scoring a round in Scrabble. "In case you didn't know, due to circumstances beyond anyone's control, the game has been forfeited."

"We can't just walk away," Charlie whispers, which sounds like a lyric from a bittersweet Cole Porter tune. I see us projected on a movie screen, two aging profiles on the telephone, a scratchy silver image split down the middle. "Paula and Donny aren't blind, Alex. At some point, I think they got scared, thinking they might lose us."

"Well, now there's nothing to fear."

"Really? No, I think we're all pretty terrified."

"Sorry, I have to go." I hear the rattle of the automatic garage door, the children running up the stairs, tripping, climbing, tripping some more. "Call back later if you want to speak to your wife."

I drag the phone cord to the front door and watch Donny and Paula walking up the path. Donny bends down to pick up the newspaper and Paula squints, lifting her flushed face toward me. She seems rejuvenated by the ordeal, not as I imagined she'd look—drained and forlorn.

"You okay?" I ask, holding the door for Paula. She brushes past me and heads for her kids, who are with mine in the kitchen.

"Just a headache," Paula answers. A headache? Why isn't she doubled over in cramps? Her hand waves in front of my face, as if to say: dismissed. She is erasing me like a drawing on an Etch A Sketch.

Donny and I lock eyes. "So, how did it go?" I ask.

"I guess she didn't tell you," he says, peering into the dark hallway. "She's decided to have her baby." What? He might as well have said, while examining her, they discovered she has a penis.

When I step back from Donny, I nearly stumble over Paula's handbag tossed on the floor.

"But she can't have a baby! Especially, *this* baby. I thought it was talked out and—"

"She's changed her mind. Alex, sorry, you have no say here. This is her decision. It turns out, Paula is anti-abortion. It's a very big deal to her."

"And what about Charlie? When was she planning to tell him?"

I look down at the receiver in my hand. The loud dial tone hums in the air. "Who was that on the phone?" Donny asks.

"What? Sorry, but that's none of your business. I am no longer your business."

Donny shrugs, walks past me, and surveys the living room. "I guess we should hang out until after dinner to see how she feels. It's been a rough day."

"Hey, know what? You stay, Donny. You don't need me here. I'll take the girls home with me, where they belong. Becky, Lana, come on, we're leaving!"

"Have it your way," Donny says, with a laser-like glare.

"If only that were possible."

Hands trembling, I dig my car keys from a collapsing pile of dusty magazines near the door. A scary Richard Nixon stares at me from last August's cover of *Time* magazine. He looks like a liar who's been defeated, downtrodden, and terribly old.

Too exhausted at bath time, I bring Becky and Lana into the shower with me for the very first time. For some reason, Lana can't take her eyes off my vagina. She crouches down to look at her sister for comparison. Then she begins clowning around, slipping and sliding on purpose, and banging heads with Becky, who pinches Lana on her butt to make her stop. Next comes this ferocious hair pulling, a scene out of Saturday night wrestling. I grab them by their wrists and dry them off before sending them to their rooms. Tired, I choose not to probe for what might be brewing in their heads.

I hear their muffled whimpers but wait until they fall asleep before

I go cover them. Sometimes I'm resigned to let things happen, to watch our lives unfold as if I were roosting under a tree, shielded from the harsh glare of sunlight. Now though, I'm stuffed with remorse, thinking I've damaged us all in some irreparable way. Just yesterday my grandmother visited me in the middle of the night. But instead of the usual smile and warmth when she entered my dream, I felt an icy draft rush through the room—then a painful sting, instead of her tender kiss stamped upon my cheek.

Two nights later, I'm at the counter making bologna and cheese sandwiches for camp. I keep checking the clock, wondering what Charlie is doing now. Is he bathing his kids or lovingly tending to Paula? Perhaps they are looking through catalogues, picking out lead-free furniture for the new nursery. My suggestion is they move Ricki and Ross down to the dungeon, far from the new baby.

Donny goes about his business, meticulously dusting his opera collection with a flannel cloth. We have not spent this much time in the same room in months. In the past, we were adept at filling most silences with talk about the factory, the usual complaints, or sweet stories about Lana and Becky—a clever line, or some remarkable plateau in their growth. Now, without a plan for Saturday night, we have very little to say.

Occasionally, Donny rises from his recliner to shout warnings to the girls, who keep sneaking out of their beds. Maybe they are listening at the top of the stairs for something to pierce the bloated silence. I secretly love the sound of their tiny feet scampering above our heads, causing the brass fixture to sway, leaving dust on the kitchen table.

Donny can't get through the evening without making a call to the Bells. "Let's see how things are going," he announces. Of course I don't stop him, not because I share his concern, but because I know Charlie will be on the other end. I bang around our kitchen, brooding. I fantasize jumping in my car and driving to the Howard Johnson's down the road. Why not call Charlie and ask him to meet me there? But it's not sex I want, no, not at all. *Show them how you feel about me,* I want to shout, but Donny's already hung up the phone. I sink into a chair and pluck the petals from a wilted yellow rose. Donny sits cowboy-style, his face inches in front of mine, his mouth taut. "Everything sounds under control over there. What do you suppose we should do?"

I wince, surprisingly revolted at feeling wedged in and close to him.

"You want me to direct you? You must be kidding." As I attempt to rise, Donny grabs my wrist. I stare at his scarlet knuckles digging into me. "Let go."

"Forget him. Forget all of it. It's over," Donny says, sounding pleased.

I think of lunging forward to claw his pretty face. The level of my fury shocks me as our chairs scrape against the floor. I must shimmy back from him.

"We knew it couldn't last, but we've learned a great deal from this." Donny cocks his head sideways, hoping to draw out my response. "Alex?"

"Leave me the fuck alone, Donny!" I bang my fist on the table so hard that the vase vibrates and the rose petals drop away, leaving only the stamen—the center of what was once so whole, so lovely. I stand and move to the sink, my tears finally released.

"Sure, whatever you say, but remember, I'm all you've got now."

A week of Swanson's TV dinners crawls up from my stomach into my esophagus. "Oh, but you're wrong about that. I've got quite a bit more. I have my children, my work, and *me*! Whatever the hell *I* decide to do with this life." I lean down and sip water straight from the faucet. Donny moves alongside me, his mouth at my ear.

"He no longer wants you, Alex."

"And I guess she doesn't want you." I tug my arm away; my aching hand has made a fist, all on its own. "If she did, we'd be together right now. Tell me, was it the money? Yup, I bet that was it."

"Wrong."

"You know what, Donny? She used you."

"Hmm, how's that?"

"Nobody paid attention to her until you, and you were a perfect mother's helper to her kids."

Purple rage flashes across Donny's face, but I don't flinch. I look at him squarely. He will have to turn from me. Walk away once and for all.

"I'm going upstairs," he finally says, banging a cabinet door so hard that he shatters two wineglasses inside.

On Monday morning, after the camp bus pulls out of the driveway, I shut the door, rinse two bowls of soggy Sugar Snaps, and climb the stairs to our bedroom. I waver between a hot shower and the softness of tousled linens. The bed wins. The August sun streaks across our double dresser and finds my face. I pull the top sheet over my head and lie there wondering what it feels like to be dead. I had a lousy night's sleep, tossing and turning next to Donny, hearing him snore while propped on pillows like a prince. I thought of leaving the room and slipping into bed with Becky or Lana, but I didn't want to scare them out of their sweet, peaceful sleep.

Lying here now, I have the distinct feeling there are weird things crawling inside me. They move up and down my legs and arms like armies of ants. I'm almost sure that I'm shrinking away, disappearing through a perforation in the mattress into the floorboards below. The smaller I get, the louder the voices outside: lawn mowers, trucks, planes—all about to crash through the roof. Years ago, there were lots of plane crashes in New Jersey. I was young then and that's all my parents talked about, that and the bomb. *Here today, gone tomorrow* was their mantra.

"Alex, are you there?" I hear a voice interspersed with chimes from someone pressing our doorbell. I leap from the cobwebs of a dream, and part the curtains to see Charlie pacing the front lawn. He's squinting up, looking for signs of life in our house. Afraid he will leave, I bang my already bruised fist on the window until he sees me. I struggle to open the window, thinking of Rapunzel, Becky's favorite heroine.

"I'll be right down," I yell, breathless with excitement.

I run a brush through my tangled hair, chew a broken Life Saver from Donny's dresser, and take the steps two at a time. Charlie walks through the door impeccably dressed, wearing a navy blue suit and red striped tie. Coming closer, I notice the smoky circles fringing his eyes.

"I'm taking a later flight so I could stop by to see you," he says, pressing his forehead against mine. Across the street, Norman and Sue are getting into their car, looking toward my house. I slam the front door, leaving us in the darkened hallway.

"Can I hold you?" he asks. His lips gently brush my neck, and my body starts to tremble. I sense this is a final goodbye, and though

I know I should tell him to leave, *right now*, I want him to touch me—one more time. I am that pathetically lonely. If I were my own best friend, I'd smack me hard.

Behind the shaky voice and mistiness in his eyes, I see a warrior on his way to do battle. And who am I, but the unfinished business muddling Charlie's concentration? "Coffee?" I ask, sounding ridiculous. Charlie shakes his head no and glances at his watch, and we walk into the living room and sit down.

"I've got a few minutes," he says, "and here's what I want to say to you." He hesitates, taking his time, and I get to see glimpses of the lawyer, as if looking to settle, but he is clearly struggling through his words. Has Charlie Bell lost his silver tongue? I've been conditioned by men who kept all emotions on simmer, never fully boiled.

"I'm not sure what the next few weeks will be like, for any of us, but I don't want you to go through this alone." He looks frustrated, as if he's given this a great deal of thought.

"So, you and Paula are okay?"

"We're civil and reporting, mostly. But there's something else now."

"Yes, I know, a baby who's fifty-fifty yours."

"And you, a constant reminder of what it feels like to connect to someone, to know real happiness. There's a cloud hanging over us," he says, "and resentment we can't seem to shake. It's hard, but I imagine, with time, you and Donny will work things out."

"Work things out?" My maniacal laugh makes Charlie bristle—this is his former lover staring at him, wild-eyed in a dye-stained bathrobe. "Oh, so that would eradicate your guilt, if we were to Krazy Glue my little family back together again?"

"I think about leaving all the time. But I can't. I promised myself I'd never jeopardize my family."

"What we did, each of us, was jam-packed with jeopardy. Did you think it was just a hop and skip around a game board? Shop and Swap by Parker Brothers. Please . . . leave now and spare me your patronizing guilt."

He grins anyway, then tilts my chin to force me to look at him. I see yearning, but something new—suffering.

"I came here to say I'm here for you no matter what."

"Please, no more," I say, standing and tying my robe so tight I can hardly breathe.

Charlie follows me to the steps and wraps his arms around me. He leans his warm smooth face into mine and kisses me lightly so that a tiny spark springs from our lips. A first kiss, a last kiss, a moment to remember when I'm old.

"Would you mind locking the screen door when you leave?" I start up the stairs, knowing he won't follow me, knowing he can't. He has a plane to catch and so many people who depend on him.

Once upstairs, sitting at the edge of my bed, I comb my fingers through my hair. I glimpse myself in the dresser mirror; a wild woman with cheeks tomato red. Outside, a car engine starts up, stops and starts before rolling past our house. I reach in my robe pocket for a tissue, and my fingers graze something smooth and metallic and cold. Dangling at the end of a long silver chain is Charlie's swimming medal he had won in high school. I'd asked about it just once, curious why he wore it after so many years.

"As a reminder," he told me—of how hard he'd practiced for that particular competition. In winning, he said he'd learned that anything in life was attainable, but you had to want it so fiercely that it took up every frame of space in your dreams.

The next morning, I force myself out of bed, and slip on denim cut-offs and my rose design T-shirt. I scribble a list of simple chores: buy cookie mix to surprise the girls, clip a few inches off my hair, check on my *pushke* account at our local bank. When I pull in to the local shopping center, I notice how most of the stores are decorated, blasphemously, hawking back-to-school specials. What is the rush? It's warm and officially still summertime.

I'm at the checkout counter at the A&P, waiting my turn, when I notice the young woman in front of me paying the cashier. She has the most exquisite body I've ever seen, topped with long, lush red hair pulled up in a tortoiseshell barrette. From her profile, revealing a tiny turned-up nose, I quickly recognize her. She is our former babysitter, Colleen. Her pale, freckled arm reaches, cautiously, over me to select a *Seventeen* magazine from a metal rack. Yes, she is finally seventeen.

"Excuse me, ma'am," she utters, so politely, that my knees nearly buckle. She hasn't looked at me at all. She looks busy and purposeful, not to mention . . . beautiful. I am so curious to watch her, to breathe in all her apparent freedom. She's placed her keys on the counter, and I have the impulse to call out, "Don't forget them, Colleen," but I can't find my voice. There's a pink rabbit foot attached to her key ring, and I imagine the teenager had finally conquered her fear of driving—the fear Donny said he'd witnessed.

The cashier hands Colleen her change, and peering down, she says: "Oh, what a delicious baby!"

That's when I notice that Colleen has been leaning against a stroller parked in front of her; it is tiny, the style that would safely cradle an infant. My arms and legs turn rubbery; my mouth becomes sandpaper. Had Colleen Byrnes learned to drive and had a baby in the same year? The year my marriage turned to crap. I tabulate the approximate dates. Of course, it is possible, of course. Trembling, I abandon my groceries in the shopping cart and follow her out of the store and into the noisy parking lot. Colleen heads toward an old Chevy station wagon. A woman who looks very much like Colleen, except a very tired version, reaches out her arms.

"Oh, sweet pea, come to your mama," this woman says, completely confusing me.

She said, *Mama*, not Grammy! I give myself a quick lesson in the branches in a family tree right here in the A&P parking lot while cars honk and doors slam around me.

"You want to give your sister a big juicy kiss, don't you angel-pie?" she says, as she lifts the bundle of pink from the stroller and holds her against Colleen's ebullient face. I watch, crouched between a dented pickup and shiny black Plymouth. I catch myself smiling, though what I really want is to lie down on the gravel and have a good cry.

I envy the woman holding her baby daughter, her joy so fresh and apparent. She looks no more than five or six years older than me. I stare as she climbs into the back seat with her baby girl. Colleen, her lovely teenage girl, is the driver. Within seconds her head begins bobbing to the hurried beat of some unfamiliar rock song. She puckers, checking her lips in the rearview mirror. She is nearly perfect, as she pulls away, squinting briefly in my direction.

I stand in the parking lot, losing all track of time. Cool breezes alternate with a steady pulse of midday heat, making me shiver. I am certain I hear Rona's melodious voice. How did she find me?

"Al-lux?" She is dressed in a sleeveless white jumpsuit, as groomed as a French poodle. Strange, how I find this comforting as my arms open in a conciliatory gesture.

"Are you okay, you've got goose bumps?" Her eyes roll over me as if she's flattening a lump of dough. Tears spring to my eyes. "Let's get out of here, quick, the coffee shop," Rona says, as if my emotional state needs to be interiorly contained—out of the light of day.

Minutes later we are sitting in a booth at the rear, straining to hear above the sweaty cook as he calls out orders to the chronically glum waitress.

Taking a deep breath, Rona begins. "I just knew something weird was going on. You've avoided me at times, Alex, but never for this long." Rona takes a sip of her iced coffee, and I am fascinated by the iridescent orange ring imprinted around the straw. I can feel her staring at me under the hood of her thick mascara.

"So, I might as well tell you that Hy heard people talking on the train. Apparently, one of your lovely neighbors on Daisy Lane has been spying on you."

Now Rona has my complete attention. Norman and Sue? What could they have seen but cars parked at strange hours, unless, of course, they had a telescope fixed on our bedroom, or a camera, hidden in my garage.

"The truth is I'm beyond caring about my neighbors, and what they think they see. I'm just glad to be sitting with you now. It feels so normal. Oh, but I forgot, you're angry with me."

"Angry, no, but do I wish you shared more with me instead of pretending you discovered this fabulous new best friend? That's a different story. You're not the only one with feelings, Alex."

"Rona, I never meant to snub you. Things happened so quickly, and then . . ."

"Don't say it—you fell head over heels in love?"

"Skydived is more like it."

"Whew," Rona says, fanning her face with a napkin. "That might have been a whole lot safer."

I can hardly expect consolation from Rona, but I can't be alone now. I need to be reminded of something—something ordinary, which was the way my life used to be before I screwed it all up.

"I don't plan to ask you a ton of questions. But I will listen to whatever you want to tell me," Rona says, pausing her missile-like lipstick tube midair. Her eyes are more hazel today, tinted with envy. When I notice the envy, something weird happens. I feel powerful again. Could I possibly have something Rona wants? I enjoy this revelation, though it's paired with an inability to trust her completely, why I had tried to escape.

Before long I begin inventing a pristine account of the last three months, a story unrecognizable, even to me. I make up a version of the love square, rich with images of candle burning and spirituality—how we came to depend on each of our "inner souls." I'm not even sure I possess an inner soul. Here I lose Rona's attention immediately. Still, I keep talking, bombarding her with a catalogue of sordid details: fantastic pot, a romantic country getaway, and triple-A sex. I omit all the miserable nights spent in the Bells' dank and dingy basement.

"You know, Rona, it's been said that everyone has only one true soul mate."

She stares at me for a second, then takes a pad and starts jotting down her grocery list. Is it possible I might have scared her to death? I squeeze out the clincher, like a great poker hand—a test to see if she's listening. "And so," I hesitate, taking in one deep, diaphragmatic breath.

"So?" Rona finishes right on cue.

"I have no choice. I've decided to . . . split."

"But how will you ever manage?" Rona gnaws the eraser at the end of her pencil. I bet she can't wait to get to a phone booth and call Hy, her mother, the entire county.

"The same way I've managed before: by working a whole lot harder and finding a good, reliable job."

"What about you and Charlie?"

I gaze out the window where there's a world of women who already know what they're serving tonight for dinner, what they'll wear tomorrow, who they'll be seeing on Saturday night—simple things, which keep the pendulum of life in a smooth, manageable swing.

"Alex, I asked about Charlie. What do you think?"

"Charlie has a budding career, not to mention, a *growing* family. I'm not about to wait for him to make up his mind about what *he* wants. I haven't yet figured that out for myself."

I'm surprised Rona hasn't asked about the chain around my neck, the smooth medal tucked between my cleavage. I wore a medal just like this in elementary school—an ID tag in case of imminent disaster. And here I am, again, twenty years later, bejeweled in case of an accident. I can't help but wonder: *Who, if anyone, would step up to identify me?*

"In the meantime, Alex, it wouldn't hurt for you to put on a few pounds. Your ribs are sticking out of your shirt. Waiter!" Rona calls, her delicate hand brushing away the remnants of our conversation as if it were an accumulation of dust. "My friend here will have a tuna sandwich on rye, no lettuce, and a large slice of apple pie. Food, the great healer of all problems, big and small," Rona says, winking her butterfly lashes.

The tables turn, and once again I envy her for the distinct tidiness of her existence.

Hours later, Donny and I sit quietly, he in our den, me in the kitchen. My head is about to explode, even though I have already swallowed two aspirins. I look up from my magazine, knowing I can't concentrate.

"I need to talk to you," I whisper loudly across the room. The girls are upstairs, reading in their beds.

Donny either doesn't hear or totally ignores me while he thumbs, vigorously, through Sunday's *Times*. The strangeness of my voice forces him to glance over at me a couple of times. His expression changes from mild curiosity into annoyance.

I try but can't get the words out. I want a d-i-v-o-r-c-e. They seem so unreal. So grand a declaration. Besides, I don't want to ask Donny for anything. I'm scared to death; I don't know one divorced couple. None except movie stars and a woman from our old apartment building in Queens who jumped from her terrace on the day her ex-husband remarried. Had she still loved him or was she so lonely she couldn't bear it anymore? For now, I try to focus on distinct realities, and facts that require small actions to change the way we live.

"Donny, can you please put down the paper for a few minutes?"

"Shoot." But he's still turning the pages, scanning, testing me.

"I spoke to Dr. Carner and he gave me the name of a child psychologist. I've already called to ask how we should tell Becky and Lana about us."

"Tell them what?" Donny asks, finally tossing the paper on the cocktail table.

"Come on, Donny, please cooperate here. We have to tell them we won't be living together anymore. That you'll be leaving. We should do it soon, before they get any more confused or upset."

"And who decided that?"

"You know we can't go on pretending everything's normal. It's as if a live wire has landed inside our home."

Donny stands and gathers the strewn newspapers, a thoughtful gesture for someone who despises me. He walks up the two slate steps into the kitchen and leans against a chair. "You're as much responsible for everything that's happened here. What's more, you haven't been so attentive to your daughters lately. Truthfully, I think *you* should leave. I'm the one who's willing to stay and save our marriage."

"You're back living in our house, that's all. Aren't you here because there's no place else for you to go? Face it—you're settling, not choosing!"

He sits down next to me, placing a heavy hand on my forearm. A blast of Freon passes between us. "I'm not leaving," Donny says, "And neither will Charlie!"

"Please take your hands off of me. I know what you're doing—don't try and scare me." I get up quickly, toppling the heavy wooden chair onto the floor. A spindle breaks and rolls away. This is what I'd hoped to avoid, and yet it's happening right before my eyes. I am filled with fury—feeling powerless in my own house. Donny's words shred my veil of strength, and smother all traces of determination. I need fresh air; I can't catch my breath. My fingers fumble with the lock on the screen door. I hear deep sighs. It's Becky and Lana crouched together on the bottom step under a tent made from Lana's blanket. Becky stares at me, her eyes silvery blue in the dimly lit hallway. Her arms are draped around Lana, whose fingers are clamped inside her mouth.

"Mommy, where are you going?" Becky cries, her perfect lips quivering.

"Oh sweetheart, no place, really. I'm upset and thought I'd take a nice walk. Walking always makes me feel a whole lot better. Would you like to come along?"

The girls shake their heads in unison. Yes, they wish to come.

"Hurry then and put on your slippers. It'll be dark soon."

From the den comes this huge audio boom. For a split second I imagine a gun, held to Donny's temple—his gelatinous brain splattered across the thick pile of the shaggy rug. But he is escaping, as well, by blasting *The Grand Canyon Suite*. I'd like to die right now, anything, so not to witness the terror unraveling in Becky's and Lana's once calm little faces.

For the next few nights, Donny stays late at the factory. This is unusual considering all summer long business has lagged. I notice brochures on top of his dresser advertising courses for everything from scuba diving to rock climbing, but they stay there for days, gathering dust. I stop myself from inquiring, letting go of a claim to Donny, his present, our present, and the future. When he *is* home, he pounds the keyboard with a fury I've never witnessed—an energy which sends peculiar stirrings through me, until I realize what I feel is the pathos triggered by his choice of music.

Downstairs, right below him, I work late into the evenings, putting the finishing touches on another new painting. I catch myself staring at the canvas as if it were a maze offering hidden clues, or a map with intricate directions. What I like about the work is that it is anything but finite. The borders are open and free to interpretation—yet the core of the painting represents such deep entanglement. *Tangled* . . . yes, that's what I'll name this.

I call Louise on Friday—her day for chores around home and town. I want to reach out to her, to tell her how, no matter what, she will always be important to me and to the girls. We haven't spoken in several days, a rare occurrence, or perhaps I've lost track of time. My weeks had been marked by the special significance I'd attached to Saturday nights. Now time seems stretched out, each hour agonizingly slow, like in school when I'd sit staring at the large metal clock above the classroom door, convinced it had jumped backward a minute, to torture me.

After several rings, Gussie answers the phone. She recites Louise's itinerary for the day: a wash and set, the dressmaker for a fitting, her weekly trip to the vault to borrow her own jewelry for an upcoming wedding. My attention becomes focused when her voice, low and gravelly, breaks in its projection. I'm stunned when she asks if I'm okay.

"So, you heard?" I ask Gussie, this person whose loyalty marches North with her employers.

"Be sure and mind your children. That's all I can say. You folks sure made a mess of your lives, and Mr. Pearl wants those little ones cared for."

Which Mr. Pearl is she referring to? "They're fine, Gussie. I've always taken real good care of them. That'll never change."

"First, you need to take care of yourself so you can do your job. I wish I could help but I can't. Should Mrs. P. call you when she gets in?"

"No, never mind, I'll try again later."

I sink down at the kitchen table. This is the first time I can remember sipping hot tea in late August, but it fails to warm me up or cease the noisy chattering of my teeth.

On Sunday afternoon, Louise and Ben show up, unexpected. Luckily, it has been a quiet weekend devoid of confrontations, but the atmosphere feels strained—the smiles and laughter fake. After dinner, I pull some of Becky's old dresses from storage to try on Lana, who is both thrilled and jittery to be starting kindergarten. Donny bangs on the piano while Lana models the outfits. There are loud applauds as Lana performs a tap dance she learned at camp over the summer. I bite the inside of my cheek, afraid I might burst into tears.

"Are you sure they have bathrooms in the classrooms, Mommy?" Lana asks, cuddling up next to Louise.

"Sure baby, little seats, a perfect fit for your tushie."

"That's cool!" A phrase Lana's picked up from Ricki Bell.

During the coffee and cake ritual, a blimp-like silence threatens to drop and crush us all. Louise looks at me and then strokes my cheek in a loving way.

"Darling, I think you could use a break," she says, surprising me. This is the nicest she's been to me in a long time. "You've lost too much weight, and when I called you back last Friday, you were napping in the middle of the day. That's not like you, Alex, not at all."

I wasn't about to tell Louise it was impossible to rest during the night with her son beside me. How we'd each drawn an imaginary boundary on our mattress, avoiding an accidental colliding of hands and feet, enough to jolt either one of us out of the pleasures of sleep.

"I admit I'm a bit tired, but that's all. I've been working late after the girls are asleep." It occurs to me that Louise has never asked to see any of my new work. To her I might always be the T-shirt lady of Wheatley Heights.

"Why not hop on a plane and go visit your folks?" She sounds certain that a few days of separation will have some magic reconciliatory power. "Don't worry, I've got Gussie to help me, and it's a perfect time—Labor Day weekend."

"But there's so much to do before school starts."

"Whatever it is, tell me and it's done. Your folks are quite concerned, Alex. They're calling all the time."

I had deliberately rushed through our conversations recently. For years, my parents' weekly call became part of the fine balance in their lives. Still, staying with them would be a total regression. All I need is to see *that look*—the one that speaks volumes in its cast-iron silence. *Look, look what you've done to us.*

Yet, strange as I feel, the next morning I pick up the telephone and call Sophie in Miami, thinking I'll book a room in one of her senior citizen hotels. Hell, I feel a bit like a senior citizen—older, yes, though certainly not wiser.

It's been months since we've spoken; we wrote for a time after Rob died, and then stopped. I didn't think she'd be in a frame of mind to hear about our involvement with the Bells, but mostly because of her friendship with Charlie's brother and sister-in-law. However, after we finish catching up on our children, Sophie boasts that she already knows the whole story. Her tone borders on congratulatory.

"Got the scoop from Cheryl and Peter," Sophie brags, her delivery matter-of-fact.

"Why on earth would they share something so private, especially about their own brother's marriage?" I ask Sophie.

"Ah, I guess you could say they have quite a bit in common with you, Donny and . . . ah, me." Sophie giggles. "Okay, I might as well spill the beans, Alex. Rob and I had our own little fling with Cheryl and Peter about two years ago. But it didn't last long. They were so incredibly boring that we had a tough time staying awake."

"What? Rob and you were the other couple?"

"Yup! Ain't that a kick in your Levi's?"

I try picturing Cheryl with Rob, Peter with Sophie. Nothing makes sense, that is, if sensibility is part of the equation. What happened to us could not possibly have been the same. Sexual attraction leading to sex, yes, but there was also the slow unraveling of affection, or maybe I'm the only one who felt that way.

"He told Charlie he'd been involved, but no names were mentioned," I answer. I realize I am more than a little pissed off. What gave Peter Bell the right to be spreading gossip and making assumptions?

I renege on Sophie's offer to stay at her home, stressing I was flying down in order to have time alone. When she made it clear she was through with mourning and ready to party, I told her my partying days were over.

Later that evening, I circle my departure date on our new calendar, remembering that it was a gift from the friendly folks at Marriage Mountain. They had sent it along with a 50 percent-off coupon, good for our October "brush-up" weekend—the one Donny and I never attended.

EIGHTEEN

I land in Miami on the stroke of midnight. But there are no gilded coaches turning into pumpkins, no handsome princes waiting on bended knee—only a pockmarked cab driver, greeting me gruffly in broken English and reeking of garlic.

"Lady, we're here," he says, startling me. He hands me my duffel bag, which, at once, feels heavier. I pay him, and without saying a word, he screeches off, leaving me standing alone on a cracked cement sidewalk. The surrounding air is nearly visible, steaming like the tunnel in a car wash. Miami in summer; Miami *is* summer.

I enter the lobby of the Betsy Ross Hotel, dimly lit by amber sconces placed too high on pea-green walls. The aroma of strong bleach masking all other odors invades my nostrils. Pop-up air fresheners stand everywhere, poised like miniature spaceships on launching pads. I am on the verge of gagging. In a far corner sits an elderly woman wearing a flowered housecoat, just like the ones Bubbe, my father's mother, wore. I bet there are hard candies with soft, fruity centers in her pocket, wrapped in a handkerchief. She is mumbling to herself, rocking and moving her fingers as if engaged in some task. An aluminum walker is propped in front of her, protecting her as if she were a toddler in a playpen.

A young Spanish man, about twenty, dangles a key in the air. He already knows who I am and seems amused that someone close to his age is alert at this late hour. His dark eyes gleam like olives as he jumps from his post—a beat-up desk on which sits a phone and small TV.

"Buenas noches, senorita Pearl. Are you sure you don't need help with that bag?"

"No, gracias." I falter. All I remember from high school Spanish is finally implemented in the somber lobby of this hotel. If I could recall how to say, *It fucking stinks in here*, I would.

At the end of a long hallway, I find the door to my room unlocked. There is absolutely nothing here to steal: a cot-like bed, a gray metal dresser, a torch-like floor lamp, and a torn vinyl chair. There's a portable burner with a greasy tea kettle stuck to its top reminding me of the YWCA where I'd lived while student teaching in Gloversville, New York—a town that catered to the workers from leather factories—where nearly every storefront was a pub.

This would be a horrible place to die, I think. I can only imagine how many poor souls gasped their final breath upon these creaky springs. My eyes trace the water stains on the ceiling, then move down to a gold plaster picture frame above my bed. I lie down with my head at the foot of the bed to get a better look. Could my eyes be playing tricks on me? I see a print of Degas's ballet dancers in recital, the very same print my mother hung above my pale pink desk when I was seven. We had just moved from an apartment in Brooklyn, and Mom kept busy accessorizing the bedrooms. It was such a joyous time for all of us: the powdery aroma of a brand-new baby brother; Dad bright-eyed sneaking up behind my mother to kiss the nape of her neck; my grandparents' Sunday visits. And me pressed against the pane of my bedroom window, counting to one hundred, again and again, until I'd see them pull into our driveway. I tripped down the stairs to get to them, my feet running in place as my grandparents struggled out of their car, Papa reeking from city sweat and cigars, Nana, not a hair out of place, her skin cool as peppermint—so much love and history pulling up to our curb in one gigantic aqua '57 Caddy.

The sound of my weeping is unrecognizable. I grab the end of a pillowcase to wipe my eyes, staring at the faded ballet print I must struggle to see. If only I could swim through these colors—the serenity of pastels, colors missing from my own oval palette. It's hard not to wonder why everything turned out so differently from what I was promised. Work hard, they said. Do well in school. Marry a nice boy from a fine family. Keep your home clean, your children tidy and polite.

I need my babies now; I have never been this far from what I truly love.

All night long, I drift in and out of an unsettled sleep. Am I awake or is this a dream? My aloneness makes me an uncertain witness. Rising from the deep gully I've made in the bed, I float like a ballerina around the room. When I lift the peeling shade, to my surprise, I find a full Miami moon, which, beyond a doubt, is a most spectacular sight. In the roundness of its melon face is an exquisite mystery: a vast landscape of shapes and shadows, and its promise to return, again and again.

Why am I here, on my parents' plant-filled terrace, sweat pouring down my neck and soaking my tank top? They offer gourmet salads, and a basket of my favorite onion pockets. But I am too hot to eat. Dad points to a stubborn cloud pattern that's been hovering in the sky. *Nimbus*, the former sailor says. *Cumulus*, I utter, forever trying to impress him.

"Better get the sun while you can, kiddo. We're headed for a downpour."

"Nah, Dad, it's too hot to bask in the sun."

"Squirt yourself with the hose, dear. You used to do that, remember?" my mother chimes in. *I have come to be with them, after all.* If only what I feel could be cured with a smear of Vicks rubbed above the heart, chicken soup, and the gift of the latest Archie comic book.

"I'm all right, just thirsty." I sip iced tea. I pick at a mound of potato salad, amazingly still chilled.

"Your hair's a pretty shade, full of golden streaks. Natie, don't you think Alex's hair looks nice?" They are being so kind and attentive, I'm certain something terrible shows.

My fork bangs on the wrought iron table before bouncing to the floor. While retrieving it, I smack my forehead and feel the hot sting that promises blood. Blaming my injury on the table, my father pats my head like he did our childhood dog. My mother moves quickly, especially for her, and wraps tiny ice cubes in a dish towel. She presses hard against the eruption above my brow, making me wince. But she sees through me, I can tell. This is not about my bump.

"It's over," I blurt out.

My mother strokes my hair, something she hasn't done in twenty years. "And if you hadn't met that other fella?"

"What? How do you—"

"Yes, of course we know. Did you not think Louise would fill us in? She jumped at the opportunity. We waited for you to tell us, week after week, that is when you decided to pick up the telephone, but all we heard was about your 'wonderful new friends.'"

"Charlie and Paula."

"Right, well now I'm asking if you hadn't started all that *messy* stuff, would it still be over?"

Dad doesn't know where to put himself. He begins shredding a luncheon napkin, but I can feel him struggling to listen, even though he's humming *Younger Than Springtime*.

"I know what happened sounds crazy. But it wasn't one of those random love affairs. We switched partners, and when doing that, we also changed our lives. I'm a different person now. I can't go back pretending with Donny."

"Some people go through an entire lifetime pretending." She turns toward my father, with a wistful look in her eyes. Dad has switched to whistling, but the tune is choppy, like a scratched record.

"Don't worry, Dad, I'm not going to become a burden to you. I can take care of myself. I just need some time."

"Kiddo, we love you, but you need to be sure. It's not easy out there, alone," my father says, his eyes brimming with tears. "Maybe, you should think about teaching again."

"Yes, dear, you once loved teaching," Mom says.

Though I nod yes, I can't dismiss the fact that everything they suggest feels like enormous pressure.

Finally, we escape the heat and go inside. In an attempt to distract me, my mother drags out several old picture albums. There are faded photos dating back to the 1920s, when my grandparents first arrived in this country from Riga. One is a group shot of my great-grandmother, my grandparents, and an assortment of aunts, uncles, and cousins taken on a sprawling lawn in the Catskills, where the clan often gathered in summertime. All heads are turned, upright and proud, toward the camera's lens. The men wear their shirtsleeves rolled at their elbows, and the women appear ethereal in bright floral dresses. I am struck how everyone touches the person next to them: leaning in with a shoulder or an arm draped over a kneecap, fingers clasped around someone's waist. Though not a single person in the photo is smiling, they appear proud, as though they are collectively thinking: *We know who we are and where we have been.* Maybe it was enough to know they were bound by blood, marriage, and an arduous past—a past that catapulted them here in order to survive. How I envy them now—the fierce pride in their apparent struggle; but more, I ache for what is evident in each and every photo: the closeness of family, and the sanctity and power sealed by that connection.

Noticing my condition, the regression I was hoping to avoid, my parents beg me to stay the night. It doesn't take much convincing. At the hotel, the night before, I lay awake listening to moaning from the wall behind my headboard. I thought about going downstairs to tell the desk clerk, but then someone's gentle shushing became audible above deep moans. I imagined an elderly couple resting side by side on their too-small bed. The husband's hand lifts damp strands of white hair from his wife's burning forehead. *In sickness and in health.* It will never be Donny and me behind some wall; we will not grow old together as we, naïvely, once believed.

It's just past six, and the Florida sky is streaked like hot pink crepe paper. I borrow Dad's car and drive back to the hotel to pick up some clean clothing, but, more important, I need to be alone. It's so easy to fall into the trap, to become immobile in my parents' presence—an anxious child, helpless, and as malleable as Play-Doh.

The clerk, whose name I've learned is Pedro, jumps up from the gray swivel chair as soon as he spots me. Two women, their thin voices croaking, are either conversing or arguing. It's hard to tell the difference. One stops to look at me and says, "There's the skinny little shiksa."

"Not me, ladies. I was once a nice Jewish girl from Brooklyn." I shrug my shoulders and walk over to Pedro, who appears to be waving me down.

"I hope it's all right, Mrs. Pearl," he whispers. "Your husband arrived about an hour ago. He looked so tired I let him in your room to rest."

"My husband?"

"Oh, I'm so sorry to ruin the big surprise. Mrs. Pearl, are you okay?"

"Fine, yes, Pedro. I just wasn't expecting him this early." I squeeze out a grin and move toward the elevator. *This is too weird,* I think, dragging my legs down the dingy hallway toward my room—a medieval chamber designed to make anyone sink into the quicksand of self-pity.

What the hell is Donny up to now, and why am I trembling? I decide to be strong no matter what he has to say, but I can't help but wonder if this visit has been orchestrated by Ben and Louise—a final grandiose attempt to save our marriage. I am pelted by a new wave of sadness. Though I try hard, I can't find a single stirring of affection for Donny. Our seven years together is like a vestigial organ, an appendage now surgically removed.

Skulking outside the door, I think of running away, but as I lean my head closer, I hear what sounds like a baseball game broadcast on TV. Donny couldn't care less about baseball, even with the World Series just weeks away. Turning the door handle slowly, I peek in and see his bare feet first. The rest of him is blocked by the bathroom partition. The television is on, the volume pumped, and some announcer is screaming about Hernandez's second homerun. *Amazing,* I think, my heart flying through the room like some high fly in center field. I don't want to feel like this anymore, about anyone, especially any man. But there he is . . . dressed in a Mets T-shirt and khaki shorts, Charlie Bell, sprawled across my disheveled bed, his eyes sealed in sleep. He doesn't flinch when I crawl from the bottom of the mattress to sandwich myself beside him. He does look terribly tired, and his chin measures more than a few days stubble. I try covering us both with a single top sheet. I lie still, eyes wide open, playing the game I learned to play—matching the rhythms of his deep, cavernous breaths. Though, after a few minutes, I grow impatient.

"The Mets won," I say, not quite sure it's true. Charlie opens his tightly shut eyes. He focuses and grins. There are gritty tears in the corners from sleep. He lifts his legs and tosses off the sheet. We lie side by side staring into each other's eyes, then he pulls me on top of him, adjusting his torso to mine.

"I didn't know you liked baseball," he says, his thick breath tickling my neck.

"Me either."

There are only strangers beyond these suffering walls of the Betsy Ross Hotel. We are truly alone: far from wives, husbands, and curious neighbors. The knowledge is tempting and more than intoxicating. Welded together, we push deeper and deeper into the sinking bedsprings. Our mouths move furiously; we don't stop to breathe. Damp clothing tangles around our ankles as sweat mixes into a hot, spicy broth. The one rusty lamp crashes to the floor. Like a dingy that's drifted from a mooring, I am tugged back to him—he who encircles my space, swallows my air, yet promises to make things better.

The phones in the Betsy Ross are ancient—black with a rotary dial and so heavy; if it fell, you'd break your foot. I call my mother to tell her I won't be having a sleepover after all.

"Ah, I have a surprise visitor."

"Oh, so you're seeing Sophie, that's good dear," she says, "I imagine she must be terribly lonely."

"No, Mom, not Sophie."

"Alex, don't tell me it's that fella. What's his name?" Could she have guessed from the timbre of my voice?

"Yes, Charlie." On cue, Charlie yanks a white Lacoste shirt over his head and makes a face like a lizard; he fans out his neck so I see all the veins.

"I don't understand. What on earth is he doing in Florida? Shouldn't he be back in New York with his family?"

"He's headed back to DC, and wanted to see me, to check if I'm okay."

"Alex, this is terribly confusing. I don't think we're doing the right thing by accepting this. Donny *is* the father of your children."

"Yes, Mom, I understand this is strange, but he's here now, and I'm not sending him away."

I think I hear my mother's deep, accepting exhale. "Well, are you sure you don't want to bring him over for dinner? I've made a nice brisket."

"Ah, thanks, Mom. But we'll probably grab a bite right down the road. He's leaving for an emergency meeting in the morning."

"Suit yourself," she says, hanging up hard before I say goodbye, leaving me with the distinct impression I've done something wrong.

Stepping outside the hotel, we are slapped with a wall of hot, humid air. The sidewalk appears to be wavering in what must be an optical illusion. Luckily, there are three eateries directly across the street, all with eye-popping signs: Wolfie's, The Rascal House, and the historical

Pumpernicks, where I'd tasted my first onion pocket during a child-hood vacation.

"They make a great Reuben sandwich," I tell Charlie, whose tongue circles his lips, while one hand moves instinctively to his belly. Charlie told me he had to deal with being overweight as a teenager and, no matter how thin he became, a nagging guilt attached itself to practically every single meal.

"No argument from me," he says. "I'm famished." His arm drapes around my shoulder as we walk, and I become uneasy and self-conscious. Was there something more alluring about locked doors and dank basements, hiding out like moles beneath dirt-filled lawns? I wish I knew why I can't seem to relax.

I slide into a tall red booth in the rear of the cool, cheery restaurant and nod at an elderly woman eating solo, hunched over her meal as if deep in prayer. As if the oval white platter before her, which held her towering sandwich, sour pickles, and the drippy serving of coleslaw, was not only sustenance, but offered some mystical clue, which might soothe her desperately fragile self.

Charlie's unshaven face is hidden by the encyclopedia-sized menu. But not his hands—hands I now know better than Donny's. My eyes are riveted to Charlie's gold wedding band; it presses into his flesh insistently, like a birthmark.

A young, sweaty busboy slams two water glasses on the table, startling us both. A comical and efficient Borscht Belt–style waiter is on his heels. The man looks as though he hasn't laughed in forty years, and he never makes eye contact with us, not once. Charlie reveals yet another side of himself. He is a split-hair away from getting the sixty-something old-timer to crack a smile with his persistence but fails when the waiter grabs our menus and darts away. I feel the nervous, vibrating motion of Charlie's left knee under the table.

"You almost had him," I say. "You get his *schtick*."

"Remember, I used to do this once upon a time with my law school pal, Ivan?"

"Oh right, up in the mountains."

"Yeah, that was way before I got involved with all the bullshit, people pretending to do right by the world." Charlie leans back against the faux leather and rubs his eyes.

"Sounds like they've gotten to you, whoever they are."

"It's a lot more than that," Charlie says, leaning in, always the cautious and sometimes paranoid attorney. "They lied." For a second my mind goes to Donny and Paula, reminding me of the small, narrow world I've come to inhabit.

"Who, Charlie? Who lied?"

"My clients, Alex, the very people I've spent the entire year defending. Every single hotshot executive from all the utility companies. They swore up and down to the commission that the power plants were absolutely safe—all the time knowing they weren't. They built these plants, promising nuclear waste would never be problematic. But the truth is they were clueless about the potential dangers to the public."

I recall the exact moment when I first learned what Charlie did for a living, how I'd felt a sharp stab of disappointment. We were at the park with all the kids. All I'd seen then was the syrupy warmth in his eyes. I'd made a scowling face just hearing the word *nuclear*, but he sloughed it off, saying it was *only* a job. I refused to focus on the serious implications.

"Are you saying the case you've been working on all this time is a sham?"

"No pun intended, but that's pretty much the case."

"Well, you can't quit now, right? There's a lot to consider. You have a family to support, a growing one, at that." We lock eyes, and, for what seems like eternity, Charlie stares back at me, until I look down at my place mat displaying a happy family of flamingos.

"I'm not about to do anything stupid, but I've already started to make plans," he says.

"You don't have to tell me any of this, really."

"No, I want you to know. I'm planning on telling the firm that I'm resigning as soon as this last case is tried. It's taken over ten years, but what I've learned, at least about me and the law, is that I'm better suited to represent people with real problems than institutions run by a bunch of faceless stockholders. But, most of all, I'm done traveling. I want to be home, though home for me is less than rock-solid, more like circling the atmosphere."

These last few words ring manipulative. Especially the look in his eyes, a little too: *You'll help me, Alex, won't you?* I find myself resisting an all too familiar pull—the need to service whatever it is that needs servicing. I sit up tall in the booth.

"I can no longer pivot my life around anyone's needs," I blurt out, surprising myself.

"Hey, of course, I know you're amazingly strong."

"It's an illusion. I'm like that bowl of Jell-O on the counter over there. You don't know me, not really, you just think you do. What's more, I don't have a grand plan like you. My *only* plan is to go slow."

I turn Charlie's wrist to check on the time. He grips my hand, lifts it to his lips, and kisses me just as our stoic waiter plops down our food along with the wet check. We hurry up and down our foot-high sandwiches (I eat a quarter of mine), then rush to find a phone booth a few doors down. Charlie plugs in his credit card and hands me the phone. He strolls down the block to give me some privacy. He already knows how anxious I am to talk to Becky and Lana. Every time I've called, previously, I was told they weren't home or were already asleep.

Gussie picks up on the fourth ring, and hearing my voice, she hesitates in her unique style, which insinuates calamity. There's a churning inside my stomach; a combo of sour pickles and corned beef struggling to assimilate.

"They're okay, Gussie, right? No one's sick or anything?"

"No. But they've been actin' up a bit."

"What do you mean? That's not like them at all."

"You know . . . a million excuses before bed . . . more juice, the potty, and those scary noises they think they're hearing."

"Can't Donny calm them down?"

"Truth is I haven't seen much of that fella since you dropped them off on Thursday. Mrs. P. gave him a piece of her mind on the phone last night. He'd better show up later or she'll be fit to be tied."

It seems my leaving has given Donny an open ticket. No restrictions, rules, or restraints. But who am I to judge? Gussie recaptures my attention. "If I were you, I'd get my hide back to New Jersey a.s.a.p. That way no one can say you're not capable of caring for your children."

"But Louise was the one who suggested I take a few days to rest," I answer, feeling the need to defend myself.

"All I'm *saying* is what I'm *hearing*. A mama ought to be with her children."

"Okay, Gussie, thanks, now please just put them on the telephone," I say, trying to keep down my last meal.

"I would but they're out with the folks seeing some new Disney movie."

"Well, that's nice, Gussie," I say, while hoping it's not the latest remake of *Bambi*.

"Yeah, they all went out after Lana had an accident on Mrs. P's bed."

"Oh, my poor girl. She was doing so much better."

"Lana bawled like the dickens, afraid they won't let her go to kindergarten next week."

"I hope someone told her that isn't true. Please Gussie, tell her, tell them both, I'll be home very soon."

"The sooner the better," Gussie says, before hanging up.

From halfway down the block I think Charlie has noticed my worried expression. His eyes widen while he puffs on a fat cigar he's purchased from a seedy bodega. He looks ten years older than he did five minutes ago, or maybe I just need him to be older. I am already queasy from the airless, yet odorous, phone booth when he asks me what's wrong.

"You'd think with me gone Donny would want to spend some more time alone with the girls."

"Where has he been?" Charlie asks, taking a drag on the monster cigar.

"Hey, now that's a really good question. Well, Gussie more than hinted that Donny has been spending his vacation time with Paula. Unless he's managed to find someone else in the day and a half I've been away."

Though there are no signs of ownership in Charlie's expression, I remind myself acting is a huge part of his job. "Why are you surprised?" he says. "Though I'm not sure either one of them knows what they want."

"Charlie, I can't worry about them, but I feel like I'm the only one who's walked out on my job. I should never have left, not now."

"You haven't, Alex. Becky and Lana are terrific girls, and you're a wonderful mom. They'll be fine."

"How can you be sure? Aren't you the one who said your parents' breakup nearly destroyed you?"

For once Charlie can't find a sufficient answer. My guess is his thoughts have drifted to Ricki and Ross, who, before long, will be sharing their parents with another sibling. Charlie snubs out his cigar on the bottom of his loafer and grabs my hand. We walk back to the hotel in total silence, but his eyes keep checking to see if I'm okay.

As soon as we enter the lobby, Pedro leaps up from his desk and smiles. I spot a couple, who must be in their nineties, sitting on a sunken couch and holding hands. They are watching a rerun of *The Fugitive*. I want to crawl between them and rest my head on the cool, chintz sleeve of her housedress.

"Have a good evening, Mr. Pearl," Pedro says, beaming, then he winks at me as if the *good* part was up to me.

"Thank you," Charlie answers, taking the key. "Funny, I don't feel like a Pearl. Do I look like a Pearl?" He tries to make me smile to no avail. "Come on, Alex, I promise everything will be fine."

"I wish there was a flight out right now," I answer.

When the elevator door opens, I step in and pivot to look at Charlie. I see how much he wants me at this moment and know that it would be such a final pronouncement to let him go— to say: *Please go away, Charlie Bell. Who needed you and this whole damn mess?*

I head toward our room. It's become our room. Charlie's dark, damp arm scoops my waist as I fumble with the key. Like a butterfly, I fold and fall backward, topple into the soft mesh of his body. His hot cheek presses the back of my neck; his lips push through the fabric of my top. But no, no! I don't want him wanting me now. All I want is solace and kind affection. Someone's hacking cough from down the hall makes us scramble inside, locking the door like runaway thieves.

"I can't. Not here, not now." I pull from his arms and prop myself on one meager, musty pillow.

"Of course, I understand." Charlie glances toward the window. He's quiet for no more than five seconds, but I've already given up on him, on all men, on hope. "Come here," he says, "let me rub your back, it'll help you fall asleep."

"Sleep, ha, you must be joking. What exactly is sleep?"

The clock radio I'd set for five reads 3:00 a.m. I slip out of bed and decide not to use the shower, afraid that he'll hear me. My hair is a twisted mass of curls from the humidity, and I pull it back with a black headband. Scampering through the room, I collect discarded clothes, stuffing them in the duffel bag I never unpacked. Charlie stirs, and I halt my breathing. I wait like I did when the girls were babies, and I tiptoed into their room, checking if they'd awakened from their long afternoon nap. He turns facedown in his pillow, one arm gorilla-like, grazing the carpet. I crouch down in a painful knee bend to open his lit bag and find a stack of legal pads and a box of ballpoint pens. I throw a few in my bag—souvenirs to remember Charlie Bell. The orange glow from the streetlight barely illuminates the sheet of paper, but I write anyway, letting the words come, jumbled in my fog of sleep.

Dear Charlie,
Thank you for seeing me through to the end of this—I wonder
will there ever be an ending, or are we bound by all our crazy
mistakes? You know how anxious I was to get to the airport,
to get home—I didn't want you to worry about me, or feel you

had to see me off. If only I'd been a counselor at the Coral Club when you were their lifeguard, things might have turned out differently. I know you will do well in whatever it is you choose. I will miss you.

Yours,

Alex

I tear the sheet from the legal pad and place the pad between stacks of others. My hand touches something smooth and slick—I slide it up from the bag and bring it into the light, now brightening through the shade. It is a picture of us that was taken at Cousin George's home in May. The lake shimmers like green glass behind us; we are smiling, but I distinctly remember holding back, afraid to have Donny, the photographer, see how happy I was the moment he snapped the picture, the instant he commanded: "Say cheese." I am touched that Charlie's hidden this picture amongst important legal papers. Yet, I wonder what he'd say if it appeared on a conference table by accident. I imagine him using his wide hands, sweeping the picture away before he would have to explain who I am. *Hey, so who's the smiling chick with the shaggy hair?* I don't want to be explained or hidden away ever again. I prop the picture against Charlie's watch on the nightstand and tiptoe out the door.

At the airport, I exchange my ticket for the first available flight to New York at 6:30 a.m. I will call my parents once I land and hear the complaint that I didn't say a proper goodbye. I am freezing from the air-conditioning blasting through the ceiling vents of the nearly barren terminal. But it is better than the inferno outside or in the lobby of the Betsy Ross Hotel. Sitting in a plastic bucket of a chair, I pull my knees to my chest and stretch my shirt over them for warmth. I close my eyes but dare not sleep. A hunchbacked janitor has been mopping the same piece of floor in front of me, over and over again, and the fumes of bleach begin to burn my eyes. *Please go away*, I want to say. *What do you find so interesting in these tiles?*

Once in the air, I'm transfixed by the rivulets of hard rain streaking my window. I think of the girls, their laughter often mixed with cautious observation as we cruise through our neighborhood car wash. And how, when I took them there for the very first time, I had to climb over the back seat to calm Lana, whose sweet little mouth turned blue from her incessant screaming.

The pilot gets on the loudspeaker to apologize for the slight delay. His cheerfulness evokes my suspicion, especially when he warns us to keep our seat belts buckled. He mentions there are severe thunderstorms reported along the entire eastern coast and considerable turbulence is anticipated. Fear pierces a hole in me, making me feel very small. "As small as Alice?" Becky would ask. I shrink back in my seat, pulling my body as far as possible from the burly man next to me. Though I pray for sleep, it's an improbable option. I might as well be in the cockpit helping the pilot. *Cockpit.* How did it get that name, and have I lost my mind entirely?

I keep glancing at my watch, counting the minutes until landing. Please, God, let me see my children again. I promise they'll be no more cursing, much more patience, large sums allotted for charity. And all the while I play this game, I'm aware of a deep deception. The one deal I do not make. To return to the life I lived before.

Bracing myself, I accept the rodeo landing as punishment. *Give me all you've got,* I telegraph the Lord, happy to be spared. My eyes open only when I hear the deafening rev of the plane's engine and the rattling of luggage stored above my head.

"What's her name?" I ask the man alongside me who's now cracking his hairy knuckles.

"Pardon, ma'am?" he says in a spongy, southern drawl.

"The plane, you know how National names their flights after women?"

"Oh yes, ma'am, guess you're right about that. Well, I believe I heard the name *Ida* mentioned. Yes, it's printed right on her wing. See? I-D-A."

"How can that be? Ida was my grandmother's name," I whisper to myself.

I wince at the glare of brilliant sunlight, the kind that follows a hard September rain. I really can't make out the letters. Maybe the man said *Edna* or *Leda* or maybe nothing at all. I fight back tears, thrilled to be on the ground and knowing that Becky and Lana are just a long taxi ride away.

NINETEEN

Forty-two minutes later, I pull up to the Pearls' sprawling Brooklyn home. I'd expected Ben and Louise to be at the club, but their cars, like old lovers, are parked side by side in the driveway. I ask the cab driver to please wait for me; I won't be that long. This way, I don't have to ask for favors, or put anybody out. There's some cash folded in my pocket, about twenty bucks, and T-shirt money stashed under the shag carpet at my house. It will be good to get home and immerse myself with everyday chores, the automatic ones—tasks that became my internal clock. Finally, school starts on Wednesday. Lana begins kindergarten, Becky, second grade. This is what to focus on.

Walking through the breezeway that separates the garage from the house, I spot Lana's flowered dolly stroller. It's lying upside down, an assortment of naked dollies scattered on the blue slate. The screen door opens before I have a chance to knock. It's Gussie balancing laundry which looks gloriously familiar: small pastel T-shirts. The girl's shirts, ones I'd tie-dyed and painted. Gussie's face is warm and welcoming, and I'm instantly relieved, aware of how badly I need a friend.

"So, where are they?" I ask, pushing past her through the kitchen, deciding not to scold her for having scared me with her dramatic premonitions.

"In the den watching some show on TV, magic something," she says.

"*Magic Garden!*" I shout, full of joy, running through the dining

273

room, hearing the familiar clinking of the china, then through the living room that opens to the den. I see them in profile before they notice me. They are standing in front of the couch, enthralled with the program, swaying slightly to the strum of a guitar. Scrubbed clean, the girls are dressed in matching lavender floral shorts sets. Lana turns toward the doorway first, her fingers mashed in her busy gums. Gussie's voice bellows behind us. "It poured like the dickens all morning. Oh, and you better call your folks. They called to see if you got home okay. They sounded real upset." My parents must have called the hotel, or else Charlie might have gone searching for me upon awakening.

Becky and Lana run to me, wordless, their arms out and up, thinner and lighter than I remember them. I scoop them up like handfuls of silky summer sand. My body trembles, when I squeeze them as tight as I can.

"My sweeties, I missed you so much."

"Missed you, Mommy face," Lana says, lifting her head, rubbing her little pug nose against the tip of mine. "Just like Eskimos."

Becky lifts a tear from my cheek. Her fingers feel sticky and sugary when I lick them.

"Were you eating candy?" I ask, in the voice of the big, bad wolf.

They widen their eyes, shaking their lying heads in unison. *Good,* I think, *I'm happy they know that often revealing small truths can have consequences.*

Gussie watches us from the doorway, still balancing the tower of laundry.

"Where is everyone?" I ask, afraid to take my eyes off Becky and Lana.

"The folks are in their bedroom watching TV. Their golf game was cancelled because of the storms."

"Yeah, Mommy, there was lots of thunder and fire," Lana chimes in.

"That wasn't fire—it was just light-ning," Becky says.

I squeeze them until they squirm away, glad they're not clinging.

"And Donny?"

"Girl, I've known that boy since he didn't have a hair nowhere, and still I can't figure how his mind works."

"Well, if he calls, tell him I took his daughters home. I've got a cab waiting outside."

At the counter, Becky helps Lana pour apple juice from a half-gallon plastic bottle. She offers me a plate of cookies that look home-baked. Not one of them is whole. The phone rings and, forgetting momentarily that Ben and Louise are home, I pick up.

"Oh, you're back," Donny says, his voice gravelly, as though fresh out of sleep.

"Hello, hello," Louise says, from her bedroom extension.

"Yes, and I'm taking *us* home. There's a lot to do. School begins this Wednesday."

"Did you just remember that? When were you planning to come back after leaving your children?"

"Hey, I'm with my children. Whose children are you with?"

I turn my back to the four frightened eyes staring at me, sucking up juice noisily through their straws. I muffle my voice, but my neck veins are popping.

"How do I know you're capable of caring for the girls in your state of exhaustion?" Donny asks. He sounds as if he's putting on a little show.

"Donny, please, not now," Louise interjects, still on the extension. "The both of you must cut this out."

The cab driver, who's been waiting outside, startles me when he taps on the kitchen window.

"Goodbye . . . I'm going home." I gently hang up the phone. Gussie hands over a shopping bag containing the girls' things, and Becky's Drowsy Doll's head pops out from the top like she's gasping for air. I look down and find Lana, beside me, performing her "sissy" dance—running circles in place, signaling she has to use the potty. Now! I rush her down the hall to the bathroom, where I splash my face with cool water.

"Come on, girls, time to say goodbye to Gram and Gramps. We're leaving now, that nice man waiting outside is our driver." As we walk toward the master bedroom, I hear the rapid clicking of Louise's heels on the ceramic tile. She pauses in front of me, her expression grave. I figure she's upset by what she's just witnessed on the phone. Still, she gives me an obligatory peck, and, forcing cheer into her voice, ushers the girls in the kitchen for a "surprise." Though anxious to get going, I allow this small indulgence.

I lean against the doorframe of their bedroom to wave both hello and goodbye to Ben. He sits tensely at the edge of the bed, motioning me to come join him. But I am not in the mood for a chat now. He points to the TV. There's something just on the news—some special report interrupting regular programming. My parched mouth gets instantly drier. I loathe all special reports. I'm always expecting the final payoff for all those duck-and-cover drills in school.

"Listen to this," Ben says, raising the volume with his remote. I stand awkwardly beside the bed. My legs turn to rubber. I have not been near that sprawling bed since I lost my virginity seven years ago.

"What? What's happened?" The "Special Report" graphic across the male newscaster's face makes my adrenaline surge, while the skin on my scalp contracts. The newscaster is wearing a yellow rain slicker. One hand holds a microphone with the station's call letters, some ABC affiliate, the other juggles an umbrella about to become airborne. I sense the words more than I actually hear them. Some picture begins to form, but still I resist and turn to Ben and ask, "So, did you all have a nice morning?" But my eyes never leave the screen.

"Alex, shhh! There's been a plane crash."

I stare at the reporter and recognize the familiar beehive dome in the background— the Capitol building. The words "Air Florida . . . Flight 91 . . . Miami . . . Washington, DC . . . thunderstorms . . . wind shear . . . Potomac River . . ." BB pellets assaulting my brain. A hand, my hand, clamps my mouth. I spit saliva when I say his name aloud. "Charlie, oh God, Charlie." My hands tremble; I bite my knuckles to make them stop.

The news anchor from New York, Bill Beutel, is firing questions to the field reporter, a young man he calls Tom.

"Bill, all we know now is Flight 91 left Miami International at nine thirty this morning heading for Dulles. The flight was due to land at approximately eleven thirty. But severe thunderstorms along the entire East Coast caused the pilot to change his normal approach upon land-ing. Eyewitnesses have told us that the plane seemed to dip unusually low before turning, and on its final descent . . . missed the runway."

"Tom, I know you said there are emergency rescue crews at the scene, the Red Cross, the National Guard. Can you tell us what's being done at this moment?"

"Well, as you can imagine, it is total bedlam at the scene. The plane went down literally yards from the runway, on the banks of the Potomac. We're cutting to Jane Meade, who's on the scene where rescue attempts are now in progress."

I get up and stand in front of the bed blocking Ben's view.

"Charlie's not on that plane, no." I am talking to myself, jabber-ing really. "He was planning to leave earlier, sometime before eight. I know, because . . ."

"Because you were together. We heard, Alex, first from your mother, then from Donny. Charlie called home before boarding to talk to Paula. She's his wife, remember?" Ben motions for me to move away from the screen.

"But he might have caught an earlier flight." I start pacing the room, looking for my shoes, needing to be completely dressed, ready, ready to go, anywhere.

"Alex, calm down and listen. He was already at the airport, waiting to board an Air Florida flight. There were delays due to heavy rain."

"Yes, yes, I know, my flight was delayed also." I should call my parents, but I can't move, can't leave this disaster unfolding in front of me.

Ben stands up and runs his hands through his silver hair. "Christ," he says, over and over again, until I want to smother him with one of the super-king goose down pillows.

Finally, Jane Meade appears on camera. "Bill, behind me there are some truly incredible scenes of team efforts to search for the survivors of Flight 91." She holds a clipboard in her hands and says they will soon announce a hotline number that families can call for further information—information that will possibly ruin their lives.

"Jane, how many have been pulled from the river?" Bill asks.

"We can confirm there were fifty-two passengers on the plane, about a third of the aircraft's capacity." Jane Meade jiggles her earphone and pauses for a few seconds. Ben tosses me his neatly folded hanky. Tears stream down my face onto my chest.

"Bill, this just in—" She smiles, and I cringe. How can she smile when a plane has crashed? "It has just been confirmed, there are 21 people who have been taken to Bethesda Hospital, most in critical condition. We are also told there are some who actually swam to shore. One unidentified man is said to have gone back three times to look for other passengers. Stand by, we're cutting to tape."

Louise rushes in the room and hands me a glass of orange juice, but I want a chug of her numbing water—the liquid cascading between ice cubes. She mumbles something about paying the man waiting outside and then, "Oh, and your folks called again. I told them you were here and perfectly all right."

"Look, there are survivors," I shout. "He'll make it. Charlie will make it."

"Those poor children," Louise says, taking a noisy gulp from her drink.

Louise and I stare at each other hard, and although her expression does not necessarily chastise, I already sense a deepening chasm, like a fault on the earth's surface. I can't remember when I sat down on their bed, but now I'm here. My body detached from my head. We watch the newscast mute. They are showing cuts from a tape taken an hour or so earlier, minutes after the crash. I'm jolted by an image on the screen—contours of a familiar body and the swiftness of its movement. Through the haze of a rain-streaked camera lens, I see a grainy silhouette: two figures attached at the shoulders, flailing through choppy waters. Then they disappear.

What's evident is the standard lifesaving technique practiced here—something which might have been taught, decades ago, on the smooth sandy beaches of the Jersey Shore, experienced by a teenage boy, a champion swimmer, taught on his first summer job. Skills he'd perfected for the one chance disaster, which, years later, would mold that boy into a hero.

I am at the sink, filling the tea kettle when Paula and Donny arrive, thirty minutes later, holding hands. I would hold their hands, too, if they reached for me. My eyes scan over Donny. He reeks from an unfamiliar spicy cologne and is wearing the shirt Paula bought for him in May—the same one I gave to Charlie when we were flirty, frivolous, but mostly selfish. No one knows where to place themselves. There is a whole lot of sighing, followed by a dreadful silence. Paula's eyes appear swollen and another sharp pain of reality intrudes. I glance down at her belly where her shirt is pulled out, but it's too soon for her to be showing.

In her softest voice ever, Paula tells Louise that Ricki and Ross spent most of the weekend with her parents. Enlightening information: Donny and Paula playing house in Wheatley Heights, me, the youngest citizen ever registered at the Betsy Ross Hotel, and Charlie: thirty thousand miles up in the turbulent air, torn between the demands of love, marriage, and work, only to wind up in the icy waters of the Potomac.

There is little validation for the aching concerns of a lover. No place to express how scared I am. Now, as Ben and Louise embrace Paula, lingering with loving touches, I slowly back away. Or maybe I don't have to; I've already slipped through the cracks in the tile. Someone's taken an eraser and wiped me from the board. I'm already residue—a hint of powdery dust.

September's golden dusk darkens the kitchen, making me cold. I take Lana's beaten-up blankie and toss it over my goose-bumped arms. As Gussie moves past me, her large hand rubs my shoulder and lingers. I'm overcome by a desperate need to be alone. I pour myself a mug of tea and slip out the side door, unnoticed into the final curtain call of daylight. The sky is smeared like a child's finger painting: reds, purples, pinks. They were the colors of Nana's smiling lips; perhaps why I always think of her somewhere in the sky. Silly, I know, to be an educated adult who believes things like this, but it soothes me to think of Nana floating miles above me, enjoying a spectacular view of those she once cherished. I've seen the headstone marking her gravesite and placed rosy pebbles on many of my visits, but it's hard to believe there's not more of her spread around the earth—molecules of her gentle soul suspended in the air. Closing my eyes, I mumble a fractured prayer.

Only when someone turns the lamps on in the den do I realize I've been outside a very long time—sitting on the wooden swing Ben had affixed to an old maple and the exact same spot where Donny proposed. Through the slatted wooden shades, I make out the familiar figures: Donny and Ben standing in front of the TV, Louise and Paula leaning against a doorframe talking.

The outside lights click on, one by one, perfectly orchestrated like a line of long-legged chorus girls kicking higher and higher. No one has called out my name or peeked for me through the screen door. I assume they sent my cab driver home or I've chalked up quite a bill by now. I think of hopping in Donny's car, sure that the keys are still in the ignition, as always.

The sky shuts down like a silent film fading to black, and I close my eyes, inviting only Charlie's face. In this fantasy, it is difficult for him to speak, but he struggles, all the while, urging me to go home:

Go home, you must go, Alex.

Where, where is home? I have forgotten each and every familiar route.

"I'll do it!" Donny announces. Instantly, Donny's ruddy complexion fades to a yellowish tinge as he volunteers to make the call no one wants to make. While the rest of us, lowering our heads, pray, mumble, breathe hard and fast, Donny paces with the phone. He slams the receiver down, more than once, having been disconnected while waiting for confirmation. A stab of fear: Was it false hope or blind wishes making me think I saw Charlie's broad shoulders moving swiftly, like oars, in the oil-slick waters of the river?

"His name is Bell, Charles Bell!" Donny yells into the phone. Again, and again, he is put on hold, and this waiting begins to bind us in a peculiar way, the simplicity of being on the same team, Charlie's team. We walk in figure eights around the kitchen, as if at a pep rally performing a routine. In the moments when I imagine him gone, I feel ill, cold-blooded, nearly amphibious. Then I drift back to the past, forcing myself to remember human things: the warmth of Charlie's eyes, the saltiness of his lips, the sharp ridges of his cheekbones.

"Yes, yes, he was traveling alone. What? One passenger, yes. Please don't put me on hold again. His family is here with me now." *His family*. Donny raises his index finger in the one-minute gesture, but his eyes are fixed on me, only me. Behind us, Ben munches on a carrot stick, and the tea kettle whistles, drowning out the percussion session deep inside my chest.

Seconds pass, then minutes. "Are you absolutely certain?" Donny asks.

Paula and I each grip one of Donny's arms. He pulls free from us and rummages a hand through the thicket of his hair. Finally, he speaks. "Thank you, sir, yes, please, tell me everything you know."

TWENTY

I will always remember the cracked parchment lampshade—how it was annoyingly tilted on this night, the night we decided to tell the girls Donny is moving out. Images of the scene, like the outline of bodies during a crime investigation, are stamped indelibly in my brain. I keep returning to the crooked lamp so to escape Becky's and Lana's dazed faces.

All the counsel in the world could not have prepared either one of us for what we have to say—the terrifying words that will sear the souls of our two innocent children. The therapist had cautioned me not to cry—"You don't want to frighten them any more than they already are, and most importantly, Mrs. Pearl, you must tell your children, emphatically, that *nothing* they said or did caused this situation to happen."

I drove home, thinking all I can do is try to keep calm and listen, minutes later, hours later, years later, while it all sinks in, when the girls finally realize their world was breakable, more fragile than the porcelain dolls that were kept, out of reach, high on a shelf.

And so now it is done. Yet, within seconds of the telling, Lana jumps from the couch with her hands planted firmly on her hips. "This is a family joke, Mommy, right? Ha!" As always, Lana eases some of the tension with her precious denial. I answer the best I can with my silence. Sucking furiously on her fingers, my baby girl lays her head against the arm of the couch and within seconds falls asleep.

"What about *Passover*?" Becky cries, lifting Donny's drooping chin with both her hands.

"Of course," I stammer, "we'll have all our holidays, sweetie. That'll never change."

Becky's voice trembles as she looks back and forth at us with begging eyes. I'm aware of a deep, sinking sensation as I realize there is a strong possibility that the Pearls and I might no longer share any holidays or celebrations.

Finally, I ignore the therapist's last piece of advice, which suggested we all linger in the den together, perhaps play a board game, or complete a puzzle. We have just talked about us splitting apart. Working together to find the missing pieces of a crossword puzzle seems like such a lie.

Later, after tucking the girls in for the night, Donny packs up a cardboard box and fills it with record albums, favorite books, and some college paraphernalia. Noticing how meticulously he wraps these items—things that have given him comfort over the years—I feel a deep sadness for him, for us both. Then, as he is about to leave, Donny lifts the carved oak hat rack from the foyer wall. Stunned, I don't say a word.

"I'll come back tomorrow for more of my things. And we can talk about the house."

"Sure, but I may need some time. I don't know where I can go and not disrupt the girls."

"Well, I can tell you it certainly won't be here."

Feeling faint, I remind myself that Donny's style is to try intimidation whenever his pride is wounded. He still can't believe I am actually going through with a legal separation. Is he holding out, waiting for me to change my mind? I was naïve to think the elation we shared over the news of Charlie's survival would change how we interfaced, and that the destruction to both families might be inoculated with a resurgence of hope.

Trembling, I hold the screen door open for Donny and the mirrored hat rack—an anniversary gift from his parents. I lock *our* front door, using the deadbolt for the first time in over three years, since we moved to this quiet little cul-de-sac—Daisy Lane. And, after almost eight years together, our life, and what we once called *family*, ends with a hard slam of a door.

The next night Donny picks up Becky and Lana to take them out for an early dinner—to give them a sense that he will always be close and readily available. I point-blank ask Donny if he knows how Charlie is doing, and whether Paula has visited him in the DC hospital. He glares at me as if insulted, and I wonder if it's crazy to think he might be envious of Charlie's near- death experience.

"Yes, of course, Alex. It was the right thing to do," Donny says.

"Well, I'm glad to hear that. He has, after all, been all alone down there."

"And she *is* still his wife. Did you forget?" Donny reminds me I'm no longer privy to any hints of Paula's devotion toward Charlie, or any intrinsic claim to their relationship. He continues to wear his insecurity like a cloak of steel.

"So, what exactly is *she* to you, Don? I'm curious, that's all."

"Our relationship is now strictly platonic, if you must know. It's one of moral support and mutually beneficial . . . particularly during this hard time."

Though I smile, my face feels hot, and my heart pounds harder than I would have expected. Donny has become Paula's white knight—wholly needed, respected, anything but a disappointment, in someone else's eyes.

Trying to keep myself busy, the next day, I'm on the floor of our garage tying up a stack of old newspapers. Next, I'll tackle the overstuffed garbage pails—the first rude awakening of Donny's departure. For weeks, I've hoarded papers, reading everything printed about the plane crash and Charles Louis Bell, a thirty-three-year-old attorney, turned hero. Though, in reality, the Potomac crash is already old news, only a few lines wedged between stories of crooked politicians and rising gas prices.

From the pile of papers cradled in my arms, I spot a thumbnail photo of Charlie speaking into a microphone. He looks so much older, weary, and forlorn. I remember that look—his need to convince, desperately hoping to be understood. From day one, the news slant seemed focused on making Charlie an anti-hero: a New York hotshot attorney who just happened to risk his life to save the lives of three strangers. This was obviously the penance for his defending the shutdown of the nuclear reactors. For days, noisy activist groups crawled from the woodwork to loiter outside his hospital. The signs they carried were a reminder of the threats of toxic waste—the dangers in by-products of all nuclear facilities. In this and other interviews, Charlie stressed he only did the job required of him; nobody gave a damn about his moral conflicts. I imagine him shrugging his shoulders, saying, "This is the price one pays when dealing with the big guys." But then a shadow curtains his face, penetrating his fierce pride.

I tie the papers in a double knot, trying to remember Donny's special method, but coupons and inserts keep sliding out all over the garage floor. The bundles should resemble a large cake box. Sweating, I kick the lopsided stack and twist my ankle. My palms are streaked charcoal and my cuticles bear remnants of purple dye from the T-shirts I'd made for the girls. This morning, when they waved from the driveway, I tried to believe their sweet, photogenic smiles meant they were happy. But I saw how they kept looking back at me, as if I might disintegrate in the doorway.

Sinking down on a mound of garbage bags, I inhale the rot of a week's worth of discarded food. My face falls into my filthy hands while I hold back tears. Sobered by the sight of Donny's windbreaker among a pile of clothing he'd forgotten, I reach for the jacket and wipe my face into its soft cotton lining. I have the strange impulse to toss his clothes in the wash. And as I've done hundreds of times in the past seven years, I empty all the pockets. There are golf tees, pennies, breath mints, a crinkled receipt, and ticket stubs. Bile races to my tongue. I shove three breath mints in my mouth before examining the stubs. They are for the movie *Dog Day Afternoon*—Donny and I haven't been to the movies in ages. I lift myself off the stinking bags and limp to the kitchen to check the calendar. The twenty-third is circled like a bull's eye—the day I'd watched Paula's children—the scorching afternoon when she changed her mind.

Irritation invades all melancholy the instant I picture Paula and Donny relaxing in a cool theater, perhaps fresh from the doctor after she decided: *Oh, what the hell, I'll have the kid.* Then, like troubled teens, they happily share a jumbo bag of buttered popcorn, a cup of Coke big enough to bathe in.

Pacing the kitchen, I see myself in the oven door and jump. I resemble a homeless orphan—my face muddied from a mix of ink and tears. I have looked in that oven door hundreds of times, but this is the first time I know who I see. I glance at the clock. Becky and Lana's bus will drop them off in a matter of minutes.

"I can do this," I say aloud. There's not a soul left to answer to.

There's a four-thirty shuttle to DC, which only takes an hour from Newark. I've memorized every departure, known them for a long time. Jumbled and insane elation has me calculating a time frame to have me back home by 11:00 p.m. That is, if I tell some white lies, and reach out for help. *Rona? Really?* But there is little time to think about pride or Rona's appraisal of me—of anyone's appraisal of me. It's faster and cheaper to drive my Dart to the airport and drop Becky and Lana at Rona's on the way.

"Mommy, you look so shiny," Lana says, "and you smell like vanilla wafers."

"Thank you, honey." I check my face in the rearview mirror. Over my faint tan is a wild cherry blush spreading down to my chest. I touch my forehead with the back of my hand like my mother used to do when checking for fever.

"Where are you going?" Becky asks, eyeing me suspiciously. For a split second I see Donny's mouth twisting up at the corners: *Yeah, tell me another one.*

"Hmm . . . where am I going?" I think aloud.

"Tell us, tell us, please." Lana bounces on the floor of the back seat. "I can keep a secret, Mommy. I go to kindergarten now."

"But it's not a secret, angel. There's something Mommy has to do . . . something good for me, and then I'm absolutely coming right home to you."

"Tonight?" Becky asks.

"Yes, tonight, and don't worry if I'm a little bit late. You can get into your jammies at Rona's."

"And what about this weekend . . . can we still go to Adventureland?"

"I don't see why not."

"Can Daddy come with us?" Lana asks, as I pull into Rona's driveway. Rona waves vigorously from her front porch, then tucks Ethan's plaid shirt inside his new khakis—images from the back-to-school issue of *Parents* magazine.

I turn around in the car to face Becky and Lana, feeling the tug of fresh raw guilt.

"I bet Daddy would love to go, but we'll have to ask him. Better not mention the Ferris wheel."

"I know," Lana giggles, "Daddy always gets the throw-ups."

My mere speaking of Donny, just a few simple words of recognition, seems to soothe them. I watch their eyes haze over as if they're already there, at the amusement park, with us, their mom and dad. Whether this is a good thing or bad, I have no idea. I will do anything to ease their aching hearts—anything, but return to a life with someone who didn't love me like I needed to be loved. Only now, do I realize Donny might be saying the exact same thing. Maybe someday my girls will understand or maybe never.

Rona and I exchange tight little smiles. I think she knows it's wise not to say too much. When I called her, only an hour ago, she'd asked if I knew what I was doing and pressed if I was certain it was over between Donny and me. She sounded like a divorce lawyer pushing for reconciliation. I didn't mind her probing—it helped me validate everything I've known for a long time. What has happened to me must terrify someone like Rona. How in less than a year, a couple, living what appears to be an ordinary life, can suffer such upheaval.

I hand over the tote bag containing the girls' pajamas and a large one-hundred-piece Sesame Street puzzle, which Rona will probably hide before allowing it to be spilled across her floor. I hug the girls so tightly I can count their ribs. They turn and wave, then run up the steps to the eager Ethan, the delicious only child who becomes buoyant in their presence.

"Thank you, Rona." I sit up tall, straightening my shoulders.

"Be careful," she says, pecking my cheek in the style of my mother. As I'm backing out of the driveway, Rona knocks on my window, startling me. I roll the glass down halfway, already tense and impatient in my rushing mode.

"I have to ask you something," she says, leaning in closer.

"Quick, Rona, or I'll miss my flight."

"Alex, that top you're wearing is absolutely stunning. Where did you find it?"

My mouth drops open. "You're joking, right?"

Rona laughs, heartily, pulling me along. If I had time, I'd squeeze her, until all her phony layers peeled away, leaving what I see more clearly now: a kind young woman needing, much like me, to be needed. I turn the corner, leaving Rona waving, rigorously, from her lush garden, where rows of emerald boxwoods stand pruned in perfect, three-foot spheres.

I consider double-parking and leaving my car with the motor running, but then some angel pulls out of the one and only spot in Newark's cramped overnight lot. I run to the gate like a zebra, the fastest I've moved my entire life, my breasts aching with each long stride. Their tenderness, coupled with a week of erratic mood swings, signals I'll be bleeding before long. I am a barge of bloat craving relief from the salty fluids pressing into my brain and belly.

Terror strikes the moment I hear the last call for my flight. I block out the image of Paula already perched on the plane flipping through *Baby Talk* magazine and rush down the cool gray corridors leading to the gate. When I arrive, out of breath, an attendant looking like the mannequin from Annie Sez, uses a stiff arm and gestures me to slow down.

"We're quite busy this afternoon, but you're in luck. No seats left on the shuttle, but we've got one seat on our regular flight . . . first class." She smiles, her lipstick clownish and curled above her mouth. I have an impulse to put a quarter in her hand, to have her emit a card predicting my fortune.

I pray that my credit card goes through and that Donny hasn't already cancelled the account. My habitual fear of flight is obliterated by the belief that another plane crash could not occur within two weeks—especially with DC as the final destination. Plus, I've run up quite the tab in the *let's make a deal and let me live* department.

The stewardess, a friendlier mannequin, serves hot towels with tongs. I blot the perspiration from my neck and inhale the soothing lemony smell; dry flecks of skin peel off me, and I scrub until the towel is cool. A painful pressure grips my loins. I unbuckle the seat belt and lock myself in the tubular cubicle called a restroom. A tinge of pink appears on my panties. The tampon dispenser is empty, so I grab a wad of tissues to create my own protective shield. Then, in the foggy mirror, I give myself a silent pep talk. I force a pleasant smile and pinch my burning cheeks. It suddenly occurs to me there is no one left to pinch my cheeks, to say, *Good for you, Alex.*

I return to my seat, leaving my practiced face behind, saying goodbye to the pretense that often looked back at me from mirrors. All those years of quiet desperation—suitcases stuffed with lies.

At exactly 6:30 p.m. my cab pulls up the ramp of Bethesda Naval Hospital. Two burly security guards are parked at the curb, downing steamy slices of pizza. I get a few curious glances, and am struck by the need to duck past them. What would I say if I was questioned? Who is this frazzled blonde visiting Charlie Bell—a well-respected attorney, husband, and father of two or three, and flawless hero? My heart gallops as I approach the double glass doors. Automated, they part on their own, causing me to lunge forward, nearly toppling to the ground. Two blue-haired ladies are in the process of changing shifts at the information desk. As one walks away, I make a timid approach, hoping she'll take pity on me and my goose-bumped arms.

"Sorry, that woman just told me the room number for Charles Bell. I think I heard wrong. Did she say 324?"

"Bell, Bell, oh yes. What a terrific thing that fellow did." She flips through a Rolodex, while peering up at me suspiciously.

"No, that's 825 . . . Third floor is maternity. Here you go—you will need this pass. Are you the Mrs.?"

Fearful I'll be tossed out as an imposter, I tell the truth, and shake my head no. I back away from her and her elfish glance and head for the elevator bank. A door opens, and a beaming young man, pushing a wheelchair holding his wife and infant, moves past me. There's a familiar striped receiving blanket, a simple pink skullcap atop the baby's head, a bouquet of wilting flowers from the usual three-day stay, and bouncy balloons, but what is most visible is an aura of immeasurable bliss. I mumble a stranger's good wishes, wishes they are too euphoric to hear. *Beginnings*, I think, *are the most beautiful of blessings.*

The elevator is empty now and immobile. Many seconds pass until I realize I've forgotten to press the button. How can a person be hot and cold at the same time? I rush down the fluorescent hallway past abandoned trays of uneaten food lined up outside the rooms: Jell-O, unopened mini milk containers, remnants of peas and carrots, smears of brown gravy. All I've eaten are peanuts, and the saltiness has parched my throat. I stop at a water fountain and gather my thoughts. What do I hope to find, and what will I see? As soon as I step over the threshold of room 825, my brain stops its incessant buzzing to take its long overdue nap.

Hunched in a huge vinyl chair, Charlie is dressed in gray sweatpants paired with a white oxford shirt, half-unbuttoned. His left arm is in a sling, and he's jotting notes on a yellow legal pad with his free hand. Before he notices me, I grab a tray from the doorway and prop a discarded daisy in a glass. If only I'd worn white—the un-color symbolizing purity, hope, and healing. But no, I'm dressed in jeans and a cherry-red blouse—a fiery reminder of our recklessness.

I clear my throat, and he squints toward the doorway. I carry the tray to him and place it on the table.

"You," he says, dropping the pad to the floor.

"Me." I grin, thinking how primitive, how Tarzan and Jane. But soon, I'm absorbed in Charlie's widening smile. Like a camera lens, he marks me as his shot, then motions for me to sit upon his lap. I shake my head no. He asks again, pleading, and I climb up, gingerly, afraid of hurting sore bones. Tears streak down his dark unshaven face. The wetness dampens my sleeve.

"Shush, okay, okay."

"Beyond what you could ever imagine," he murmurs. His lips

graze my ear, sending chills down my spine. He pulls back to stare at me. I'm holding my breath, wanting to give him all of my air.

"There was no time to think. Everything happened within seconds."

"What you did, Charlie, was unbelievably brave. Most people would think only of themselves, their own survival."

"No!" he yells, scaring me. "I could have done more. So many didn't make it."

"But three people did because of you." His sadness jolts me; I kiss his deeply etched forehead, realizing all traces of the young Charlie are gone. As we sit quietly, I feel him drifting away, perhaps reliving scenes only he can see—something that must occur daily, if not all the time.

He looks puzzled when I explain I can't stay and that I'm catching the last shuttle back tonight. Sounding like I'm on speed, I spill out the events of the last few weeks. Charlie's eyes flutter and roam until he's able to fix his gaze. He strokes my lips with his fingers, then tilts my face, halting my banter with his mouth. His lips are dry but his kiss is warm and soft. I'm reminded of our first kiss in the living room of my home, while Donny and Paula were alone together in the den, and I had cared, but not enough to stop them—to maybe stop us all. In an instant, I knew I had relinquished my safety—what I'd always believed to be safe.

A young Indian doctor comes in to check Charlie's blood pressure. Charlie jokes with him, saying, because of me, his pressure has probably surged. I wonder what this stranger knows, what Charlie has shared in the name of loneliness and vulnerability. Embarrassed, I climb from his lap and read a row of greeting cards propped above the air conditioner. *We miss you, Daddy* is scrawled in big yellow letters next to a crayon drawing of the sun. A beautiful floral arrangement sits among the cards. It is from Paula's parents. *We are so proud of you, son.* I swallow hard. In the stark, spare message is a truth I guess I'd hidden from myself. Had I pictured Charlie stripped of his past life by the crash, a man who emerged from the river void of a history? I scan the room but can't find any of the cards or letters I'd sent. I imagine them tucked in a drawer, sandwiched safely between sterile gauze and a cold metal bedpan—my existence under wraps.

The doctor leaves, and Charlie motions for me to come to him, but I'm anxious about the lack of time. Fidgeting, I feel a whole new wave of despair. I try to remember my reason for coming here. *It was for him, for Charlie,* I tell myself again. We stare at each other for several seconds, holding hands, without words. Over the intercom a voice announces visiting hours will be over, shortly, and Charlie struggles to stand. He steadies himself by leaning in and grasping my shoulders. We are nose to nose, and I see tremendous strain spreading across his face, an indication of pain.

"Listen to me," he says, impatiently, like he's about to scold.

"No, please, let me talk, Charlie. I had to see you, to know that you're going to be all right, that's all."

"Really, that's all?" He takes my face in both his hands—forcing me to look at him. I am surprised by his intensity, and a new sense of responsibility wraps around me like a shroud. "I'm not screwing around here, Alex. I want to be with you—but I'm twisted inside, pulled in a hundred different directions."

"That's the point, Charlie. You don't have to fix anything. I can take care of myself. Turns out I've been doing that for a very long time."

He strokes my chin. "Oh, I get it. You don't want me to do anything I don't want to do."

"No, it's not about *you*, or Donny, or Paula." I look away from those soft, dark eyes to gather my thoughts, not wanting to cause more hurt or confusion. "This is also about me. I've got to focus on what I want, but more than anything . . . what will be best for Becky and Lana. I won't be pushed into a corner or corralled by anyone's whims and desires."

"This is going to be tough, Alex. No one walks away from a marriage without serious problems."

"Charlie, please, you're not hearing me."

"I've never felt this deeply about anyone. If I had, none of this could have happened," he says, making me wonder if it's the painkillers talking, dulling his ability to focus.

"But you still love her, Charlie. I know you do."

"Alex, we met when we were so young—teenagers. I was still in school and overwhelmed by a hailstorm of responsibility at home. Yes, for a long time, marriage made my life feel normal. That is, until I met you, and knew what I'd wanted, maybe what she wanted as well. And what neither of us ever had. Night after night, it's you who I dreamed about walking through that door, *you* I love."

"You sound really mad at me, Charlie. Why are you always mad when you talk about loving me?" Charlie places butterfly kisses along my neck, then moves to my shoulder. When he spots his silver chain clasped around my neck, he tugs at it carefully, as if reeling in a fish. For months I'd been afraid to take it off, superstitious that something bad might happen. I am, once and for all, done with superstition. I lift the swimming medal over my head and hand it over.

"Please take this medal and put it in safekeeping for one of your children."

"So, does this mean you're breaking up with me?" The corners of Charlie's mouth quiver, yet he holds fast to a smile.

The overhead speaker booms a final warning. I move sideways toward the door in small reluctant steps, avoiding Charlie's face.

"I really have to go now. Please take care of yourself." I rush back and kiss his cheek, inhaling his reliable citrus aroma.

"Alex," Charlie yells, hobbling toward the door, but I can't turn back. I saw what I had to see. He is, and has always been, extraordinarily strong. No matter what the future brings, one thing's for sure: Charlie Bell, now a beloved national hero, will be just fine.

Six Months Later

I am sprawled across the linty shag rug, packing for Saturday's move to Cresthaven Gardens, better known in neighboring communities as "Crestfallen Gardens." Located just minutes down the road from Wheatley Heights, it's a place for transition—targeted to singles, families in limbo, and people taking slow, cautious steps toward new lives.

This change, undoubtedly, will be hardest on Becky and Lana, but here they can count on the consistency of the same school, enjoy former playmates, and depend on midweek visits with Donny. At least that's what one of me keeps reminding the other. I try shooing the annoyance away, but here I am again circling outside myself, watching every move I make—a built-in security guard, perched to snag me at my own door.

The phone rings, and I'm glad for the break—any distraction from the wind pummeling the glass doors. Donny's on the line, asking how it's going and if I would like some "extra" help. I chuckle, which is kinder than the sarcastic response itching to escape: *Oh, so it must be pretty hectic over there at Paula's house, huh? Not exactly a party since the baby boy arrived?*

This child, keeping with Paula's affection for the *R* consonant, is named: *Randy*. Though, perhaps, a more appropriate name might have been *Raunchy*. I haven't seen the baby yet; I mean, why would

I? Though, I've heard from the girls that Randy has fuzzy sprouts of reddish hair and the palest skin: "Like pink tissues, Mommy," Lana has mentioned.

"Well, isn't that something?" I answered. Any day I expect Donny to change his story. He might even lay claim to baby Randy, if perhaps at age three, the child suddenly banged out a Beethoven sonata.

"Thanks, Don, but I prefer going this alone," I answer. "Besides, I think it might be better if you keep the girls occupied for a while longer. I haven't finished packing up their rooms yet."

"Okay, so I'll bring them home after dinner like originally planned. Should I bathe them here? You know, since they have school tomorrow."

"No, Donny, I can bathe them. Our bathroom is fine. The soap and towels haven't been packed away, but I appreciate the offer."

Since our legal separation, finalized on Valentine's Day, sharing Becky and Lana has become my most difficult challenge. I had always looked forward to enjoying them with the people I loved and those who loved me back. But now the same exact people, Louise, Ben, and Donny, and most of their family, get to see and enjoy this blood of mine separate from me—my physical presence is no longer required. Because I still have deep feelings for these folks, this is by far the most painful adjustment. Yet, I am often touched by my children's deep, intuitive caring—how both Becky and Lana seem to prop open an imaginary swinging gate, as if inviting me to tag along and peek inside. I'm hoping not because they worry about me, but because they love me.

I try to remember what *our* den (still stuck on that pronoun) looked like before it became a warehouse of bubble wrap and cartons. Rushing now, I wrap the last of the picture frames from the mantel, ignoring the taunt to linger and reminisce, to make myself miserable. But misery is no longer affordable.

What I am, however, is starving; my stomach a quartet of acidic sounds. There's nothing to eat except a strawberry yogurt dated March '75, exactly one year old, oh, and a frozen slice of my birthday cake, last week's leftover from Carvel. Of course, I'll eat it, having already emptied the fridge and scrubbed the fruit and vegetable bins of all seepage for the new owners so they won't complain and say things like: *Alex Pearl left her home like a pigpen.* They seemed like a nice enough couple, the Murphys, in their twenties, and expecting their first child.

So not to jeopardize the sale and fearing the mention of *divorce* a bad omen, the broker told the young couple that her clients, the Pearls, were moving to a bigger house across town. That's when I remembered the Pittaros who we'd bought this house from just three years before—and how amiably they'd greeted us with a spectacular fire in the fireplace, then offered mugs of eggnog, the entire family dressed in identical red plaid robes.

Soon after we'd settled in, Norm and Sue, our welcoming committee, enlightened us: The Pittaros were splitting up; Mrs. Pittaro was in the throes of a torrid affair with the middle-aged Sicilian hunk who'd built the cedar deck and barbecue pit, which became the number one selling point for us. Whoever this guy was, he'd done a meticulous job. How could I know that in a few short years, we, The Pearls, would be following a similar path?

On a chilly, wintry day we filed into court, heads down like a couple of shy shorn sheep. *Court* has a knack for making the most upright citizen feel derelict. For me, the day telegraphed the one clear message I had avoided: how unlikely it was for Donny, his parents, and me to maintain an attachment beyond the boundaries of financial obligation. Of course, the Pearls' loyalty would naturally belong to Donny and whoever shared his life, but it hurt to have to sell my house so soon—the reason being Donny's income had decreased dramatically.

However, the clincher was when the judge startled me with his inquiry about my personal savings account, its sum miraculously exceeding $10,000—the nest egg I'd begun as a young teen, and what became the precious *pushke* my grandmother had urged me to keep as a married woman. This, the only secret I'd shared over coffee with Paula Bell. The judge ordered the account be split in half, and though I was initially upset, I rationalized the money would go to good use, considering there were innocent children involved.

I clear the shelves of the wall unit, which I'm leaving behind, and pack the last of the books, games, and assorted items—mostly handmade gifts like heart-shaped doilies, and clay impressions of the girls' hands. One drawer is jammed, and when I yank hard, out falls my copy of *A Sensuous Life in 30 Days*. Should I wrap it up and bring it along: helpful tips for what lay ahead? Maybe I should give the book to Rona. I bet she could handle it now, even surprise Hy once in a while. I glance through the dog-eared pages and cackle aloud. Almond oil massages, saltine crackers in bed? Nah . . .a bit too messy for Rona. I tuck the book in a slat above the drawer, hoping it will, one day, be discovered by the hopeful young woman who bought this house, who might actually think to herself: *What an interesting woman, that Alex Pearl.*

Next, I gather my T-shirt supplies into one cardboard carton. It is filled to the brim with bottles of dyes, markers, rubber bands, and stencils, many of which I have duplicated dozens of times. I promised to help Becky and Lana create their own designs, so they can give gifts to all their friends, both old and new. "But can't we sell them, Mommy?" Becky asked. "We need to make extra money now."

"Why's that, honey?" I was surprised and proud of her seven-year-old entrepreneurial spirit.

"So you and Daddy won't have to work so hard."

"Oh, sweetie, thanks, but there's nothing bad about working hard. Sometimes it's the best thing a person can do."

Then, the same day the library called to inform me that an anonymous corporate client bought my painting *Tangled*, I had decided to make a call of my own. I gave Cleo four weeks' notice, though she refused to hear me when I said I could no longer service her boutique. I shared the news: *my artwork* had been chosen for display at our town's new million-dollar library, and when I sold just one painting (which I had already done), that equated to tie-dying, at least, thirty T-shirts. Besides, I would be making a contribution to the community by sharing my earnings.

"Cleo," I sang out, "there are *soooo* many women making these T-shirts now. You won't have a problem replacing me. Not at all."

Though skeptical, I agree to meet him at four, before the sun goes down, and only in a public place.

"I'm a lawyer, Alex, not a serial killer," Charlie said, trying to disarm me, as always. I am hard to nudge these days, stony to frivolity in any shape or form. Last week, when he called, I was thrown off-balance; it seemed like a thousand years since I heard his voice, since I said I needed time. I hung up, aware of my heart banging around my chest like a finch trapped indoors.

"Well, how much time is enough time?" he'd asked, over and over again, in phone messages and letters. But I had no answer, not really. All I knew was I yearned for the safety of distance—some vast open field to scatter the remnants of sadness and regret. Shouldn't a beginning feel like a beginning: free of guilt and condemnation?

After he and Paula split, Charlie made the decision to remain in DC, at least, until the end of his trial. Now, each weekend he picks up his kids, looks in on the new baby (a child he agreed to support through college), then drives back to the city where they all stay with his old Catskill's buddy, Ivan—a devoted bachelor and terrific friend.

Charlie has seen everyone else but me. When he comes for his children, he gets glimpses of Becky and Lana. Once he gave each of them an American Indian doll, and on Valentine's Day, a box of heart candy for *their mommy*. I imagine him chatting with Donny, the two shaking hands, hard as it is to acknowledge Donny's presence there—watching Ross and Ricki grow up. I am not surprised Donny seems to thrive in the role of conduit for Charlie and his former world. Overnight, it became a new course of study, something Donny strived for and hopefully he will continue to do well.

I take a quick shower, letting my hair air-dry. My face is flushed from the tedium of packing, and some struggle going on inside me—a silent urging to hold on. I drag four bags of garbage to the curb before hopping in my car. Spotting me, Norm and Sue, with their three girls, wave wildly. How I will miss the consistency of their *Father Knows Best* existence—my favorite childhood show.

I arrive to find the park brimming with families enjoying the remnants of an early spring Sunday afternoon. A howling wind subsides, leaving the high-pitched squeals of frolicking children. I claim my favorite bench, the one always bathed in sun at the bottom of the hill. We sat on that bench once, together, and I can recall every detail of that day, that moment: how the air smelled of sweet cherry tobacco, the sharp squawk of a hovering crow, the roughness of his hand the first time it accidentally grazed mine. I stand and sit, stand and sit. I have an itch between my shoulders that is hard to reach. I get angry, euphoric, then terribly sad. It is ten past four, and as I start my ascent up the hill, back to my car, I spot him. Charlie Bell. He is carrying something bulky, wrapped in ordinary brown paper. I don't know what is bigger, the package or his smile. Now, as I walk toward him, I am elevated by a familiar magnetism. Charlie props the package alongside the trunk of an old tree and holds out his arms. Warm, like a Papa, a Dad, a friend—the man he is, and likely will always be.

"Happy birthday, kiddo," he whispers, sending chills down my back. I can't believe he remembered, even I nearly forgot this one. Thirty-one seemed mediocre, except for the fact it will always be the age I was when I divorced.

Charlie seems nervous, as though he's practicing restraint, trying not to clutch me hard. But it is me who folds easily into his outstretched arms. His fresh air aroma has not disappeared with time.

"Okay, so what's that?" I ask, stepping back to balance myself against the sturdy oak.

"Well, why not open it and find out." He hands over his tiny Hoffritz knife, warning me to be careful. His breathing is hard, while his body emanates a safe, familiar heat. I tear at the package, clumsily, having seen enough brown wrap in the past weeks to last a lifetime.

Then right beneath a thin piece of foam core, I find my painting, the one I'd entitled *Tangled*.

I am shocked, yet thrilled, to see the work again—like a surprise reunion with a dear old friend. Secretly, I was glad to be able to visit *Tangled* whenever the girls and I visited the library, to watch people stop and scratch their heads, or wrinkle their noses, or smile with enlightenment before moving on.

"But this is *my* painting, Charlie. I don't understand."

"It was me. I'm the person who bought it from the library."

"You? You were the mysterious client?"

Charlie beams. "I remembered this was the one you'd finished after a really long time. But, more than that, this painting represents you—it's your self-portrait, Alex, like a blueprint of who you used to be. Did you really want some stranger to buy it to cover a plaster wall, or to coordinate your colors with their furnishings? Of course, I'm not saying whoever bought this wouldn't have loved it. But, for so many reasons, I love it a whole lot more."

This gesture renders me speechless, and I take a few seconds just to breathe. There's a jumble of emotions swirling around me, all funicular and new. I understood that when I had given the canvas to the library so someone might purchase it, I no longer needed the work as hard evidence of my talent or ability. I'd already let it go.

"I'd like for you to keep it, Charlie," I say, never surer of my words.

"I think we should both sit down and talk about this," he says, lightly taking my hand, leading me back to one of the benches. We leave the painting propped against the tree but in full view. After about a minute, he speaks, though his voice is a bit shaky.

"Hey, how's this? Why don't you keep the work for me until I find a place of my own?" A request delivered without an ounce of pressure, and so instead of my usual hesitation or stalling gesture, I nod yes.

What follows is a long and peaceful stretch of silence, a chance to view one another in the bold starkness of just an ordinary day. We are no longer stowaways in the night, or pawns on a chess board of some crazy marital game. When I look at Charlie now, I see part of my past—my former self—an already lived life. I don't know a damn thing about the future, except, I am ready to move on. The thought comes like a gust of wind, forcing me, just for a second, to close my eyes. In the background are sporadic bursts of children's laughter and older voices delivering soft demands. I lean in to the bench, my shoulder grazing Charlie's, and point upwards—to the swirling colors of the crisp March sky—an endless stream of pastel light.

ACKNOWLEDGMENTS

During the months and years while writing *Split-Level*, pausing to complete another book in between, I kept returning to my tale of a young woman lost in the mire of ideas others had conjured for her future. One day I realized how those expectations both contrasted and conflicted with what she wanted for herself, and once that became clear, the mighty pen took over.

I am forever grateful for the support of many writers' groups over the years, which include the NYC's Writer's Voice, workshops and conferences at Marymount College, and The International Women's Writers Guild, where I formed valuable relationships with teachers and writers, many which have continued for decades. A special thanks to my NYC writing group with talented authors: Beth Schorr Jaffe, Bridget Casey, and Carol Gaunt, early readers of *Split-Level*.

I owe much gratitude to Stonybrook Southampton College's stellar MFA program, which encouraged writers, like myself, to follow lifelong dreams. Early readers who inspired me include Meg Wolitzer, Nahid Rachlin, Lou Ann Walker, Roger Rosenblatt, and the late Frank McCourt, who allowed me in his class even though I was writing fiction. To my dear friend, author Elizabeth McCourt, for her constant enthusiasm and warm support. Much gratitude to friend and editor, David Groff, for believing in this story and sharing his wisdom and honesty.

A huge thank you to the dedicated team at She Writes Press: led by my publisher, Brooke Warner, including Caitlyn Levin, Krissa Lagos, Samantha Strom, and amazing book designer Julie Metz for all their guidance and enthusiasm for this novel. And a special thanks to Liza Fleissig and Andrea Robinson for their early cheering!

Unceasing gratitude to my family who have bestowed my life's truest blessings, and my proud and patient husband who urged me to push through whenever I threatened to return to gymnastics . . . (I joke). Last, but not least, in loving memory of Franny—the sister I never had, who I tell my stories to each and every day.

1. When we first meet Alex Pearl, she is having a phone conversation with her new best friend, Rona, who seems to have adjusted to suburbia successfully. What are the clues that Alex might be having a more difficult time making that same adjustment?

2. Early on, Alex receives a phone call that sends shockwaves into her essentially happy and organized domestic life. Do you think she handles the incident in the best possible way? How might you react in the same situation?

3. During the 1970s, many couples attended retreats hoping to improve communication in their marriages. Describe Alex and Donny's experience at Marriage Mountain. What aspects did you find revealing? Sad or touching? Humorous? Have you ever attended a similar retreat?

4. Alex's trip to Florida alone with her girls brings a few new surprises. What are some of the triggers that cause both malaise and mistrust in her marriage? How is she affected by her own parents' relationship?

5. Meeting Charlie Bell and his wife initially serves Alex with an example of a marital relationship to compare against her own. How are they different as couples? What are some of the early danger signs in each marriage?

6. What is the pivotal point in the relationship between the two couples? How does that change Alex? Does her focus shift or remain the same? What does she hope for in the end? What might you see in her future?

7. It's been said that many who marry in their twenties ultimately go through transitions that may cause them to desire more in their thirties. Discuss.

8. Which parts of *Split-Level* did you find most insightful?

ABOUT THE AUTHOR

For as long as she can remember, libraries have been Sande Boritz Berger's safe haven and books her greatest joy. After two decades as a scriptwriter and video producer for Fortune 500 companies, Sande returned to her other passion: writing fiction and nonfiction full-time. She completed an MFA in writing and literature at Stony Brook Southampton College, where she was awarded the Deborah Hecht Memorial prize for fiction. Her short stories have appeared in *Epiphany, Tri-Quarterly, Confrontation,* and *The Southampton Review,* as well as several anthologies, including *Aunties: Thirty-Five Writers Celebrate Their Other Mother* (Ballantine) and *Ophelia's Mom: Women Speak Out About Loving and Letting Go of Their Adolescent Daughters* (Crown). She has written for the *Huffington Post, Salon,* and *Psychology Today.* Her debut novel, *The Sweetness,* was a *Foreword Reviews* IndieFab finalist for Book of the Year and was nominated for the Sophie Brody award from the ALA. Berger and her husband live in NYC and often escape to the quiet of Bridgehampton.

SELECTED TITLES FROM SHE WRITES PRESS

She Writes Press is an independent publishing company founded to serve women writers everywhere. Visit us at www.shewritespress.com.

The Geometry of Love by Jessica Levine. $16.95, 978-1-938314-62-9
Torn between her need for stability and her desire for independence, an aspiring poet grapples with questions of artistic inspiration, erotic love, and infidelity.

Fire & Water by Betsy Graziani Fasbinder. $16.95, 978-1-938314-14-8
Kate Murphy has always played by the rules—but when she meets charismatic artist Jake Bloom, she's forced to navigate the treacherous territory of passionate love, friendship, and family devotion.

Slipsliding by the Bay by Barbara McDonald. $16.95, 978-1631522253
A hilarious spoof of academic intrigue that offers a zany glimpse of a small college at a crossroads—and of the societal turmoil and follies of the seventies.

Play for Me by Céline Keating. $16.95, 978-1-63152-972-6
Middle-aged Lily impulsively joins a touring folk-rock band, leaving her job and marriage behind in an attempt to find a second chance at life, passion, and art.

Appetite by Sheila Grinell. $16.95, 978-1-63152-022-8
When twenty-five-year-old Jenn Adler brings home a guru fiancé from Bangalore, her parents must come to grips with the impending marriage—and its effect on their own relationship.

Beautiful Garbage by Jill DiDonato. $16.95, 978-1-938314-01-8
Talented but troubled young artist Jodi Plum leaves suburbia for the excitement of the city—and is soon swept up in the sexual politics and downtown art scene of 1980s New York.